The
JENSEN BRAND

The
JENSEN BRAND

WILLIAM W. JOHNSTONE
with J. A. JOHNSTONE

PINNACLE BOOKS
Kensington Publishing Corp.
www.kensingtonbooks.com

PINNACLE BOOKS are published by

Kensington Publishing Corp.
119 West 40th Street
New York, NY 10018

PUBLISHER'S NOTE
Following the death of William W. Johnstone, the Johnstone family is working with a carefully selected writer to organize and complete Mr. Johnstone's outlines and many unfinished manuscripts to create additional novels in all of his series like The Last Gunfighter, Mountain Man, and Eagles, among others. This novel was inspired by Mr. Johnstone's superb storytelling.

All Kensington titles, imprints, and distributed lines are available at special quantity discounts for bulk purchases for sales promotions, premiums, fund-raising, educational, or institutional use. Special book excerpts or customized printings can also be created to fit specific needs. For details, write or phone the office of the Kensington sales manager: Kensington Publishing Corp., 119 West 40th Street, New York, NY 10018, attn: Sales Department; phone 1-800-221-2647.

PINNACLE BOOKS, the Pinnacle logo, and the WWJ steer head logo are Reg. U.S. Pat. & TM Off.

ISBN-13: 978-0-7860-4063-6
ISBN-10: 0-7860-4063-7

First printing: July 2017

10 9 8 7 6 5 4 3 2

Printed in the United States of America

First electronic edition: July 2017

ISBN-13: 978-0-7860-4064-3
ISBN-10: 0-7860-4064-5

THE JENSEN FAMILY
FIRST FAMILY OF THE AMERICAN FRONTIER

Smoke Jensen—*The Mountain Man*
The youngest of three children and orphaned as a young boy, Smoke Jensen is considered one of the fastest draws in the West. His quest to tame the lawless West has become the stuff of legend. Smoke owns the Sugarloaf Ranch in Colorado. Married to Sally Jensen, father to Denise ("Denny") and Louis.

Preacher—*The First Mountain Man*
Though not a blood relative, grizzled frontiersman Preacher became a father figure to the young Smoke Jensen, teaching him how to survive in the brutal, often deadly Rocky Mountains. Fought the battles that forged his destiny. Armed with a long gun, Preacher is as fierce as the land itself.

Matt Jensen—*The Last Mountain Man*
Orphaned but taken in by Smoke Jensen, Matt Jensen has become like a younger brother to Smoke and even took the Jensen name. And like Smoke, Matt has carved out his destiny on the American frontier. He lives by the gun and surrenders to no man.

Luke Jensen—*Bounty Hunter*
Mountain Man Smoke Jensen's long-lost brother Luke Jensen is scarred by war and a dead shot—the right

qualities to be a bounty hunter. And he's cunning, and fierce enough, to bring down the deadliest outlaws of his day.

Ace Jensen and Chance Jensen—*Those Jensen Boys!*
Smoke Jensen's long-lost nephews, Ace and Chance, are a pair of young-gun twins as reckless and wild as the frontier itself . . . Their father is Luke Jensen, thought killed in the Civil War. Their uncle Smoke Jensen is one of the fiercest gunfighters the West has ever known. It's no surprise that the inseparable Ace and Chance Jensen have a knack for taking risks— even if they have to blast their way out of them.

CHAPTER I

The Sugarloaf Ranch, Colorado, 1901

A thin sliver of moon hung over the mountains bordering the valley, casting such a feeble amount of light that it did little to relieve the pitch blackness cloaking much of the landscape.

A rustlers' moon, Smoke Jensen thought.

"Are they there?" Calvin Woods whispered next to Smoke. "I can't see a blasted thing!"

"They're there," Smoke told his foreman. He raised the Winchester he held in both hands but didn't bring it to his shoulder just yet. A shot would spook the men who had been stealing his cattle, and he didn't want them to take off for the tall and uncut before he had a chance to nab them. "Hold your fire . . ."

Hidden in the trees along with Smoke and Cal were half a dozen more Sugarloaf hands, all of them young and eager for action, like frisky colts ready to stretch their legs. One reason cowboys signed on to ride for the Sugarloaf was the prospect of working for Smoke Jensen, quite possibly the most famous gunfighter the West had ever known. They figured just being around Smoke upped the chances for excitement.

That was true. Even though Smoke had put his powder-burning days behind him more than two decades earlier and settled down to be a peace-loving rancher, things hadn't quite worked out that way. Trouble still seemed to find him on a fairly regular basis, despite his intentions.

That was the way it was with Jensens. None of them had ever been plagued with an abundance of peace and quiet.

In recent weeks, for example, Sugarloaf cattle had begun disappearing on a regular basis. Only a few at first, then more and more as the thieves grew bolder. Smoke was in his fifties, and it only made sense to believe that he might have slowed down some. Some might have figured he wasn't the same sort of pure hell on wheels he had been when he was younger.

Those rustlers were about to find out how wrong they were to assume that.

"There to the right," Smoke whispered as he looked out across the broad pasture where a couple hundred cattle were settled down for the night. "Coming out of that stand of trees."

"I see 'em," Cal replied, equally quiet. He had started out as a young cowboy, too, twenty years earlier. Back then, the reformed outlaw known as Pearlie was the Sugarloaf's ramrod, and he and Cal had become fast friends. Pearlie was also a mentor to Cal, who'd learned everything there was to know about running a ranch. When it came time for Pearlie to retire, it was only natural for Cal to move into the foreman's job.

He still looked a little like a kid, though, despite the mustache he had cultivated in an attempt to make himself seem older. However, no one on the crew failed to hop when he gave an order.

On the other side of the pasture, several riders moved out of the trees and rode slowly toward the cattle. It was too dark to make out any details about them or even to be sure of how many there were. But they didn't belong and there was only one reason for them to be there.

Calling out softly, slapping coiled lassos against their thighs, they started moving a jag of about a hundred head along the valley, toward the north end.

"I've seen all I need to see," Cal said. "Let's blast 'em outta their saddles."

"I'd rather round up a few of them if we can," Smoke said. "I'd like to know if they started this wide-looping on their own or if they're working for somebody."

"You got suspicions?"

"No . . . but if there's a head to this snake, I'd just as soon know about it so I can cut it off." Smoke leaned his head to indicate they should pull back, although it was doubtful Cal saw the gesture in the thick shadows. "Let's drift on back to the horses."

"If we go chargin' out there, we'll scatter those cows all over kingdom come," Cal warned.

Smoke chuckled. "They can be rounded up again."

Silently, the men moved through the trees until they reached the spot where they had left their horses and swung up into the saddles. Over the years of his adventurous life, Smoke had learned to trust his gut. He'd had a hunch the rustlers might strike again that night, so he, Cal, and some of the hands had gone out to a likely spot for more villainy where they could stand watch and maybe catch the cattle thieves in the act.

"Are you gonna give those varmints a chance to surrender, Smoke?" Cal sounded like he hoped the answer would be no.

"Yes . . . but not much of one. They'd better throw

down their guns and get their hands in the air in a hurry. Otherwise . . ." Smoke didn't have to elaborate.

All the cowboys would be checking their guns before they rode out into the pasture.

He gave instructions. "We'll swing around and come up behind them. I'll hail them. If they start the ball, you fellas do what you have to. Like I said, it would be nice to take some of them alive, but I'd much rather all of you boys come through this with whole hides. Now let's go."

With Smoke and Cal in the lead, the men rode slowly through the trees until they reached the edge of the growth. The dark mass of the cattle was to the left, moving away as the rustlers pushed the reluctant animals along. Smoke and his companions moved out into the open and started after them, still not hurrying but moving fast enough to catch up to the plodding cattle.

The sounds made by the cattle and the hooves of the rustlers' horses were enough to muffle the advance of Smoke and his men. At least Smoke hoped that was the case. The rustlers hadn't panicked yet, at least.

The group from the Sugarloaf closed in.

Smoke had his Winchester in his right hand and the reins in his left. He looped the reins around the saddle horn, knowing he could control the rangy gray gelding with his knees. With both hands gripping the rifle, he shouted, "You're caught! Throw down your guns!"

Instead of surrendering, the rustlers yanked their horses around. Spurts of gun flame bloomed in the darkness like crimson flowers as they opened fire.

In one smooth motion, Smoke brought the rifle to his shoulder, aimed at one of the spurts of orange, and squeezed the trigger. The Winchester cracked. He barely felt the weapon's recoil. Working the lever to throw another round in the chamber, he shifted his aim, and swiftly fired a second shot then kneed his horse into motion and charged toward the rustlers.

Around him, Cal and the other Sugarloaf hands galloped forward, yelling and shooting.

The thieves scattered in all directions, abandoning the cows they were trying to steal.

Although it was difficult to see much, Smoke and his allies continued aiming at the muzzle flashes of their enemies. Of course, the rustlers were doing the same thing. The air was filled with flying lead.

Smoke always hoped his men would come through such encounters unscathed, but knew better than to expect it.

He made out one of the fleeing rustlers and closed in on the man, who twisted in the saddle and flung a shot back at him. Smoke felt as much as heard the slug rip through the air not far from his ear. That was good shooting from the back of a running horse. He leaned forward to make himself a smaller target and urged his mount to greater speed.

As he drew close to his quarry, the rustler turned to try another shot, but Smoke lashed out with the barrel of the Winchester. It thudded against the rustler's head and swept him out of the saddle. Both horses galloped on for a few strides before Smoke was able to swing his mount around. Elsewhere in the big pasture, gunfire still crackled.

He swung down from the saddle and let the reins drop, knowing the horse was trained not to go anywhere. Keeping his rifle pointed at the dim figure on the ground, Smoke approached him. The fallen rustler didn't move.

Smoke ordered, "Put your hands in the air!" but there was no response. Wary of a trick, he lowered the rifle and drew the Colt on his right hip. The revolver was better for close work. Almost supernaturally fast with it, he was confident he could put a bullet in the varmint before he had a chance to try anything.

"On your feet if you can, and keep your hands where I can see 'em!"

The rustler remained motionless. He appeared to be lying facedown. Smoke hooked a boot toe under his shoulder and rolled him onto his back.

The loose-limbed way the man flopped over spoke volumes. The fall from the running horse had either busted the rustler's head open or broken his neck, more likely the latter. Either way, he sure looked dead.

Or he was mighty good at playing possum.

Smoke backed off and holstered the Colt. He'd return later and check on the rustler. At the moment, his men needed his help elsewhere.

He mounted up quickly and rode toward the sound of the guns, which had become intermittent. The shots died out completely as Smoke approached several dark shapes that turned into men on horseback as he got closer.

He had his rifle ready, but he recognized the voice that called, "Smoke? Is that you?"

"Yeah, Cal, it's me. Are you all right?"

"Fine as frog hair. How about you?"

"A few of those bullets came close enough for me to hear, but that's all. How about the other fellas?"

"Don't know. Randy and Josh are with me and they're all right, but I can't say about the rest."

"And the rustlers?"

"We downed a couple. Don't know about the rest of *them*, either."

Smoke said, "The fight seems to be over. Let's see if we can round up the rest of our bunch."

"Then we can round up those cows," Cal said. "They scattered hell-west and crosswise, just like I figured they would."

"But they're still on Sugarloaf range," Smoke pointed out. "Those rustlers didn't succeed in driving them off."

"They sure didn't!"

Smoke drew his Colt and fired three shots into the air, the signal for his riders to regroup. Over the next few minutes they came in. One man had a bullet burn on his arm, but the others were unhurt . . . until the last two horses plodded up. One man rode in front, leading the other horse.

Smoke could make out a shape draped over the second horse's saddle, and the sight made his jaw tighten in anger. "Who's that?" he snapped.

"I'm Jimmy Holt, Mr. Jensen." With a catch in his voice, the young cowboy said, "That's Sid MacDowell behind me. He . . . he cashed in his chips. One of those damn rustlers drilled him right through the brisket. I ain't sure Sid had time to know what happened."

"Might be better that way," Smoke muttered. "What about the rustlers? Did any of them get away?"

"I think one of them did," another cowboy reported. "I'm pretty sure he was hit, but he managed to stay on his horse. Do you want us to see if we can trail him, Mr. Jensen?"

"The best tracker in the world couldn't follow a trail on a night like this, and I've known a few who could lay claim to that title." Smoke shook his head. "No, we might see if we can find any tracks in the morning, but right now, some of you boys start gathering those cows and the rest of you come with me and Cal. I want to see if any of the rustlers are still alive."

For the next half hour, Smoke, Cal, and a couple other men rode around the pasture, hunting for the bodies of the rustlers. Smoke hoped to find at least one of them only wounded and still able to talk, but as thief after thief turned up dead, that hope began to fade.

Finally they rode over to the man Smoke had knocked out of his saddle. Smoke knelt beside him, struck a lucifer, and saw by its flaring light that the rustler's wide, staring eyes were sightless. The unnatural twist of his head told that his neck was broken. Smoke had tried to take him alive, but fate had had other ideas.

Smoke straightened and told Cal, "You can bring a wagon out here in the morning and collect the bodies . . . if the wolves haven't dragged them off by then. Haul 'em into Big Rock to the undertaker. I'll pay to have them put in the ground if they don't have enough money on them to cover the cost."

Cal nodded. "Should I get Sheriff Carson to take a look at them?"

"Wouldn't hurt. Chances are some of them are wanted. You fellas might have some reward money coming to you."

Cal rubbed his chin. "I'm not sure I'd want to take blood money. On the other hand, the world's probably better off without these varmints, and that's worth something, I guess."

"Up to you." Smoke wouldn't be taking any reward money. Between the Sugarloaf's success and the lucrative gold claim he had found many years earlier, he was one of the wealthiest men in Colorado, although no one would ever know it to look at him. He still dressed like a common cowhand.

"We'll make sure none of those cattle ran too far when they spooked, then head back to the bunkhouse," Cal said. "How about you?"

Smoke had already turned his horse. He said over his shoulder, "I'm headed home."

CHAPTER 2

The small ranch house that Smoke had built when he and Sally first settled on the Sugarloaf had been added onto many times over the years, until it was a big, sprawling, two-story structure surrounded by cottonwoods and oaks. He always felt good when he rode up to it. He couldn't help but think about all the fine times he and his wife and their children had had. More often than not, the house had rung with laughter.

As he approached the house, he saw that a lamp still burned in the parlor despite the late hour. The glow in the window was dim enough he knew the flame was turned low. More than likely, Sally had waited up for him. That came as no surprise.

Movement on the porch caught his eye. Out of habit—one that had saved his life on occasion—his hand was close to the butt of his revolver. He relaxed, though, as he recognized Pearlie's tall, lanky figure.

"Thought I heard shots up yonderways a while back," the retired foreman said as he came down the steps from the porch. "You must've had a run-in with those wide-loopers."

"We did." Smoke dismounted. "They figured on chasing off a hundred head. We changed their minds."

Pearlie reached for the reins of Smoke's horse. "I'll take care of that for you. I ain't forgot how to wrangle a cayuse. How's the kid?"

Even though Cal wasn't that far from being middle-aged, he would always be a kid to Pearlie. The two of them had shared many adventures, had been through tragedy and triumph together, and were fast friends.

"Cal's fine," Smoke assured him. "We lost one man. Sid MacDowell."

"Blast it! I didn't really know the younker—Cal hired him, not me—but he deserved better 'n a damn rustler's bullet."

"That's the truth. We tried to even the score for him, though. Five carcasses are still out there for Cal to haul into town in the morning."

"Didn't manage to take any of 'em alive?"

Smoke shook his head. "Nope. And one got away, although he might've been wounded. We'll do some tracking in the morning and see if we can turn up another body."

"Even if you don't, killin' five out of six practically wipes out the gang," Pearlie said.

"Only if there were just half a dozen of them to start with," Smoke pointed out.

"No reason to think otherwise, is there?"

"Not really," Smoke admitted. "If the rustling stops now, I reckon we can assume that was all. But if they were just part of a bigger gang—"

"We'll probably know that soon enough, too," Pearlie said in a gloomy voice. He started toward the barn, leading Smoke's horse, and added over his shoulder, "Miss Sally's waitin' up in the parlor."

Even though Smoke was tired and the smell of gun

smoke clung to him, he was smiling as he stepped into the house.

Wearing a soft robe, Sally was sitting in one of the rocking chairs beside the table where the lamp burned. She was reading a book, but she set it aside on the table and looked up with a smile as he stepped into the parlor.

She was on her feet by the time he reached her. Her arms went around his neck and his arms encircled her trim waist. Their mouths met in a passionate kiss that had lost none of its urgency despite the time they had been together.

He lifted his lips from hers and said, "You ought to be in bed getting your beauty sleep . . . not that you need it."

That was certainly true. There might be a few more small lines on Sally's face, and if you looked hard enough you could find a strand of gray here and there in her thick, lustrously dark hair, but to Smoke she was every bit as beautiful as when he had first laid eyes on her in the town of Bury, Idaho, all those years ago.

Smoke knew he hadn't changed much, either. If there was gray in his hair, its natural ash blond color made that sign of age hard to see. Most men on the far side of fifty were past the prime of life, but not Smoke Jensen. He was still as vital as ever, his muscular, broad-shouldered frame near to bursting with strength. He attributed that to fresh air, sunshine, clean living, and being married to the prettiest girl alive.

"I didn't see any bloodstains on your clothes when you came in," Sally said, "so I assume you're all right."

"How do you know there was even any trouble?"

"You went out looking for it, didn't you? If there's one thing Smoke Jensen is good at, it's finding trouble."

He chuckled. "I'd like to think I'm good for more than one thing."

"Well, we might find out about that in a little while, but first, tell me what happened."

Smoke grew serious as he said, "Those rustlers made a try for the stock in the big pasture up north of Granite Creek, just like I had a hunch they might. We killed five out of the six of them and probably wounded the one who got away. No telling how bad." He paused a moment. "But Sid MacDowell was killed in the fight."

Sally took a step back and put a hand to her mouth. "Oh, no. Sid was a fine young man. I'll have to write to his mother and sister down in Amarillo."

Smoke hadn't known that the young cowboy had a mother and sister in Amarillo, but he wasn't surprised Sally was aware of it. She made it a point to be a good friend to every member of the ranch crew.

"We'll send them the wages he had coming, and more besides," Smoke said. "Of course, that won't make up for losing him."

"No, but it's all we can do, I suppose."

He changed the subject by gesturing toward the book on the table. "What are you reading?"

"Charles Dickens's *A Tale of Two Cities*. It's very good."

"Maybe I'll read it one of these days," Smoke said.

She reached for the book. "There's something else in here you'll want to see right away." She opened the volume's front cover and took out a small, square sheet of yellow paper. "Late this afternoon, right after you and Cal and the others rode out, a boy from town brought me this telegram that had just come in."

"Telegrams are usually bad news," Smoke said with a slight frown.

"Not this one, I'm happy to say. Denise Nicole and Louis Arthur are coming home!"

Smoke's frown disappeared. He reached for the

flimsy and scanned the words printed in block letters by the telegrapher in Big Rock.

ARRIVING BIG ROCK 27TH STOP
COMING HOME FOR GOOD STOP
LOVE TO YOU BOTH STOP LAJ AND DNJ

Smoke's heart beat faster as the news soaked in on him. His kids were coming back to the Sugarloaf, and according to the telegram Louis had sent, they would be staying. That was enough to quicken the pulse of any man who loved his children and missed them when they were away.

For most of their lives, Louis and Denise had indeed been away from the Sugarloaf. Twins, they had been inseparable as youngsters, and when sickness had threatened Louis's life and forced Smoke and Sally to seek treatment for him in Europe, Denise had gone along. Sally had taken the children back east to her parents' home, and then John and Abigail Reynolds had sailed across the Atlantic and delivered Louis to top specialists in France.

Through their efforts, the boy had been saved, but his health had remained precarious enough that he had remained in Europe to be closer to the medical help he might need.

That wasn't the only reason the twins had stayed in Europe, living on an estate in England owned by Sally's parents. They had traveled all over the continent and soaked up all the education and culture available to them. Smoke's mentor, the old mountain man called Preacher, thought such behavior was plumb foolishness, and to be honest, at times Smoke felt sort of the same way, but it seemed important to Sally and her folks, so he had gone along with the idea. He missed his kids, but he wanted what was best for them.

They had come back to Colorado for frequent visits to the Sugarloaf, and each time Smoke had harbored the hope in the back of his mind that they might decide to stay. Judging by the telegram in his hand, it looked like that might finally come to pass.

"It'll sure be good to have the kids around again," he said as he placed the telegram on top of Mr. Dickens's novel.

"I'm not sure we can think of them as children anymore," Sally said. "They're twenty years old. They're grown, Smoke."

"Twenty's not grown."

"Think of all the things *you* had done by the time you were twenty years old."

Smoke scowled. He had killed more than two dozen men and been forced to battle for his life countless times. He had married a woman, fathered a child, lost them both to vicious murderers, and avenged their deaths by tracking down those killers and blasting them to hell. He had been a wanted outlaw and worn a lawman's badge.

Yes, it was safe to say that Smoke Jensen had grown up fast. Too fast.

But his children hadn't lived that sort of life, thank God. Instead of dodging the law and shooting it out with gunmen, they had spent their time in clinics and universities and concert halls. They had learned mathematics and natural science and literature instead of how to track an enemy and reload a gun in the heat of battle and stay calm with bullets whipping around their heads.

Smoke was glad they hadn't had to endure such hardships. To his way of thinking, that easy life meant they were still kids. Nothing wrong with that.

Instead of arguing with Sally about whether or not the twins could be considered grown, he said, "The twenty-seventh is only a couple days away. Can we be ready for them by then?"

"There's no getting ready to do," Sally said. "I keep their rooms just like they've always been. They can move right in."

"It's been a while since we've seen them. I wonder if they've changed much."

"Probably not. Louis Arthur will still be handsome and Denise Nicole will be as beautiful as always."

Smoke smiled. "I don't doubt it." They had always been beautiful to him, even as red-faced, squalling babies.

Louis Arthur was named for two of Smoke's oldest friends, the gambler and gunman Louis Longmont and Preacher, whose real name was Arthur. The name was also a way of honoring Smoke's first son, the one who had been murdered, who was named Arthur as well. Along with the old Reynolds family name Denise, Nicole, Smoke's first wife, had inspired the middle name given to his daughter.

Smoke would never forget his first family, the one that had been ripped brutally from him. That tragedy had forged his steel-hard determination to see evildoers brought to justice, and he was more than willing to deliver that justice from the barrel of a gun whenever and wherever necessary.

He wasn't one to dwell on the violence of the past, though. It was more his nature to look ahead to the future with optimism and a friendly smile.

Sally put a hand on his arm. "Would you like a cup of coffee before we go upstairs?"

Smoke slid his other arm around his wife's waist again, feeling the supple warmth of her body under the robe, and smiled "No, I reckon not. If I'm going to be kept awake for a while, I'd rather it was by something else besides coffee."

She laughed and linked her arm with his as they turned toward the parlor entrance. They had gone up only a few steps when she said, "Do you think the rustling is over?"

"I hope so. There's no reason to think otherwise, but we'll just have to wait and see. I can trust Cal and the others to keep a close eye on the stock and let me know if any more turn up missing."

"I hope that's the way it turns out. I'd hate to have a bunch of trouble going on just as Louis Arthur and Denise Nicole finally come home to stay."

"Yeah," Smoke agreed. "Jensens and trouble just don't mix."

She laughed and swatted him lightly on the shoulder, and they continued on their way upstairs to their bedroom.

CHAPTER 3

Louis Arthur Jensen reached out and caught hold of his sister's arm as she started to get up from the bench seat in the train car. He said in a low, urgent voice, "Blast it, Denny, do you always have to cause trouble?"

"I didn't start it," Denise Nicole Jensen replied through clenched teeth. "That son of a—" She caught herself before the oath could slip out. "That scoundrel in the derby hat started it, and you know it, Louis!"

As she pulled her arm free from her brother's grip and stood up, the train went around a fairly sharp curve and swayed. Denny lost her balance, but her hand shot out and gripped the back of the seat, and she steadied herself before Louis could steady her.

Then she took off up the aisle after the man who had leered at her and made an improper suggestion. "Sir!" she called, although "Hey, you!" would have been more appropriate for such an uncouth hombre.

He had a broad, beefy face and a mustache that curled up at the tips. His attire, as well as his general demeanor, suggested that he was some sort of traveling salesman. The man stopped and turned to look at her. A stub of a cigar protruded from thick lips that curved in a smile. "Well, howdy again, little missy. I didn't expect you to take me up on my offer. At least not so soon. But I'm happy you did. Let's go on up to the club car and have that drink." He put out a hand as if he intended to take her arm.

She caught hold of his little finger, twisted it enough to make him let out a little yelp of pain, and leaned in close. "I can snap this off before you can stop me, mister. And I'm mighty tempted to. So maybe you'll think twice before making inappropriate remarks to young ladies again!"

His eyes bulged as he said, "I-I didn't say anything like that! I just asked you if . . . if you'd like to have a drink with me in the club car."

"And then you said maybe we could find someplace more private and you could show me something you thought I'd like!" She put more pressure on his finger and made him breathe harder.

"I was talking about hats! I-I sell ladies' hats. I've got my sample case in the next car—"

"Hats?" Denny said. "You were talking about hats?"

"Yeah. Honest, lady. I didn't mean anything forward. I mean, sure, you're a pretty girl, and I'd enjoy having a drink with you, but I can tell you've got good taste and might be interested in buying a hat. I wholesale 'em to stores, but I don't mind sellin' to an individual if I think she'd like—"

"Are you married?" Denny cut into his babbling explanation.

"What? Married?" He looked pained again, and by more than his finger. "Yeah . . . I got a wife and four kids back in Kansas City."

"Then you shouldn't be acting forward with young women on trains."

"You're right," he said hastily. "You're absolutely

right. I was out of line. I'm sorry. If you could . . . could let go."

"Just remember this," Denny said as she released his finger and moved back a step.

He rubbed the painful digit. "I will, lady. You can count on that. And if your brother was offended, please convey my apologies to him, too."

"How do you know he's my brother?"

"Well, hell. Uh, I mean, the two of you are sort of like peas in a pod, aren't you?"

"Not hardly." Denny turned back toward her seat, well aware that many of the other passengers in the car had been watching the confrontation and were looking at her like she was some sort of crazy woman. She didn't care. Let them think whatever they wanted to, she told herself.

If she worried about what other people thought of her, she'd never have time to do anything else.

Things like that bothered Louis, however. He looked like he wanted to crawl under the seat rather than sitting on it.

Grudgingly, Denny had to admit that she and Louis did look considerably alike. They had the same fair hair, a legacy from their father, and the fine-boned features of their mother. Smoke Jensen was handsome in a rugged way, and Sally was a true beauty, so both Louis and Denny were attractive. Denny was levelheaded enough to acknowledge that.

Her face had a golden tan to it that Louis's lacked. He spent most of his time indoors, poring over books, while Denny preferred to be outside riding horses or practicing her marksmanship. Derringford, the butler at her grandparents' estate in the English countryside, had been appalled at first to see a young woman wearing trousers, riding astride, and carrying a rifle around. He had grown more accustomed to

Denny's behavior over the years, but he would never fully accept it.

Old Rosston, the estate's gamekeeper, had been impressed by Denny's ability to shoot from an early age. It came naturally to her. Her father was Smoke Jensen, after all.

She sat down next to Louis again. "See? I didn't make too much of a scene."

"Well, you didn't break the poor man's finger," Louis said. "So I suppose we should be thankful for that. His spirit may be broken beyond repair, though."

Denny snorted, knowing it was an unladylike sound and not caring. "He needed to learn a lesson. He can't just go around flirting with any young woman who takes his fancy. And you know good and well he wasn't just talking about trying to sell me a hat!"

"No, probably not," Louis admitted. "Anyway, it's over, so let's try to maintain some decorum the rest of the way to Big Rock."

"Decorum's overrated," Denny muttered as she looked past her brother and out the window at the plains of eastern Kansas rolling by.

Tomorrow they would be able to see the mountains, she thought, and that would be a most welcome sight indeed.

That would mean they were almost home.

Sheriff Monte Carson was leaning against one of the posts holding up the awning over the boardwalk when he saw the wagon rolling down the street. Calvin Woods was at the reins, and another of the Sugarloaf hands was on the seat beside him.

Monte straightened up from his casual stance as the wagon went right on past the general store. He had expected the Sugarloaf's foreman to stop there and pick up supplies. As the wagon drew closer, though, Monte spotted several blanket-wrapped shapes in the back, and that brought a frown to his weathered face.

Once an outlaw but for the past two decades a dedicated lawman, he was getting on in years. Before too much longer, he knew he was going to have to give some real thought to retiring as Big Rock's peace officer. His draw, never as fast as his friend Smoke Jensen's but pretty darned swift, had slowed down in recent months. Monte knew that age was catching up to him. It happened to everybody and was inevitable.

But that didn't mean he had to like it.

He was still sheriff, and when somebody brought in a load of dead bodies—he was pretty sure that was what Cal had in the wagon—it was still his job to find out what in blazes had happened. He stepped down from the boardwalk and moved out into the street to intercept the wagon.

As Monte raised a hand, Cal hauled back on the reins, brought the vehicle to a halt, and nodded. "Mornin', Sheriff."

"If I'm not mistaken, that's sort of a grim load you got there, Cal."

The Sugarloaf foreman shrugged and turned to jerk his head toward one of the shrouded shapes that was placed a little apart from the others. "That's Sid MacDowell, one of our hands. I don't have names for the others, but they're all no-good rustlers."

Monte let out a low whistle. "Five of 'em, eh?"

"Yeah, and one got away, damn it. But we came close to makin' it a clean sweep."

"I take it they hit the Sugarloaf last night?"

"Tried to," Cal said. "I'm takin' them down to the undertaker's, but if you want to have a look at them, see if you recognize anybody from the reward dodgers you've got, I can uncover them."

Monte shook his head. "No, you go ahead. I'll come down there and have a gander at them before they're planted. In the old days, we would have strapped the carcasses onto planks and stood them up so the whole town could gawk at them, but I reckon Big Rock is too civilized for that now."

Cal grinned. "You sound like you think that's a bad thing."

"You get to be my age, you start missin' the old days, whether they were really all that good or not." Monte stepped back so Cal could drive on.

He would allow some time while the bodies were prepared and laid out in cheap pine coffins, then check them before the lids were nailed on. Simon Rone, who had taken over Big Rock's undertaking business, knew to send a boy to fetch him before burying any outlaws.

Monte was a bit surprised the slain Sugarloaf man wasn't being laid to rest in the little cemetery out at the ranch. Maybe the fellow had kinfolks elsewhere, and Cal was going to have the body sent back to them. Monte put those thoughts out of his head for the moment. It was time for a second cup of coffee. He wondered sometimes how people ever lived before they started drinking coffee.

As he ambled toward the café, he noticed a man walking toward him, and the instincts that had kept him alive through a lot of long, dangerous years warned him that the hombre intended to brace him. Monte's eyes, still keen as ever even though his gun hand was slowing down, took in the man at a glance.

Late twenties, more than likely, which was still young to Monte. Medium-sized, but he moved with a sort of wolflike grace. He wore denim trousers, a soft buckskin shirt with a drawstring neck but no fringe, and a light brown hat with a rounded crown. A fine layer of trail dust covered the outfit.

A gun belt with a single holstered Colt attached to it was buckled around the stranger's lean hips. He had a pleasant smile on his face, but a certain hardness in his eyes.

The lawman recognized that look. He had seen it in Smoke's eyes many times. The stranger wasn't the sort to call attention to himself.

The truly dangerous ones usually weren't.

The man raised his left hand in an innocuous gesture of greeting as his right hand remained close by the revolver on his hip. "Excuse me. You're Sheriff Carson, aren't you?"

Monte pointed toward the badge pinned to his vest. "That's what this tin star says. What can I do for you?"

"I was hoping I could talk to you for a minute, maybe in your office."

"You have business with the law?"

"You could say that." The stranger lowered his left hand to his waist, slid his fingers behind his belt, and brought out something he concealed in his palm. He turned his hand just enough for Monte to catch a glimpse of a badge.

"You're a lawman?" Monte asked, pitching his voice quietly so that no one else could overhear.

The stranger's attitude made it plain he didn't want his true identity spread around town. His answer was equally quiet. "Deputy U.S. marshal."

"Come on, then," Monte said as he turned toward the sheriff's office. He tried not to sigh. "There'll be a pot of coffee on the stove. I warn you, though, it won't be as good as what we could get at the café."

"As long as it's coffee, that's good enough for me. I started out from Denver early this morning."

The two men walked to the square stone building that housed the sheriff's office and jail. The front office was empty, the two deputies who were on duty at the moment being out walking around town. Monte went over to the potbellied stove in the corner and took down two tin cups from the shelf on the side wall. Using a piece of leather to protect his hand from the heat, he picked up the pot and poured strong black brew into both cups.

"You know who I am." He handed one of the cups to the stranger. "Now, who are you besides somebody who packs a badge for Uncle Sam?"

"My name is Brice Rogers," the young man said. "I'm told you've got a rustling problem around here, and I've come to solve it."

CHAPTER 4

Monte managed not to laugh in his fellow lawman's face, but it wasn't easy. "You have, have you?"

"That's right. We've had reports that cattlemen around here have been losing stock, and my boss, the chief marshal, wants it stopped."

"Since when is stealing cows a federal crime?"

"When those ranchers have contracts to sell those cows to the army, as most of the ones located in this valley do. Anything that interferes with that puts the case under federal jurisdiction."

Monte blew out a breath. "Sounds like a pretty far reach to me."

"You can take that up with Chief Marshal Horton if you'd like."

Monte waved a hand dismissively. "No, there's probably no need to go to that much trouble. Anyway, there's a good chance Smoke Jensen has already solved that little rustling problem his ownself."

"Smoke Jensen? The notorious gunman?"

"Smoke's one of those ranchers you were just talking about. That gang of outlaws tried to hit his spread last night, but Smoke and his men were ready for them.

Did you see me talking to that fella who brought the wagon into town?"

Rogers nodded. "I noticed that, yes."

"That was Cal Woods, the foreman of Smoke's ranch. The bodies of five dead rustlers were in the back of it."

"Jensen executed them?" Rogers asked with a frown. "Was it a lynching?"

"Not hardly. There was a fight when the rustlers tried to drive off some stock. One of Smoke's men was killed, too, but the Sugarloaf came out on top."

"That's Jensen's ranch? The Sugarloaf?"

"Yep. You see now why I said Smoke may have taken care of your problem for you?"

Rogers didn't look convinced. "How do you know there aren't more rustlers?"

"I don't," Monte admitted with a shrug. "In fact, Cal told me that one of the bunch got away, although it's likely he was wounded . . . no telling how bad."

"So the problem may not be over after all. My boss won't like it if I come back without being sure. It looks like I'll be sticking around here for a while, at least until I'm convinced that's nothing else to interfere with those beef contracts."

"Suit yourself, Marshal. I appreciate you letting me know that you're here, as well as what brings you to Big Rock."

Rogers took a sip of his coffee. He didn't make a face at the taste, but he glanced down into the cup as if he'd never encountered anything quite like it before. "You know, now that I think about it, I seem to recall reading quite a few reports about outbreaks of trouble in these parts. Would that have something to do with Smoke Jensen?"

"Smoke's not the kind to start trouble," Monte said.

"But if it comes along, he can damn sure finish it in a hurry."

"He was a wanted man at one time, wasn't he?"

"So was I." Monte's tone was curt. "But that was a long time ago for both of us. I reckon if you care to go back to Denver and dig deeper, you'll find that he's done a lot of good for Colorado, including helping out the governor on occasion."

Rogers lifted his eyebrows. "You're not telling me to get out of town, are you, Sheriff?"

Monte shook his head. "No, just saying you shouldn't jump to any conclusions about Smoke on account of stories that may have been told about him. I've never known a finer, more decent man in all my life. If my word's not good enough for you—"

Rogers raised a hand to stop him. "It's plenty good enough for me. I'm just trying to get a handle on what's going on around here. I'll be around for a while. Marshal Horton didn't put any time limit on this assignment. Actually, I think he'd like to have a man in this part of the state on a semipermanent basis. Times are changing, you know. Civilization has spread all across what used to be the frontier, and it's up to us to make sure that it stays that way. The lawless elements aren't going to go away quietly, though."

"No, I reckon you can count on that," Monte agreed. "From the looks of the way you showed me your badge, I get the idea you don't want it spread around town that you're a lawman."

Rogers nodded. "Yes, I'd rather keep that quiet. I get better results if not everyone in the area knows who I am. I have a little pocket here on the back of my belt where I cache my badge and bona fides."

"Be happy to. If you need a hand with anything, let me know."

"I will, Sheriff." Rogers lifted the cup in his hand. "I'd thank you for the coffee, but—"

"Yeah, I know. Don't worry about—" He stopped when the door opened.

Phil Harrigan, one of his deputies, hurried in. "Sheriff, looks like trouble at the Brown Dirt Cowboy."

Monte bit back a groan. "Again? Blast it. If this keeps up, I may have to ask the town council to shut that place down. It was always a little wild, but since Emmett Brown died and his nephew took over, it's gettin' to be a damn nuisance!"

"What's the Brown Dirt Cowboy?" Rogers asked. "A saloon?"

"Yeah. The second biggest one in town. And the roughest."

Harrigan nodded toward Rogers. "Who's this?"

"Brice Rogers," Monte said. "He's new in town. Just thought I'd have a word with him, let him know how we do things around here."

"You don't have to worry, Sheriff," Rogers said, playing along with Monte's response. "I'm a peaceable man."

"I wish everybody was. See you around, Rogers." Monte headed for the door with Harrigan following him. He asked over his shoulder, "What's going on down there?"

"The Gunderson brothers are at it again."

"Oh, Lord," Monte said. "I should have known."

Arno and Ingborg—who went by the nickname Haystack—Gunderson were a pair of bachelor Swedish brothers who had a farm east of Big Rock, where the terrain was more suitable for growing crops. They were both big, blond, and heavy with muscles from hard work. Normally they were as peaceful as could be. Even when they lost their tempers, they never bothered anyone else . . . they just tried to beat each other to death.

And it was usually over a woman. Not the same woman every time, just one in a succession of soiled doves who found themselves working at the Brown Dirt Cowboy.

Whenever they started a ruckus, Monte had to arrest them to keep them from wrecking the place. They were so big and hardheaded, they could pound on each other for a long time without doing any real damage, but in the process, they fell over tables and chairs and busted them to pieces. Sometimes bottles flew and broke windows and mirrors. It could turn into a real mess in a hurry.

"Who are they fighting over this time?" Monte asked as he and the deputy strode along the street toward the saloon.

"That soiled dove called Cindy."

"I can't keep up with them, the way Claude Brown runs them through there. Is she the one with the red hair and the big . . . uh—"

"That's her all right, Sheriff," Harrigan said.

"Well, I can see how she could get a man riled up." Monte was happily married, but he wasn't blind. "Especially fellas like those Gundersons, who spend so much time by themselves out on that farm, working so hard. When they do come into town, they like to have themselves a good time."

"Cindy can sure provide that." Harrigan added hastily, "Uh, from what I've heard. I wouldn't really know."

As Monte stepped up onto the boardwalk in front of the saloon, a crash came from inside, followed by a scream. He picked up his pace, slapping the bat-wings aside as he plunged through the entrance. Two massive figures were lying on the floor amid the wreckage of a table as they kicked and gouged and punched at each other. A lushly built redhead in a short, spangled dress stood not too far away, her hands pressed to her mouth. She was trying to look horrified by the violence, but her eyes watched the battle with avid interest.

The saloon's other patrons had abandoned their tables and drawn back around the walls to give the combatants plenty of room. Some of them were casually fondling the scandalously clad serving girls who stood with them.

Claude Brown, the current owner of the establishment and the nephew of the man who had started it, stood behind the bar. A florid-faced man in a collarless shirt, he had a bungstarter in his hand, as did the bartender in a grimy apron standing next to him. Monte figured that if either of the Gundersons had come close enough, Brown or the bartender would have leaned over the hardwood and walloped him. Neither of the Swedes had strayed into that danger zone, however.

Spotting Monte, Brown said, "Thank God you're here, Sheriff! You've got to put a stop to this!"

"I intend to." Monte drew his gun as the brothers rolled close enough that they were almost under his feet. He leaned over and shouted, "Hey! Arno! Haystack! That's enough!"

They ignored him, got sausagelike fingers around each other's necks and started squeezing. Both faces under disheveled blond hair began to turn red.

Monte thought about clouting them with his Colt, but he knew it might do more damage to the gun than to their heads. He jammed the revolver back into its holster and called to Brown, "Gimme that bungstarter!"

Brown tossed the mallet to Monte, who caught it and

then stood there watching for an opening to use it. He told the deputy, "Phil, get the other bungstarter."

Harrigan hurried over to the bar. Arno and Haystack suddenly lurched up from the floor and crashed into the sheriff's legs, knocking Monte down. It was an accident. They hadn't even noticed him standing there, as intent on choking each other to death as they seemed to be. But whether it was deliberate or not, he found himself on the sawdust-littered floor, trapped between what seemed like two wild bulls.

Monte swung the bungstarter at a slablike Swedish jaw but missed. The Gundersons rolled on top of him as they continued to struggle, and upwards of four hundred pounds pinned him to the floor. He couldn't breathe, and he didn't have enough air to shout for help.

A shot blasted. The brothers broke apart and rolled off him. That was a huge relief. He could drag breath into his lungs again, but he hoped Phil Harrigan hadn't shot one of them. They might be a couple crazy Scandihoovians, but they weren't outlaws.

Monte looked up. Brice Rogers stood there, gun in hand. A tendril of smoke curled from the revolver's muzzle.

Yelping in outrage, Claude Brown said, "Sheriff, that stranger just shot a hole in my ceiling!"

"I . . . I almost did the same thing . . . myself," Monte said as he sat up, still gasping for air. "Reckon I . . . should have . . . instead of trying to pound some sense . . . into these two."

"You bane all right, Sheriff?" one of the Gundersons asked. Blood leaked from his swollen nose. The other one's mouth was bloody.

"I'm fine," Monte snapped. "Give me a hand, Phil."

Harrigan helped Monte to his feet. "Sorry, Sheriff.

I was tryin' to figure out what to do when this fella barged in and let off that shot."

"And it's a good thing he did. Those two oxes might've crushed every bone in my body if they'd rolled around on me for a while." Monte looked at Rogers. "I'm obliged to you, mister."

Coolly, Rogers returned his Colt to its holster. "Seemed like somebody needed to break it up. That seemed like the quickest way of doing it."

Claude Brown leaned both hands on the bar. "Damn it, somebody has to pay for fixin' that hole in my ceiling."

"The damage will come out of Arno and Haystack's pockets." Monte glared at Cindy. "Were you the cause of this, young woman?"

"I didn't mean anything, Sheriff. I just sat on Arno's lap . . . or was it Haystack's? . . . and then they started arguing—"

"All right." Monte suspected she had been trying to stir up the Gundersons enough to get both of them to pay for her favors, but it didn't really matter.

A soiled dove was never going to take the blame for anything.

He turned his attention to Arno and Haystack, who had climbed to their feet. "Here's what we're going to do. You pay Brown for the damages, and I won't throw you in jail."

"They ought to be fined for disturbing the peace!" Brown protested.

Monte ignored that. "I won't throw you in jail on the condition . . . that the two of you don't come into town together anymore. One at a time, got it?" He knew that given their generally placid nature, they wouldn't likely start fights with anybody except each other.

"But we are brothers," Arno said.

"We do things together," Haystack said.

"You *work* together," Monte said. "From now on you come into town alone. Or you can be locked up together. Your choice."

Arno looked at his brother. "I do not like being locked up."

"Neither do I," Haystack said. "Should we do what the sheriff says?"

"Yah, I think maybe we should."

Both of them looked at Monte and nodded solemnly.

Arno said, "Thank you, Sheriff. You bane a good man."

Monte grunted. "I just don't want to have to feed you. The two of you could bankrupt the town if I kept you behind bars for very long." He leaned his head toward the bar. "Go settle up with Brown. And Claude, you charge those boys a fair price for what they busted up."

Brown scowled, but he didn't argue.

Monte nodded to Rogers, said, "Thanks again," and started toward the door with Harrigan following him.

Outside on the boardwalk, the deputy started making excuses for not acting quicker to stop the fight. "I really didn't have much of a chance to, Sheriff. That fella who came in, he had his gun out mighty slick and fast. I hardly even saw him draw before he squeezed off that shot."

"Is that so?" Monte said. "That's interesting."

So Brice Rogers was fast on the draw. Some lawmen were and some weren't. Those who weren't generally relied on shotguns or lots of deputies.

"You think he's a gunfighter like Smoke?" Harrigan said.

"No," Monte said. "There aren't any gunfighters like Smoke Jensen."

CHAPTER 5

Standing in the parlor, Smoke held up the pieces of frilly fabric, one in each hand. He felt a little ridiculous, but Sally had asked for his help and he couldn't turn down such a request from his wife. It would be all right with him, though, if she would make up her mind pretty soon which one she wanted to use for the new curtains in Denise Nicole's room. As long as Cal or Pearlie didn't come in and find him standing there . . .

Sally cocked her head a little to the side as she mulled over the decision. After a moment, she said, "All right, I think I like the one on the right the best. Or—no, wait a minute. I'm not sure. Now the one on the left looks better to me."

"You know it's not going to make much difference to her, don't you? She never was one to care much about curtains and things like that."

"She's a young lady, and she's going to want something nice in her room."

Smoke didn't argue with her, but he knew that Denise Nicole was a tomboy. He hadn't tried to encourage her in that direction during her visits to the Sugarloaf, but it had become apparent at a pretty early age that she was more interested in riding and roping than she was in frilly, fancy things. Smoke wouldn't have minded if she *hadn't* been that way—his kids were Jensens, and Jensens made up their own minds about things, by God—but he had always enjoyed seeing his daughter take to the outdoor life.

At the same time, she had been a beautiful girl and he knew she had grown into a beautiful young woman. She would be breathtaking in a ballroom, clad in silk and lace and with her mass of blond curls done up in an elaborate hairstyle.

"It's kind of late to be making new curtains, too," Smoke pointed out. "The kids will be here tomorrow morning if the train's on time."

"I know that. I may not have them ready for a few days . . . but I can get started on them, anyway." Sally nodded decisively. "The one on the left. That's what I'm going to use."

Before Smoke could put the two pieces of fabric down, the front door opened and Cal stepped into the foyer. He looked through the arched entrance into the parlor and saw Smoke and Sally standing there. "I can come back later if you want." The Sugarloaf foreman's face was solemn, but Smoke thought he saw a glint of amusement in the younger man's eyes.

"No, that's fine. We're done here," Sally said. "Aren't we, Smoke?"

"Yeah." He handed the fabric to her and thought he caught a glimpse of laughter in her eyes, too. At least she hadn't been using him for a dress dummy or anything that undignified, he thought. He wasn't sure he would ever go that far, even for Sally. "What is it, Cal?"

"Me and some of the boys rode out to the pasture where we had that dustup last night and looked for the tracks of that rustler who got away. We found them, all right, along with some blood."

"You said you thought he was hit."

"Yep, and it appears he was. We were able to follow the trail for a few miles before we lost it. Sorry, Smoke. I was hoping we'd find the fella. Either that or his carcass."

"How much blood was there?"

"Enough to make me think he was ventilated pretty good."

Smoke nodded. "You did what you could, Cal. Chances are, even if the hombre survives his wound, he won't be in a hurry to come back to the Sugarloaf."

"We'll have more of the same to give him if he does," Cal declared vehemently. His forehead creased in a frown. "What worries me is not knowin' if there are any more of those wide-loopers out there somewhere. This varmint could make it back to them and tell them what happened . . . and cause even more trouble in the long run."

"If there are more of them, and they planned on hitting us again, it won't make any difference," Smoke said. "I suppose there could be some personal reason for them to come after us even harder, but I don't know any way to predict that when we don't know who's behind it."

"I reckon we'll find out in time," Cal said, looking gloomy.

"You can probably count on that," Smoke said.

There was only one way into the narrow, twisting box canyon, and it was guarded around the clock. Two men with rifles were always stationed at the entrance, hidden in a clump of boulders that provided good cover for them if they had to shoot at any would-be invaders. As if the sound of shots wouldn't be enough of an indication that something was wrong, signal fires had been laid at each bend in the canyon, and a man was posted at each of those as well. In the event of an attack, each man would light his fire until the warning reached the gang's headquarters at the far end of the canyon, a little over a mile from the entrance.

At that end, the canyon widened into a roughly circular basin half a mile across. Most of the canyon was just stone and dirt, but some scrubby trees and quite a bit of hardy grass grew in the basin, enough to support the small numbers of cattle that grazed there from time to time. A spring-fed pond provided water for men and cattle alike.

As the crow flies, the place was about ten miles north of the Sugarloaf's northern boundary, but a man would have to ride more than twice that far on twisting trails to reach it. Those trails serpentined their way through an area of badlands butted up against the mountains.

Sound traveled pretty well in the thin air of the high country, but the landscape was so rugged it created a lot of echoes, which made it difficult to tell for sure where a sound was coming from.

The guards posted at the canyon's entrance heard the slow, steady hoofbeats of a horse plodding along, but they couldn't be certain it was coming toward them.

They weren't sure until the horse came into sight between a couple boulders on a shallow ridge about a hundred yards away. The man in the saddle leaned forward, and as the horse started down the slope, the rider lost his balance and fell. The guards saw dust puff up from the trail where he landed. The horse shied away a few steps but didn't bolt.

"What the hell?" Turk Sanford said.

From behind a rock on the other side of the canyon entrance, Muddy Malone squinted toward the ridge.

"Fella must be hurt. I thought for a second he might be sleepin', but he didn't jump up when he landed."

"No, he's still there," Turk agreed. "Say, that paint pony looks a little like Blue's."

"You think?" Muddy said. "Lemme get my spyglass. I know the pattern on Blue's horse pretty well." When he had settled down in the rocks for his shift, he had placed his canteen, the telescope—taken from the body of a cavalry lieutenant he had shot in the back a couple years earlier—and a pouch of chaw in a little niche where they would be handy. He picked up the telescope, extended it to its full length, and peered through the glass for a moment. Then he exclaimed, "Son of a *bitch*! That's Blue's pony, all right, and it sure looks like Blue layin' there on the ground. Nick's gonna be loco mad!"

"We knew there was a chance something had happened to him and the other boys," Turk said. "When they didn't come back last night, I had a bad feelin' about it. So did Nick, I reckon. He just wouldn't show it."

"We'd best go see about this," Muddy said.

"And leave our posts?" Turk shook his head. "We're on guard duty, you infernal idiot. What if this is a trick or a trap? Nick'll take that bowie of his and peel our hide off in one-inch strips if we desert our post."

Muddy pointed. "But that's his little brother out there!"

"You don't know that for sure. Could be a lawman, dressed in Blue's clothes, ridin' Blue's horse, and pretending to be Blue to take us by surprise and get us to leave the canyon wide open. Even worse, it could be Smoke Jensen."

"I never heard tell of Jensen doin' anything that tricky, but I suppose it's possible." Muddy gnawed at his lower lip as he continued to frown. "But damn it, there's blood on the fella's shirt, Turk, and you saw the way he toppled off that horse. He's either dead or out cold. He's not playin' a trick."

"Then you go see about him," Turk said. "As for me, I'm stayin' right here."

Muddy stayed where he was, grimacing as he tried to figure out his best course of action. He knew how much store Nick Creighton set by his younger brother Blue. If Blue was lying out there in plain sight, hurt or maybe even dying, and Creighton's men didn't do anything to help him . . . well, that might be more dangerous than abandoning a guard post. "I'm goin'," Muddy told Turk.

"Fine with me. I'm still staying where I was told to stay."

Muddy swallowed hard, tightened his grip on his Winchester, and stepped out of the rocks. He started toward the fallen figure, moving slow and wary at first, but as his nerves tightened and started jumping around more, he began to hurry. After a few quicker steps, he broke into a run.

Nobody shot at him. That was good, anyway.

His boot soles slapped against the hard ground. That and the pounding of his pulse inside his head and the slight wheezing of his breath were the only things he heard. As he got closer, he was able to make out the light brown hair and young face that looked considerably more innocent than Blue Creighton really was. Muddy skidded to a stop, turned, and shouted to Turk, "It's him, damn it! It's Blue!"

Even from a distance, Muddy could hear Turk's bitter curses. Now that Muddy hadn't been ambushed and he knew the wounded man was the gang leader's brother, Turk couldn't very well just stay where he was like a bump on a log. He had to help or risk Creighton's wrath. None of his men wanted to do that.

Without waiting to see what Turk was going to do, Muddy hurried on to Blue's side and dropped to a knee. The youngster lay hunched up, mostly on his left side. The right side of his shirt was dark with dried blood. Muddy saw the brighter red of fresh blood, too. Blue's life was still seeping out.

"Damn, Blue. What happened?" Muddy asked, even though he had a pretty good idea. Carefully, he pulled the shirt up and saw the angry, black-rimmed hole in Blue's belly.

If Blue had been shot the night before when he and the men with him rode down to the Sugarloaf to make off with some more cattle, as seemed likely, he ought to have been dead already. A gut-shot man took a long time to die, but usually not that long. Blue's eyes were closed and his face was covered with sweat. His breath rasped in his throat. He was alive but no telling how much longer that would be true.

Turk pounded up, raising some dust with his hurried steps. "What happened? Is he shot?"

"What do you think?" Turk was a fine one to be calling anybody an idiot, Muddy thought. It was plain as day that Blue had been ventilated.

"Well . . . well, hell! What can we do for him?"

"Get him up on his horse, I reckon, and take him on to the basin. Ain't no point in tryin' to patch him up, but he'd probably like to see his brother before he crosses the divide. Nick'll want to see him, too."

They set their rifles aside and got hold of Blue. Putting the Winchester down made Muddy even more nervous, but he needed both hands free for the grim task.

As they struggled to hold Blue's horse in place and

lift the young man into the saddle, Turk said, "Jensen done this."

"Of course he did."

With much grunting and straining, they got Blue on his horse. Turk held the animal's reins while Muddy kept the wounded man in the saddle.

Muddy went on. "Jensen must've sprung a trap on the boys or just happened on 'em while they were tryin' to drive off that stock. Either way, since Blue's the only one who made it back here, it looks pretty bad for the rest of the fellas."

One at a time, they picked up their rifles, then Turk slowly turned the horse toward the canyon mouth. Muddy kept a hand on Blue to prevent him from sliding off again. They started toward the canyon at a careful pace.

As they went through the entrance, Turk bellowed, "Light the signal fires!"

The signal would ensure that Creighton would send somebody else out to take over the guard post, and they would be ready in the basin for trouble.

They wouldn't be expecting what was coming toward them, though. Anybody who rode the owlhoot trail knew that death could catch up to them at any time, but Blue Creighton had always had such an air of carefree, youthful invincibility that no one in the gang had really believed that he might be killed or even badly hurt. His big brother Nick just wouldn't allow it.

But Nick hadn't been able to stop that slug from burying itself in Blue's gut, and the young outlaw's life could probably be measured in minutes.

Somebody would pay for what had happened to Blue. Muddy felt like he was walking straight into the mouth of a mountain lion's den. He just hoped

Creighton wouldn't go loco and take out his rage on the men who brought his brother in.

Muddy licked his lips and turned to Turk. "You reckon we should've left him out there after all?"

"I reckon we were damned no matter what we did."

CHAPTER 6

Nick Creighton was the only member of the gang who had brought a woman to the hideout. If any of the others resented Molly being there, Creighton didn't know about it—and wouldn't have cared if he did. He was the boss man of the bunch, and his word was law.

He had the only permanent dwelling in the basin, an old cabin probably built by some prospector searching for gold. When Creighton had found the box canyon, realized its proximity to the Sugarloaf, and recognized that it was perfect for his plans, he and his second in command, Lupe Herrera, had set to work right away fixing up the place. The roof had been falling in, but they had repaired that, cleaned up the mess and damage done by time, the elements, and wildlife. Then Creighton had sent for his brother and the rest of the men.

And Molly.

Creighton sat on a stool in front of the cabin, cleaning his rifle. He was a medium-sized man with a hawklike face and a closely clipped, dark mustache. Just to look at him, he didn't seem that impressive. A black hat was shoved back on his head. He wore a black vest over a white shirt, and his gun belt was black as well.

He heard a shout and looked up from what he was doing. Gazing out from under bushy brows, his eyes were cold and reptilian.

Herrera trotted toward him and called, "Nick, the signal fires are lit!"

Creighton closed the Winchester's breech and stood up. He took cartridges from a pocket on his vest and began thumbing them into the rifle's loading gate. Word was already spreading through the camp. He saw men hurrying among the tents, getting ready for trouble if it was about to come calling.

Molly appeared in the doorway and asked, "What's going on?"

Creighton glanced over at her. She wore a plain cotton dress that hugged her well-shaped body. Her long, straight brown hair was parted in the middle. Her jaw was a little too strong and her nose a little too big for her to be called beautiful, but she had an earthy, sensuous appeal that slapped a man right across the face and made him want her.

Creighton had taken her away from a lynch mob in a small Wyoming settlement that wanted to hang her because she had killed one of her customers at the local whorehouse. The dead man was a well-liked local and she was just a soiled dove, so even though the bastard had been beating on her and might have hurt her badly or even killed her, his friends had wanted to string her up.

They had abandoned that idea pretty quickly when Creighton shot a couple of them.

Molly had been with him ever since, almost two years, the longest Creighton had been with any woman . . . well, ever. He wouldn't have gone so far as to say he loved her, because he didn't really love

anybody except his little brother Blue, but Molly was a
pretty good ol' gal, to his way of thinking.

"Signal fires are lit," he told her. "I don't know what
it's about. Lupe, go and see."

Herrera nodded and ran toward the men bristling
with rifles and revolvers who were gathering where the
canyon widened into the basin.

"This is bad," Molly said.

"One of those feelings you get again?"

She frowned. "Don't make fun of them, Nick. I've
always been able to tell when something bad was about
to happen."

"I'm not making fun of them," Creighton said.
"Hell, I have hunches, too."

"This is more than just a hunch, though. It's like
somebody's talking to me."

Creighton sometimes thought she really was a little
touched in the head, that maybe she actually heard
voices that weren't there. She'd had a hard life before
their trails crossed, and it hadn't always been pleasant
since then. That was enough to make a person not
quite right.

Or maybe it was all true and she really did have
some sort of power. Creighton didn't know and couldn't
see that it really mattered one way or the other.

"It's Blue," she said.

Creighton's head jerked toward her again. "Hell,
no. The boy's all right. He's got to be."

"He and the others didn't come back last night
when you expected them."

"That doesn't mean anything's happened to him.
The cattle could have stampeded after Blue and the
boys drove them away from Jensen's ranch. They
could still be down there, trying to gather them up."

Molly just looked at him like he was a little boy

whistling past a graveyard. Creighton bit back a curse and waited to see what was going to happen.

He didn't have to wait long. A few minutes later he saw a commotion at the canyon mouth, then the men broke apart and let two more men and a horse enter the basin. Creighton's breath hissed between his teeth as he inhaled sharply. One of the men was leading a horse while the other guard walked alongside and braced the rider in the saddle.

The horse was a paint pony just like the one Blue rode.

No, it *was* the one Blue rode, Creighton realized, and he felt a cold, hollow spot form in his belly as the certainty of who the rider was sunk in on him. "No."

"I'm sorry, Nick," Molly said.

His head jerked toward her again as his lips drew back from his teeth in a snarl. Rage boiled up inside him, and he wanted to smash his fist in the middle of her face.

Then he brought the murderous fury under control. Molly might have predicted it, but she hadn't caused it. Whatever had happened to Blue, it wasn't her fault.

As the men with the paint pony came closer, Creighton recognized them as Turk Sanford and Muddy Malone. They'd been standing guard all the way out at the other end of the canyon. He figured Blue had made it that far on his own, and they had brought him the rest of the way.

Creighton walked out to meet them, revealing how he limped heavily on his left leg. The hobbled gait made him rock and forth as he walked. He knew it probably looked comical to his men, but none of them ever said anything about it. They knew better.

Each awkward step reminded him of Smoke Jensen and the blood debt owed to him.

That blood debt had just grown larger, Creighton thought as he swallowed hard. He could see Blue's pale, pain-wracked face, as well as the dark blood on the youngster's shirt.

It had never occurred to him not to send his brother out on jobs like the one the previous night. One day Blue might be running the gang, and he had to know how things were done. Anyway, he had been in plenty of shooting scrapes and come out of them all right. He knew how to take care of himself. Creighton had figured that would continue.

From the looks of it, though, Blue's luck had run out.

"Boss, I'm sorry!" Turk called when they were close enough. "It's Blue!"

"I can see that, you damn fool." Creighton waved them on. "Take him to the cabin!" In a mixture of hope and despair, he added, "Maybe Molly can do something for him."

When Turk led the paint past him, Creighton saw the location of the wound and how much blood had soaked into Blue's shirt. Any hope he might have had disappeared. Blue was shot in the belly. Nobody recovered from a wound like that without immediate medical attention, and even then such a recovery was mighty rare.

Still feeling cold and empty inside, Creighton limped after the pony.

Molly was waiting at the cabin. "All of you men get hold of him and bring him inside. Be careful with him."

Four men lifted Blue down from the saddle and carried him into the cabin. Following Molly's commands, they lowered him onto the room's single bunk. His head lolled loosely on his neck. He looked dead, but Creighton could hear and see that he was still breathing, although pretty raggedly.

"I need hot water," Molly said. "You—Muddy—you stay and help me. The rest of you go back outside."

"He's my brother, damn it," Creighton said.

"And that's why you're too upset to be of any use to me. He probably doesn't have a chance, but we're not letting him go without a fight."

A fierce note had entered Molly's voice as she spoke, and Creighton had a pretty good idea why. He had come back to the cabin one night and found Blue there, grunting and thrusting on top of Molly. Any of his other men, he would have put a bullet in their heads—well, maybe not Lupe—but he couldn't do that to Blue. A whore was a whore and a brother was a brother, he had told himself, then said to hell with it and went away for a while. As far as he knew, they never had any idea he'd been there.

Maybe they had been together from time to time since then. Creighton wasn't sure. But he knew Molly was fond of the kid, and she would do her best to save him, even though the attempt was almost certainly futile.

Why wouldn't he have shot Lupe if he'd been the one with Molly? Lupe was a good segundo.

Outside again, Creighton asked Turk, "What happened?"

"Muddy and me were standing guard just like we were supposed to, Nick, when we saw Blue's pony come over that ridge in front of the canyon mouth. Looked like he was barely hanging on, and he fell off when the horse started down the slope. When we saw who it was, we went out to help him."

"You mean you abandoned your post and left the entrance to the canyon wide open." Creighton's voice had a knife's edge to it.

Visibly nervous, Turk said, "We talked about that, boss, we really did. I stayed at the canyon mouth while

Muddy checked on him. When he was sure it was Blue, and that he was still alive, I went to give Muddy a hand. We were pretty sure by then it wasn't a trick or a trap."

"Pretty sure," Herrera repeated with an undertone of menace of his own.

Anger made Turk's face flush slightly. "It was Nick's little brother lyin' out there. We couldn't just leave him, no matter what our orders were. I don't reckon you would have, either, Lupe."

Creighton waved away Turk's protests. "Forget it. You were in a bad spot, Turk. I know that."

"When we got to the first signal fire, we told the fella there to go on out to the canyon mouth and keep his eyes open as soon as he lit the blaze," Turk said. "So it's not like the entrance was completely unguarded for long."

"I said forget it."

"All right, boss. Thanks."

Creighton looked around the basin. Things appeared to be getting back to normal. Men were lounging in front of their tents, cleaning guns, drinking, playing cards. On the other side of the basin, a pole fence with a gate closed off part of the area keeping the stolen stock before they drove it to an outlaws' rendezvous where shady buyers took the cattle off their hands.

That pasture was empty . . but it should have had some of Smoke Jensen's cattle in it.

And Blue should have been laughing and joking about how they'd rustled that stock from the Sugarloaf, instead of fighting for every breath.

From the cabin doorway, Molly said, "You'd better come in here, Nick."

The grim tone of her voice and the frozen set of her face when Creighton turned to look at her told him everything he needed to know. She moved aside so he could limp into the cabin.

Muddy stood to one side and shook his head. "Boss, I'm sure sorry—"

"Get out," Creighton said.

Muddy hastened to follow the command.

Creighton approached the head of the bunk.

Molly stood at the foot. She said quietly, "I cleaned away some of the blood, enough to see that there was nothing I could do."

"He's still alive?"

"Yes, but I don't see how. He was conscious a minute ago, but he may have slipped away again."

Creighton dropped to a knee beside the bunk. That wasn't easy with his stiff left leg, but he did the best he could. He gripped Blue's shoulder hard.

The boy's eyelids fluttered at the touch and after a few seconds stayed open. "N-Nick . . . ?" he whispered.

"I'm right here, little brother. You just take it easy. You're going to be all right." He knew that was a lie.

So did Molly. Blue probably did, too. But it was what was said at a time like that.

"Nick, I . . . I'm sorry. We didn't get those cows . . . from the Sugarloaf. Somebody . . . jumped us. Must've been . . . Jensen and his men."

"Yeah, bound to be," Creighton said. "What happened to the other boys?"

"Don't . . . know . . . Never saw 'em . . . after the shootin' started . . . but I reckon . . . they never made it out."

"Don't worry. Just that much more Jensen has to answer for. We'll settle the score for them."

"And . . . for me," Blue said.

"You're going to be fine—"

"I . . . know better. Nick, is . . . is Molly here? I can't see her . . ."

"I'm here, Blue." She leaned down and rested a hand on his leg.

"You take . . . good care o' her, Nick. She's . . . a fine lady."

A tear welled from each eye to roll down Molly's cheeks. More than likely, she hadn't been called a lady very often, and probably no one had ever meant it as much as Blue.

Blue swallowed and started to breathe harder. "Nick, I'm scared. I can't see nothin' anymore." He lifted his head a little. "I can't—" His head fell back and the air emptied from his lungs in a rattling sigh. His eyes were still open, but they weren't seeing anything anymore.

Creighton's hand tightened on his brother's shoulder even though Blue couldn't feel it. "I'll make Jensen pay, Blue," he promised. "Him and all the rest on that damned ranch. I'll wipe Smoke Jensen and everyone he loves off the face of the earth!"

CHAPTER 7

The westbound train was supposed to roll into Big Rock at 10:17 in the morning. Trains were never early, but Sally wanted to be in town by 9:30 anyway, so she climbed onto the wagon seat and took up the reins herself in plenty of time to arrive by then. She could handle a team as well as or better than most men, Smoke thought as he swung up into the saddle and nudged his horse alongside the wagon. He had tied a second mount to the back of the wagon for Louis.

"You're never prettier than when you're happy like this," Smoke said to his wife.

"How can I not be happy? My children are coming home, and this time they're going to be staying!" She grew more serious. "I just hope Louis's health doesn't force him to return to Europe later on, despite his intentions."

"Doctors are getting better all over, including here in the States," Smoke said. "If he needs help, maybe he can just go to Denver, or back to Philadelphia or Boston if necessary. Even that's a lot closer than France!"

Of course, it could be that breathing in all the

clean Colorado air might be as much of a restorative as anything else, he thought. Fresh air and hard work couldn't cure everything, but they sure never hurt.

The previous night had passed quietly on the Sugarloaf. After the battle with the rustlers, Smoke hadn't expected another raid so soon, although one could never tell what owlhoots might do. Smoke wasn't going to let his guard down. For more than thirty years, he had been ready for trouble, and he didn't see any point in changing that attitude.

It was a beautiful morning with huge white clouds floating over the mountains to the west and just a hint of coolness in the air in the valley. Smoke and Sally didn't talk much on their way into the settlement. They had been together for so long, and their love for each other was so deep, that quiet companionship was normal.

They reached Big Rock in plenty of time, as Smoke had figured they would.

Sally brought the wagon to a halt in front of the train station. "I'm going to walk back up to the dress shop," she informed Smoke as he dismounted and tied his horse to one of the station's hitch rails. "I want to see what Mrs. Bannister has. Denise might want some new outfits."

"That's a fine idea," Smoke said. "I see Monte over there at the hardware store, so I'll go talk to him."

They went their separate ways for the moment. Smoke stepped up on the boardwalk on the opposite side of the street from Sally and ambled along to Reese's Hardware, where Sheriff Monte Carson was looking at a plow sitting on the walk.

"Going to turn in your badge and take up farming, Monte?" Smoke asked with a smile on his face.

"Not hardly," the lawman said. "I'm too old to be

wrestling a plow all day. Never did care much for the idea of farming. That's why I, uh, took up other occupations."

"Went on the owlhoot, you mean."

"I made some bad decisions in my life," Monte allowed. "Backing your play all those years ago wasn't one of 'em. Never would've had this job and my wife if I hadn't." He slapped the plow handle. "No, this just made me think of a run-in I had yesterday with Arno and Haystack Gunderson."

Smoke let out a low whistle. "Those two were at it again?"

"Yeah, they tangled over some redheaded calico cat and busted up the Brown Dirt Cowboy a little. When I was trying to bust them up, they accidentally knocked me down—and then Haystack fell on me!"

Smoke winced. "That must've hurt."

"My ribs are still a little sore today," Monte said with a rueful smile. "Luckily, I had some help handling those two Scandahoovian buffaloes."

"Help from your deputies?" Smoke knew that Monte was relying more and more on his assistants as age began to catch up with him. Eventually, Big Rock would have to have a new sheriff . . . but not just yet, Smoke thought.

"No, that fella over there pitched in to give me a hand." Monte nodded to someone across the street.

Smoke looked in that direction and saw a mild-looking young man in a brown buckskin shirt and a brown hat walking toward the depot. As it happened, the man met Sally going the other way just as Smoke looked in that direction. He smiled, reached up and tugged his hat brim, and nodded. Sally returned the smile and the nod and said something to him. He replied to her and moved on. The encounter was brief but apparently pleasant.

"Stranger in town, isn't he?" Smoke said.

"Yeah. I think he just rode in yesterday. Name is Brice Rogers. Mean anything to you?"

Smoke thought about it for a moment, then shook his head. "No, I don't reckon it does. Should it?"

"I don't know of any reason why it should," Monte said.

That was kind of an odd thing to say, Smoke thought, but Monte didn't offer an explanation and Smoke didn't press him for one.

He shrugged. "I thought I'd go up to Longmont's and get a cup of coffee. Want to come along?"

"That sounds good. Won't find a better cup of coffee in Big Rock than at Longmont's." As the two men started along the boardwalk, Monte went on. "What brings you and Sally to town this morning, Smoke? I saw her drive in with the wagon."

Smoke grinned. "I'm surprised you haven't heard, the way you keep your ear to the ground. Louis Arthur and Denise Nicole are coming home today."

"The twins? You don't say! That's good news. Coming for a visit, are they?"

"Actually, according to the telegram we got, they're going to be staying."

"Well, what do you know," Monte said. "That's not good news, Smoke, it's great news. Those two are as fine a pair of kids as anybody could ever want." Monte and his wife had no children themselves, but they had been an unofficial aunt and uncle to Smoke and Sally's young-sters when Louis and Denise were little . . . before they'd gone to Europe. "How's Louis's health these days?"

"Good as far as we know," Smoke said. "I'd like for him to be able to take over the ranch one of these days. I don't know if he'll ever be up to that, though."

"Just have to wait and see, I reckon. They're on the train coming in this morning?"

"That's what the telegram said."

They turned in at Longmont's Saloon. The place was more than just a drinking and gambling establishment. It was also one of the finest restaurants in Big Rock, maybe *the* finest. And as Monte had said, the coffee couldn't be beat. Louis Longmont, with his Cajun heritage, saw to that.

The dapper gambler, gunman, and saloonkeeper was sitting at one of the tables in the rear of the big room, sorting through some papers. In the middle of the morning, the saloon wasn't busy, so he had no trouble spotting Smoke and Monte when they came in. A gesture of his elegant hand motioned for them to join him.

Smoke looked over at the bar and told the red-jacketed man behind it, "Coffee for the sheriff and me, Stewart."

"Coming right up, Smoke," the bartender replied.

Louis already had a cup sitting on the table. He took a sip from it as Smoke and Monte pulled out chairs. "Good morning, gentlemen. Smoke, it's been a while since I've seen you. How are you?"

"Doing fine. Better today, because your namesake is supposed to be on this morning's train, along with his sister."

Longmont's eyebrows rose. "The children are coming home? Excellent news, my friend. I'll be glad to see them again. I'm sure they've grown into fine young people by now."

"I hope so," Smoke said as the bartender placed steaming cups of coffee in front of him and Monte.

"How could they have done anything else, with parents like you and Sally?" Longmont said.

The men sipped their coffee and conversed pleasantly for a while. Smoke kept an eye on the time. It wouldn't do to be late to the train station. He would probably hear the locomotive's whistle when it rolled in, but it wouldn't hurt to be on the safe side.

When he knew he ought to be getting back down there, he drained the rest of the coffee from his cup and stood. "Time to go."

"I'll come with you," Longmont said, getting to his feet as well.

"And so will I," Monte added. "Anyway, it's my job. I have to keep an eye on departures and arrivals, you know."

Longmont got his flat-crowned black hat from a hook on the wall, then joined Smoke and Monte in strolling toward the train station. As they approached, Smoke spotted Sally going into the big, red-brick building ahead of them. She was eager to see her kids again, and Smoke couldn't blame her. So was he.

The three men entered the lobby and crossed it to the doors leading onto the long, covered platform next to the rails. As they emerged onto the platform, Smoke saw Brice Rogers standing at the far end, leaning against one of the pillars that held up the roof.

Nothing suspicious about that, Smoke thought. *Maybe Rogers was meeting somebody. No reason to think otherwise.*

And yet something about the young man made Smoke's instincts kick into gear. Although Rogers's stance seemed completely casual, he appeared ready to move instantly if need be. His right thumb was tucked behind his belt, meaning that hand was very close to the walnut grips of the revolver holstered on his hip.

Smoke had seen enough savvy gun-handlers to recognize one when he saw him. Again, he knew that didn't have to mean a thing.

He also knew that he was going to be watching Rogers from the corner of his eye.

Sally went over to Smoke and his companions with a big smile on her beautiful face. She said hello to the sheriff and the saloonkeeper, then told Smoke, "I asked at the ticket window. The train is supposed to be on time. So it shouldn't be much longer—"

The shrill blast of a whistle in the distance interrupted her hopeful statement.

Smoke grinned. "Here they come now."

CHAPTER 8

Denny hadn't run into any more trouble since the encounter with the derby-wearing lech the day before. She had seen him once since then, at the opposite end of a passenger car she and Louis were entering on their way to the club car. The man had taken one look at her, turned around, and hastily went the other way.

Almost home, Denny could feel her excitement growing. Soon she would be on the Sugarloaf again. She was grateful to her grandparents for everything they had done to help Louis, and she had enjoyed living on the Reynolds estate in England and touring the continent.

Even though she had been born back east in Boston, the Sugarloaf was in her blood. Her heart leaped and the blood raced in her veins as she looked out the window beside her at the snowcapped mountains. That wild, magnificent land was where she was meant to be, and she hoped never to leave it again, at least not for very long at a time.

Something bumped her shoulder. She looked over to see that Louis had dozed off and was leaning his head against her. How in the world could he sleep at a time like this, Denny asked herself?

But that was Louis for you. He was a lot stronger than he had been as a child, but he was still tired a lot of the time. He would probably never be able to lead the sort of adventurous outdoor life she craved . . . but who could tell about such things? The doctors at the clinic, during Louis's last visit, had in fact advised him to return home, saying that they had done all they could for him. Their hope was that being out in the fresh air and nature would strengthen him even more.

Denny hoped that, too. She would do anything she could to help her twin.

She nudged him with an elbow. "Wake up, sleepy-head. We'll be home in another few minutes."

Louis stirred, lifted his head, and murmured, "What?" He looked around, blinked a few times, and said, "Oh. We're almost there, aren't we?"

"We certainly are. You don't want to sleep through it."

"Not much chance of that." He regarded his sister thoughtfully. "Before the day's over, you're going to be wearing jeans and riding a horse, aren't you? Back in the saddle, toting a rifle around, searching for excitement."

Denny laughed. "I have to admit that sounds pretty good to me. But I don't have to—"

"Oh, no. Don't let me stop you," Louis said, holding up a hand to forestall her protest. "You should get out and run wild. You've been waiting patiently long enough for a chance to do that."

"I don't figure Mother will let me run wild."

"Father might, though. He'd understand if you did, anyway. After all, he took off for the West and started fighting Indians and bad men when he was still just a boy."

"A boy who grew up quick." Denny knew the basics of her father's adventurous life. Smoke had always answered her questions honestly because he wanted her to know the truth, not what came from the fevered imaginations of whiskey-addled dime novelists, as he put it. Even so, she was sure he had tried to shield her from some of the more sordid details. That would be a father's natural instinct.

Louis patted his sister's hand and said dryly, "Don't worry, Denny. I'm sure you'll have your own adventures."

"I wouldn't count on that. Nobody's going to dare mess with Smoke Jensen's daughter."

So that was the notorious Smoke Jensen, Brice Rogers thought as he looked along the platform at the small group of people clustered at the other end. He had seen photographs of Jensen in newspapers. At first glance the man didn't *look* like one of the deadliest gunfighters the West had ever known. He was more likely to be taken for a successful, middle-aged rancher.

Rogers supposed that was what Jensen actually was since he owned the vast, lucrative Sugarloaf Ranch. After Marshal Horton had given him his current assignment, Rogers had gone to the Denver Public Library and done some reading up in the newspapers on the area and its prominent citizens before he rode up there.

He took a closer look at Smoke Jensen. It revealed the pantherlike tread with which he moved and the obvious strength packed into that impressive broad-shouldered frame. Also, he wore a holstered Colt on his hip, something not many men did anymore. It was a new, modern century, and normal men didn't pack iron, even where the law still allowed it.

The very attractive woman with Jensen had to be his

wife Sally. She appeared to be charming and elegant. Rogers knew that she had been a teacher at one time.

Sheriff Carson was there, too, and a dark-haired, well-dressed man Rogers didn't recognize. If he had to guess why they were all there, he'd say they were meeting someone.

He hoped the Jensens planned on staying in town for a while. That would give him a chance to ride out to the Sugarloaf and have a look around without having to worry about running into Jensen and needing to explain himself. He didn't want to reveal his true identity to anyone except Sheriff Carson, and he sure didn't want to have to swap lead with a notorious gunfighter!

The locomotive's whistle blasted again. Rogers could see the smoke billowing up from the stack as it rose above the trees just outside town and hear the rumble of the engine as it drew nearer. A moment later the train came into view and its brakes began to squeal as they clamped down on the drivers.

The big Baldwin locomotive rolled past and slowed to a perfect stop with the passenger cars lined up next to the platform. Jensen and the others moved toward one of the cars. Maybe they had spotted whoever they were waiting for through the car's windows.

Rogers straightened from his casual stance. He had no real reason for being there other than a lawman's natural curiosity about who was getting off the train. As he had told Sheriff Carson, he might be around those parts for a while, and he wanted to get a good grip on what went on in Big Rock and the surrounding area. As he waited for passengers to get off the train, he remembered his conversation with the chief marshal in the federal building in Denver.

* * *

"*Monte Carson is getting old. Of course, when his term's up, the people can elect a new sheriff if Carson decides not to run again, or replace him if he does. Or maybe they'll keep him in the job. There's never any telling what voters will do. But either way, that's a prosperous, growing area up there, and it needs law and order!*"

"*That's why you're sending me, Marshal,*" Brice said with quiet confidence. Despite his relative youth, he had been a lawman for a few years and had been successful in the job. He didn't doubt that he could handle whatever task Horton assigned him.

The white-mustachioed old chief marshal started fiddling with his pipe. "*Your first order of business is to get to the bottom of the rustling that's been going on around Big Rock. Find out who's responsible and then bust up the gang. Once you've done that, you can send me a wire, and I'll tell you whether you should come back or stay where you are.*"

Brice shifted the hat he had perched on his knee. "*You make it sound like this might be a permanent assignment, Marshal.*"

"*That valley is a hotbed of trouble!*" Horton said as he thumped a fist on the desk. "*It has been for a long time. You know how Big Rock got started, don't you?*"

"*Same way as any other settlement, I reckon,*" Brice replied with a shrug.

"*Not exactly. There was another town in that area called Fontana. An outlaw town. The fella who ran things came up against Smoke Jensen. Jensen got the honest, respectable folks to move out of Fontana and start themselves a new settlement. That's the one wound up bein' called Big Rock.*"

"*What happened to Fontana?*"

Finished packing his pipe, Horton scratched a kitchen match to life on the sole of his boot and lit it. When he had the pipe going good, he blew out a cloud of smoke and said, "*Smoke Jensen and his friends blasted all those owlhoots to hell and burned down their town. He had already started his*

Sugarloaf ranch by then, so he kept it going. Trouble's broken out more times than I can count, and Jensen was right in the middle of it every time."

"Sounds to me like he might be an outlaw himself," Brice commented.

Horton shook his head vehemently. "No, there have been rumors about him, but men I trust have told me that Jensen's as honest as the day is long. The man's just a lodestone when it comes to trouble! He attracts it. There's plenty of potential for it up there in those parts, too. You've got big ranches all around, farming to the east, mining in the mountains to the west, pilgrims passing through all the time . . . I've been thinkin' for a while now it'd be a good idea to have a man up there to sort of keep the lid on things. Could be you, Brice. We'll see how it goes with this rustlin' job."

"You can count on me, Marshal."

"Hell, I know that! Why do you think I called you in here this mornin'?"

Those memories faded from Rogers's thoughts as he saw a young woman step onto the platform at the rear of one of the passenger cars and start down the steps a porter had set in place. She wore a blue traveling outfit with a matching hat that sported a small feather. Thick blond curls seemed barely contained under the hat. They looked like it wouldn't take much to send them spilling down around her shoulders.

That would be an interesting sight to see, he found himself thinking.

The young woman was slender but shapely, with a golden tan on her face that was set off by a small beauty mark near her mouth. He was no real judge of female beauty but knew he was having a hard time taking his eyes off her.

Jensen and his wife moved forward to greet her as

she reached the bottom of the steps. There were happy smiles all around as they hugged her.

It was a family reunion, Rogers realized. He could see the resemblance between the young woman and both of the older Jensens.

Then a young man followed her out of the railroad car and down the steps. He had fair hair, too, and wore a suit and a bowler hat. Pale, narrow-shouldered, and downright skinny, he wasn't nearly as impressive physically as Jensen, but again, there was enough of a resemblance for Rogers to make the connection. And the man looked enough like the young woman that it was obvious they were twins.

Jensen youngsters coming home to visit their parents, Rogers decided, wondering if they knew about the rustling.

The young man was greeted with handshaking and backslapping by the men and a hug from his mother. The entire group moved toward the station lobby, talking animatedly. Back at the baggage car, porters were unloading bags and placing them on a cart. Rogers figured they would roll it around the depot and load the bags on a wagon for the new arrivals. No one else seemed to be getting off the train.

Instead of going through the station, Rogers ambled along the platform to its end, went down the steps, and started around the brick building that way.

CHAPTER 9

Denny liked to think she was grown up and knew how to keep her emotions under control, but when she saw her parents, she suddenly felt like a little girl again. It was wonderful to hug her mother, to have her father pat her gently on the back. She felt her eyes growing damp with tears of happiness and tried to banish them.

Then Louis came down the steps from the railroad car and said with a grin, "Let me in on that."

Sheriff Monte Carson gravely shook hands with Denny and said, "Welcome home, Denise."

Louis Longmont wasn't satisfied with that. He took Denny's hand, bent over it, and pressed his lips to the back of it. "I always knew you would grow up to be a beautiful woman, Denise," he said as he straightened. "I see I was right. I couldn't be prouder of you if you were my own niece."

"Thank you, Mr. Longmont."

He waved a carefully manicured hand. "You're old enough to call me Louis now."

"Then I might get you confused with my brother. He's Louis, too, you know."

"Of course." The gambler smiled. "All right, then, Mr. Longmont it is."

Sally said, "We're having a big dinner out at the ranch tonight to welcome the children home. You and your wife should come, Monte, and you, too, Louis. You're all invited."

"We'll be there," the sheriff promised, and Longmont nodded his agreement as well.

Smoke started herding them toward the station lobby. "Let's go. They'll have the bags loaded pretty soon, and then we can head for the Sugarloaf. It'll sure be good to have you kids home."

"It's good to be home," Louis said.

"And you're really here to stay this time?" Sally said as she linked her arm with her son's.

"As far as I'm concerned, we're here to stay," Louis said. "How about you, Denny?"

"As much as I appreciate everything Grandmother and Grandfather Reynolds did for us, I'm a Western girl," Denny declared. "Reckon I always will be."

"Denny?" Sally repeated. "Louis called you Denny?"

"That's right. Denise Nicole sounds too formal. Pa used to call me Denny when I was a little girl."

Smoke grinned. "I sure did."

"Anyway, I like it," Denny said.

"I suppose I can get used to it." Sally looked at her son. "Are we supposed to call you *Louie* now?"

"I'd really rather you didn't," Louis said.

That brought a hearty laugh from Smoke as he slapped Louis on the back. "Come on, son."

The Brown Dirt Cowboy was open for business, but there wouldn't be much of it until later in the day. At the moment, only two customers were inside, and one of them was passed out facedown at one of the tables, snoring blissfully with his cheek in a little puddle of spilled beer.

The other customer was Haystack Gunderson, who stood at the bar talking to the buxom soiled dove called Cindy.

"No, damn it. I don't want to go upstairs, Haystack," she said in response to his plea. "It's too early! Hell, I've only had one cup of coffee. I'm barely awake. I should still be asleep at this unholy hour. I'm only down here because Claude likes to have at least one girl around all the time."

"But that's why you're here," Haystack insisted. "To work, yah?"

"No, I'm here so any fellas who come in lookin' for a little hair of the dog will have somethin' pretty to look at." She gave his broad chest a push as he leaned closer to her on the stool where she sat. "Now you go on and get outta here. Claude said you and your brother weren't allowed in here for a week after all the hell you raised yesterday, and if he wasn't asleep you never would've made it through the door. Git!"

"I will not," Haystack declared stolidly. "Not until I have spent time with the girl I love—"

The batwings slammed open. Work boots thudded loudly on the floor as the broad, towering figure of Arno Gunderson stomped into the saloon. "Ingborg!" he shouted at his brother. "When I saw you bane gone, I knew where you'd sneaked off to! You bane go behind my back with Cindy, yah?"

Haystack thumped a big fist against his chest and bellowed, "Cindy is my girl!"

Arno sneered. "That's not what she told me the last time I was with her!"

"Not again!" Cindy wailed.

Haystack lowered his head, roared in outrage, and charged like a maddened bull. The brothers crashed together with such force the floor practically shook. Haystack had built up enough steam to drive Arno backwards through the batwings. As they grappled, they stumbled across the boardwalk and then fell into the street. They rolled over a couple times and then surged to their feet, dust-covered giants whaling away at each other with hamlike fists.

Caught up in the heat of battle, the two men paid no attention to their surroundings. Arno sent a straight right to his brother's jaw that landed with such power Haystack was thrown back against a team of four horses hitched to a wagon parked at the edge of the street.

The collision spooked the animals. One of the leaders let out a shrill whinny and lunged against its harness. The other horses followed suit. As the wagon jerked forward, its front corner clipped Haystack and spun him off his feet. He barely avoided being run over by the wheels as the team stampeded down the street toward the train station.

Directly in their path, a woman was crossing the street with two small children, a boy and a girl, each holding one of the woman's hands. At the sight of the crazed team barreling toward them, her scream shattered the peaceful morning. She broke into a run, tugging the children with her.

One hand slipped, though, leaving the little girl crying and frozen in the path of the stampeding horses and the bouncing, rattling wagon.

Denny and the others had angled toward one of the boardwalks as they left the depot, but they hadn't gone far when the commotion broke out. She heard the scream, looked toward the center of the street, and saw the little girl standing there while the child's mother hesitated, unsure what to do.

Denny didn't wait. Instinct took over. The high-buttoned shoes she wore under her traveling outfit weren't really made for running, but that didn't stop her from lifting her skirt and flashing out into the street. She thought she could grab the little girl and get her out of the path of the runaway team.

She was only halfway there when somebody tackled her.

Denny went down hard in the dirt. The impact knocked the breath out of her and left her stunned. All she could do was lift her head and watch as the man who had knocked her down scrambled back to his feet and practically flung himself toward the child. He reached out, plucked the girl from the ground, pulled her against him as he landed on his shoulder and rolled.

The slashing, iron-shod hooves missed them by inches.

The team was still stampeding. Although breathless, Denny forced herself to her feet and took a couple quick steps as the wagon rocketed past her. She leaped and caught hold of the tailgate. She thought she heard someone shouting at her, but she ignored it and concentrated on pulling herself up. Finally, she managed to hook a foot over the tailgate.

That allowed her to lever herself up and over, into the wagon bed. The vehicle was empty. On hands and knees she crawled forward, muttering to herself about how it would have been a lot easier and quicker if she'd been wearing pants. She climbed over the back of the seat, grabbed the reins where they had looped around part of the wagon's frame, and hauled back on the lines as she braced her feet against the floorboards.

"Whoa!" she called to the horses. "Whoa there, you crazy varmints!"

As the team slowed a crazy thought crossed her mind. What would they have thought of her back in England or on the continent if they could see her now? A tight smile curve her lips as she sawed on the reins and the spooked team finally came to a halt.

Hearing shouts behind her, she turned on the seat and looked back along the street. Her mother, father, and brother were hurrying toward her, followed by Louis Longmont. Farther up the street, Sheriff Carson was haranguing the two big, sheepish-looking men who had stampeded the wagon team. A few yards from them, a man in a buckskin shirt handed the sobbing little girl to her equally distraught mother while the little boy clung to the woman's skirts.

"Denise Nicole!" Sally Jensen cried as she ran up to the wagon. "What in the world were you thinking?"

"That someone had to get that little girl out of the way of those horses before they trampled her, of course," Denny answered as she lifted a hand and pushed her hair out of her eyes. That made her aware her hat was gone and her hair had come loose from its pins and fallen around her face and shoulders. She didn't care about that. A toss of her head got it out of the way.

"Your father could have—"

"Denny reacted faster than I did," Smoke said. "In fact, that was pretty fast for anybody."

Denny jumped down from the wagon. "Yes, and I would have gotten there in time if somebody hadn't interfered with me." She stalked past her parents and headed for the man who had tackled her.

"Denise!" Sally said.

"You'd better let her go, Mother," Louis advised. "She's got blood in her eye, and when she looks like that there's no stopping her."

Denny thought she heard her father chuckle at that comment, but she wasn't sure. Then she was out of earshot and she didn't care anymore. She was about to confront the man who had come out of nowhere to knock her down. He had just bent over, picked up his hat from the street, and started to swat it against his leg to get some of the dust off it.

Denny grabbed his shoulder and jerked him around. "Hey! What the hell did you think you were doing?"

CHAPTER 10

Rogers's first instinct when he was grabbed was to reach for his gun, but he controlled the impulse and was glad he did when he saw who was confronting him. He wouldn't want to throw down on anybody as pretty as the young woman in front of him.

Her hat had fallen off and her hair had come loose and her neat traveling outfit was rumpled and covered with dust from the street. But her bluish-green eyes flashed with angry fire as her intriguingly curved bosom rose and fell quickly.

Despite that, his voice was cool as he answered, "You were about to get yourself killed, miss. I figured I'd better stop you."

"I was trying to save that little girl!"

He shrugged. "I figured I could do both of those things. And I did."

"You were that sure of yourself, even though a child's life was at stake?"

"I reckon."

"Then you're an idiot," Denny snapped. "I was closer."

"I was faster."

"Fast enough to stop this?" Her right hand suddenly streaked toward his face as she tried to slap him.

His left hand shot up and caught her wrist, stopping the blow a couple inches short of his cheek. "Evidently," he drawled, trying not to smirk . . . but he did a little bit.

Less than a foot separated their faces, so she couldn't miss the expression. "Ooooh," she fumed. "Let go of me!"

"You promise not to try to slap me again?"

She glared at him for a second, then said through clenched teeth, "I promise."

"Good." He released her wrist. "I—"

Her knee came up and slammed into his groin. Pain exploded through his body and doubled him over. As she stepped back, she said coldly, "I didn't promise not to do *that*, though."

He stumbled over to a nearby hitch rail and leaned on it, grateful it was there. Otherwise he would have crumpled up in the street. Breathing hard from the pain, he managed to lift his head and watch her walk away, stiff-backed with fury.

Damn, he thought through his pain. If that was Smoke Jensen's little *girl*, he didn't want to clash with any other members of the Jensen family.

"Denise Nicole, you should be ashamed of yourself."

"Why? For putting an arrogant son of a—" Denny caught herself. "For putting a scoundrel in his place?"

"She does that sort of thing," Louis said dryly.

Sally blew out an exasperated breath. "I've been married to your father for too long to worry that much about propriety when something needs to be done. You acted instinctively and I can't complain about that. But then you deliberately confronted that man."

Denny shook back a stray curl that insisted on getting in her face. "He had it coming."

Sally might have continued, but Smoke put a hand on her shoulder and said, "I don't reckon you're going to win this argument. We might as well see if the bags are loaded up and head for the ranch."

"Yes, I can tell I've certainly got my work cut out for me," Sally said as she looked at her daughter.

Denny just returned the gaze coolly. As they walked back toward the train station, she asked the group at large, "Who was that fella, anyway?"

"His name's Brice Rogers," Smoke said.

"I don't recall seeing him around Big Rock before."

"He just drifted in lately, according to Monte. I don't know anything else about him."

"I know he's pretty cocky. He's got a mighty high opinion of himself."

"He moved fast," Smoke pointed out.

"Don't you start going on about that, Pa. He just took everybody by surprise, that's all." Denny's jaw tightened. "It won't happen again."

"It's entirely possible you'll never see him again," Sally pointed out.

"And that'll be just fine with me." Denny glanced over at her brother and saw him smiling. "What are *you* laughing about?"

"Not a thing," Louis said, holding up his hands as if in self-defense. "Not a blessed thing."

After the excitement in town, the ride out to the Sugarloaf was uneventful. Denny headed for the extra saddle mount Smoke had brought along, but Sally said, "The horse is for Louis. That's not a sidesaddle, and you're hardly dressed for riding astride, Denise. I mean, Denny."

Denny wouldn't have had a problem with hiking up her skirts and swinging into the saddle, but she might as well let her mother have her way on this one, she decided. She nodded and climbed onto the seat alongside Sally, who took up the reins and handled the team expertly, reminding Denny that she wasn't the only female who could do such things.

It wouldn't hurt for her to remember that Sally Jensen wasn't exactly a typical female herself.

Smoke rode to the left of the wagon, Louis on the right. Louis was a decent rider, even though he had never spent as much time outdoors on the English estate as Denny had.

Smoke asked, "What do you two intend to do now that you're home?"

"They just got here, Smoke," Sally said. "I don't think the children have to plan their future right away."

"On the contrary," Louis said, "I have a pretty good idea what I'd like to do. I got well acquainted with the barrister who handles some of Grandfather's business and legal affairs in England, and that made me think I'd be interested in studying the law."

"It sure would be good to know more about such things," Smoke said. "When your mother and I started the Sugarloaf all those years ago, there wasn't much law in these parts."

"There was the law of the gun," Denny put in.

Smoke shrugged. "Most of the time, that's what it amounted to, all right. But things are different now. There's real law, and it's getting to be more important all the time. A man can't run a business without knowing something about it, and when you get right down to it, that's what a ranch is—a business."

"Yes, but I'm not going to be running the Sugarloaf," Louis said.

Denny saw the frown that creased her father's forehead.

"You're not?" Smoke said. "I reckon that's the way a man's mind runs. He figures that one of these days his son will take over everything that he's built . . ."

"I'm sorry, Father. I don't think my health will ever be good enough for that. My heart's stronger now, but I'll never be able to spend all day in the saddle like you do. Just this ride out to the ranch is going to be taxing enough."

"Then we need to stop right now," Sally said. "Louis, you can get in the wagon and ride the rest of the way."

"You should have let me have the horse," Denny muttered.

Louis held up a hand. "No, no, I'm fine. I'll just rest a bit once we get there and it won't be a problem. I just want to be sure both of you understand that I'm not cut out for running a ranch. A profession like the law will be much more suitable."

"He's smart, that's for sure," Denny said. "He could have stayed in England and gone to Oxford."

"I didn't want to go to Oxford. I wanted to come home." Louis grinned. "And here we are." He gestured at the mountains and the rugged, tree-covered hills around them. "There's no more spectacular place in the world than the Sugarloaf. I may not live up to the Jensen legacy, but it's still home to me."

"Don't ever say you don't live up to the Jensen legacy," Smoke told him sharply. "Everybody's different. You're not me, but nobody expects you to be. You're every bit a Jensen, though. No doubt about that in my mind."

"Well, I hope I don't disappoint you, Father. I'll do my best not to."

Smoke grinned. "Actually, there have been times

when it would have come in handy to have a lawyer in the family."

"You mean when you were accused of being an outlaw?" Denny said.

"That's right. Of course, I wasn't married to your mother yet, so you two weren't even a twinkle in her eye back then."

Sally laughed. "I'm not the one who had a twinkle."

"Well, now, that's not the way I remember it—"

"You hush, Smoke Jensen." Sally turned to her daughter. "How about you, Denise . . . Denny? I'll get used to that sooner or later. Maybe."

"You mean what do I plan to do?"

"That's right."

Denny shook her head. "I haven't given it that much thought. I'm not like Louis. He plans everything out to the smallest detail. That's why he'll be such a good lawyer. I just sort of go along and do whatever strikes me at the time."

"I believe you'd make an excellent teacher," Sally said. "And with the way the population of the West is growing so fast, I'm sure there'll be more and more schools and a need for more and more teachers."

"I don't know," Denny said slowly, then glanced at her brother and saw Louis smiling. "You quit smirking over there, Louis Arthur Jensen."

"I'm just trying to imagine you in a classroom full of unruly little scamps," Louis said. "You'd probably take a bullwhip to them to make them behave."

"I would not!" Denny made a face. "They wouldn't let me have a bullwhip in school, anyway."

"Well, you don't have to make up your mind now," Smoke said. "There'll be plenty of time for you to figure things out. For now, I remember how much you liked helping out around the ranch when you visited before. I don't see any reason you can't do that again for a while."

Sally said, "You mean you intend to put her to work as a member of the crew?"

"I don't mind taking orders from Pearlie," Denny said.

"Pearlie's not the foreman anymore," Smoke said. "He's retired, but he's still living at the ranch and giving Cal advice. Cal's the ramrod now."

"Fine by me. Give me a pair of trousers and a saddle and a job to do, and I'll do it."

"I'll see what can be arranged," Smoke said with a smile. "After you and Louis have your homecoming dinner tonight."

"First thing in the morning," Denny prompted him.

"First thing," Smoke agreed.

Denny nodded and sat back on the seat as the wagon rolled along. Despite what she had just told her parents, she *did* have a long-term plan, and working with Cal Woods and the other hands fit right into it.

Louis might not want the job, but one day Denny was going to run the Sugarloaf herself.

CHAPTER 11

Cal, Pearlie, and all the hands crowded into the ranch house that evening for the magnificent dinner Sally had prepared. Monte Carson and his wife came from Big Rock, along with Louis Longmont. The long table in the dining room was packed, as well as being heavily laden with food. Sally had left a side of beef roasting slowly over a fire pit behind the house that morning, tended to by Pearlie and Inez Sandoval, the Mexican woman who worked as cook and house-keeper. Smoke figured that Pearlie and Inez would get married eventually, but that didn't stop them from squabbling over things, such as how best to cook that side of beef and get the rest of the meal ready.

The first time Smoke had met Pearlie, the older man had been a hired gun working for one of Smoke's enemies. He had ridden the owlhoot trail and seemed destined for a bad end, like most of that breed. Hard to believe, back then, that he and Smoke Jensen would become fast friends and that Pearlie would spend many years riding for the Sugarloaf brand.

The Jensen brand, really. Men were drawn to it, and it was powerful enough to turn bad men good and make good men better.

And those bad men who wouldn't put aside their evil ways . . . the Jensen brand had a way of dealing with them, too.

Smoke wasn't going to think about any of that, though. He was so glad to have his children home that he wasn't going to worry about anything else.

Laughter and good fellowship filled the room as family and friends feasted. After a while, when everyone was sitting back, pleasantly stuffed, Smoke stood. Gradually, the group around the table quieted.

He lifted his coffee cup. "We're here to celebrate the homecoming of Louis and Denny, but right now I'd like to drink a toast to the person who made this wonderful evening possible by giving birth to a little boy and girl who grew up to be two of the finest young people you'll ever know. Here's to my wife Sally!"

"To Sally!" the group around the table chorused as they lifted their cups.

Smoke bent over and kissed the top of Sally's head. She looked a little embarrassed by the attention.

Then even more so when Cal put two fingers in his mouth, whistled shrilly, and called, "Speech!"

"You want *me* to make a speech?" Sally said. "How often have I done anything like that?"

"Always a first time for everything, darlin'," Smoke said with a smile.

"All right." She got to her feet and looked around the table, then settled her gaze on Louis and Denny. "I just want to repeat what Smoke said about these two. No mother could ever wish for finer children."

"I'm not sure what you were wishing for this morning in Big Rock," Denny said.

"Maybe that my beautiful daughter wasn't quite so impulsive," Sally said. "But what you did was motivated by a desire to save the life of a child, even at the risk of your own life, so no one can say you shouldn't have done that. That's what Jensens do—we try to help. And so do our friends." Sally beamed at everyone. "To all of our friends . . . thank you for being part of our lives."

Warmth suffused the room as she sat down. People went back to talking.

Smoke settled into his chair and leaned over to say quietly to his wife, "We're mighty lucky folks, you know."

She smile. "I've never doubted it for a second."

Even though the long journey from England, by steamship and then by train, had been tiring, the brisk mountain air worked wonders to restore Denny's energy. She woke up early the next morning in her old room—with new curtains—and got dressed in denim trousers, a butternut shirt, and a dark brown vest that she took from the big wardrobe on the other side of the room. She reached into it and pulled out boots and a hat as well. She put on socks and worked her feet into the boots, then stood in front of the mirror attached to the dressing table as she piled her hair on top of her head and then stuffed the cream-colored hat down over it. A few curls tried to escape, but she poked them back into place.

A glance out the window, through a gap in those new, lacy curtains, told her the sun wasn't up yet, but a gray, predawn light was creeping across the sky. She had intended to be up even earlier. The hands were probably eating their breakfast already. They might even be out on the range. She didn't want to miss out on anything and hurried downstairs and into the kitchen.

No one was there, but a pot of coffee sat on the stove along with a pan of biscuits. Denny got a cup from the cabinet, poured some of the strong black brew in it, and picked up two biscuits from the pan. She had started toward the back door when a footstep sounded behind her.

"Señor Louis, wait," Inez said as she came into the kitchen. "I will fix you a proper breakfast—" She stopped short as Denny looked back over her shoulder and grinned.

"Not Louis, Inez, sorry. And I don't really have time for breakfast. I have to get out to the corral and see about a horse—"

Smoke walked into the kitchen in time to hear what Denny was saying. "Sit down and eat. No ranch hand passes up a chance for grub."

"But the crew's probably getting ready to start out on the day's chores, if they haven't already."

"They rode out just a little while ago."

Denny rolled her eyes. "See? That's what I was afraid of! I just want to be part of the crew, and already I'm late to work!"

Smoke pointed at the kitchen table and said again, "Sit."

She heaved a dramatic sigh and pulled out a chair.

Smoke took the cup of coffee that Inez handed him and sat down opposite Denny. "There's something you need to get through your head," he told her. "You're never going to be just another ranch hand."

"Don't you think I can handle the job?"

"That's not it," Smoke said. "There are two reasons. One is that your pa owns the spread."

"And the other?" Denny asked in a challenging tone.

"You know it as well as I do. You're a young woman, and a pretty one at that."

"I'm pretty sure there's no law saying a woman can't rope and ride and shoot, but I can ask Louis to look it up for you if you want."

"Don't sass me too much, young lady, and don't make fun of your brother."

Denny shrugged. "Sorry. And I wasn't trying to make fun of Louis. He's a demon when it comes to looking things up."

"Maybe so. The law I'm talking about is a natural law, the one that says young cowboys are going to sit up and take notice any time there's a pretty girl around."

"I just want them to treat me like one of them."

"They won't do it," Smoke said. "They *can't* do it. It's just not in their nature."

"So you're saying I can't work here on the ranch after all."

Smoke shook his head. "Not at all. Just take it easy and don't be in such an all-fired hurry to do everything at once. It's been a while since you were here. I figured this morning you and I would just ride some of the range and have a look around."

"I don't think the valley and the mountains have changed much since I was here last," Denny said. "They tend not to do that."

"You might not remember every detail about them, though." Smoke gestured toward the plate of bacon and fried eggs Inez put in front of Denny. "Now dig in, and after you've eaten, we'll go saddle up."

Denny hesitated, then said, "If this didn't smell so good, I might argue with you."

"It probably tastes even better than it smells."

A grin broke out across Denny's face as she reached for the fork Inez set beside the plate. "I guess it wouldn't hurt anything to find out."

"That dun's a good horse," Smoke said as he leaned on the corral fence. He nodded toward the animal he was talking about.

"How about that buckskin?" Denny asked, indicating a rangy horse with a darker mane, tail, and legs.

Smoke cocked his head a little to the side. "I don't know. He's pretty spirited."

"So am I, if you haven't noticed."

"Don't see how I could have missed that," Smoke said with a chuckle. "If you really want to give it a try, I'll throw a saddle on that buckskin cayuse for you."

"I can saddle my own horses," Denny said as she started for the barn.

Ten minutes later, she had cut out the buckskin, lassoed it, led it to a snubbing post, tied it securely, and then put on the saddle blanket and saddle she brought from the barn. The saddle was a double-cinched rig. Denny tightened it, then got the headstall and bit in place. So far the buckskin had been as cooperative as it could be.

"I thought you said this horse was spirited," she said to Smoke, who was saddling a big gray gelding.

"Maybe he takes to you," Smoke said. "Or maybe he's just working up to it."

"Well, he certainly doesn't act like he's going to give me any trouble." Denny loosened the lasso and slipped the loop over the buckskin's head. She kept a good grip on the reins with her other hand just in case the horse got any ideas. The buckskin still stood there calmly. She gripped the saddle horn, put her left foot in the stirrup, and stepped up, swinging her right leg over the horse's back and then settling down in the saddle.

Her right foot had just gone in the stirrup when the buckskin sunfished.

The horse arched its back in that violent buck.

Denny let out a startled yell as she came up out of the saddle. She still had hold of the horn and her feet didn't leave the stirrups, so she wasn't thrown, but she came down hard. The buckskin crowhopped toward the corral fence, pounding at her with each spasmodic jerk. Denny hung on as best she could.

Smoke watched anxiously. He hadn't mounted up yet and was ready to dash in, grab the buckskin's reins, and help her bring the animal under control if he needed to, but he saw the angry grimace of determination on his daughter's face and hung back to give her room. She had been startled at first but had settled down, and the contest of wills between horse and rider had commenced.

"Get right with me, will you, you jughead!" she yelled at the horse as she tightened her grip on the reins.

The buckskin tried sunfishing again, but Denny was ready with her knees clamped firmly to the horse's sides. She didn't budge in the saddle. Smoke grinned. She was stuck to that buckskin like a tick.

The horse jumped again, then raced straight at the corral fence as if it intended to crash into the poles at full speed. Suddenly, it stiffened its legs and lowered its head. That move sometimes made experienced cowboys fly forward out of the saddle.

Not Denny. She stayed right where she was, and as she pulled the buckskin's head up sharply, she said, "Don't try that again, you loco horse, or you'll be sorry!"

The buckskin stood still, trembling a little. Then it gave an all-over shake and let out a disgusted snort.

"Why don't you sigh?" Denny said. "I won."

The buckskin just stood there. But when she clucked to it and pulled its head around, the horse followed her commands willingly enough.

"Reckon you showed it who's boss," Smoke said.

"Maybe it'll remember next time." Denny patted the buckskin's shoulder. "Seems like a pretty good horse."

Smoke laughed again and swung up into his saddle. He opened the corral gate and they rode out. Denny headed the buckskin toward the house while Smoke closed the gate.

When he looked around, he called after her, "Where are you going?"

"Back in a minute," she said as she drew up in front of the porch. She dismounted, looped the reins around the hitching post there, and went quickly into the house.

When she came back out a minute later, she was carrying a Winchester carbine and a box of cartridges. She slid the carbine into the sheath strapped underneath the fender on the right side, tucked the shells into one of the saddlebags, and mounted again.

She rode to Smoke and told him, "Now I'm ready."

CHAPTER 12

They rode north up the valley away from the ranch house. Towering, rocky, snowcapped peaks stood to the west and smaller, tree-covered slopes to the east. The sun was up, casting its golden light over the landscape as it climbed, but the air was still crisp and cool. Denny had never felt more like she was where she was supposed to be, where she belonged.

Smoke started pointing out landmarks.

Denny told him, "I know, Pa. I've been here before."

"Yeah, I know you have, but it doesn't hurt to refresh your memory."

"Where was it you had that shoot-out with those rustlers?"

Smoke slanted a look at her. "Where'd you hear about that?"

"I overheard some of the hands talking about it last night at the dinner table." Denny's face was solemn as she added, "You lost a man."

"We did," Smoke said with a nod. "Sid MacDowell. I don't think you ever knew him. He signed on after you and Louis were here the last time."

"I don't recognize the name. I'm sure he was a good man, though, if he rode for the Sugarloaf. Cal wouldn't have hired him otherwise, and you wouldn't have let him stay around the place."

"He was a fine fella. Young and raw, but a hard worker. He would've made a top hand one of these days, if he'd gotten the chance."

"Did you manage to round up all the rustlers?"

"One got away," Smoke said. "We don't know what happened to him. Cal and some of the boys tracked him for a ways, but his trail petered out."

"I hope he went off somewhere to die."

The viciousness in his daughter's voice made Smoke look at her again. "I don't feel any sympathy for rustlers and killers, but that doesn't sound like you, Denny."

"This is still a hard land, isn't it, Pa?"

"It can be," Smoke admitted.

"Then if I'm going to live here, I've got to be hard sometimes, too."

After a moment, Smoke nodded. "I don't reckon I can argue with that. An hombre's just not used to hearing it come from his daughter, I reckon."

"Ma fought side by side with you several times, didn't she?"

"She sure did," Smoke said.

"Well, any time you need me, I will, too."

"I'll keep that in mind," Smoke said dryly. "I figure on handling any of the rustling or other lawbreaking problems around here, though. And if it gets too bad, it'll be Monte Carson's job to step in as sheriff."

"Just remember what I said," Denny declared.

"I'm not likely to forget."

They continued riding the range all morning, seeing a number of cattle and some of the Sugarloaf crew. Inez had packed sandwiches for them, using some of the roast beef left from supper the night before. Smoke and Denny stopped beside a creek for lunch, washing down the food with cold, sparkling clear water from the stream.

Afterward, Smoke stretched out on the grass underneath a tree and tipped his hat down over his eyes. "I think I'll doze for a while. I'm not as young as I once was, you know."

Denny let out an unladylike snort. "You could stay in the saddle longer and work harder than any of those twenty-year-old cowboys, and you know it."

"Well, it's a good day for a nap anyway. Reckon you can find something to occupy yourself with for a spell?"

"You trust me to wander around by my lonesome?"

"You know how to use that Winchester carbine you brought along, don't you?"

"You know I do," she said.

"Then I don't suppose you'll run into any trouble you can't handle," Smoke said. "If you do, though, fire three shots in the air. Won't take me too long to get there, wherever you are."

Denny nodded. "All right."

"I really am craving a nap, though," Smoke said, "so don't get spooked for no reason."

Denny blew out a disgusted breath as she walked to her horse. "That'll be the day."

She rode on north, following the creek. The buckskin had been cooperative ever since leaving the corral, but she could tell that he was eager to run. When she came to a long, flat stretch beside the stream, she reined in long enough to take her hat off and shake her hair down.

She put the hat back on and tightened the chin strap. "All right, horse. If you're hankering to stretch your legs, get to it." With that, she kneed the buckskin into a run.

The horse surged forward, legs flashing as it galloped along the creek bank. Denny's thick blond hair streamed out behind her from the wind of their speed.

It was an exhilarating ride, but it was over too soon. Denny slowed the buckskin and gradually brought it to a halt. Horse and rider were both breathing harder.

She leaned forward and patted the horse on the shoulder. "You're a good saddle mount. You just had to figure out who's boss."

The buckskin tossed its head as if to argue that point.

Denny laughed. "Oh, *you're* just tolerating *me*, is that it?"

She grew serious as she spotted movement from the corner of her eye. Across the creek, the ground sloped up sharply to a flat ridge where a thick stand of pine grew. Denny wasn't sure, but she thought she had seen someone up there in those trees. Without being obvious about it, she looked closer. She continued talking softly and stroking and patting the buckskin's sleek shoulder so that if she really was being spied upon, the lurker wouldn't realize that she was on to him.

Nothing. Maybe she had seen a bird flitting from branch to branch or a squirrel making a daring leap from one tree to another, she told herself.

Some instinct told her it wasn't something that innocent. She turned the horse and rode back the direction she had come from, although that made the hair on the back of her neck prickle. She had put her back to the unknown, and she didn't like it. Even though it was very unlikely anyone would threaten her on her father's ranch, there was no guarantee of that.

Somebody could be drawing a bead on her. She felt

like there was a nice, fat target painted on the middle
of her back . . .

"You're being silly," she muttered to herself.

That might well be true—but when she reached the
next bend in the creek and had gone around it, out of
sight of that wooded ridge, she turned the buckskin
and rode across the stream. The water was only about
a foot deep and the creek bed was rocky, so the horse
had no trouble fording it.

Now that she was on the east side of the creek,
Denny headed north again. The trees and brush were
thicker away from the stream, so she angled into that
cover as she rode. She pulled the carbine from its
scabbard, levered a shell into its chamber, and rode
with the weapon in front of her, across the saddle.

She didn't get in any hurry. Rushing headlong into
trouble was a stupid thing to do. She paralleled the
creek and stayed out of sight in the trees as much as
possible, stopping now and then to listen intently. She
didn't hear anything, not even the tiny sounds made
by birds and small animals, but it was possible they had
fallen silent because of her approach.

They might have quieted down because somebody
else was skulking around, too, Denny reminded herself. She pushed on until the ground began to rise.
She was climbing onto that ridge.

If somebody had been watching her, she hadn't run
into them so far. She wondered again if she had been
mistaken, or even just imagined the whole thing. She
had come home halfway expecting adventure. Maybe
she was trying to manufacture some.

No, she decided, she was too levelheaded for that.
At least, she liked to think she was.

The piney growth became denser. Denny reined in
and dismounted. Leading the buckskin, she went forward on foot. She reached a spot where she could look

down and see the open bank on the far side of the creek where she had let the horse run. It was some forty feet lower than where she stood. It was a perfect place for someone to spy on her, she realized.

She wrapped the buckskin's reins around a sapling. Holding the carbine in both hands, she eased along the ridge. Her keen eyes searched the ground, looking for any signs of the watcher she suspected. After a few yards, she came to a spot where the carpet of pine needles was disturbed. Some of them had been kicked aside, leaving scuff marks.

Someone had walked up and stood there, she thought. She looked across the creek again and compared her position on the ridge to where she had been earlier and was sure she was standing where she had seen that faint movement.

Somebody *had* been spying on her! She had no doubt of that now.

The question was . . . who?

She thought about what her father had said about young cowboys and pretty girls. Denny wasn't afflicted with false modesty. She knew she was an attractive young woman. It was entirely possible one of the Sugarloaf hands had spotted her riding along the creek and decided to get a better look. They might be risking Smoke Jensen's wrath by sneaking around like that, but they could have decided it was worth it.

Denny wasn't satisfied with that assumption, though. She hunkered beside the tracks and studied them, trying to see if anything was distinctive about them.

Unfortunately, they were just smudges in the pine needles, without anything to make them recognizable if she ever saw them again.

All right. The lurker must have had a horse up there. She walked back away from the edge of the ridge and searched for signs that a mount had been tied up to wait while its rider peered across the creek at her.

After a few minutes, she found hoofprints and a fresh pile of horse dung about fifty yards back where the trees thinned out somewhat. Again she studied the tracks. Those were more distinct. She was able to make out the markings made by that particular set of horse-shoes, and she tried to commit all the telltale nicks and scratches and bent nails to memory.

A frown put lines in her forehead. Whoever had shod this horse hadn't done a particularly good job of it. If it was a Sugarloaf animal, her father wouldn't have tolerated such sloppiness. Of course, some cowpokes had their own mounts and didn't always use ranch stock. Still, it was an indication that the lurker might not have been a member of her father's crew.

If that was the case, then the hombre probably had no business being on the Sugarloaf—and he sure hadn't had any cause to be spying on the boss's daughter.

Denny was pondering whether to try backtracking the sneaky son of a gun when she heard her buckskin whinny. Knowing the animal probably wouldn't react like that unless some other horse was around, she quickly got to her feet. Her pa might have come along looking for her, or it might be someone else. Was the lurker coming back for some reason? she wondered.

She started in the buckskin's direction, moving through the trees and brush as quickly as she could and still be relatively quiet about it. She didn't hear her horse make any other sounds.

She wondered suddenly if some horse thief had come along and stolen the buckskin. That would be a stroke of bad luck. She was several miles from the ranch headquarters, and it would be a long walk in riding boots.

Of course, she could always fire those signal shots Smoke had mentioned, and he or one of the hands would show up to help her.

But damned if she wanted to be one of those helpless females who was always in need of rescuing, she told herself. She'd encountered way too many of them in books and was always annoyed by such characters.

To her relief, the buckskin was still there, she saw a few minutes later. Denny looked around and didn't see anyone else, man or horse. Maybe some other animal had spooked the buckskin. A prowling bobcat, maybe.

She patted the horse's shoulder and murmured, "What's wrong? You smell some varmint?"

As she spoke, she heard a faint rustling in some nearby brush. She stiffened slightly but managed not to show any other reaction. Watching from the corner of her eye as she continued to talk softly to the buckskin, she saw some branches shiver a little. The movement was more than a small animal would have made by rooting around.

A man was hiding over there, she thought, and she had no doubt he had been checking out her mount a few minutes earlier. The thought that she was so close to whoever had been spying on her made her nervous, but it angered her as well. Without putting the carbine back in its sheath, she untied the buckskin's reins and swung up into the saddle.

Then, without any warning, she sent the horse plunging straight at the brush where the stranger was lurking.

CHAPTER 13

It was a loco thing to do, and Denny knew it. She was too angry to do anything else, though. Whoever was hiding, she was going to teach him that spying on her was a bad idea.

She heard a startled yell as the buckskin crashed into the brush. A figure leaped aside, diving out of the way. In the sharply contrasting pattern of shadow and light cast by the trees, Denny couldn't see the man very well, but she slashed at him with the carbine's barrel. She wasn't going to open fire without knowing who she was shooting at.

The lurker might have been surprised by the unexpected charge, but he recovered quickly. As Denny tried to wallop him with the carbine, his hand shot up and grasped the barrel, stopping the blow in midair. He wrenched at the carbine, and since Denny wouldn't let go, she abruptly found herself being pulled out of the saddle. She yelled in surprise and dismay as she came crashing down in the underbrush.

The man loomed over her, still trying to wrestle the carbine away from her. From the ground, Denny kicked upward, but the man twisted so her boot heel thudded against his thigh rather than into his groin where she had aimed it. She writhed around, trying to get away from him, but all that succeeded in doing was knocking her hat down over her eyes so she couldn't see.

She lashed out blindly with her other leg, and when her foot hooked behind something, she yanked on it as hard as she could. She heard a surprised curse, then more brush crashed as her attacker toppled, his legs swept out from under him by her swift move.

Denny rolled over. The wrist of the hand holding the carbine banged against a tree trunk with such force that her hand went numb for a second. That was long enough for the Winchester to slip out of momentarily nerveless fingers. Denny scrambled after it, but just as she slapped her other hand down on the stock, the stranger grabbed her from behind with both arms around her middle. He jerked her back away from the carbine and struggled to his feet as he hung on to her.

It was like trying to hang on to a wildcat, or at least she tried to make it as much like that as she could. She writhed and kicked and flailed, and as she drove an elbow back she felt it land solidly. The man started gagging and choking. The point of her elbow had gotten him in the throat and at least distracted him for a moment, if not worse.

Denny tore free, but instead of running she whirled around, lowered her head, and butted it against the man's chest as she tackled him around the waist. His hat flew off, and the tackle knocked him off balance. As she drove as hard with her feet as she could, she forced him backwards. The two of them crashed through the brush and then out of it, into the open along the edge of the ridge. Denny kept pushing and never slowed down.

Suddenly, there was nothing under their feet. She

had driven them both off the edge, and she let out a
startled yell as she realized her mistake.

A split second later, they hit the slope, were jolted
apart by the impact, and started to bounce and roll.
The slope was steep, but it wasn't a sheer drop or the
fall probably would have killed them.

As it was, they tumbled like thrown-aside rag dolls
toward the creek below.

Denny grunted and yelped as she banged into rocky
knobs protruding from the slope. She tried to grab
some of them to slow her fall, but her fingers slipped
off. Sky and earth changed places with dizzying speed
as she rolled, until finally she landed in the creek with
enough force to drive all the breath from her body. It
didn't help that immediately after that, water splashed
in her face and went down her throat. She came up
coughing and spitting and gasping.

At least she hadn't landed facedown and knocked
herself out. She wasn't going to drown. She sat in the
cold, swiftly flowing water and lifted a shaky hand to
push ropes of sodden hair out of her face. She probably looked like a wet rat, she thought.

That started her brain working again. She remembered how she had come to be in this predicament to
start with, and anger blazed to life inside her again as
she looked around for the man who had attacked her.

She spotted him about ten yards away from her. He
was floundering around in the creek, too, with his
back toward her. He seemed to be having trouble
catching his breath.

She would give him even more trouble, Denny
thought as she felt around under the water on the
creek bed and closed her hand around a rock that was
just about the size of her two fists clenched together.
She pulled it free from where it was wedged in with
some other rocks and lunged to her feet. She lifted the

rock and splashed toward the enemy, vaguely aware that she hurt in a lot of places, but she was too mad to worry about that.

He heard her coming, of course, and twisted around to see her looming over him with the rock upraised, ready to stove in his skull. He ducked toward her so that as she struck, she fell over his back and sprawled face-first into the creek.

She jerked her head up out of the water and tried to turn around and get her feet underneath her again. He grabbed her wrist and wrenched hard enough that she cried out as she dropped the rock. She tried to punch him with her other hand, but he caught hold of that wrist, too.

"Stop it! Settle down, you . . . you hellcat!"

Denny's chest heaved as she gritted her teeth and glared at him. "Let go of me, you son of a bitch!" she raged.

"That's no way for a rich young lady to talk."

She blinked water out of her eyes and stared at him, realizing that he wasn't a complete stranger, although she didn't know much about him. She knew his name, though. "Let go of me, Rogers."

"Are you gonna keep trying to kill me if I do?" he asked.

"I'll kill you if you don't!"

"How do you figure on doing that when I've got hold of both your arms?"

She snarled. "I didn't say I'd do it right now! But I swear, one of these days when you least expect it—"

"You can get in trouble threatening to kill a—" He stopped short.

When he didn't go on, Denny demanded, "Kill a what? An insufferable, perverted *sneak*?"

He frowned in evident confusion. "What?"

"You were spying on me! What else would you call a man who skulks around to stare at young women?"

Rogers shook his head slowly. "I don't know what you're talking about, Miss Jensen."

Denny jerked her chin to point toward the open area where she had been running the buckskin earlier. "You were up on the ridge watching me while I was over there about half an hour ago."

"What were you doing?" He smiled. "Having a swim?"

Denny felt her face growing warm. "Oh!" and tried to pull her wrists free again. "Let go of me, blast it. You're hurting me."

"I don't want to hurt you," he said, his face growing solemn. "But you knocked me off that cliff and then tried to brain me with a rock, so I'm not sure I feel like running the risk of letting you go."

She breathed hard for a couple seconds, then ground out, "I won't fight anymore. All right?"

"I have your word on that? Your word as Smoke Jensen's daughter?"

"That means something to you?"

"From what I've heard about him, he's a mighty honorable man," Rogers said. "I figure that sense of honor might extend to his kids, too."

"I give you my word," Denny snapped.

Brice let go of her wrists. For a second she thought seriously about punching him anyway, then decided she couldn't do that after she had given her word. He was right about that assumption, anyway, damn it.

"You realize we're sitting here up to our, uh, waists in icy cold water, don't you?" he said.

"Going numb, are you?"

"Well, I wouldn't mind getting back on dry land." He got to his feet, wincing. "Reckon my bruises are gonna have bruises by the time tomorrow morning rolls around." He extended a hand to her. "Let me help you up."

"Go to hell," she muttered. She climbed upright, awkwardly and painfully. But she made it without any help from him, and that pleased her.

"Now, what's this about somebody watching you from the ridge?"

"You were," she said flatly.

Rogers shook his head. "No, I wasn't. I rode up, found a saddled horse tied to a tree, and was about to look around for whoever owned it when I heard somebody coming. I pulled back into the brush to wait and see who it turned out to be. That's the first time I laid eyes on you today, Miss Jensen."

"You're lying," Denny insisted.

"Why would I lie?"

"Because you're a low-down, good-for-nothing—"

He held up a hand to stop her. "I reckon we've established that you don't have a very high opinion of me. But even so, I'm not the sort of fella who goes around spying on young ladies. You don't have to believe me if you don't want to, but it's the truth."

She frowned at him for a long moment, then said, "You mean somebody else was sneaking around here?"

"If you're sure you saw somebody, then yeah, there had to be."

"I found some tracks up there," Denny said, pointing to the top of the ridge. "I found where he tied his horse, too."

"But you never got a good look at him?"

"No, I just saw some movement in the trees, enough to make me suspicious. I went back down the creek, forded it, and circled around on this side to try to find out who it was. Then I ran into you."

"And you just assumed that I had to be the varmint you were after."

"You don't have any other good reason for being out here, do you?" Denny said. "This is Sugarloaf range, and the last time I checked, you don't work for the Sugarloaf."

"You object to people riding across your father's ranch?"

"Unless they have a good reason to, I do."

Rogers shrugged. "Fair enough, I suppose."

"I don't care if you think it's fair or not. What *are* you doing here?"

His voice tightened as he said, "That's my business. I can tell you this much, though—I mean no harm to you or your family."

"I'm supposed to just believe that?"

"Like I said before, believe it or don't, whatever suits you. But it's the truth." He took a breath. "Now, I need to get on about my business and let you get on with yours . . ."

Denny pointed to the top of the ridge again. "The problem is that's where our horses are. It's a long way back around if we have to walk it."

Rogers regarded the slope for a few seconds and then said, "I reckon if we're careful, we can climb this ridge. We came down that way, we might as well go back up. I can give you a hand if you want—"

"I've been climbing hills and trees and anything else that needed climbing since almost before I could walk," she said. "Just stay out of my way and I'll be fine."

"Suit yourself, then." He waved a hand at the slope. "Up you go."

Denny glared at him and wanted to say something else but couldn't think of anything. She turned toward the ridge while he began feeling around behind his belt. He suddenly seemed agitated about something and she heard him mutter, "Now where in blazes did that—?"

"Looking for something?" she asked.

"Yeah, but it's nothing for you to worry about. You go ahead and climb on up—"

Denny was already looking around on the ground. A glint of something caught her eye, and before he could stop her, she reached down and plucked an object from the rocks at their feet. "Is this what you're looking for?" she asked as she held out her hand with a deputy United States marshal's badge lying on the palm.

CHAPTER 14

Rogers caught his breath as he looked down at the badge in Denny Jensen's hand. He wasn't sure how it had slipped out of its pocket on the back of his belt, but the way he had been tumbling head over heels down the ridge, he supposed anything was possible.

But why did it have to wind up where this crazy young woman would find it?

For a second he thought about denying that it was his, but he realized she probably wouldn't believe him. The way he had been pawing at his belt made it obvious he was looking for *something*, and it would be too much of a coincidence for the lost object to be anything else.

He started to take it from her, but she quickly closed her hand around it and drew it back. "Wait just a minute. You haven't told me this belongs to you."

"It does. And I'd appreciate it if you'd hand it over."

"You're a deputy U.S. marshal."

She didn't make it sound like a question, but he answered it like one anyway. "That's right, and I'd be mighty grateful to you, Miss Jensen, if you could keep that to yourself."

"Does my father know?" she asked sharply.

"No, he doesn't." Might as well spill the whole thing, he decided. Denny was stubborn enough to keep after him until he did. "The only one around here who knows is Sheriff Carson. I had to tell him who I am."

"Professional courtesy, you'd call it."

"Something like that."

She still had her hand closed around the badge. That was better than waving it around out in the open, he thought. There was no telling who might be watching. After all, she had said that someone was spying on her earlier. But what he really wanted was to have it snugged away in that hidden pocket where it belonged.

"My boss, the chief marshal, sent me out here from Denver," Rogers went on. "He assigned me to look into the rustling that's been going on in this area. I assume I can trust you, Miss Jensen, otherwise I wouldn't be telling you about official government business."

"You're wasting your time," she said. "My father's already taken care of that gang of rustlers."

"He eliminated some of them. We don't know if he got rid of the whole bunch."

"What business is it of the federal government if some cattle are stolen?"

She was pretty sharp, he thought. That was the same question Sheriff Carson had asked.

"The rustling jeopardizes beef contracts with the army. Anyway, the marshal's office has a stake in maintaining law and order in general."

"My brother knows a lot about such things. Maybe I should ask him about any jurisdictional questions."

"I'd really rather you didn't say anything to anybody," Rogers began quickly but stopped when Denny laughed.

She stuck her hand out. "Here. Take your blasted old badge. I don't care what you poke your nose into.

I guess you had a good reason for being out here, instead of just spying on me."

He took the badge from her. "I wasn't spying—"

She held up a hand to stop him. "Forget it. You can go on searching for clues or whatever you were doing, and I'll get back to my father. I don't want him to come along and find us like this, looking like we've been rolling around together in the creek."

As he slid the badge back into its hiding place, he said, "We *were* rolling around together in the creek."

"Don't remind me. Anyway, we were both in the creek at the same time. That doesn't mean we were *together*." Denny turned toward the ridge and studied it for a second, found some handholds she liked the looks of, and started to climb. She had lifted herself only a few feet when she slipped a little.

Without thinking, he raised a hand to brace her, but she caught herself before he could touch her. He realized the palm of his hand was positioned only a few inches away from the curve of her denim-clad bottom.

"Don't you dare," she said coldly as she looked back over her shoulder and down at him.

He backed off a step. "Wouldn't think of it. You can fall down and bust your . . . whatever you land on." With that, he moved over a few yards, found another spot to climb, and started up.

Going up the ridge took a lot longer than coming down had, and despite the fact that the day wasn't very warm, Rogers was sweaty when he pulled himself over the edge and rolled onto the pine needles. He had passed Denny on the way up—the route she had chosen proving to be more difficult—so he got to his feet, went over to kneel at the brink, and called to her, "I'll give you a hand when you get close enough for me to reach."

"I don't want a hand!" she said.

"There's no point in being stubborn about it."

"I'm not stubborn! I'm determined."

"All right. Suit yourself. Be careful, though. We both managed not to break any bones when we tumbled down, but there's no point in pushing your luck." He looked around and found his hat. Hers was lying nearby, too. He picked it up and dusted pine needles off of it.

"That's . . . mine," she panted as she reached the top and saw him holding the hat.

He held it out to her. "You're welcome."

She snatched it away and crammed it on her head.

As disheveled and bedraggled as she was, he had to admit that she still looked pretty good. He was sure she wouldn't want to hear that, so he kept the opinion to himself and said, "You claimed you found some tracks left by the hombre who was watching you. How about showing them to me?"

"Why?"

"I'm a lawman. Sounds like this fella was a suspicious character. Sort of my job to check it out."

"What I found isn't going to tell you much," she said with a shrug, "but I reckon I can show you if you're interested."

It took her a few minutes to locate the rough footprints she had seen before. He knelt next to them and studied them, but Denny was right. Other than proving that someone had been there, the tracks didn't mean a thing.

"His horse was tied back there," she said, pointing through the trees. "I can show you the droppings if you want."

"I can find them."

"You're really going to look?"

He rubbed his chin. "I'm a halfway decent tracker.

I might be able to follow and see where he came from."

"I was thinking about doing that myself. In fact, I was going to get my horse when I heard you rustling around in the brush and figured the varmint had come back."

"I didn't think I made that much noise."

She snorted. "Enough for me to hear. And I've lived in England for years."

He wasn't sure what she meant by that. "I'll see what I can find out, and if it's anything important, I'll let you know."

"I could come with you . . ." He was about to veto that idea when she went on. "But my father's probably wondering by now where I've gotten off to. I'd better go see if I can find him and let him know I'm all right."

"Maybe your clothes will be dry by then."

"You let me worry about that. Don't worry, I won't compromise your reputation. And . . . I won't say anything about you being a deputy marshal."

"Thanks."

"I really think you're wasting your time, though. After what happened a few nights ago, there's probably not a rustler within a hundred miles of here."

The sun had almost set and shadows were already thick when Muddy Malone rode up to the canyon mouth.

One of the guards stepped out from behind the rocks, rifle leveled, then relaxed and lowered the weapon. "Oh, it's just you."

"Just me?" Muddy said with a snort. "What do you mean by that, Wilkins?"

"Means I don't have to shoot you. Go on in, Malone. You got news for the boss?"

"If I do, it's him I'll be tellin' it to."

"Don't get a burr under your saddle just because I'm doin' my job. Go on now."

Muddy snorted again but rode on through the entrance. He followed the narrow, twisting canyon past the other guard posts. Those men hailed him, too, but didn't challenge him since they knew no intruder could have gotten that far without gunplay to alert them.

Muddy reached the basin a few minutes later. Cook fires were already burning, and lamplight glowed from the windows of Nick Creighton's cabin.

Off to one side, invisible in the gloom, was the grave where Blue Creighton had been laid to rest. Several of the men, acting under Nick Creighton's orders, had wrestled a big slab of rock from the canyon wall and rolled it into place to mark the grave. Nick claimed he was going to chisel Blue's name into the stone, when he got around to it.

Muddy rode over to the rope corral where the gang kept their mounts.

Turk met him there and reached for the reins. "I'll take care of your horse for you. Nick's been waitin' for you. You'd better go see him right away."

Muddy dismounted. "What sort of mood is he in?"

Turk made a face. "It's been less than forty-eight hours since his little brother died. What sort of mood do you think he's in?"

Muddy sighed. He didn't have much to report. His steps were reluctant as he approached the cabin, but he knew he needed to get it over with. He knocked on the door, which had been repaired when the gang moved in. It no longer hung askew on its thick leather hinges. He waited, hoping that Nick wouldn't be mad and take the anger out on him.

After a moment, the door swung back and Molly stood there. "Come on in. He's been waiting for you."

Respectfully, Muddy took off his battered old hat as he entered the cabin. Nick Creighton was sitting at the rough-hewn table, legs stretched out in front of him, crossed at the ankles. His right elbow rested on the table, and he had a glass of whiskey in that hand. A half-full bottle sat on the table beside him. He scowled as he looked up at the newcomer. The look made Muddy's gut tighten.

"Muddy," Creighton said. "What's going on down at Jensen's place?"

"Not a lot, boss," Muddy reported. "His hands are out ridin' the range and doin' their chores as usual. They're all carryin' rifles and packin' irons on their hips, though. From the looks of it, Jensen's told them not to let their guard down, so I reckon he ain't convinced he's in the clear yet."

Creighton tossed back the whiskey in the glass, then nodded slowly. "We'll let him stew a while longer. We've done all right with the cattle we've lifted from there so far, so we're not short of money. There's no rush."

Muddy hesitated. Creighton had accepted what he had to say without losing his temper, so the smart thing to do would be to get out while the gettin' was good. But he didn't want to fail to report everything he had seen. That might come back to cause him trouble later. "There's one more thing, Nick. I saw a girl."

Creighton frowned as he glanced up from pouring himself another drink. "A girl?" he repeated.

"Yeah. A, uh, really pretty girl. Lots of curly blond hair. She was dressed like a man and she rode like a man, but she was a gal, all right, there was no mistakin' that."

Molly laughed softly. "You sound a little smitten, Muddy."

"No, ma'am," he said, shaking his head. "I just hadn't

seen her there before and figured Nick might want to know about her."

"Seems like I've heard that Jensen has a daughter," Creighton mused. "Maybe that was her you saw."

"Could've been, Nick. She was ridin' around like she owned the place, sure enough. I watched her for a while, but then I spied somebody else comin' and lit a shuck. You told me not to get caught on the Sugarloaf, so I figured I'd better be careful."

"Was it Jensen?"

"The fella who was comin'?" Muddy shook his head. "I don't know for sure. Never got a good look at him. But I don't think so. Even if it had been, I know you don't want him bushwhacked."

Creighton took a sip of the liquor. "That's right. When the time comes to kill Smoke Jensen, it's going to be my finger that pulls the trigger while I look him in the eye and make sure he knows why he's dying. That's the only way Blue will be avenged. Although"—Creighton stroked his chin—"if that *was* Jensen's daughter you saw, that makes me think of some other ways he could be made to suffer before I put him out of his misery."

Molly frowned. "You wouldn't hurt a woman, would you, Nick?"

Creighton's hand tightened on the glass as he said, "I'd hurt anybody if it caused Smoke Jensen pain. He's going to pay for happened to Blue . . . pay in blood!"

CHAPTER 15

"What in the world happened to you?" Smoke asked as Denny rode up and dismounted. She should have known he was too keen of eye not to notice the signs of her little misadventure. "That horse didn't spook and throw you off into the creek, did it?"

"Of course not," Denny replied tartly. "I'm too good a rider for that."

"Well, you managed to get a dunking somehow. Your clothes are still damp, and your hair's gonna take a while to dry."

She shrugged. "I fell in all on my own. I was getting a drink and my foot slipped on a rock."

"Oh. Well, that was careless of you."

"Yeah." She wasn't sure if her father believed the story, but he didn't press her about it.

They mounted up and headed back to the ranch house.

After a while, he said, "Any time you want to go swimming, there's a good swimmin' hole farther up the creek. I can make sure none of the hands are around that part of the ranch."

"I can take care of myself. Anyway, none of the cowboys who work for you would dare spy on Smoke

Jensen's daughter, no matter how much it's in their nature."

"You're probably right about that," Smoke said with a chuckle.

That left the question of who *had* been spying on her, Denny thought, and she had no answer for it. Maybe Brice Rogers would be able to backtrack the lurker and find out. If he did, would he let her know? Maybe, she decided, if it suited his purposes. Otherwise he'd probably keep it to himself and shut her out. He wouldn't want her interfering with the job that had brought him there.

By the time they got back to the ranch house, Denny's clothes were dry and she had straightened them up so the beating they had taken wasn't as noticeable. She tucked her still-damp hair under her hat, the way it had been when she and her father had ridden out earlier.

"You're trying to make sure your mother doesn't notice that you fell in the creek," Smoke said as they dismounted.

"Well, it's sort of embarrassing," Denny said. "You won't say anything, will you?"

"I reckon not. Like Sally keeps reminding me, you're a grown woman now. We can't keep track of where you are or what you're doing every hour of the day, so there's no point in trying." Smoke paused. "We sort of missed that when you were growing up, because you *weren't* here so much of the time. You were way off over there in England and France and all those other places you went. You spent your childhood away from us, for the most part. It had to be that way, for Louis's sake and for the benefits you got out of it, too, but you can understand why we want to spend as much time around you now as we can."

"Sure, Pa," Denny said as she rested a hand on his

shoulder for a second. "Louis and I are just used to being on our own a lot."

"The two of you grew up pretty fast, I reckon," Smoke said.

"Not like you."

"Well, no, and thank goodness for that!"

They turned their horses over to the wrangler who'd come out of the barn to take them, then, smiling, they went into the house. Denny didn't see her mother, so she headed right upstairs to put on some clean clothes and brush out her hair while she had the chance, all the time wondering if Brice Rogers had found anything when he trailed the man who'd been skulking on the ridge.

If nothing else, Rogers thought as he rode through the rugged foothills, the job of tracking was giving him a better idea of the Sugarloaf's layout. Back in Denver, he had studied the ranch's boundaries on a map, but that wasn't the same as actually laying eyes on the landscape.

The trail was fairly easy to follow at first, as if the watcher didn't know that Denny had spotted him and hadn't been trying to conceal his sign. But as the tracks led more and more toward the mountains and the terrain got rougher, Rogers had a harder time following them. The ground was rocky for long stretches, and he had to cast back and forth quite a bit before he was able to pick up the tracks again. Several times he was convinced he had lost the trail, then he found it again.

His search would be easier if he wasn't distracted by thoughts of Denny Jensen, he told himself. Sure, she was pretty, but she was also reckless, headstrong, and even a little arrogant. He supposed that was understandable in a girl who had grown up rich and beautiful.

His thoughts turned to memories of his childhood. He'd certainly never had the same sort of advantages.

He grew up on a hardscrabble ranch in West Texas, pressed into service helping his father run the place almost as soon as he was old enough to stay in a saddle. By that time, the threat from Comanches and Apaches was over for all practical purposes, although bands of bronco Apaches were rumored to still be hiding in the mountains across the border in Mexico. It was said that from time to time they crossed the Rio Grande to raid isolated ranches, but no renegades ever bothered the Rogers family.

They had enough to handle without any bloodthirsty savages showing up. The elements were brutal—drought in the summer, blizzards in the winter, never enough water or grass to sustain a herd. Throw in rattlesnakes and scorpions and all the other things that could kill you, and life was hard, with little or no promise of a reward somewhere in the future.

He was fifteen when a fever had claimed both his parents. The oldest of four children, he figured he would keep the ranch running, but folks from the church in the nearest settlement, thirty miles away, had showed up to take his little brothers and sister away. They would find new homes for the youngsters, they said. People were willing to take him in, too. At fifteen, he didn't argue. The church folks had a sheriff's deputy with them.

He told them all to go to hell and rode off on his own, leaving the ranch behind for good. He had done nothing his whole life except work hard and take orders, and he was damned if he was going to live with some new family and take orders from them.

* * *

He mused about his past with one part of his mind while the other concentrated on following the tracks.

Making his way in the world alone wasn't easy. Eventually, he found a job sweeping out a jail up in the Panhandle, and that led to pinning on a deputy's star. Law work seemed to suit him and he did that for a few years, working in various settlements. He met a deputy U.S. marshal who suggested that he try to get a job with Chief Marshal Horton in Denver. He followed the suggestion and succeeded in becoming a deputy U.S. marshal, working hard as always.

The tracks had disappeared again. Rogers stopped his musing and focused all his attention on the search, thinking about his assignment to clean up the rustling around Big Rock. For more than an hour, he continued to ride through the foothills, his eyes intent for any sign of his quarry, until he was finally forced to admit it was no use. He'd lost the trail.

He hated to give up, but at least there was one good thing about the situation. Denny Jensen wasn't there to witness his failure. The next time he ran into her, whether it was in Big Rock or on the Sugarloaf, he was willing to bet she would ask him what he had found, and he wasn't looking forward to having to tell her.

Even though it might be nice to see her again . . .

Things were calm on the Sugarloaf for the next week. Some branding needed to be done, and Denny insisted on being right in the middle of it, working with the men amid the dust and the smoke from the branding fire and the stink of burned hair when the iron sizzled its mark into hide. Smoke turned her loose to do what she wanted, but discreetly he asked Cal to keep an eye on her.

"I'll try," the foreman promised, "but if she thinks I'm givin' her any special privileges, she's liable to light into me. I'm not sure I want that."

Smoke laughed and slapped his old friend on the shoulder. "Just do the best you can, Cal."

During that week, Smoke spent quite a bit of time with Louis. The young man wanted to learn all he could about the business end of running the ranch.

They were in the office going over the tally books and ledgers.

"I may not be able to bulldog steers or use a branding iron like Denny, but I assume there's more than that to what goes on around here," Louis said.

"There sure is," Smoke agreed. "And there's getting to be more of this part all the time. Your mother's helped me out with some of it, but I'm sure she wouldn't mind giving up that chore if you're interested in taking it on."

"Well . . . I intend to practice law at some point, but I don't see why I can't do that and help with the ranch's business affairs at the same time."

"Let's do some studying, then." Smoke chuckled as he opened one of the ledgers. "There was a time I never dreamed I'd be saying something like that."

"When all it took to run a ranch was an iron fist and a fast gun?"

"Something like that," Smoke admitted. "Although I never went in much for the iron fist part. I figured if I always treated my crew decent, they'd do a better job of riding for the brand."

He enjoyed spending the time with Louis, working with him and getting to know him better. The boy had a quick mind and a wry sense of humor, usually self-deprecating, unlike Denny, who took herself pretty seriously most of the time. Smoke had a hunch that Louis would make a success of himself as a lawyer, ranch manager, or really anything he put his mind to, as long as it didn't take a lot of hard physical work. Louis's heart couldn't stand up to that and probably never would.

As the days went by, he had a little more color in his face, at least, and seemed to feel good most of the time.

One evening after supper, while Smoke was sitting in a rocking chair on the front porch enjoying the fresh air, Cal walked over from the bunkhouse and said in a quiet voice, "Need to talk to you for a few minutes, Smoke."

"Privatelike?" Smoke asked, sensing that whatever Cal had to say, he wanted to keep it between the two of them.

"I reckon that'd be better, at least for now."

Smoke stood up. "Let's take a walk down to the barn, then," he suggested.

They ambled in that direction, neither man speaking until they were inside the big, cavernous structure. The barn was dark and quiet and filled with the scents of straw, horseflesh, and manure.

To a man like Smoke, that wasn't a bad smell. "What's on your mind?" he asked his foreman.

"I was riding up by Aspen Springs today and saw a couple tracks."

"Animal tracks?"

Cal grunted. "More like a two-legged varmint. Boot marks, along with a few hoofprints."

"So one of the boys stopped to water his horse."

Cal shook his head. "None of our crew have been over there in the past week . . . and the tracks I saw were less than a day old."

"Still could've been a pilgrim just passing through," Smoke suggested.

"Passing through to where? You know there's nothing around there except that big box canyon we sometimes use as a holding pen during roundup. Somebody stopped to water his horse, all right, but he wasn't a pilgrim and he wasn't one of ours."

Smoke ran a thumbnail along his jaw a moment. "That doesn't leave much."

"It sure doesn't. We've got a good-sized bunch of cattle less than a mile from there, Smoke."

"And you think this hombre was scouting them for the rest of his gang."

"It makes sense," Cal said. "They've left us alone for a while. They wanted us to think that after we dealt them such a hard blow last time, they were finished in this part of the country, so we'd let our guard down. But they're not finished. They've just been bidin' their time."

Smoke nodded. "I tend to agree with you. I halfway expected that very thing."

"I know you did, and I trust your hunches. How soon do you think they'll hit us?"

"Now that they've found some stock to go after, they won't waste any time about it," Smoke said. "There's a good chance they'll try to pull a raid tonight. Go round up half a dozen of the boys."

"I've got a couple ridin' nighthawk out there already," Cal said with a grim note in his voice. "Will Dugan and Chet Parkhurst. I sure don't want anything happenin' to them."

"It won't if we have anything to say about it. Can you be ready to ride in ten minutes?"

"You know we can, Smoke."

"I'll meet you out here then."

"You gonna tell Sally where you're goin'?"

Smoke thought about it for a second and then shook his head. "Despite our hunches, this might all turn out to be nothing. No need to get anybody worried until we see for sure what's going on. Tell Pearlie and the boys who stay here, though, just in case they have to come after us. We'll leave Sally and Inez and the kids in the dark about it for now."

"Whatever you say, Smoke."

They left the barn together and split up, Cal hurrying toward the bunkhouse while Smoke's long strides carried him back to the house. Neither of them saw the figure that came up to the edge of the thick shadows inside the barn and peered after them.

"Leave us all in the dark, eh?" Denny whispered to herself. "We'll just see about that!"

CHAPTER 16

Denny had heard the whole conversation between Smoke and Cal. Clearly, they hadn't known she was in the barn. She hadn't intended for anyone to know, which was why she had slipped out of the house's rear door and circled around. Her mother had said something earlier about playing the harpsichord so they could all sing. Denny knew she had a tin ear and couldn't carry a tune in a bucket, so she didn't see any point in embarrassing herself.

She'd taken a carrot from the kitchen to feed to the buckskin in the barn. After a week of her riding him out on the range every day, the two of them had become good friends.

She'd been about to light a lantern when she heard someone approaching, so she had put the match back into her pocket and drawn back deeper into the shadows until she found out who it was. Once her father and Cal started talking, Denny knew she didn't want to reveal her presence.

They would talk a lot more freely if they didn't know she was there, she thought.

Sure enough, Cal had spilled the news about the rustlers being back.

Denny realized there wasn't any real proof of that yet, but she agreed with what Smoke and Cal's instincts told them—that rustlers were the most logical explanation.

She wished there was some way for her to get word to Brice Rogers. It would be good for his career as a lawman if he was part of breaking up the gang he had been sent after. If a local rancher took care of the rustlers, it could look bad . . . like Rogers didn't really know what he was doing.

On the other hand, she told herself, it wasn't her job to take care of him. He was a big boy. He could look out for his own career.

She started toward the tack room, intending to get her saddle and put it on the buckskin, knowing she could handle that chore without any light. Then she realized her father would be back in a minute or two to saddle up one of his own string of mounts. He probably *would* light the lantern hanging from a nail on one of the beams that held up the hayloft, and Smoke Jensen was keen-eyed enough to spot the buckskin being gone right away.

She would have to wait, Denny told herself, then saddle up and follow Smoke and the others after they were gone. She could only hope they would still be within earshot.

Whatever excitement happened, she planned to at least witness it . . . if not wind up right in the thick of it. She bypassed the tack room and slipped through the small door at the rear of the barn and disappeared into the thick shadows under the nearby trees.

Smoke was able to retrieve his gun belt, holstered Colt, and Winchester from his study without running into Sally, but he encountered Louis in the hall as he headed for the front door.

The young man nodded toward the hardware in Smoke's hands and asked, "Trouble?"

"Maybe, maybe not. Where's your mother?"

"She went upstairs to look for Denny, I believe." Louis smiled. "Would you prefer that I not mention to her that you left out of here armed for bear?"

"That would probably be a good idea. No need to worry her or your sister."

"What if she looks for you and realizes you're gone?"

"Maybe you could tell her that I went out to the bunkhouse to talk to Cal for a while?" That wasn't a complete lie, Smoke thought. He was going to be with Cal.

"Lying for a client . . . I suppose that would be good practice for when I start practicing law."

"I'm a client?" Smoke said, cocking an eyebrow.

"Give me a dollar. We'll call it a retainer, and that way we'll be bound by attorney-client privilege."

Smoke chuckled. "I think that only works in court, not with mothers, but you can give it a try if you want." He took a silver dollar from his pocket, and flipped it to Louis, who caught it deftly.

"You'd better go while you've got the chance," Louis advised. "There's no telling how long she'll be up there."

Smoke nodded, clapped a hand on his son's shoulder for a second, and then hurried out of the house. It would have been nice to have Louis ride out with him to face down trouble, he thought briefly, but on the other hand, he wouldn't have to worry about any rustler lead maybe finding his offspring.

Cal and six members of the crew were waiting at the

barn. Their horses were saddled and they were ready to ride.

Cal held out the reins of Smoke's big gray stallion. "I went ahead and threw a hull on him for you, Smoke. Figured that would be all right."

"More than all right," Smoke said as he took the reins. "I'm obliged to you." He swung up into the saddle and the others followed his lead. They rode out of the ranch yard, heading north toward Aspen Springs, which was near the boundary of Sugarloaf range. It was a dark night, but they didn't need much light to find their way. They knew every foot of the ranch, especially Smoke and Cal.

The stars twinkled brilliantly in the ebony sky. The air was cool enough that the breath of men and horses fogged slightly in front of their faces. As he rode, Smoke listened intently, hoping he wouldn't hear any gunfire in the distance. Like Cal, he was worried about the two men riding nighthawk. The night was quiet, but they had no guarantee it would stay that way.

Anything could be lurking in the dark.

Muddy Malone's heart pounded in his chest as he rode hard along the trail between the Sugarloaf ranch house and the spring where he had left the tracks that morning. It had been a tricky business, leaving that sign where it would look realistic without it being too obvious what he was doing. Then he'd had to find himself a good hidey-hole farther up the slopes where he could wait and watch to see if they were discovered.

Sure enough, one of Jensen's men had come along and acted real interested in the tracks. Muddy had stayed out of sight, even though he could have plugged the fella without any trouble. After a while, the rider had gone on about his business. Muddy had stayed where he was until nearly dark, when he started drifting carefully toward the Sugarloaf headquarters to see if he'd stirred up any excitement around the place.

That was all Creighton's idea, of course. He was a pretty cunning hombre. If Jensen thought the rustlers were back, he'd have to do something about it.

Muddy watched from the trees as some of Jensen's men saddled horses and readied to ride. So far, it appeared that everything was going according to plan. They wouldn't be going out at night unless they were trying to head off a raid by rustlers.

Certain that was what was going on, Muddy led his horse and eased back away from the ranch headquarters, not mounting up and galloping northward until he was out of earshot. Creighton and most of the other men were waiting for him in the box canyon just south of the springs.

In sight of the canyon, Muddy slowed his horse. The canyon mouth resembled a dark, sinister maw, opening into a long ridge like a giant step up to the mountains. He didn't think any of the boys would get trigger-happy, but it never hurt to be careful. He pulled his mount down to a walk and stopped to call softly, "Hey, fellas. It's me!"

"Get in here," Creighton ordered sharply.

Muddy nudged his horse forward. The darkness closed around him, so thick he wasn't sure he could see his hand even if he held it right in front of his face. He could hear the faint sounds of horses and men shifting around nearby.

Creighton asked, "Are they on their way?"

"They're a few minutes behind me, boss," Muddy replied. "Fifteen, at the most, I'd say."

"And Jensen is with them?"

Muddy hesitated. Lying might get him in more trouble than telling the truth, he decided. "I'm not sure. I think so. He was talkin' to his foreman, the fella who found those tracks you had me leave, and then he went into his house like he was goin' to get his guns. So he must be leadin' the bunch."

"But you don't know that for sure?" Creighton's question had a cold edge to it.

"Noooo . . . I reckon not. But you know, boss, Smoke Jensen wouldn't just send his men up here without comin' along himself. That ain't the way he does things."

"You'd better be right, Malone," Creighton snapped.

Muddy swallowed hard. He hoped he was right, too.

Creighton went on. "Jensen and his men will be bound for the springs, where we left the bodies of those two men of his. We'll let them ride past us, then we'll hit them from behind. We outnumber them two to one, but I want to take as many of them alive as we can, including Jensen."

Lupe Herrera spoke up in the shadows. "That may be hard, Nick. Once the bullets start to fly, we won't know who's dying and who isn't."

"I understand that," Creighton said, "but if I order you to hold your fire, everybody had better hold their fire, got it?"

Murmurs of agreement came from the assembled outlaws.

"Jensen's mine, if I can manage it," Creighton went on. "But the most important thing is that Smoke Jensen dies tonight."

Denny wasn't sure how far behind her father and the other men she was, but she knew they were still up ahead because she could hear their horses. She had saddled the buckskin as soon as they rode off from the ranch and gone after them, relying on her knowledge of the Sugarloaf to keep from getting lost. She didn't know the ranch as well as Smoke, Cal, and the others did, so she worried they might get away from her and closed up the gap between them as much as she could and still not alert them to her presence.

A quarter moon was peeking over the hills to the east. Soon it would be high enough to cast some light over the valley. It might be enough for her father to spot her if he looked back, Denny thought, so she slowed her pace. She risked losing them by doing that, but it couldn't be helped.

Anyway, she had overheard enough of the conversation between Smoke and Cal that she knew where they were going. She thought she could find the place, even in the dark.

Denny reached the southern end of the long, broad pasture that ran all way to the Sugarloaf's northern boundary. It was some of the best grazing land on the whole ranch, and it was dotted with dark masses of cattle clumped together to doze through the night. She reined in and peered at the landscape ahead of her, searching for Smoke and the others. That quarter-moon in the sky cast silvery fingers across the valley, and she spotted the riders several hundred yards ahead of her.

More movement caught her eye and made her forehead crease in a puzzled frown. Off to the left, between her and the group she had followed, lay the dark mouth of the box canyon Cal had mentioned. Men on horseback were emerging from it and swinging north, falling in behind Smoke and his companions.

It appeared to her they outnumbered her father and his men. She knew they weren't from the ranch headquarters as the rest of the crew was back there.

She stiffened in the saddle as she realized there was only one logical explanation for the presence of those strangers—they were up to no good. And they were closing in on the Sugarloaf party from behind.

Without thinking about it any more than that, Denny grabbed the stock of her Winchester carbine and hauled it from the saddle boot. She worked the weapon's lever, pointed the barrel at the sky, and pulled the trigger as she drove her boot heels into the buckskin's flanks and sent the horse lunging forward. The carbine cracked three times as fast as she could work its lever. The sharp reports rang out across the valley as she charged the sinister band of unknown riders.

CHAPTER 17

Smoke heard the shots and the swift rataplan of running hoofbeats and knew instinctively that he and his men had ridden into a trap. That possibility had lurked in the back of his mind, but he had known that he had to check out the situation anyway.

As he wheeled around instantly, with Cal and the other cowboys following suit, Smoke spotted the riders charging them from behind. Without even stopping to think about it, he knew they had been hidden in the box canyon. It was the only place they could have been lurking in order to get behind the group of Sugarloaf riders. Muzzle flame bloomed in the darkness as the raiders opened fire.

They had launched their attack too soon, he thought. They should have waited until they were closer if they wanted to make sure of their prey.

That was all the confirmation Denny needed that the strange riders were indeed up to no good. She drove the buckskin forward, guiding the horse with her knees as she pressed the carbine's butt firmly against her shoulder and started raking the intruders with lead.

Since they were between her and her father, she worried a missed shot might go on past them and hit someone it wasn't supposed to. She aimed low, knowing she was more likely to hit innocent horses, but that couldn't be helped. Downing some of them would put the riders on foot, making it easier for the Sugarloaf men to round them up.

With his rifle already in his hands, Smoke flung it to his shoulder and sprayed lead into the mass of riders charging toward him and his small crew.

His men opened fire as well. For a long moment, the darkness was torn asunder by orange streaks of light that geysered from the barrels of rifles and pistols. A deadly storm of lead lashed back and forth between the two groups. Then they came together, and chaos erupted as the battle shattered into numerous individual fights.

Smoke found himself facing two shadowy riders who charged him from different angles. He shifted his grip on the Winchester and thrust it out using only his left hand, while his right palmed the Colt from its holster and brought it up. The gray was used to the sound of gunfire, so it stood fairly steady while Smoke squeezed off shots with both weapons. The revolver boomed and bucked in his right hand, and the attacker on that side flew backwards as the .45 slug swept him out of the saddle.

The rifle was harder to fire one-handed, and the recoil kicked the barrel high. As Smoke was bringing it down, he felt the heat of a bullet whipping past his cheek, and then in the next split second, a hammer blow smashed into his left side, high up just below the

shoulder. The impact twisted him halfway around in
the saddle. His left arm went numb with shock, and the
rifle slipped from his fingers.

Even caught in the crossfire, only a few of the
rustlers wheeled around and opened fire on the threat
coming up from behind them. Most charged ahead,
intent on overrunning and overwhelming the group
from the Sugarloaf.

Denny heard slugs whining through the air near
her head. She would have been scared half to death—
if there had been time for that. She allowed her instincts to take over, veered the buckskin to the left, and
kept shooting. Her bullets spooked the attackers. They
peeled away and circled back toward the main fight.

The dark maw of the canyon mouth loomed on
Denny's left. She could have darted in there and
hidden until the battle was over, thus staying fairly safe
from stray bullets. But there was no guarantee that
Smoke and his allies would win. From what she had
been able to see, they were outnumbered. She wanted
to help so pressed on.

The battle had broken down and spread out into
smaller confrontations. Muzzle flame spurted here
and there like a sprawling cloud of deadly fireflies.
Denny raced toward one of those clashes, hoping she
would be able to tell friend from foe. If she couldn't,
she would have to hold her fire.

Since he was already slewed to the side, Smoke
didn't have as far to bring the Colt around to meet
the remaining threat. A flood of pain washed away the
numbness that had gripped him when he was hit, but
he tightened his jaw against it and triggered a pair of

swift shots. Only a few yards away, the man who'd wounded him rocked backwards in the saddle but didn't fall. His horse charged on, wild and out of control.

Sensing the imminent collision between the two horses, Smoke kicked his feet free of the stirrups and was thrown clear when they crashed together and went down. Unfortunately, he landed on his wounded shoulder, which caused such a blinding explosion of agony that for a moment he was unaware of anything else and unable to move.

In one of the split seconds of glare that ripped the night apart, Denny saw two horses crash together and one of the riders fly through the air, land hard, and roll over a couple times. She watched as another rider spurred toward him.

When his senses came back to him, Smoke lifted his head and saw a huge dark shape looming above him, blotting out the stars and the moon.

It was a man on horseback, who shouted, "Now you'll die for what you've done, Jensen!"

The barrel of a pistol swung swiftly toward Smoke.

Denny knew the only other Jensen out there was her father. The carbine flashed up to her shoulder and barked as soon as she lined the barrel on the shadowy target. The man cried out in pain as the slug raked him somewhere. The pistol fell from his hand.

Denny worked the carbine's lever and fired again, but the man had already bent forward in the saddle to make himself a smaller target, or he slumped that way because he was wounded. The bullet whipped harmlessly over his head. He was able to yank the horse around and jab his spurs viciously into its flanks. The animal let out a shrill scream but leaped away. Denny fired again and grimaced because she knew she had missed.

She sent the buckskin pounding toward the fallen man, leaped down while the horse was still moving, staggered forward a step, and dropped to her knees beside him. He was struggling to sit up. He had lost his hat when he fell, and in the moonlight she was able to make out the familiar features. "Pa, are you hit?" she asked as she pressed a hand against his right shoulder.

"Denny?" he exclaimed. "What the hell—" He let out a groan and twisted, favoring his left side.

Denny saw the dark stain on Smoke's shirt and set her carbine aside so she could take hold of him and carefully eased him back to the ground. "Just lie there. You're hurt."

"Denny, what in blazes . . . are you doing here?"

"Saving your bacon, from the looks of it." She groaned inwardly. Maybe that wasn't the wisest reaction, but she was too worried about him to be thinking straight at the moment.

She turned her head and looked out across the valley. Shots still flashed here and there, but most of the fighting seemed to be over. As she watched tensely, the last of the gunfire died away. And it was too dark to tell who had won the battle.

"Denny—" Smoke began again, but she hissed at him to be quiet.

"We don't want to bring them down on top of us," she whispered. "Was it those rustlers who jumped you?"

"Had to be," he said, keeping his voice as quiet as hers.

She heard the pain in his tone. Uncertainty over how badly he was hit gnawed at her, but she couldn't risk a light to examine the wound.

Hoofbeats thudded not far off in the darkness. Denny tensed and picked up the carbine. She couldn't remember if, in the heat of battle, she had worked the lever after the last shot she fired. There might be a round in the chamber, or there might not be, but she couldn't risk cocking it. Not with an unknown rider so close.

A familiar voice called softly, "Smoke! Smoke, you around here?"

A shudder of relief went through Denny. Still not knowing if any of the rustlers were still around, she kept her voice quiet as she responded, "Cal! Over here!"

Horse and rider loomed out of the shadows. Cal said in evident amazement, "Miss Denise? Is that you?"

"I'm here, Cal. So is my father. He's hurt."

She heard a muttered curse from the foreman as he reined in. Cal dismounted in a hurry and let his horse's reins dangle as he knelt on Smoke's other side. "How bad is it?"

"Blast it, I'm all right," Smoke said, but his voice sounded weak. "I caught a slug in the left side . . . just under my shoulder, but it missed my heart . . . else I'd be dead already. I don't think it broke any bones. I'm just . . . bleeding like a stuck pig . . . You'd better get . . . Denny out of here—"

"The hell with that. I'm not going anywhere without you, Pa." She looked across him at Cal. "What about the rustlers?"

"I'm pretty sure they all lit a shuck, except for the ones we killed." He added grimly, "We lost some men, too, I think. I'll round everybody up and see how bad the situation is, but right now we need to get Smoke on his horse and the two of you back to the house as quick as can be."

"I'm going to risk a light," Denny said. "You get

ready to shoot if anybody opens up on us. Probably need to do something about this wound, though, or he's liable to bleed to death on the way back."

Smoke said, "She sure does . . . take to giving orders . . . doesn't she, Cal?"

"I reckon she's right." Cal stood up and pulled his Winchester from its scabbard. "You go ahead, Miss Denise, and see if you can patch him up a mite. If anybody tries to give us trouble, I'll deal with 'em."

Denny found the little waterproof packet of matches she had taken to carrying since she got back to the ranch and struck one of them. Squinting against the glare, she looked at her father's side and saw that his shirt was soaked with blood from just below his shoulder to the waist. He had lost a lot of it already, and it still seemed to be welling from the wound.

The match burned down. Working by feel, Denny ripped the bloody shirt and pulled it aside, then struck another match. She saw the hole where the bullet had gone in and lifted his shoulder enough to make sure there wasn't a matching wound on Smoke's back.

There wasn't. The slug was still in him somewhere.

Well, that wasn't good, she thought, but at the same time it meant she only had to stop the bleeding from one hole. She dropped the second match as the flame reached her fingers, then pulled her shirttails out from behind her belt. She had a folding knife in her pocket. It took her only a minute to use the blade to cut a piece of cloth from her shirttail.

She wadded the cloth into a ball, told her father, "This is going to hurt," and jammed it into the wound, pushing down until it completely filled the hole.

Smoke's breath hissed between his clenched teeth, but he didn't say anything or let out any other noise.

"Hold it there," Denny told him.

He used his right hand to do that while she cut long

strips from the bottom of her shirt and bound the makeshift plug in place with them.

"Somebody coming," Cal warned. He had his rifle ready.

A couple seconds later, a man called, "Cal? Mr. Jensen?"

"That's Rick Yates," Cal said, relief plain to hear in his voice. "Rick! We're over here!"

A couple riders pounded up.

One of them asked, "Are you all right, Cal?"

"Yeah, but the boss is here, and he's hit."

"Son of a—! Is that Miss Denise?"

"What about those rustlers?" Denny asked as she stood up wearily.

"Gone," Yates replied.

"Good. You can help me get my pa on his horse."

They found Smoke's gray, which didn't seem to have been injured in the collision with the rustler's mount. As carefully as possible, the cowboys lifted Smoke into the saddle.

"I'll ride behind him to make sure he doesn't pass out and fall off," Denny said. "Somebody give me a hand getting up there."

Yates held his hands to make a step for her. Denny settled herself on the horse's back behind the saddle, put one arm around her father's waist to steady him, and used the other hand to take the reins.

"Here's Smoke's Colt," Cal said. "Looks like he dropped it."

"Reload it," she said.

When Cal had done so, using cartridges from his own shell belt, she put the reins between her teeth for a moment and held out a hand. "Give it here," she ordered around the reins.

Cal handed her the revolver, butt first. She stuck it behind her belt.

"Miss Denise . . . ?" the foreman said uncertainly.

"Anybody tries to stop us, they'll be sorry," Denny declared and then heeled the big gray into a run. They disappeared into the night, heading south toward the ranch headquarters.

CHAPTER 18

That ride was as nerve-wracking as anything Denny had ever experienced. During the gun battle she had been too busy to be scared. Instinct and anger had fueled her actions. Now that the danger was over, reaction was setting in. She felt herself trembling inside, especially when she thought about how many bullets had slapped through the air near her head.

Not only that, but the danger wasn't over for her father. However serious his wound was, she knew he had lost a lot of blood and that could be fatal. She tightened her arm around him and said urgently, "You hang on, Pa. Don't you even think about dying. You hear me?"

No telling where the bullet was inside him. He had said he didn't think it had broken any bones, but it could have glanced off one and lodged who knows where. Because of that uncertainty, she didn't want to jolt him around too much. She didn't run the gray at a full gallop but kept the horse's pace at a ground-eating lope instead. Even at that, Smoke groaned from time to time, sometimes muttering words, but Denny couldn't make them out except a couple times she heard him say her mother's name. "Sally . . . Sally . . ."

"You'll see her soon, Pa," she told him, but she didn't know if he heard her or not.

No one tried to stop them, so the revolver remained behind her belt. They didn't encounter any other riders on the trip.

Finally, after what seemed like days, lights came into view up ahead. Denny knew they came from the ranch house and the other buildings at the ranch headquarters. "Almost there," she told Smoke as she urged the horse on.

As the gray pounded up in front of the house, Denny eased back on the reins. "Ma! Louis! I need help out here! It's Pa! Hello, the house!" She breathed heavily. She could feel Smoke breathing, too, so she knew he was still alive . . . but how much longer that would be true, she had no idea.

Even though she had been apart from him for most of her life, the time she had spent around him had impressed her so much that she couldn't imagine a world without Smoke Jensen in it. He was a towering figure in her life.

The front door slammed open and Sally rushed out, a cry springing to her lips as she caught sight of the bloody, slumped figure in the saddle. She wore a silk dressing gown, and her hair was loose as if she'd been ready for bed. For a second she stopped short and raised the back of a hand to her mouth in horror, then she brought that reaction under control and visibly steeled herself to do what needed to be done. "Denny, is that you?"

"Yeah, Ma. I—"

"Explanations later. Right now we need to get your father into the house." Sally turned and called, "Louis!"

He was already there, emerging from the house. "Mother, what is—Good Lord! Father?"

"Run out to the bunkhouse and fetch the men who are there."

"We can get 'em here quicker than that." Denny pulled the gun from behind her belt, pointed it at the sky, and thumbed off three shots, the universal signal for distress on the frontier. The gray danced around a little, but not much.

Men in long underwear tumbled out of the bunkhouse, some in boots but most barefoot. They all had guns and were ready to shoot it out with anybody who had dared to invade the Sugarloaf. Louis quickly set them straight, running out to meet them as they charged across the ranch yard, and telling them that Smoke had been wounded.

Callused but gentle hands reached up, took hold of him, and lifted him from the saddle. With Sally giving orders briskly, the men carried Smoke into the house and placed him on a sofa in the parlor.

She lit a lamp and looked around. "Where's Cal?"

Denny said, "He's with the rest of the crew, up in the big pasture by Aspen Springs. There was a fight with some rustlers. That's how Pa got wounded." She didn't go into any more detail than that. The rest of the explanation could wait. "I tried to stop the bleeding as best I could."

Sally thrust the lamp into Louis's hands and told him to hold it where she could examine the wound. "I can see what you did," she said to Denny. "It looks like a good job. I need to get that off of there and clean up all that blood, though. Inez!"

"Here, señora," the cook and housekeeper said from behind the group of half-dressed cowboys. They parted hastily to let her through.

"Clean cloths and hot water," Sally said.

"The pot is already on the stove, señora. When I

heard shouting I put it on to heat. Any disturbance this late at night is likely to require hot water."

Sally laughed, but there wasn't much genuine humor in the sound. "That's right. You men, thank you for your help. Now clear out and give us room to work."

"You'll let us know if you need anything else, Miz Sally?" one of the hands asked.

"Of course." Sally looked at her children. "Denise, Louis, you stay here."

The cowboys shuffled out of the parlor, some of them looking sheepish because they were dressed only in their underwear.

Sally turned to Denny. "You have blood on you."

"It's Pa's," Denny assured her mother. "I wasn't hit."

"You were in the middle of that fight?"

Louis murmured, "Somehow I'm not surprised."

Smoke startled them all by saying in a faint voice, "She . . . saved us."

Sally turned quickly to him. "Smoke, I didn't know you were awake."

"Just . . . came to," he forced out. His eyelids fluttered for a second, then stayed open. His face twisted in a grimace of pain. "There were some shots . . . warned us we were . . . about to be ambushed . . . I reckon you . . . fired them . . . Denny?"

"That's right," she said as she knelt beside the sofa. "I was trailing you and saw a bunch of hombres come out of the blind canyon behind you. I knew they had to be bushwhackers."

"That's because"—a faint smile curved Smoke's lips—"because . . . you're my daughter . . ."

Inez came in with clean rags draped over her arm and a pan of hot water in her hands.

Sally said, "Let me get to work on him."

Denny moved aside. "Somebody needs to go to Big Rock for the doctor."

"I imagine one of the crew is saddling up to do that right now. Louis, can you check and see about that?"

"Of course, Mother."

"What about me?" Denny asked.

Sally said, "It sounds like we have you to thank for keeping him alive this long. Now it's up to me to keep him that way until the doctor gets here."

"You can do that?"

Sally glanced at her daughter and gave Denny a bleak smile. "You don't think this is the first bullet wound I've patched up, do you? For heaven's sake, I've been married to Smoke Jensen for more than twenty years!"

True to her word, Sally took good care of Smoke. She cleaned all the gore away from the wound and saw that the bleeding had stopped except for a little seepage. Since she didn't know for sure how long it would be before the doctor arrived, she got a bottle of whiskey from a cabinet, soaked a rag with it, and swabbed the outer edges of the wound. That stung enough to make Smoke mutter in the stupor that had set in.

"This will hurt even worse, darling." She turned the bottle up and poured some of the fiery liquor into the bullet hole. "Hold him down!" she told Denny and Inez as Smoke groaned and arched his back against the whiskey's bite.

Louis said, "There are other ways to disinfect a wound, you know."

"Bourbon's good for what ails you," Sally said. "Preacher taught us that. Of course, he claimed there are more medicinal uses for it than there really are . . ."

Denny and Inez had hold of Smoke's shoulders. His reaction subsided as the pain eased. He opened his eyes, raised his head, and rasped, "I could use a little of that . . . internally."

"You've never been much of a drinking man, Smoke," Sally said.

"I make an exception . . . when I'm shot."

She held the bottle to his lips and eased a little of the whiskey into his mouth. Smoke swallowed, sighed, and let his head sag back. His chest rose and fell regularly.

"He's more asleep now than passed out," Sally said quietly. "That's good." She stepped back and motioned for Denny to come with her to the other side of the room. "Now, tell me what happened. What in the world were the two of you up to tonight?"

Denny explained everything that had happened, starting with her overhearing the conversation between Smoke and Cal in the barn. Sally and Louis listened with grave expressions on their faces.

"Smoke should have told me what was going on," Sally said when her daughter was finished. "*You* should have told me."

"There wasn't really time," Denny said. "Anyway, it might not have amounted to anything, and he didn't want to worry you unnecessarily. Neither did I."

Sally sighed and shook her head. "I suppose I ought to be used to it by now . . . and it looks as if you're turning out to be just like him, Denise."

"I'll take that as a compliment," Denny said.

"As would I, if I were in your circumstances," Louis added. He turned his head. "I think I hear something. Might be the doctor coming. I'll go see." He went out onto the porch. Denny followed him, leaving Sally to keep an eye on Smoke.

"Don't be offended at anything she says," Louis murmured to his sister. "She's just upset and worried about him."

"I'm not upset. I meant it when I said I'd take it as a compliment."

"As did I." Louis gestured toward the revolver. "That's his iron you're packing, you know."

"Yeah." Denny wrapped her hand around the plain walnut grips and pulled the Colt from behind her belt. "Feels pretty good. Natural."

"Yes, you're Smoke Jensen's daughter, all right."

"Did you really hear somebody coming?"

"No, but I thought it might be a good idea to get out of there for a while and let the two of them be alone. Mother feels like she has to be strong—she *is* strong—but it won't hurt for her to sit down and let her guard down, maybe even cry a little, for a few minutes."

"You think of things I never would," Denny said.

Louis smiled. "That's why we make a good team."

Less than half an hour later, the doctor arrived from Big Rock. Youngish and bespectacled, Enoch Steward was the current medico. He followed several physicians since Big Rock's first doctor, Colton Spaulding, had arrived. He examined Smoke while Sally, Denny, Louis, and Inez looked on anxiously, then straightened from his work. "You've done an excellent job of taking care of your husband, Mrs. Jensen. If you hadn't stopped the bleeding when you did, I don't believe he would have survived."

"That was Denny's doing," Sally said with a nod toward her daughter. "She already had the bleeding practically stopped when she got here with Smoke."

"But you cleaned and disinfected the wound."

"I did." Sally smiled. "With bourbon. I applied a little internally, too, at Smoke's request."

Dr. Steward chuckled. "It can't have hurt. Now,

though, that bullet is still in there, and it needs to come out. Mr. Jensen is asleep, but I'll use ether to put him under deeper so he won't feel it while I'm probing for the slug."

"Can you remove it?" Louis asked.

"I'm almost certain I can. Of course, I'll have to locate it first."

Sally said, "Do we need to move him?"

"He'll do fine right where he is. Your sofa already has blood on it, I'm afraid—"

"To hell with the sofa," Sally said. "Just save my husband's life."

"That's exactly what I intend to do," the doctor declared. "I'll need to sterilize my instruments . . ."

"There's hot water already on the stove," Inez told him.

Steward chased everyone out of the room except Inez while he was performing his surgery. Sally, Denny, and Louis went out onto the front porch to wait. They were there only a few minutes before Cal came out of the night, jogging up on horseback.

He reined in and jerked his hat off. "Miss Sally, how's Smoke?"

"The doctor is working on him now. It looks like he's going to be all right."

"Well, thank the Lord for that! When I saw all the blood on his shirt—" He stopped and put his hat on again, wearily thumbing it to the back of his head. "You were mighty cool under fire out there, Miss Denny. Your pa's gonna be proud of you."

"I hope so," Denny said. "What about the rustlers?"

"We found five of 'em shot to pieces. The rest of 'em sloped, looks like." Cal grimaced. "We lost five men, too, countin' the two nighthawks those sons of . . . those varmints shot down in cold blood. Killin' five good boys who rode for the Sugarloaf and puttin' a bullet in Smoke"—he shook his head—"we've sure got a big score to settle with those rustlers."

"That score will be settled," Denny said with anger blazing inside her. "It'll be settled as sure as my name is Jensen."

CHAPTER 19

"You're gonna be all right, boss," Muddy said as he rode alongside Nick Creighton.

From time to time, the boss outlaw reeled in the saddle, and it was Muddy's job to reach over and steady him. Turk was leading Creighton's horse.

Muddy went on. "Once we get back to the hideout, Molly'll fix you right up, I'll bet."

"Shut up, Malone," Creighton grated. "I'm in enough pain without listening to you yammer." He used his left arm to cradle his right arm against his body. His shirtsleeve had been torn away and then wrapped around his right forearm as a crude bandage to slow down the bleeding from the long furrow left behind by a bullet. The wound wasn't that serious, but Muddy knew it had to hurt like hell.

Even worse, as far as Creighton was concerned, was that the injury had happened just as he was about to blast the life out of Smoke Jensen. The slug had ripped along his arm and made him drop his gun an instant before he could have squeezed the trigger and avenged his brother Blue.

Muddy knew that because the boss had been complaining bitterly about it for most of the ride back to the basin at the end of the box canyon. That missed opportunity to kill Jensen seemed to bother him more than the five men they had lost during the botched ambush.

Muddy still wasn't sure what had gone wrong. One of Jensen's men had gotten behind them somehow. Maybe the fella's horse had had trouble and he had fallen behind. All that really mattered was that he had started shooting and spoiled the trap and then all hell had broken loose.

Jensen and his men were fightin' fools, that was for damn sure, Muddy thought. Even outnumbered, they had killed nearly half a dozen of the rustlers and routed the others.

The rest of the men straggled along behind Creighton, Muddy, and Turk. Some of them were wounded, which led to an occasional groan or curse in the darkness. With Creighton being wounded, Turk didn't want to set too fast a pace and bounce him around in the saddle. Also, it wasn't easy finding his way through the rugged landscape at the edge of the mountains.

Finally, they reached the entrance to the canyon. Knowing that guards had been left on duty there, Turk called out, "Hold your fire, boys! It's us."

One of the riflemen came out from behind the rocks. "Where are the cattle? I thought you were gonna drive some more stock up here after you killed Jensen and his men. Where's the boss?"

"I'm right here, you damned fool," Creighton snapped. He used his knees to nudge his mount out from behind Turk. Muddy moved up, too, in case the boss needed his help.

"Sorry, Nick," the guard said hastily. "I didn't see you."

"Get out of the way," Creighton ordered. "Has there been any trouble here?"

"Nope, quiet as can be." The guard stepped back but fidgeted.

Muddy thought he wanted to know what had happened but was too leery of getting Creighton mad at him to press the question. Anyway, he would find out soon enough. All the men who had been left behind would.

The group rode through the twisting canyon and came out in the basin. A large fire had been built, and the flickering light spread out almost from one side of the basin to the other.

Molly stood in the cabin's open doorway, lantern light silhouetting her shapely body. She started walking out to meet the returning men, then began hurrying when she saw how Creighton was slumped forward in the saddle, his shoulders hunched as he protected his wounded arm. "Nick! Nick, are you all right?"

Turk reined in and brought Creighton's mount to a halt as Molly ran up. She caught hold of Creighton's left leg.

"The boss got grazed by a bullet," Turk told her. "It left a pretty good scratch almost the length of his forearm."

"Get him down off of there and into the cabin," Molly said. "I need to take a look at it."

Muddy and Turk swung down and helped Creighton dismount. They would have picked him up and carried him in, but he barked, "I can walk, damn it! It's my arm that's hurt. There's nothing wrong with my legs."

That wasn't strictly true, considering his limp, and he wasn't very steady on his feet. He had lost a lot of blood. Muddy helped him stumble into the cabin. Creighton stretched out on the bunk.

Molly knelt beside him. "Let me see your arm." She

started unwrapping the makeshift bandage. Some of the blood had dried and stuck to the wound.

Creighton cursed as she carefully worked it free.

"Muddy, hand me that bottle of rye on the table."

"Yes'm."

Molly reached under her skirt and tore a strip off her petticoat, then poured rye onto the cloth. She began cleaning the blood from the wound with it. Creighton grimaced and muttered more curses.

"Oh, hush," Molly told him. "This isn't going to kill you, but if that wound festers, it might."

"I know that, damn it. Go ahead."

"What about Jensen?"

That question brought another stream of profanity from Creighton. Muddy edged toward the door, figuring he didn't need to be around while the boss told Molly what had happened.

Creighton saw him trying to slip out. "Malone!"

Muddy turned back. "Yeah, boss?"

"Find your buddy Turk. Tell him that he's second in command now that Lupe's dead."

"Really?" Muddy was glad to hear that, hoping it meant he might get some of the easier chores, having been Turk's pard for several years. He knew Turk would be glad to hear it, too. Then he said, "We don't actually *know* that Lupe's dead—"

"He didn't make it out of that fight. Maybe he's just wounded and Jensen took him prisoner. It doesn't matter. He can't help us anymore, either way."

"Come to think of it," Muddy said, "you told us you saw Jensen get hit and go down. Even though you didn't get to blow his brains out, boss, could be he bled to death."

Creighton shook his head. "No, I don't believe that. I'd sense it somehow if he was dead. I'd feel like the debt for Blue had been paid. I don't feel that, so I know that Jensen's still alive . . . for now."

Talking about sensing things like that seemed just too spooky to Muddy. He didn't put any stock in it. But Creighton obviously did, and his word was law. So they would proceed as if Smoke Jensen were still alive.

"What you're sayin' is . . . this ain't over."

"Not by a long shot." Creighton looked down at his wounded arm. "I may be laid up for a little while, but it won't take me long to recover from being winged like this. And once I have . . . Smoke Jensen had better look out, because I'm coming for that son of a bitch."

They had already tried that and not accomplished anything except to get several men killed, Muddy thought. Even though he wasn't known far and wide for being smart, he had enough sense not to say that as he slipped out of the cabin and went to give Turk the sort-of good news.

"I'm afraid you're not going to be getting up and moving around for at least two weeks, Mr. Jensen," Dr. Steward said the next morning as he finished his examination of Smoke's wound and changing the dressings.

"That's not going to do," Smoke said as he frowned and shook his head.

"It'll have to. Actually, as much blood as you lost, you really shouldn't even be alive. I'm not quite sure how you survived, unless it's just sheer stubbornness on your part. At this point, however, if you insist on continuing to be stubborn and ignore my orders, it *will* kill you."

Sally crossed her arms and looked sternly at Smoke. "It's not going to happen, Doctor. I can give you my word on that. My husband is going to do exactly what you say, right to the letter."

"I hope you can convince him of that, Mrs. Jensen."

"Oh," Sally said, giving Smoke a warning frown to match his own, "I have my methods."

Smoke blew out an exasperated breath. "If Preacher was here, he'd go out and gather some moss and herbs, make a poultice, and slap it on the wound, and I'd be good as new in a few days."

"I don't know who Preacher is," Steward said, "but it would take a miracle to do such a thing."

"That old man's got a few miracles left in him."

"Don't worry, Doctor," Sally went on. "Smoke will behave. He'll complain up one way and down the other about it, but he'll follow orders for once in his life."

Steward summoned up a tired smile. "I'll leave the patient with you, then, madam." He rolled his sleeves down. He had spent the night dozing in a rocking chair in Smoke and Sally's bedroom, where Smoke had been moved after the long and bloody operation to remove the rustler's bullet that had lodged in his body. Steward had confirmed that no bones were broken, and the slug hadn't touched any internal organs, just torn up some meat and severed numerous blood vessels.

Denny, Louis, and Cal were also in the room, standing out of the way and observing while Steward finished up and got ready to go back to Big Rock. As the doctor turned to pick up the coat he had laid aside during the night, he smiled at Denny. "Any time you'd like to consider a career in medicine, Miss Jensen, I'd be glad to put in a good word for you. I believe your quick action saved your father's life."

"You mean be a doctor?" Denny said. "Me?"

"I've heard of several women who practice medicine. I believe there will come to be more of such in time."

"Maybe so, but not me," Denny declared without hesitation. "Shut up inside all the time, taking care of sick folks . . . not hardly."

"Well, sometimes it's a wise person who knows when they're *not* called to a certain profession." Steward shrugged into his coat, picked up his hat, and nodded to everyone gathered in the room. "I'll be back out to check on Mr. Jensen this evening. In the meantime, that dressing will need to be changed every four hours, without fail."

Sally nodded. "We'll take care of it, Doctor."

"Good day, then," Steward said with a tug on the brim of his hat.

"I'll see you out, Doctor," Louis said.

As they went out, Smoke called after them, "I'll be laid up for a week! Maybe!"

Sally laughed. "Now you're just being contrary, Smoke."

"That fella just didn't know who he was talking to." Smoke turned his head on the pillow to look at his foreman. "Cal—"

"Don't you worry about a thing, Smoke," Cal broke in. "The ranch will keep running nice and smooth."

"Under normal circumstances, I figure that would be true," Smoke said. "But there are a couple things that make this situation anything but normal, and you know as well as I do what they are."

Cal's jaw tightened. "The rustlers who got away."

"And the varmint who called me by name just before he tried to kill me."

"He must have a personal grudge against you, Smoke," Sally said. "Did you get a good enough look at him to recognize his face or voice?"

Smoke shook his head. "No, I don't have any idea

who he was. But he got away, and if he didn't die from Denny winging him, he's almost certain to come back and try again."

"You reckon I'd better hire some extra men?" Cal asked. "Pearlie could put the word out that we're paying fighting wages. He's still got some friends who rode those trails with him in the old days."

"No, it's the twentieth century," Smoke said. "Those days are over and done with."

"Maybe," Cal said. "Maybe not."

"It probably wouldn't hurt to take on a few extra hands. But the Sugarloaf doesn't hire gun-wolves, even if you could find any. Never has."

"All right, Smoke. Laid up or not, you're still the boss."

"I won't be laid up long," Smoke vowed. "Not near as long as that pill pusher thinks."

Sally said, "Dr. Steward seems to be a very competent physician. He's not some quack, Smoke."

"I'll do what he says," Smoke said grudgingly. "Within reason." He took a deep breath and then winced as the movement caused a twinge of pain, even as tightly bandaged up as his torso and shoulder were. "I don't know why I'm . . . getting sleepy . . ."

"Because you were shot and nearly died and need your rest." Sally drew the covers up tighter over him. She cast a meaningful glance over her shoulder at Denny and Cal, and the two of them started to withdraw.

"If you need anything, Pa, you let me know," Denny said before she went out.

"I will, darlin' . . . Thanks for . . . everything you've done . . ." Smoke's eyelids drooped closed.

"It's got to be the hardest thing in the world for a man like your pa," Cal said as he and Denny went down the stairs. "He's used to always bein' right in the middle of the action, no matter what's going on. And now he's got to just take it easy." Cal shook his head. "He'll go plumb loco."

"No, he won't. My mother will see to that."

He chuckled. "You're probably right. When it comes to strong-willed folks, those two are a good match."

Denny agreed with that. She had inherited that strong will, too. She was already thinking about her next course of action. Her father probably wouldn't like it, and her mother damned sure wouldn't, but Denny knew what she had to do.

While Cal headed outside to see to the day's chores, Denny went into the parlor. She picked up Smoke's Colt revolver from the table she'd set it on the night before and checked the cylinder. Five rounds, with the hammer resting on the empty chamber, just the way she had heard him say many times.

Dressed in clean riding clothes, she slid the Colt into the waistband of her jeans and went outside, looking for Pearlie. She found him in the barn where he spent a lot of his time, mending tack.

"Howdy, gal," he said as he looked up from the saddle he was working on. "How's your pa?"

"The doctor says he'll be all right, but he has to stay in bed for the next two weeks and take it easy for who knows how long after that."

Pearlie let out a bray of laughter. "Smoke Jensen layin' in bed and takin' it easy . . . That'll be the day!" He noticed the gun at her waist and a slight frown creased his weathered forehead. "What do you have there?"

"Pa's .45."

"He know you're carryin' it around?"

"I've got a good reason for carrying it," Denny said, not really answering Pearlie's question.

"Oh? What's that?"

Denny wrapped her hand around the gun butt and drew the weapon. She looked down at it for a moment as she held it, then she raised her gaze to the former pistoleer. "Teach me how to use this."

CHAPTER 20

Standing next to a line shack in the high country about five miles from the Sugarloaf headquarters, Pearlie said with a worried frown, "I ain't sure about this, girl. I don't much think your pa would want you doin' this." He'd made the same argument about Smoke not liking the idea when Denny had first confronted him with her request, but she'd pressed him until he had agreed to meet her up there.

"It'll be all right," Denny insisted. "If anybody ought to understand about having to pick up a gun and do what's right, it's Smoke Jensen. He was doing that when he was younger than I am."

"Younger, maybe, but he was still a man full-growed, not a—"

Denny glared at him as he stopped short. "Not a mere woman. Is that what you were about to say? Is there any rule that says a woman can't use a gun? I know my mother has, more than once."

They had left headquarters separately, half an hour apart, Pearlie departing first. By the time Denny got there, he had scavenged half a dozen empty tin cans from the trash dump behind the shack and set them up on the poles that supported the corral fence. He looked down at the holstered revolver and gun belt he held. The rig was one of his old ones.

The gun was Smoke's.

Pearlie didn't have an answer for Denny's questions, so when she held out her hand he sighed and passed over the Colt.

She took the belt, buckled it around her hips, and smiled. "It's a good thing you're a scrawny old cuss, Pearlie, or this might have been too big for me." She adjusted the holster and then reached for the rawhide thongs at the bottom of it.

"Wait just a minute," Pearlie said. "You're wearin' that too dang low."

"I thought gunfighters always wore their holsters low."

"You ain't one of them dime-novel gunfighters. Anyway, wasn't never much truth to those yarns. You don't want to carry your gun so low you have to bend over to reach it. That'll just slow you down. Of course, speed ain't the most important thing."

"It's not?"

"No, it ain't. Bein' able to hit what you're shootin' at, that's the main thing."

"Smoke Jensen is famous for being one of the fastest guns alive. Maybe *the* fastest."

"One thing you best get through your head right now," Pearlie said with a stern frown, "you ain't Smoke Jensen. You ain't never gonna *be* Smoke Jensen. He's one of a kind. I ain't sure there's ever been anybody who could shoot as fast and as accurate as him. Frank Morgan, maybe. On a good day, Falcon MacCallister and Matt Beaudine. John Wesley Hardin and Ben Thompson might come close, but no see-gar."

"How about you, in your prime?"

Pearlie snorted. "Not hardly. I could get my gun out quick enough, mind you, but I won many a fight where

I got off the second shot. The other fella got off the first one . . . but missed." He gestured at the holstered gun on Denny's hip. "Now, pull that up a mite, say four or five inches, and then tighten the belt so it stays there. Then you can tie the holster down."

Denny followed his instructions, positioning the Colt to Pearlie's satisfaction.

That done, he waved toward the cans balanced on the poles. "All right. Shoot them empty airtights."

"We're only fifteen feet away from them. Shouldn't I back off?"

"You won't have any business shootin' at anything farther away from you than that with a handgun. If it is, use a rifle. I know you're a good shot with a long gun. You creased that rustler who was about to do your pa in."

Denny spread her feet a little, hunched her shoulders, and let her hand hover over the butt of the gun. "Should I do a fast draw?"

Pearlie rolled his eyes and sighed. "No. Stand up straight. Just pull the gun and shoot. Don't rush it."

It seemed wrong to Denny to be so nonchalant about it, but she did as Pearlie said. She drew the gun from the holster and lifted it, then hesitated. "Am I supposed to cock it?"

"It's a double action. All you have to do is pull the trigger."

Denny raised the gun more, thrust it straight out, closed her left eye, squinted over the barrel with her right, and pulled the trigger. The gun boomed and she said, "Ow!"

None of the cans went flying.

"Your arm was too stiff," Pearlie said. "Bend your elbow just a little. Keep both eyes open, and don't squint. You ain't the villain in some mellerdrama. And if you need to, use both hands to hold the gun. It's heavier than what you'd think it'd be."

"I can hold it with one hand," Denny muttered. She aimed again, taking Pearlie's advice. When she pulled the trigger, the first can in line leaped into the air and flew several feet before dropping to the ground.

Pearlie grunted. "Actually, that ain't bad. You got three more rounds in that gun. See what you can do with 'em. Take it nice an' slow an' steady."

Denny sent two more cans flying with her next two shots, then missed with the third and exclaimed in disappointment.

"You weren't more 'n an inch off with that last one," Pearlie said. "You can reload whilst I fetch the cans and set 'em up again."

For the next hour, shots boomed out again and again, echoing over the shoulder of the mountain where the line shack was located. Gradually, the reports began to come faster. Denny's increasing confidence in what she was doing could be heard in the sounds.

"You're doin' good, girl," Pearlie told her as she reloaded yet again. "You've burned a heap of powder. Don't you reckon you've done just about enough for today? They've likely missed us back at the ranch by now."

Denny snapped the loading gate closed on the Colt and pouched the iron. "I've hit my last fifteen shots in a row, and thirty-seven out of thirty-eight. Don't you think we ought to work on my speed a little?"

"Plenty of time for that. After everything that's happened, it's liable to be a good while before those rustlers come back, if they ever do."

"You heard about what the one I shot said to my father," Denny reminded him. "He's got a personal grudge. He's not going to just abandon that. He'll be back."

"Well, by the time that happens, you'll have had a chance to practice plenty, I reckon. Ain't no reason to rush things."

There was a very good reason, Denny thought . . . but she wasn't going to tell him what it was. As much of an argument as he had put up over just teaching her how to use a handgun, he really would pitch a fit if he knew what her ultimate plan was.

"I'll just go ahead and set them cans up again, so they'll be ready for next time," Pearlie said as he walked over to the corral fence. The gate was open, so he was able to walk inside and pick up the cans Denny had shot off the posts. As he looked at them, he chuckled and added, "Looks like I may have to hunt up some new targets 'fore too much longer. You've just about shot these to pieces."

He balanced the cans on the posts, then walked over to join her near the horses they had tied to a hitching post in front of the shack. She had her back to the corral fence.

Without any warning, Pearlie barked, "Shoot them cans! *Fast!*"

Denny whirled around, her hand dropping to the gun on her hip. The Colt came out and up and began to roar. With barely a pause between each shot for her to shift aim, the blasts rolled out in an almost continuous wave of gun-thunder. Cans flew in the air.

When the sixth shot exploded and the echoes danced across the landscape, two cans remained on the fence posts. But the other four were lying on the ground inside the corral with fresh bullet holes in them.

Denny was breathing hard as she slowly lowered the empty revolver. She had reacted instinctively to

Pearlie's unexpected command. The suddenness of it had kept her from thinking about what she was doing.

"Reload!" Pearlie snapped. "Standin' around with an empty cutter will get you killed. You can't take the time to admire your gun work. Reload and make sure there ain't no more threats."

"Those cans were never really a threat," Denny said.

"But you treated 'em like they were, just now. You didn't think about it, you just acted. That's what you got to do. It's got to come natural to you, like breathin'."

"It did," Denny said with a note of satisfied amazement as she thumbed fresh rounds into the Colt's cylinder. "That's exactly how it was."

"You're the pure quill Jensen when it comes to gunhandlin', I reckon," Pearlie admitted. "I seen it there in flashes, plain as day. Four outta six ain't bad . . . but if you were facin' six enemies, them two you missed woulda killed you, more than likely. And you're still slow as mud compared to any real gun-handler."

"I just started practicing today!" Denny protested. "And you just said I have some natural talent."

"Natural talent, sure. But it still needs a lot of honin'." Pearlie sighed. "Anyway, havin' a natural talent for drawin' and shootin' a gun ain't somethin' a young woman ought to be proud of. You oughta be doin' other things. You know . . . woman things."

"I want to do what I'm good at." Denny slid the Colt back into leather. "And this is it."

"You'd be a heap more likely to land a husband if you concentrated on cookin' and suchlike."

"Who said I wanted to land a husband? And I *can* cook, thank you very much."

"Well, what is it you intend on doin'?" he asked.

"You'll know when the time comes." Denny couldn't

tell anyone what she had in mind, not even Louis. Certainly not her mother and father.

Whoever that rustler was, whatever his grudge against Smoke Jensen might be, Denny was going to see to it that he never again threatened anyone she loved.

CHAPTER 21

Denny and Pearlie met at the unused line shack for the next three days. She was a little surprised that her mother didn't seem to have noticed her leaving the ranch headquarters for several hours every day, but she supposed Sally was too busy taking care of Smoke and worrying about him to pay attention to much of anything else.

The first night after firing so many rounds, her wrist had ached almost intolerably from the recoil and from supporting the weight of the Colt. The next day, it was still sore but better, and since then the overtaxed muscles and ligaments had begun to strengthen and improve. According to Pearlie, it was just a matter of getting used to the experience.

Most of the time, the old gunman insisted that she work on her accuracy. By the third day, she could make forty or fifty shots in a row without missing. She could knock cans off of posts, clip branches from trees, hit knotholes in a cottonwood's trunk. Pearlie tossed cans in the air, and with a little practice she was able to hit those, too.

What she liked best was working on the skills that would keep her alive in a gunfight: a speedy draw, swift reflexes, cool nerves. Pearlie would call out a target with no warning, sometimes off to the side and sometimes behind her, and she had to whirl toward it as fast as she could, get the Colt out, and plant three or four slugs as close to the mark as possible. At first she was more than a little wild, but as she grew accustomed to the task, her accuracy improved.

Her speed was good from the start. She had been born with that, Pearlie declared. The long hours of practice improved that, too.

"To think that gunhandlin' knack was in you all along," Pearlie commented one afternoon after Denny had just spun around, dropped to one knee, and shot three cans off a stump about twenty feet away. He had modified his fifteen-foot rule. Denny had demonstrated she was good enough that he had extended her effective range with a handgun.

He went on. "We all knowed you could ride. Smoke put you in a saddle pretty much before you could walk, and he let you start usin' a lariat when you was just a little bitty thing, too. We all figured out early on you'd have had the makin's of a top hand if . . . uh . . ."

"If I wasn't a girl?" Denny said. "That's what you were about to say, wasn't it?"

"Well, that ain't it exactly. It's true there ain't many gals who work cattle on ranches out here, but there's some. There's enough work around a spread that sometimes a fella's wife and daughters will have to pitch in. It's more like . . . you ain't just a gal, Denny. You're the daughter of Smoke Jensen, who, in case you didn't know it, is one of the richest fellas in this part of the country, and not only that, you was livin' most of the time in England. Everybody figured you'd go to some fancy school over there and then marry up with a duke or an earl or somebody like that. You'd be the lady o' some big ol' manor, livin' in a house like a dang castle."

Denny looked at the earnest old foreman for a moment, then threw her head back and laughed. "Honestly, Pearlie, I can't think of anything that sounds worse! Louis might not have minded staying over there, but once I got old enough to compare life in England to life out here on the frontier, there was never any question which one I preferred. I'm a Western girl, plain and simple."

Pearlie shrugged. "Anyway, we knew you could rope and ride, and when you was a mite older Smoke took you huntin' with him and me and some of the other fellas. You were a good natural shot with a rifle the first time you ever had one in your hands. You knocked over a big ol' jackrabbit at fifty yards." He smiled at the memory. "Then you cried for an hour once you realized you'd killed it."

"I did?" Denny shook her head. "I don't remember that."

"It happened. You were the saddest little girl I ever did see. Of course, that didn't stop you from eatin' some of that rabbit when we cooked it that night. You said it was mighty good, too, even though you were still sorry it had to die to feed us. That's the way it is with life, I reckon. It's all a mixture of good and bad, and there ain't nothin' that don't come without a price."

Denny nodded. The men who had wounded and nearly killed her father owed a price for that, she thought, and she intended to collect.

A few minutes later, while she was reloading after burning some more powder, she heard a horse coming.

Pearlie heard the hoofbeats, too, and stiffened. "Dang it! Somebody heard all the shootin' and come to see what it's all about."

Denny slid the loaded Colt into the holster, turned

toward the sound, and waited with her hand resting on the gun butt. On the ranch, the chances of the new arrival being a threat were pretty small, but she was going to be ready if he was.

Pearlie was thinking the same thing. He moved over to his horse and slid his Winchester from the saddle boot. He worked the repeater's lever and stayed where he was by the horses instead of going back to rejoin Denny. "You know why I'm stayin' over here, don't you?" he asked quietly.

"So whoever it is can't get both of us at once. If he aims to start shooting, he'll have to go for one or the other—and whoever he doesn't go after will kill him."

"Yeah, you're your pa's daughter, all right."

Denny squinted at the spot where the trail to the line shack emerged from some nearby trees. After a second she said disgustedly, "Yes, and that's my pa's son. My stupid twin brother."

Louis rode out from the shadows under the trees on a brown mare. He wore canvas trousers tucked into high-topped boots, a white shirt, and a broad-brimmed straw hat. He wasn't wearing a gun, and he didn't have a rifle or any other weapon as far as Denny could see. That was worth being called stupid all by itself. Riding out unarmed that far from the ranch headquarters was dangerously careless. Even if you didn't run into any two-legged varmints, there were plenty of four-legged ones—from mountain lions to bears—in those parts that could kill you.

As he came up to them and reined the mare to a halt, Denny said, "Louis, what in the hell are you doing here?"

"I could ask the same of you," he replied coolly. He glanced at the other man. "And of you, Pearlie. I take it this isn't some sort of . . . romantic rendezvous? I don't have to feel compelled to defend my sister's honor, do I?"

Pearlie's eyes opened as far as they could go in a look of horror. "Good Lord, no!" he exclaimed. "I mean . . . it ain't that she ain't pretty . . . I mean . . . Good Lord! I'm old enough to be her pa! Pert near old enough to be her grandpap! Yours, too, you . . . you ornery little—"

Louis held up a hand, palm out, to stop him. "I'll take your word for it, Pearlie, since I never really assumed otherwise. But you should probably stop blustering now, or else I might start thinking thou doth protest too much."

"No need to talk fancy," Pearlie said with a scowl.

"Let's talk plain, then," Louis suggested. He looked at his sister. "What *are* the two of you doing here, Denny? From the sounds I heard while riding up here, it seemed a bit like a war had broken out."

"I was just practicing," Denny replied, looking and sounding surly.

Louis pointed to the gun on her hip. "With that?"

"Yeah, that's right. Anything wrong with that?"

"Oh, I can think of any number of things, starting with the fact that Mother and Father wouldn't like it." Louis looked closer at the Colt. "That's Father's gun!"

"Yes, it is. I'm damned good with it, too."

He sighed. "You don't have to curse just to prove how tough you are, Denny." He looked at Pearlie. "Or have you been teaching her that, too?"

Pearlie opened his mouth, but before he could say anything, Denny snapped, "Oh, leave him alone. He's been a perfectly proper gentleman every second of the time we've spent together. And just so you'll know, he argued very persistently about meeting me up here and helping me learn how to use a handgun. I practically had to force him to do it."

"Maybe he should have been a little more persistent. Are you going to invite me to get down off this horse?"

"Why would I? This isn't some social. We're not having refreshments."

"Well, since I have just as much right to be here as you do . . ." Louis swung down from the saddle and stood holding the mare's reins. "I noticed today that both of you were gone, and that made me realize I couldn't remember seeing either of you around during long stretches over the past few days. That struck me as suspicious."

"How'd you follow us?" Pearlie asked.

"I know a few things about following a trail. I used to listen to Preacher when I was young. My body may not be very strong in some respects, but there's nothing wrong with my eyes. I found two sets of tracks heading in this general direction. They looked like they weren't made at the same time, but that fit with the theory I developed that the two of you were meeting somewhere away from the ranch. Once I got close enough to hear the shots in the distance"—Louis shrugged—"it wasn't difficult to find you."

"So now what are you going to do?" Denny asked. "Run and tattle to Ma and Pa?"

"We're not eight years old anymore, Denny. I figure whatever you're doing is your own business."

"Well, that's a relief."

He grinned. "It may be your business, but I'm nosy enough to blackmail you into telling me what it's about. You can explain it to me, or you can explain it to Mother and Father. It's your choice." He paused, then added, "And I should think you wouldn't want to give Father anything extra to worry about, since he's in the middle of recuperating from a very serious gunshot wound."

She glared at him. "You are a—"

"I told you, you don't have to curse. I know you're a rough, tough cowgirl."

While Denny seethed, Pearlie slid his Winchester back into the scabbard strapped to his horse. "I'm gonna mosey on back and leave you two to hash this out amongst your ownselfs. Louis, I'd take it as a personal favor if you didn't say nothin' to Smoke about this."

"That'll depend on what Denny has to say—unless she's made you privy to her plan . . . ?"

Pearlie shook his head. "She asked me to help her practice with that Colt. That's all I know, and all I'm likely to know." He untied his horse and mounted up. "See you young'uns back at the ranch."

As he started to ride off, Denny called after him, "Pearlie, tell my brother that I'm good with a gun!"

Pearlie looked back. "She's good, all right. Mighty good. But what else would you expect when it comes to gunhandlin'? She wears the Jensen brand."

CHAPTER 22

Once Pearlie was out of sight, Louis looked at Denny and said, "Whatever you're thinking about doing, it's a crazy idea, and you should put it out of your head immediately."

"How do you know I'm thinking about doing anything except learning how to shoot better? That's a *good* idea, not a crazy one. With somebody out there who has a grudge against Pa, and probably by extension everybody else on the Sugarloaf, it wouldn't hurt if *you* learned how to handle a gun."

"You remember when I went out with old Rosston on the estate and he let me fire his fowling piece? It knocked me flat on my *gluteus maximus*. I thought you were going to pass out, you were laughing so hard."

Denny smiled. "It was a pretty funny sight, now that I think about it. You looked so shocked."

"That was enough gunplay to last me a lifetime. However, you're trying to change the subject. I don't believe for a second that self-defense is the only thing you have in mind by coming out here and firing off enough ammunition to supply a small army."

Denny shook her head and said stubbornly, "I don't have any idea what you're talking about."

Louis regarded her with an intent expression for a long moment, then said, "You're going after them, aren't you?"

"Going after . . . what? I don't know what you mean."

Louis sighed. "Denny, you should have learned by now. You can lie with a good deal of success to just about anybody but me. You can't lie to me. I always know when you attempt it."

"You just think you're so smart," she snapped. "You're tricky, that's all it is. You act like you know something you really don't, and you fool people into admitting things. You're cut out to be a lying, sneaking lawyer, all right. That's *your* natural talent." She snorted. "But it's sure not a *Jensen* talent."

Louis's face hardened in anger. "But killing people with a six-gun is?"

"Well, it seems to be, and not just Pa, either. Look at Uncle Luke and Uncle Matt. Matt's not even a Jensen by blood, but he took the name and he's a man to stand aside from. Then there's cousins Ace and Chance—"

He held up a hand to stop her. "You've made your point. We Jensens are a violent bunch. But you're just making *my* point for me. When something bothers you, Denny, you don't wait for it to go away. You go after it and confront it. That man on the train had already passed us by. You could have let him go. Instead you went after him."

"The lecherous scoundrel had it coming," Denny said.

"Yes, in your opinion, anyway. And so do the men who ambushed Father and nearly killed him."

"Well, I'm glad that you understand that much, anyway."

"What I don't understand is what you think you're going to do about it."

Denny didn't offer an explanation. For one thing, her plan wasn't completely formed in her head. She still had some thinking to do about it. For another, if she told Louis even the notion that had come to her, he was liable to go to their parents and try to ruin everything. He didn't have the right to do that, she thought. She was grown, and he couldn't boss her around.

"Just forget it," she muttered as she turned away. "You're right. I was just being reckless and impulsive, as usual. It's not going to hurt anything for me to be able to handle a gun, though. If there's more trouble in the future, that might come in handy."

"It might," he admitted. "Although there are other people on this ranch who are good with guns. *Very* good."

"You can never have too many." Denny reached for the reins of her horse.

Louis stopped her by asking, "Are you really any good?"

Denny turned her head to squint at him. "Am I any good?" she repeated. "You see those cans on the ground?"

"Yes . . ." Louis said dubiously.

"Go over and put them on the fence posts."

"You're not going to shoot at them while I'm over there, are you?"

"Don't worry. You'll be perfectly safe."

He didn't look completely convinced of that. Casting a few nervous glances in her direction, he did as she said and balanced four cans on top of the posts.

Finished, he scurried back out of the line of fire. "There. What are you—"

She turned her back to the fence and crossed her arms.

"Denny? I thought—"

Her turn and draw were almost too fast for the eye to follow. The gun in her hand exploded with flame and noise. Louis let out a shocked yell. Each of the four cans leaped from its post. As the last one flew up in the air, she fired twice more, and each time the can jumped higher before finally thudding to earth with its fellows.

Louis's eyes seemed about to bulge out of their sockets. Casually, Denny shucked the empty shells from the Colt's cylinder. She blew through the barrel. It was a dime-novel thing to do, strictly for show to impress Louis. Then she began reloading.

"I . . . I never saw such a thing," he was able to say after a moment. "How did you . . . When did you . . . Just how long have you been practicing, anyway?"

"Three days. It comes natural to me." She closed the revolver's cylinder. "I'm a Jensen, like Pearlie said."

"But that's insane! No one ought to be able to shoot like that without years of practice!"

"I'll bet Pa could, the very first time he picked up a six-shooter," Denny said. "Preacher always said Smoke was the best he'd ever seen—and that old mountain man had seen just about everything!"

"Maybe. Maybe. But this . . . and you're . . ."

"You're not about to say something about me being a girl, are you? I'm getting a mite tired of hearing that."

"I don't care. It's not natural."

"Tell Annie Oakley that."

Louis frowned. "Who?"

"The girl sharpshooter in that Wild West show we saw in London," Denny said.

"Oh, yes. I remember. But that was a show, Denny. It wasn't real life. No outlaws were shooting back at her."

"I told you, I'm not going after those rustlers. I'll admit, I thought about it, but really, when you come right down to it . . . what could I do?" Denny motioned with her head. "Come on. Let's get back."

Louis nodded slowly and moved over to get his horse. They mounted up and started to ride away from the line shack.

"You sound like you're being very sensible and reasonable," Louis said. "I should be happy about that."

"But . . . ?"

"But you worry me when you're being sensible and reasonable, Denny. You really do."

As they rode, Louis promised not to say anything to Sally and Smoke about what Denny and Pearlie had been doing up at the old line shack. He even said he could understand if Denny wanted to keep practicing with the Colt, but he warned, "Sooner or later, Father's going to want to know where his gun is. You'll have to give it back to him."

Denny shrugged as she rocked along in the saddle. "I can always get another gun."

"That's true. And yet another reason to worry."

He kept his word when they got back to the Sugarloaf headquarters. To anyone who might have noticed them, it looked like the siblings had come back from a ride together.

Inez was waiting for them when they came into the house . . . or waiting for Denny, rather. The housekeeper said, "Your mama and papa want to see you upstairs, Señorita Denise. They asked me to tell you as soon as you came into the house."

Denny felt a worried shiver go through her. Was it possible her parents had discovered what she was up to? Louis hadn't said anything about telling them his suspicions. When she glanced at him, he gave a tiny shrug and returned her look with a blank stare, as if he had no idea what it was about.

There was only one way to find out. she said, "Gracias, Inez," and headed up the stairs, taking off the gun belt on the way. She left it and the holstered Colt in her room, then went down the hall to her parents' bedroom.

A knock on the door brought Sally's response: "Come in."

Denny opened the door and stepped into the room to find her mother sitting in a rocking chair next to the bed while Smoke was propped up on pillows, looking stronger than he had that morning before she rode out. He was still quite pale, especially for him, and she knew he had a ways to go before he recovered from that serious wound.

"Where have you been all day, Denny?" Sally asked. "It seems like you're hardly ever around anymore."

"I'm around all the time. Or at least, I'm here on the ranch. I've been riding the range quite a bit, getting more familiar with it and making sure everything's done that needs to be."

"I trust Cal to see to that," Smoke said. "If he wasn't, Pearlie would notice and set him straight . . . but I'm not worried about that."

Pearlie hadn't been around much, either, Denny thought, because he'd been up at the line shack helping her. But since Smoke didn't seem to know about that, she didn't see any reason to tell him. "Why did you want to see me? Is there something you need me to do?"

"As a matter of fact, there is," Sally said. "Can you ride into Big Rock tomorrow?"

"Sure, I suppose so," Denny replied with a slight shrug. The request took her by surprise.

"Good." Sally picked up a piece of paper from the bedside table and held it out. "Your father would like for you to send these telegrams for him."

"Reckon I can speak for myself," Smoke said. "I wrote out those wires. Just need you to take them to the telegraph office and see that they're sent, that's all."

Denny took the paper from Sally and looked at the words written on it. "What is this? It looks like the same message is going to Matt, Ace, and Chance." She glanced up sharply. "This is a call for help."

"That's right," Smoke said. "I hate being laid up more than anything, but sometimes a fella's got to face facts. I'm not as young as I once was, and it's taking me longer to bounce back than I thought it would."

Sally said, "You thought you could lose enough blood that by all rights you should have died, then hop out of bed the next morning as if nothing had happened."

Smoke chuckled. "Well, I was hoping . . ." He grew more serious as he went on. "If that's not going to happen, we've got to take steps to make sure the Sugarloaf and everybody on it is protected. I told Cal I didn't want a bunch of hired guns around, but Matt and your cousins are different. They're family."

"You're worried those rustlers will come back," Denny said.

Smoke's face darkened with anger. "They're more than rustlers. I'm sure they've been making a profit off that stock they've wide-looped from us, but the reason they started stealing cattle in the first place was to get back at me for something. Likely they don't all feel that way, but their boss sure has a grudge against me, I'm thinking."

"But you don't know why."

Smoke shook his head. "I don't have any idea. That doesn't matter, though. What's important is that there's still a threat hanging over this ranch, and it's got to be dealt with."

"By Matt, Ace, and Chance," Denny said.

"I can't think of anybody better."

She could think of somebody else. The question was whether or not she would be better at it than her uncle and cousins. She had to admit, Matt, Ace, and Chance all had formidable reputations. They had been drifting and adventuring for many years, and as seemed to be true of all Jensens, they'd never had a problem with finding themselves in the middle of some trouble.

"You've got addresses for them," she said, "but you don't know if they're still at any of these places. The way they drift around, they could all be long gone."

"That's true," Smoke said, nodding. "It may take a while for those messages to catch up to them. But I reckon we've got a little time. We shot that bunch up pretty good, including the boss. They were hit hard the last two times and lost a good number of men. More than likely, they'll try to recoup those losses by recruiting more hardcases. The frontier's not really what it used to be, twenty or even ten years ago, but there are still plenty of bad men around if you know where to look for them. I'm betting that boss rustler does."

"So you're just going to call for help and hope it shows up in time."

"I don't see what else I can do," Smoke said, starting to sound a little irritated by Denny's attitude.

She shrugged. "All right. I'll see to it that these messages get sent out tomorrow morning. I'll ride to Big Rock first thing." She paused. "I'm a little surprised you didn't just send one of the hands."

"So was I," Sally said, "but your father claims this is

family business, so a member of the family ought to handle it."

Smoke said, "I thought, too, you might like a chance to go to town. You've been cooped up here on the ranch for several days. You're probably not used to that."

"I like being on the ranch," Denny said. "I've kept myself busy. I sure don't mind doing this for you, though."

"One more thing," Smoke said. "Take your brother with you, if you don't mind."

Denny blew out a breath. "I don't need Louis along to protect me."

Smoke grinned. "No, it'd more likely be the other way around."

Sally frowned at him, and Smoke went on. "Well, it's true. Louis is smart as a whip, but he's not a fighter, and that's not his fault. I just thought the ride and the fresh air might do him some good."

"Well, that can't hurt him, I suppose," Sally said. "Just be careful, Denise. Both of you should be careful. I know it's only a few miles to Big Rock, but you never know when you might run into trouble."

"Nothing I can't handle," Denny said confidently. More confidently than she would have a few days earlier, before she had spent long hours practicing with her father's revolver.

That Colt would be on her hip tomorrow when she and her brother rode into Big Rock.

CHAPTER 23

Sheriff Monte Carson was at his desk in his office when the door opened and Brice Rogers ambled in. Monte glanced up at the young federal lawman, greeted him with a grunt, and went back to the unpleasant chore before him, which was finishing up a detailed report for the town council on the sheriff's office expenses for the past six months.

Paperwork was the bane of almost any star packer's existence. Monte would have rather faced down a gang of outlaws than such a report. Somewhere, there might be some peace officers who didn't mind such tasks, but he had never encountered them.

Rogers went over to the stove, got a tin cup from the shelf beside it, and helped himself to a cup of coffee from the pot. He had visited the sheriff's office several times since he'd been in Big Rock.

He just made himself at home, Monte thought, annoyed. Or maybe he was just grumpy because of what he was doing. He finished the section he was working on, then pushed the document away from him and set the pencil aside. "What can I do for you, Rogers?"

The deputy U.S. marshal leaned a hip on the corner

of the desk. "Tell me where to find the worst outlaws around here."

Monte blew out a breath disgustedly. "If I knew that, don't you think I'd be rounding them up myself?"

Rogers sipped the coffee and shook his head. "I don't mean men you'd necessarily have reward dodgers on. I was thinking more of the ones who might not be wanted but are still pretty bad. The sort who drift around looking for not-so-honest work but haven't ever been caught at it, or who at least don't have any charges against them at the moment."

Monte leaned back in his chair and nodded in understanding. "The sort who might throw in with a bunch of rustlers?"

"That's what I was thinking," Rogers said.

"Well . . . it's not a bad idea. Smoke's tangled with that gang twice and nearly a dozen of them have wound up dead. The undertaker's been kept busy planting 'em, that's for sure. I don't know how many were in the gang to start with, but their ranks are bound to have been thinned considerable. Whoever's running it is liable to be looking for men. You figure to get a line on him that way?"

"The thought occurred to me."

Monte laced his hands together over his belly and frowned. "There's a place north of here, up near the Wyoming border, called Elkhorn. I've never been there, but I've heard about it. It's not a very big settlement, and from what I've been told, it owes its existence to the owlhoots and gun-throwers who drift through there. If somebody was looking to replace members of his gang who'd been wiped out, he might head for Elkhorn."

"How far away is it?" Rogers asked.

"A three- or four-day ride, depending on how fast a fella wants to push his horse."

Rogers nodded slowly. "I might mosey up there, have a look around. You say you've never been there?"

"It's out of my jurisdiction," Monte said, shaking his head. "And back in the old days, when I was known to ride a dark trail or two myself, the place didn't exist. Others served that purpose . . ." Monte sighed. "All gone now. And the world's probably better for it. Still, sometimes you can't help but miss the old days a little."

Rogers didn't look like he missed anything about the old days.

Of course, he was young, Monte thought, and nobody was more shortsighted than a kid. Age might not always grant a man wisdom—some people were born damn fools and would stay that way their whole lives—but it sure as hell changed his perspective on some things.

"You being a federal lawman, I reckon you can go wherever you want," Monte went on. "You'd better be careful up there, though. They don't cotton to star packers."

"I'll keep that in mind. I sure haven't found anything around here. I've searched the Sugarloaf and the surrounding area. If those rustlers have a hideout somewhere in these parts—and my hunch says they do—they've done a good job of hiding it." Rogers drained the rest of the coffee from the cup, then asked, "Have you heard how Jensen is doing?"

"I ran into Doc Steward at the café a while ago. He was out there at the ranch early this morning to check on Smoke. According to him, Smoke's progress is remarkable—but it's not good enough to suit him. Smoke, I mean. He wants to be up and around again, and the doctor says it's still going to be a week or more before he can even get out of bed, let alone start moving around much. No matter how restless Smoke gets, though, Sally will do a good job of keeping a tight rein on him."

"The longer he's laid up, the more chance that gang will try something else, as soon as they've gotten back up to full strength again."

"Yeah, it's just a matter of time," Monte agreed. "When do you plan to head for Elkhorn?"

"I'm going to pick up some supplies and ride out today. No point in waiting, and a delay could just cause more trouble."

Monte stood up and extended his hand. "I'll wish you good luck, then. I don't envy you, riding into that rat's nest."

"It's just part of the job, isn't it?" Rogers said as he shook the sheriff's hand.

"A job that'll get you killed if you're not careful—and lucky. Just remember, you won't have any help up there. You'll be on your own."

Rogers grinned. "Just the way I like it. I'd rather play a lone hand."

Denny made sure she was up before the crew ate breakfast. Pearlie usually took his morning meal with Cal and the rest of the men, and she wanted to catch him before he set off on his chores for the day. Retired he might be, but he still liked to keep busy around the ranch headquarters. She couldn't count on always being able to catch him in the barn or the bunkhouse.

Mixing flapjack batter in a big bowl, Inez looked surprised when Denny came into the kitchen. "You are all right, señorita?"

"Why?" Denny asked with a smile. "Because I'm usually not up this early?"

"You are not in the habit of sleeping as late as your brother, but it is still an hour until sunup."

"The biscuits smell good. I just thought that maybe I'd give you a hand."

Inez didn't look totally convinced by that answer, but she held out the mixing bowl "All right. You can stir this until it's mixed well and then start cooking the flapjacks." She nodded toward the stove. "The pan is heating and will be ready by the time you are."

Denny set to work. She had cooked pancakes before, so she wasn't completely lost in what she was doing. She had never been a particularly good cook, though, certainly not as good as her mother or Inez. Sally Jensen's bear sign was legendary in that part of the world. In the past, Denny had seen Cal and Pearlie almost come to blows over the sweet, fried doughnuts.

Sally came in while Denny was taking flapjacks from the pan and stacking them on a plate. She looked as surprised as Inez had been to see Denny working in the kitchen. "Well, this is a nice development."

"What, me being domestic?" Denny asked.

"That's right." Sally cocked an eyebrow. "Of course, you *are* still dressed like a cowboy."

"Lots of cowboys can cook. It was always a man in charge of the chuck wagon on trail drives, wasn't it?"

"That's true," Sally admitted. "Anyway, it's nice to see you giving Inez and me a hand." She took down an apron from a hook, tied it on, and picked up a basket to gather some fresh eggs from the small henhouse.

By the time the crew tramped across from the bunkhouse in the predawn light to sit down at the long table in the dining room that was loaded down with food, Denny was hot and tired. She had never realized how much work it was to feed nearly two dozen hungry young cowboys. Not only that, Inez had also prepared sandwiches of biscuits and roast beef for them to take with them out onto the range for their midday meals.

Pearlie was with the rest of the crew. Denny caught

his eye and gave him a tiny nod, hoping he would realize that meant she wanted to talk to him. She thought he understood, because he frowned worriedly, as if wondering what in the world she was up to.

Breakfast was a boisterous event, full of loud talk and laughter. Stoked on mounds of food and gallons of coffee, the crew left the house to set out on their day's riding chores. The sun still hadn't peeked above the horizon, but it was close enough to cast a bright orange glow across the heavens in the east.

Denny had managed to get out onto the porch before the cowboys emerged. Some of them bid her a raucous farewell. The shy ones just smiled and nodded or awkwardly ignored her completely.

Pearlie was the last one to come out of the house, and he did so with obvious reluctance. "Thought about sneakin' out the back so's you wouldn't catch me," he admitted candidly. "What is it you want, Miss Denny? I figured since your brother found out about it, we were finished goin' up to that old line shack."

"I just want to talk to you, Pearlie . . . about the days when you were an outlaw."

He frowned and shook his head. "I don't like to talk about that. Tweren't nothin' to be proud of, that's for sure. I'm just glad Smoke and me crossed trails when we did. That changed everything. Without that, there's no telling how bad I might've become, what terrible things I might've done."

"I don't believe that," Denny said. "You always had a good heart. I can tell."

His bony shoulders rose and fell. "I'd like to think so . . . but I know how it was. I could've easy had a short, miserable life as an owlhoot, and when I finally died in a gully somewhere with a bullet in my gut, nobody would've missed me. Instead, I've found good friends . . . a family, really . . . here on the Sugarloaf.

Seems to me I'm just about the luckiest son of a gun around, and that's why I don't like to talk about what could've been. It don't never pay to tempt fate."

"I want to know about the places where the outlaws and the hired guns gathered."

Pearlie squinted suspiciously at her. "Why would you care about that? Sure, there were places like the Hole in the Wall, the Dutchman's, Blind Pete's, Mean Pete's—they was different Pete's, mind you—Skeleton Ranch, the Duchess's place . . . Lord, just thinkin' about those days makes a shiver go through me."

"Are any of them still around?"

"Those owlhoot hangouts, you mean?" Pearlie blew out a disgusted breath. "No, and it's a good thing. This is the twentieth century, girl. All those places are gone. If there's anything left of 'em, it's just some crumblin' ruins. Blind Pete and the Dutchman are dead. The last I heard, Mean Pete was locked away in some madhouse up in Minnesota. The Duchess . . ." He sighed. "I don't reckon anybody knows for sure what happened to the Duchess. She just sorta dropped outta sight. I hope she found her someplace quiet and peaceful to live out her life."

"You were sweet on her, weren't you?" Denny said. "I can tell by the way you say her name."

"What? Me, sweet on a hellcat like the Duchess? Naw! . . . Well, maybe a little." Pearlie waved a knobby-knuckled hand. "Anyway, all that's a long time in the past. A long time. No use thinkin' about it now."

"There aren't any places like that around today?"

"Naw, I expect not. Your pa got rid of two of 'em himself, Bury up in Idaho and Fontana, not that far from where we're standin' right now. Outlaw towns, they were. Nothin' like that around today. Closest thing to it is probably Elkhorn, up along the Wyomin' border."

"Elkhorn? I never heard of it."

"No reason you would have," Pearlie said. "It's just a wide spot in the trail. It's far enough from anywhere that there ain't no real law there, from what I've heard, and that means fellas who don't want to be bothered can stop there for supplies or a drink or, uh, other things that, uh, fellas on the drift have to stop for."

"Women of easy virtue," Denny said with a smile. "That's what you mean."

Pearlie's face turned red, and it wasn't from the rising sun. "Never you mind about that. Don't know why we're talkin' about such things in the first place."

"I'm just interested in the way things used to be," Denny said. "It doesn't do anybody any good to ignore the past. It's still there, casting its shadow over what goes on today, whether folks want to admit it or not."

"Yeah, I reckon." Pearlie rasped his fingertips over his beard-stubbled chin. "Was that all you wanted?"

"That's all. Louis and I are going into Big Rock today. Pa wants some wires sent, and we're going to take care of it for him."

"All right. The two of you be careful."

"We will be. And I'll be ready for trouble. I'll have my rifle *and* Pa's Colt. You know I can use both of them just fine."

"You've only been shootin' that handgun a few days. Don't get cocky."

"We're not going to run into anything bad between here and town."

"Not likely," Pearlie admitted. "I could saddle a horse and come with you, if you want."

"No, Louis and I can take care of it."

"All right, then." Pearlie went down the steps and started toward the barn.

Denny leaned on the porch railing and watched

him go. It was true that she didn't expect to encounter any trouble between the Sugarloaf and Big Rock.

Elkhorn was a different story.

What her father had said the day before about the rustlers needing to recruit more men before they made another move against the ranch had started Denny to thinking. She knew he was right. She trusted his hunches more than anything in the world. She had been trying to think of some way to get on the trail of the man who had almost killed him, and although that certainly hadn't been his intention, his comments had been the key that unlocked her plan. What she had just learned from Pearlie had filled in the missing pieces.

Elkhorn was the closest place those rustlers could find more men, so that was where she had to go. That was where the vengeance trail would start.

But she couldn't go there as Denise Nicole Jensen.

CHAPTER 24

"You seem to have something on your mind this morning," Louis said as they rode toward Big Rock a couple hours later. He wasn't an early riser by any stretch of the imagination. Denny could have rousted him out of bed so they could have started earlier, but she didn't see any point in it. They would get to Big Rock in plenty of time to send off Smoke's telegrams.

"A lot is going on since we got back," Denny replied to her brother's comment.

"That's true. I'm a little surprised you were willing to take time off from practicing your gunplay."

"Practicing is something I intend to do from now on. Now that I'm just starting to know what I'm doing, I don't want to slack off and get rusty."

"You know, Father is going to find out about that one of these days and put a stop to it."

"You think so?" She looked over at him. "Seems more likely he'll be proud of me."

"Instead of disappointed, like he is in me?"

"I've never heard him say a thing to make me believe he's disappointed in you," Denny said. "He's always done everything he could to make sure you got what you needed."

"Yes . . . but he always went out and *took* whatever it was he needed. I've never had that capability."

Denny shrugged. "Everybody's different. They've got their own talents and liabilities. Pa's plenty smart enough to understand that. If you want to talk about somebody being disappointed, it's Ma, and I'm the one she's disappointed in." Denny gestured at the denim jeans, checked shirt, and buckskin vest she wore. "All decked out in cowboy duds instead of some fancy dress."

Louis looked at the rugged, tree-covered landscape around them. "This is no ballroom in some French count's mansion. You're dressed appropriately for where you are and what you're doing."

"Yeah, but in the back of her mind, she would have liked it better if I was more of a girl."

Louis didn't argue. He rode along in silence for several minutes until he said, "You're armed for bear today, aren't you?"

"I've just got a rifle and pistol with me."

"And that big knife."

Denny looked at the bowie knife she had taken from Smoke's study. It rode in a leather sheath she had strapped to her belt on the left side. "Might come in handy."

"I saw you putting several boxes of ammunition in your saddlebags. Just another precaution?"

"Better to have too many shells than not enough, I reckon."

"You have an answer for everything, don't you, Denny?"

"What do you mean by that?" she said.

"I mean you're up to something. I can feel it in my bones. I just don't know what it is."

Denny scowled but didn't say anything. She needed her brother's help to carry out her plan, but she was beginning to wonder if she could get it. Louis had the ability to ruin everything if he wanted to. Even though they had always been close, she wasn't sure she could count on him a hundred percent.

She thought it might be best to change the subject. "You've got the message we're supposed to send, don't you?"

Louis patted the breast pocket of the coat he wore. "Right here, along with the last addresses Father had for Uncle Matt, Ace, and Chance."

"See, that's why you ought to be running the ranch one of these days. You're organized. You always know where all the paperwork is and what you need to do with it. You can hire somebody to ramrod the crew and take care of the stock and everything else that needs doing."

"I assume that's what you'll be doing."

Denny let out a snort. "You think a salty bunch of cowboys will take orders from a woman?"

"They'll take orders from a woman they respect, one who's willing to get right in there and do the same jobs they do, no matter how dirty it makes her." Louis laughed. "But of course, this is sheer speculation. Father is going to be around for a long time yet, and by the time he's not able to run the ranch, I'll be busy with my law practice and you'll be married, taking care of your husband and eight children."

Denny laughed, too, and exclaimed, "That'll be the day!"

And yet, the idea wasn't that unappealing, she thought. Not the part about eight children, that was just loco. But to have a husband and children, a family of her own, that didn't sound too bad. Someday. Not soon.

Sometime long after she had done the job she had set for herself, the job of settling the score for what had happened to her father and to the members of the

Sugarloaf crew who had been killed. Justice for them still awaited.

They reached Big Rock late in the morning and went to the train station, which was also where the Western Union telegraph office was located.

Sheriff Monte Carson was lounging outside the depot. He nodded to Denny and Louis as they dismounted and tied their horses to the hitch rack. "Mornin', you two," he greeted them. "What brings you to town?"

"We need to send some wires," Louis replied as he pulled the folded sheet of paper from his coat pocket. "Father's getting in touch with our Uncle Matt and our cousins."

"Those Jensen boys, Ace and Chance?" Monte said with a frown.

"They're not really boys anymore," Denny pointed out. "They must be forty years old by now."

"Yeah, but it's hard to think of them any other way than as those two young hellions who kept getting in one scrape after another. You know, they were right in the thick of trouble around here several times, even before Smoke knew they were really his brother Luke's kids. I don't think anybody in the family knew that when they first popped up, even them."

"Yes, we've heard the stories," Louis said. "Father should have known right away they were blood relatives, the way people kept shooting at them." He grinned. "Jensens are natural-born targets for trouble, after all."

The sheriff grunted. "Truer words were never spoken, I reckon. But they're natural-born trouble *busters*, too."

Denny and Louis chatted with Monte for a moment longer, then excused themselves and went into the station. No train was due to arrive in the near future, so the place wasn't busy. They went to the Western Union window and got a couple telegraph forms. Louis handed one of the flimsies to Denny. "Here, you can fill out this one."

She picked up a pencil and leaned on the counter next to the window to print the message on the form. She had read it often enough to memorize it and didn't need the paper Louis had. She asked, "Who am I sending this one to?"

"I've started putting Uncle Matt's address on this one, so yours can go to Ace and Chance." He glanced at the paper. "That's care of Sheriff Braxton Humboldt, Scorpion Valley, Texas."

"If they're not there anymore, maybe this sheriff will know where they went," Denny said as she wrote out the address.

"That's the idea." Louis shuddered slightly. "Scorpion Valley. What a terrible-sounding place."

"I don't know. I'll bet they found some adventure there."

"No doubt."

Finished, they took the forms to the window and handed them to the telegrapher, a middle-aged man with a green eyeshade over his well-fed face. He counted the words and then told them the price.

"Pay the man," Denny said to her brother.

"Ah, so that's why you really wanted to bring me along," Louis said with a smile. He dug out several coins and slid them across the counter.

"You two are Smoke Jensen's young'uns, aren't you?" the telegrapher said.

"That's right," Louis said.

The man nodded. "I can't tell you how much this town appreciates Smoke and Sally. There wouldn't even *be* a Big Rock if it weren't for them. Us old-timers will never forget how Smoke took on Franklin Tilden and his wild bunch at Fontana. That town's gone now—can't even find where it was anymore except maybe a bit of busted foundation here and there—but anybody who lived through those bloody days will never forget them. Sure is a lot tamer now."

"Most of the time," Denny said. "Not always."

As they were walking away from the telegraph office, she checked the train schedule chalked onto a board beside the ticket window and saw that an eastbound train was due to come through at 1:17 that afternoon.

Louis paused outside the station. "Well, I suppose we should get some lunch before we start back."

"You can if you want to, but I'm not going back to the ranch."

He looked over at her with a surprised frown and repeated, "Not going back? What do you mean? Are you staying here in town?"

"No. I have some things I need to do. And I need your help, Louis."

He leaned back slightly and frowned even more as he said, "I don't like the sound of this, Denny. You've got some crazy idea in your head again, and I don't want any part of it."

"Listen to me." She gripped his arm, and her voice was taut with urgency as she went on. "You know there's no telling how long it'll take before those messages catch up to Matt, Ace, and Chance. It could be weeks before they show up in these parts, maybe even months. Or . . . they might not show up at all."

"They wouldn't ignore a request for help from Father unless . . ."

"Yeah," Denny said, nodding. "Unless they were dead or shot up like Pa is. And that could be the case. You know it's possible."

Louis shrugged. "I suppose it is. On the other hand, there might be return wires from all of them before the day is over, saying that they'll be here in a week or less. We just don't know, Denny. Anyway, what do you think you're going to do? Track down those rustlers and kill them yourself?"

She didn't say anything, and after a couple seconds Louis's jaw dropped in amazement. "You *do* think that! That's your plan, isn't it?"

"Not exactly. But you heard what Pa said about them looking for men to replace the ones they've lost."

"Yes. *Men.* Gunmen. Not . . . not . . ."

Denny smiled slightly. "Not a loco girl? That what you're thinking?"

"Well, you hardly look like some ruthless outlaw!"

"Maybe I could. With my hair up and my bosom bound down tight, I reckon I could pass for a young man. And I can use a gun like one, too."

"You've been practicing for less than a week!" Louis threw his hands in the air. "You've lost your mind!"

"A lot of outlaws aren't great gunfighters," Denny argued. "They shoot their victims from behind or from ambush. And I can ride and work cattle as well as or better than any rustler, you know that."

"Maybe, but—"

"I don't intend to wipe them out or anything like that. I just want to get into the gang and find out where the hideout is. Then I can slip away and get help. I'll either head for the Sugarloaf and fetch Cal and the rest of the crew or I'll tell Sheriff Carson and he can get a posse together. Maybe both. But I'm not crazy enough to think I can wipe out a couple dozen hard-cases by myself, Louis."

"Just crazy enough to believe you can fool them into thinking you're a man," he muttered.

"It can work. If you'd just stop thinking of me as your sister, you'd see that I'm right."

Louis squinted at her. "What about Mother and Father?"

"What about them?"

"What am I supposed to tell them when I ride back to the ranch without you?"

"Tell them I caught the eastbound train. Tell them I decided to go back to New Hampshire and see Grandmother and Grandfather Reynolds. That I wanted to surprise them."

Louis shook his head. "They'll never believe that. And what about your horse? They'll see that I came back without it."

"I sold it to pay for the train ticket," Denny said.

"You have answers for everything, don't you? Just not *good* answers. They'll both know that you're up to something wild and crazy, and they'll make me tell them what it is."

"You'll have to tell them you don't know, that all you know is what I told you about going east."

"Do you really expect me to be able to make them believe that?"

"You just have to make them think *you* believe it."

"They'll send a wire to New Hampshire and find out you're not there."

Denny shook her head. "Even if I was really going there, it would take me several days to arrive. Maybe my plan will have worked by then, and the threat of those rustlers and killers will be over and done with."

"That's a pretty slim chance, I'd say."

"Jensens don't need more than a fighting chance."

Louis looked at her intently for a long moment and then said, "Is there any way you're going to be talked out of this?"

"Nope," Denny said.

"What if I put you on your horse and tie you into the saddle and take you home that way?"

She couldn't stop the laugh that came from her. "We both know you can't—" She stopped short at the sight of the hurt in his eyes. "Damn it, Louis, I didn't mean—"

"Yes, you did." He looked down at the ground. "You mean it's ludicrous to think that I could actually force you to do anything. I'm too weak."

"That's not your fault—"

He held up both hands to stop her. "No, you're right. And you're right that Father shouldn't have to rely on his brother and nephews to help him out when he has children of his own. One capable child, anyway."

"You're capable of a lot of things."

"Not of masquerading as a drifting hardcase and gunman."

"Well, maybe not—"

"You'll be risking your life, you know, and even worse. I hate to be so blunt, but you know what's liable to happen to you if your true identity is exposed."

"No man would dare harm a respectable woman, not even outlaws."

Louis scoffed. "You've been listening to too many tall tales. Maybe it was that way twenty or thirty years ago, but times have changed. Anyway, if you go among them wearing trousers and packing a gun and pretending to be a man, they're not likely to take you for a respectable woman."

"I can take care of myself," she said stubbornly.

"You'll have to. Won't be anybody else to do it."

With nothing left to say, Denny and Louis stood in strained silence for a long moment, then she reached for the buckskin's reins. "I'd better get started."

"Do you know where you're going?"

"I do. I've got a pretty good idea where that gang will be looking for new recruits."

"What about supplies?"

"I was able to pack some without Ma or Inez seeing me. And I can hunt if I need to. I know how to skin and roast a rabbit."

"You could do that when you were six years old, as I recall."

"See?" Denny smiled. "I was born to do this."

"Actually . . . I think you may be right. There's something in the Jensen blood . . . Damn it, Denny, I almost envy you! I wish I was coming with you. I'm afraid I'd be more of a hindrance than a help, though."

"I'll feel better knowing that you're keeping an eye on things at the ranch."

"For what it's worth, I will." Acting as if on impulse, he put his arms around her and hugged her tightly against him. "Insanity must be contagious," he went on in a voice choked with emotion. "Otherwise I'd never agree to this."

"Take care of yourself . . . and Ma and Pa."

"And you take care of *your*self. Part of me would be missing if anything ever happened to you."

She put her hands on his shoulders and smiled. "It'll be okay. You'll see." Without delaying any longer, she put her foot in the stirrup and swung up into the saddle. "So long, Louis."

"So long." He swallowed hard. "Denny."

She turned the buckskin and nudged it into a loping gait that carried her quickly away from the train station. She didn't look back—she didn't trust herself to. If she did, her resolve might waver. It *was* a crazy plan, but sometimes those were the ones that worked, she thought. The ones that nobody would ever expect.

Heading north, it didn't take her long to leave Big Rock behind. She didn't know exactly where Elkhorn was located, but Pearlie had said it was near the border between Colorado and Wyoming. That was a big stretch of territory. She could ask questions along the way to find out where she was going.

She had one more thing she needed to do. Finally well out of sight of the settlement, she took her hat off, shaking her hair out so it fell loosely around her shoulders. Then she drew the bowie knife, gathered up a handful of hair close to her head, and started cutting. When the hair came loose, she tossed it in some brush at the side of the trail.

Within ten minutes, a pile of thick blond curls was hidden by the brush and Denny was riding on with her hair crudely hacked off. She tried not to cry, telling herself that would be a foolishly female thing to do, but she felt the wet streaks on her face anyway.

CHAPTER 25

Dark, jagged clouds formed over the mountains that afternoon, and a blustery wind began blowing. Winter was still weeks away, but the chill in that wind was a potent reminder of its inevitable arrival.

Denny was glad she had brought along a sheepskin jacket. She took it out of her saddlebags, put it on, and was more comfortable. She hadn't brought a bedroll because that would have made it too obvious what she was doing. All she had was a blanket. The nights might be pretty cold and miserable, she thought, but she could put up with some discomfort if it meant she was able to help protect her father and the Sugarloaf from any more attacks.

There would be other little towns along the way where she could outfit herself more properly. She had a money belt strapped under her clothes and a poke of double eagles in one of the saddlebags. She would just have to be careful not to reveal that she had quite a bit of money with her. That would ruin her pose as a saddle tramp and all-around disreputable character.

A coffeepot . . . that was something else she would need to buy, she thought as she hunkered next to a tiny fire, trying to use her body to block the wind from the tiny flames so they wouldn't go out. She had fried some bacon for supper, but some hot coffee sure would have washed it down nice.

Eventually the wind died down enough that she was able to stop protecting the fire, heap up some fallen pine boughs as a makeshift bed, and wrap up in the blanket to go to sleep with her saddle as a pillow. The night passed slowly and uncomfortably, just as she expected, but she was tired enough that sheer exhaustion allowed her to doze off and get a little rest.

The air the next morning had a touch of frost in it, but the clouds had blown over, the sun was out, and the temperature rose quickly. Denny was able to put her jacket away by midmorning. Late that afternoon, she spied smoke rising into the sky ahead of her and a short time later came to an actual hard-packed dirt road. Thinking there might be a town ahead, she rode into the concealment of some trees and dismounted to take another precaution against having her identity discovered.

As she stripped to the waist, she was glad that cold wind wasn't blowing anymore. She took out the strips of cotton material she had brought with her and began winding them around her torso, pulling them as tight as she could so her breasts flattened under the pressure. She had never been abundantly blessed in that area to start with. She thought wryly that for the first time she had to consider that a good thing.

She tied the bands in place and then donned her shirt and vest again. She looked down at herself, then ran her hand over the roughly close-cropped hair on her head. She could pass for a boy in his late teens, she told herself. She would have to remember to lower her voice, maybe put a harsh rasp in it to further disguise it. People had a tendency to see what they expected to see . . . or at least she hoped that would be the case.

Before she mounted up, she put the jacket on again. She didn't need it to stay warm, but it would help conceal her shape even more.

Slouching in the saddle like she'd had a long, hard day—which was true—she followed the road up a hill and then down the far side toward a settlement that was nothing more than half a dozen buildings on either side of the trail, plus a few houses and cruder cabins scattered around. Denny had no idea what the place was called or if it even had a name.

To the right was a barn, then a blacksmith shop, then a rambling log structure with a board nailed over its door with the letters *S-A-L-O-O-N* crudely burned into it. Across the street was a frame building with an actual painted sign that read CARTER'S STORE. Another frame building had ASSAY OFFICE in gilt letters on its front window, but it appeared to be empty. That told Denny the settlement had probably gotten its start when mines in the nearby mountains were still producing. Those veins must have played out, and the town was just hanging on. One of these days it would dry up and blow away.

She angled the buckskin to the left, toward the mercantile. A couple horses were tied up at the hitch rail in front of the saloon across the street, but their owners seemed to be the only other visitors to the settlement. No wagons or buggies or other saddle mounts were in evidence.

Before approaching the town, she had gotten a couple five-dollar gold pieces from her poke and put them in a pocket. She didn't want to seem rich. The buckskin was a fine horse and the saddle was good quality, as were her gun belt and holster and boots, but nothing she could do about that. A fellow could be decently outfitted and still mostly broke and in need of a job.

She tied the buckskin in front of the store and

went up the steps to its high porch. When she opened the door and went inside, the air smelled dusty and disused, like nobody had been in there for a while. The shelves were half empty. A man stood behind the counter at the back of the store, leaning on it with an elbow as he propped a hand under his chin. His eyes were closed, and they didn't open even when Denny walked along the aisle toward him, her boot heels thumping on the plank floor.

"Mister?" she said, remembering to make her voice low and rough.

He caught a sharp breath as he jerked a little. His eyes blinked open. He had graying brown hair and a long, horselike face. He straightened slowly, looking like it pained him, and looked at her in apparent confusion. Finally he said, "What do you want?"

"This is a store, ain't it?" Denny asked.

"Yes, but . . ." The man opened his eyes wider. "You mean you want to *buy something*?"

"That's the general idea." She didn't have to fake the impatience and annoyance in her voice.

"Oh. All right. I'm sorry, it's just that it's been a while . . ." The man fidgeted with the canvas apron he was wearing. "What can I do for you?"

"I need a coffeepot, some coffee, flour, sugar, and salt, and a bedroll and a couple blankets."

"How have you been gettin' by without all that? Must not have been on the trail long."

"Long enough," Denny snapped. "I had to, uh, sell some of my gear to get enough money to keep goin'."

"Oh. Well, it's none of my business anyway—"

"That's right. You have what I need?"

"I sure do. Give me a few minutes and I'll have the order put together for you. How much you want of the staples?"

"How far is it from here to Wyoming?"

The man frowned in thought. "'Bout a three-day ride, I reckon. Dependin', of course, on which part of Wyomin' you're headed for."

"Place called Elkhorn."

"Ohhhh." The storekeeper sent a nervous glance in her direction. "You have friends there?"

"Don't know yet. I hope to."

"Well, it's still in Colorado, but it's just a mile or two shy of the border. You've never been there before?"

Denny shook her head.

"Nice young fella like you, you might want to think twice about it," the man said. "It's got a reputation as a mighty rough place. Lots of bad sorts hang out there."

A cold smile curved Denny's lips. "How do you know I'm not a bad sort myself?"

"Well, you don't . . . I mean, you're just a young fella . . . Hate to see you go down the wrong path—"

Denny reached quickly across the counter, caught hold of his apron, and jerked him forward. She put her face close to his, drew her lips back from her teeth, and said in a low, menacing tone, "You let me worry about my own damn path, mister."

Maybe she shouldn't have gotten so close to him. She was risking him noticing that those cheeks and jaws had never sprouted whiskers.

But his eyes were wide with fear and didn't seem to be noticing much of anything as he stammered, "I . . . I'm sorry! I didn't mean to poke my nose in where it don't—"

"Just get the supplies." She shoved him away. "Don't worry about nothin' else. Except maybe you can tell me how to find this Elkhorn place."

"I . . . I never been there myself. Wouldn't go. Just heard about it. But if you head north and keep the mountains on your left, after a few days you'll see some other peaks off to the right. Those'll be the Prophet

Mountains. Elkhorn's supposed to lie about halfway between them and the big peaks to the west."

"Reckon I can find it," Denny said, nodding.

"Reckon you can, if you want to. If you're bound and determined to go there."

"I said that was what I was doing, didn't I?"

"Sure, sure." The storekeeper took a canvas sack from under the counter and opened it. "So you want enough of the staples to get you to Elkhorn?"

"That's right," Denny said. "Enough to get me where I'm goin'."

The storekeeper's name was George Carter. He prattled the whole time he was gathering up Denny's supplies, including introducing himself. After he told her his name, he looked at her as if expecting her to return the gesture. She started to tell him to mind his own business, then decided it wouldn't hurt anything to start establishing the identity she was going to use.

"Name's West," she said. "Denny West."

Denny was more often a boy's name, so that was believable enough and she wouldn't have to worry about remembering it. When her father, as a young man, had been on the run from the law because of bogus murder charges filed against him, he had used the name Buck West. That provided a last name for her.

"Good to know you, Denny." Carter sighed. "Although I reckon what with you just passin' through, I'll likely never see you again."

"Likely not," Denny agreed.

"Especially if you go to Elkhorn."

"Figure I'll get killed up there, do you?"

Carter didn't say anything, just looked gloomy as he packed the supplies in the canvas sack. Done with that, he got the extra blankets and a canvas tarp and rolled them up together, tying the bundle with rawhide thongs.

He tore off a piece of brown wrapping paper, picked up a stub of pencil, and totaled up the bill, pausing between each figure he wrote down to lick the pencil until the habit began to gnaw on Denny's nerves.

"Just add up the numbers, all right?" she said.

"Huh? Oh, oh, sure, I got it right here . . . That'll be seven dollars and thirty cents."

Denny took the two five-dollar gold pieces from her pocket and slid them across the counter. Carter gave her a couple of silver dollars in change, along with the smaller coins.

"You ridin' on out?" he asked as Denny picked up the sack of supplies with one hand and tucked the bedroll under her other arm.

"What business is that of yours?"

"None, but I thought you might want a drink before you go. My brother owns the saloon across the street."

"You got another brother who owns the blacksmith shop?"

"As a matter of fact, I do."

Denny frowned. "What about the stable?"

"It belongs to my Uncle Thad."

Denny grunted. "They must call this place Carterville."

"How'd you know?"

Denny ignored the question and went out. With coffee, biscuit makings, and extra blankets, the night promised to be more comfortable than the previous one had been. She tied the sack of supplies onto the saddle, then lashed the bedroll behind it.

She glanced across the street at the log saloon. She had never been much of a drinker—it didn't seem to run in the family—but she could nurse a beer along for a little while and maybe find out some more about Elkhorn from the other customers. Just two horses were still at the hitch rail, but some of the citizens of Carterville could be in there, too.

She untied the buckskin, led him across the dusty street, and looped the reins around the rail on that side. The door of the saloon stood open, but it was dark enough inside to make the entrance look like the mouth of a cave.

That thought made her hesitate, but only for a second. She walked inside and looked around as her eyes adjusted to the dimness of the room.

The bar, which consisted of thick planks laid across the tops of barrels, ran across the back. Rough-hewn tables were in the front part of the room. Off to the left was, of all things, a roulette wheel, but it looked dusty, like it hadn't been used for a long time. It might not even work anymore, Denny thought. That was another sign the settlement was just barely hanging on to its existence.

A lantern stood on a shelf behind the bar, and another hung on a long nail driven into one of the logs that formed the wall. They were turned low enough that their flames were feeble and flickering.

Two men in range clothes stood at the bar, obviously the hombres who had ridden those horses up to the saloon. Behind the planks was an aproned bartender who bore a strong family resemblance to the storekeeper across the street. One table was occupied by a man in a dusty black suit, a collarless shirt, and a battered derby. He had a pack of greasy cards and lazily dealt himself a hand of solitaire, but his eyes were bleary and didn't seem to be focusing too well on the pasteboards. Denny figured he was drunk.

The two cowboys at the bar looked around when she came in. They were curious, especially when they realized she was a stranger. Any break from the monotony in these little frontier settlements was welcome.

One of them motioned with his head and said, "Come on over and have a drink, pard."

Denny hooked her thumbs in her gun belt as she crossed the room. She made an effort not to cough from the smoke that hung in the air. Some of it came from the oil lanterns, the rest from the quirlies the two punchers were smoking.

She nodded to the bartender, who said, "Something I can do you for?"

"Beer," Denny said. "Probably be a waste of time to ask if it's cold, wouldn't it?"

That brought laughter from the cowboys, who appeared to be a few years older than her. The one who hadn't spoken before drawled, "You're wise beyond your years, kid."

"You'll be lucky if it's only got one snake head floatin' in it," the first cowboy added.

"Ha, ha," the bartender said. "You boys are sure funny." He filled a mug from one of the barrels holding up the bar and set it in front of Denny. "See? No snake heads."

"Is that extra?" Denny asked.

The cowboys howled with laughter. One of them, stocky and redheaded, pounded the bar.

"Reckon the kid got you good, Grady!" he told the bartender.

With a long-suffering sigh, Grady said, "The beer's two bits."

Denny gave him one of the quarters she had gotten in change from his brother and then picked up the mug. The beer was pretty bad, but she hadn't bought it because she wanted it.

"You lookin' for a ridin' job?" the redheaded puncher asked. "Dill and me, we work for the Six Deuce spread, northeast o' here. Could put in a good word for you if you want. Ain't heard nothin' lately about the spread hirin', but our word counts a heap with the boss, don't it, Dill?"

"Oh, sure it does." Dill giggled, which pretty well put the lie to the boast.

"I'm not interested in a riding job," Denny said. "I got some other possibilities lined up. That's why I'm heading for Elkhorn."

No sooner had the words come out of her mouth than the man at the table who had been playing solitaire bolted to his feet. His chair crashed over behind him. "Elkhorn!" he cried.

Denny's head jerked around in time to see him clawing under his coat for a gun.

He shouted, "Draw, you son of a bitch!"

CHAPTER 26

Everything happened at once.

Fear and surprise made Denny's heart leap so hard it felt like it was going to rip right out of her chest. At the same time, muscles and nerves reacted as they had while she was working with Pearlie the past few days. It was like one of his sudden, unexpected challenges. Her hand dropped to the gun on her hip. The Colt was out before she knew it, roaring and kicking back against her palm as she pulled the trigger.

The man in the derby jerked under the bullet's impact. His gun was out, too, and it went off with an ear-numbing blast. The barrel was pointed down at the table in front of him, though, and the bullet didn't do anything but scatter the cards he had dealt a few minutes earlier. He took a stumbling step forward. The gun slipped from his fingers and thudded onto the table next to the bullet hole. He followed it, falling facedown and then rolling to the side to land on his back with his arms flung out.

Denny stood absolutely motionless, not even breathing for a long moment while the blood thundered in her head, even louder than the echoes of the two shots that filled the room. When she finally did breathe again, it was to draw in a ragged gasp.

"*Sheee-it!*" the cowboy called Dill exclaimed. "I never seen nothin' like that draw before!"

"I think that fella's still alive," the redheaded puncher said. He hurried across the room to kneel next to the man Denny had shot, then announced, "He is! He's alive! Don't think he will be for much longer, though."

Denny swallowed hard. She still couldn't seem to catch her breath. Dill went over to join his friend beside the wounded man while Denny turned her head to look at Grady Carter. "I . . . I didn't have any choice. He made me draw—"

"He went for his gun first, no doubt about that," Grady said, nodding. "We all saw it. Won't be no trouble about the law, mister."

He looked scared, and his eyes kept cutting downward. Denny realized she was still holding the Colt. She started to pouch the iron, then remembered one of the things Pearlie had drummed into her head. She turned the cylinder, opened the loading gate, dumped the empty shell, and thumbed in a fresh round, then rotated the cylinder more until the hammer rested on the empty chamber.

Then she slid the weapon back into its holster.

Trying to keep from showing how unsteady she felt, she crossed the room to stand over the wounded man and the two cowboys. The man she had shot had his eyes open wide. He was breathing hard, and a large red stain marred the front of his dirty white shirt.

"Has he said anything?" Denny asked. "Do you know his name?"

"No idea what his name is," the redhead replied, "but he said somethin' about his wife runnin' off with a man from Elkhorn. Said he's been lookin' for 'em for years, and he'd just about given up until you come in, mister."

"But I'm not *from* Elkhorn. I'm going there. Anyway, I never saw him or his wife before!" Denny looked around helplessly at Grady.

"Don't worry about it, kid," the bartender said in a gruff voice. "He's been sittin' there playing solitaire and drinking for nearly a week, ever since he rode in. His horse is over in my uncle's livery stable."

"Yep," Dill said, "I reckon his brain was plumb pickled in tarantula juice. He didn't know what he was doin'. He just heard the word Elkhorn and that made him go loco."

"Drunk or not, he was still pretty slick on the draw," the redhead said. "He got his gun out in a hurry. But he was no match for you, kid."

Denny swallowed again. She was starting to feel sick. Even though she'd had only a couple sips of the beer, they threatened to come back up her throat. She wanted to look away from the face of the dying man, but she couldn't seem to do it. Her eyes were still fastened on his agonized features as he opened and closed his mouth a couple times like a fish out of water. Then his face went slack and air rattled in his throat.

"He's done for." Dill looked up at Denny. "You want me to go through his pockets, kid? Might find a letter or somethin' with his name on it."

"Why . . . why . . ."

"Well, I figured you might want to know who it was you just killed."

Denny ran out the door. She made it before the contents of her belly spewed from her mouth, but just barely.

* * *

"Fella owed me three dollars for stablin' his horse," Thad Carter told Denny. "Pay me that, and the nag is yours if you want it, son."

"What use would I have for it?" she asked.

Carter, who looked like an older version of his nephews who ran the store, the saloon, and the blacksmith shop, shrugged. "I dunno. Pack animal, maybe?"

Denny looked at the horse, a squat but sturdy paint. She supposed if she moved all her supplies over onto it, that would make the journey easier for the buckskin. She nodded. "All right. I'll get your money."

"The horse and me will be here waitin'."

Denny stepped out of the livery barn into the late afternoon sunlight. She still had a bad taste in her mouth from throwing up but didn't trust her stomach to behave if she put anything else in it. Her nerves were settling down, though. She could feel that. Killing a man was a damned hard thing, but as she had told Grady Carter, she hadn't had a choice. She could accept that. She *had to* accept that.

It was late enough in the day she could have spent the night in Carterville. Grady had a couple rooms in the back of the saloon that he rented out. It was the closest thing to a hotel.

Denny wanted to leave the settlement behind her, though, even if she traveled only a few more miles before making camp. She couldn't stay there without thinking about what it had felt like to kill that man.

Her father had slain countless men who had been trying to kill him or someone else. Had their deaths eaten at him like this one kept gnawing at her? She had never seen any sign that Smoke Jensen was anything other than a happy, contented man with a clean conscience. Maybe he was good at hiding it . . . or maybe that was the way he truly was. Maybe he could accept the harsh realities of life without dwelling on them. She needed to develop that same ability.

She didn't have enough money on her to pay Carter for the horse, so she went to the buckskin and got another gold piece from her poke. As she turned away, Dill and the redhead, whose name was Stovall, came out of the saloon and saw her.

Stovall said, "Well, hello, kid. You gonna hang around here for a while?"

"I don't think so. Why?"

"Stovall's the name, and well, this is the most excitement Carterville's seen in a long time," Dill said. "I just wish Stovall and me could hang around for the buryin' in the mornin'. We got to get back to the ranch, though."

Stovall added, "We never did find nothin' with that fella's name on it, and he never told his name to anybody around town as far as we know. Gid Carter, who handles the buryin' around here, will have to carve *Unknown* on the marker, I reckon." He shook his head. "Won't be the first hombre who winds up in an unmarked grave. Been a few dark nights when I've worried about the same thing happenin' to me."

"Hell, no, it won't," Dill told him. "I know who you are."

"What if you're gone under before I am?"

Dill frowned. "Hell, I hadn't thought about that. Sorta wish you hadn't mentioned it."

Still muttering among themselves, the two punchers went to their horses, mounted up, and started to ride out of Carterville. At the edge of the settlement, Dill began singing, *"Oh, bury me not, on the lone prairieeeee . . . where the coyotes howl . . . and the wind blows freeeee . . ."*

Denny shivered a little, then went back to the stable to pay Thad Carter for the dead man's horse.

* * *

She rode out of Carterville with more supplies, a bedroll, and the knowledge that she had killed a man. Bringing his horse with her probably wasn't a very good idea, she reflected as she followed the trail north. The paint would be a constant reminder of what she had done.

On the other hand, maybe it was better that she remember. How much worse would it be if she could end a man's existence and then just forget about it . . . as if it had had no meaning at all? She didn't want to ever be that callous. It ought to be possible to acknowledge the gravity of what she had done without actually losing any sleep over it, she thought.

She supposed she would find out when she crawled into that bedroll later on.

It was almost dark by the time she found a suitable place to camp next to a tiny creek that would provide water for her and the horses and allow her to fill up her canteens before she departed in the morning. She built a small fire, glad for all the times she had gone hunting and camping with Smoke, Cal, and Pearlie during her visits to the Sugarloaf. She knew it had bothered Sally to have her adolescent daughter out there in the wilderness with a group of men, but they'd always been careful to act properly around her. With Smoke there, nobody would have dared to do otherwise. And of the things Denny had learned, how to make a fire had already turned out to be valuable. Having learned how to skin and dress game might turn out to be *invaluable*.

She had gone along on those trips simply because she enjoyed them, but she realized they had been part of her education, just as much as any of those fancy schools in England and France and Switzerland were.

She put coffee on to boil and made batter for biscuits that she could cook for breakfast in the morning, after they'd had a chance to rise. She fried bacon and ate it with some crackers she had bought back in George Carter's store before leaving the settlement. It was sparse, plain fare, but the Arbuckles' made all the difference. As the fire burned down after she had eaten, she sat and sipped a second cup and listened to the little sounds around there—the horses cropping at grass; the stream bubbling through its rocky bed; small animals rustling in the brush, going about their nocturnal business again now that they had figured out she wasn't a threat. Somewhere far off a coyote howled, and that put her in mind of the song Dill had been singing as he and Stovall rode out of Carterville.

The man in the derby hat wouldn't be buried on the lone prairie, but he would lie in an unmarked grave in a cheap pine coffin, unknown and unmourned. If the few brief sentences he had gasped out as he was dying were true, he had been married once. Denny supposed the man and his wife had loved each other, at least some. She had left him, though, which meant that even if she knew he was dead, she probably wouldn't care anymore. Denny wondered if they'd ever had children. And what had become of the woman and the man from Elkhorn she had run off with?

Maybe none of it was real. Maybe that sordid history was just the fevered imaginings of a whiskey-addled brain. Denny had heard it said that the human mind sometimes made up stories to help it cope with things that were just too painful to face head-on, to the point that a person might not be able to tell the difference between what was real and what wasn't. Louis had told her about some doctor in Vienna who studied things like that.

She had no answers, she thought as she threw the dregs of the coffee into the fire and listened to the drops sizzle. What she had was a job to do, a gang of rustlers to find, a threat to her family that needed to be eliminated. She spread out the bedroll, wrapped herself in the blankets, and listened to the faint crackle of the flames.

Sleep came swiftly, and the dreams of blood and death she had halfway expected stayed far away.

CHAPTER 27

Brice Rogers had seen a few hellholes in his time, but he wasn't sure any of them had been as bad as Elkhorn.

Some decent folks probably lived here, but if that was the case, none of them seemed to be out and about in the settlement. As he rode slowly along the main street, everybody he saw in the light spilling through the doors and windows of the buildings he passed was either a beard-stubbled hardcase, a slinking gambler, a sloppy, stumbling drunk, or a garishly painted lady of the evening.

Raucous music and bursts of laughter came from the saloons. Seemed to be more of them than anything else, at least a dozen in a town that boasted only a three-block business district along its lone street. The other establishments included several cheap hash houses, a couple livery stables, a Chinese laundry, and a pair of general stores.

Elkhorn was off the beaten path. That was, in fact, the reason for its existence. In the old days, a settlement like this sprang to life because of the wagon trains and the other immigrants on their way west.

With railroads reaching just about everywhere and civilization advancing across the country at a break-neck pace, a town like Elkhorn had to cater to another element—the breed of men who still rode dim trails, who skirted the border of lawlessness and often bar-reled right over it.

Theoretically, the county sheriff had jurisdiction over the settlement, but the county seat was sixty miles away and no deputy had set foot in Elkhorn for several years. If one had tried to, it would have cost him his life. There was no city marshal, either. The men who ran things didn't want one, wouldn't have stood for one. If a fellow had a problem, he had to handle it himself. If that meant killing—or getting killed—then so it went, to the way of thinking of those who lived there.

No, Rogers mused, if there were decent folks in Elkhorn, they shut themselves up in their houses when the sun went down and didn't come out until the next morning, when the other denizens of the town crawled into their holes to sleep off the night's debauchery.

He seemed to feel that deputy marshal's badge burning like fire in its hidden pocket. If the men he was riding past ever caught a glimpse of it, his life would be immediately forfeit.

As long as the badge stayed concealed, he appeared to fit right in. He hadn't shaved since leaving Big Rock several days earlier, and he had deliberately kept his rations short enough that a hungry cast had settled over his features. He looked like he'd been riding the owlhoot trail for months.

One place was as good as another to get started on the job that had brought him there, he thought as he reined to a stop in front of a saloon called the Silver Slipper. That was a pretty gaudy name, considering the saloon's squalid appearance.

As he tied his horse at a rather crowded hitch rack, he wondered just how safe the animal would be. Probably fairly safe. He didn't really believe in the concept of honor among thieves, but the hardcases who drifted into Elkhorn had to have some sort of code of behavior. If they stole freely from each other, the resulting shoot-outs would plunge the settlement into bloody chaos overnight. For their own benefit, they were better off keeping any larcenous impulses in check.

He stepped up onto the boardwalk, pushed the batwings aside, and walked into the saloon. The atmosphere inside the Silver Slipper was thick with heat and unpleasant odors. The smells of unwashed human flesh, spilled beer and whiskey, vomit, and piss vied with the blue-gray clouds of tobacco smoke that hung in the air. He had to make an effort not to grimace at the stench. Most of the people in the saloon spent so much time in places like that they didn't even notice the smell anymore.

Nobody paid much attention to his entrance—or at least they pretended not to. He saw eyes flicking unobtrusively in his direction, though. Wherever they were, men on the dodge had to check out everybody who walked in, just in case the newcomer was an old enemy . . . or a lawman who was braver than he was smart, looking to get himself ventilated.

The gamblers and the soiled doves assessed him as a potential source of income. Rogers ignored them as he walked to the bar, found an empty space, and eased himself into it.

A craggy-faced bartender in vest, string tie, and boiled white shirt came down the hardwood to stand across from him. "What'll it be, mister?"

"Whiskey and then a beer." Rogers wasn't a big hombre, but he had a considerable capacity for liquor and knew that much wouldn't muddle his thinking or slow down his reflexes.

Of course, that was probably what all drunks believed, he thought wryly.

The whiskey was raw enough to make him cough a little, despite his best effort not to.

The bartender chuckled. "Don't worry, mister. It affects most fellas the same way. I reckon it's all the gunpowder and strychnine we put in it for flavoring."

"That's a good joke," Rogers said hoarsely.

"Yeah, a joke, that's what it is," the bartender said. "Want another?"

"Not just yet." Rogers picked up the mug of beer the man had set in front of him. "I'll chase it with this." He took a swallow.

The beer actually wasn't bad. It was cool enough to soothe his whiskey-tortured throat.

He downed another swallow and said, "What's going on around here?"

"What do you mean?" the bartender asked with a frown.

"Well, there's got to be some kind of action—"

"We got poker and faro games going, and of course there's always women."

Rogers shook his head. "I don't see any profit in that. I'm looking to make some money, not spend it."

The bartender leaned both hands on the bar. "You've come to the wrong place, then. Elkhorn's a plumb peaceable settlement. It welcomes all sorts, as long as they're not looking to cause trouble."

That went along with what Rogers had thought earlier about the settlement. There was an unspoken truce. The men who drifted through wanted to be able to ride in again the next time they needed supplies or a drink or a card game or some female companionship.

"Fair enough. Trouble's sure not what I'm looking

for. Some job that might be worth doing, though . . . that's a different story."

"Well, if you're looking for work, there's a fella you might want to talk to. He's sitting back there in the corner. You better tell me your name first, though."

"That seems a mite on the nosy side."

The bartender shrugged. "Seems more like just being careful to me."

Rogers had known that was likely to happen. His reluctance to provide a name was more for show than anything else. After a moment, he said in a slightly surly tone, "My name's Lon Williams."

"Whereabouts are you from?"

He stiffened. "Hell, that's going too far!"

The bartender chuckled again. "Take it easy, Williams. I was just funnin' with you. See that brown-haired hombre back yonder in the corner?"

Rogers turned his head to look, then asked, "You mean the fella with the pug nose and the freckles? Looks like he ought to be on a farm somewhere?"

"That's no farm boy," the bartender said. "You go on back and talk to him. I'll give him the high sign so he'll know you strike me as the right sort of gent."

"Obliged to you," Rogers said with a curt nod.

"Take your beer with you."

Rogers picked up the mug with his left hand and walked toward the table in the back corner where the pug-nosed man sat alone. He wore a denim jacket and flannel shirt, and had a bottle and an empty glass on the table. His black hat was thumbed back on thick, tousled brown hair.

Rogers saw the man's eyes dart past him and figured the bartender was giving the signal. He stopped at the table. "Howdy. The drink juggler says you're the man I need to talk to about hunting some work."

"He does, does he?" the man asked in a mild voice.

"That's right. Mind if I sit?"

"It's a free country, amigo. Last time I checked, anyway."

Rogers set his beer down, pulled out a chair, and eased into it. "I expect you'll want my name."

The man held up a hand, barely lifting it from the table. "Names are like shirts. You can change 'em when you need to. I'm more interested in where you've been and who you might know."

Brice was prepared for that. "You want to know my bona fides. I drifted this way from Kansas. Rode with Edgar Bell and his cousin Jim Poole for a while."

The brown-haired man squinted at him. "Bell's in jail and Poole's dead. The rest of their bunch is behind bars, too. Seems I recall they tried to rob a bank and found themselves in the middle of a hornet's nest instead."

"That's right. I pulled my freight a couple weeks before that happened, or else I'd be looking out through some gray bars, too—or holding up six feet worth of dirt."

"Not many people knew that Bell and Poole were cousins," the man mused. "They sorta kept that quiet."

Rogers nodded. "I know."

"What about before that?"

"I grew up in Missouri. Too civilized back there, though. Me and another fella got into a scrape over a girl. He figured he could get away with pulling a knife on me. I blew his lights out and had to leave those parts in a hurry."

"Where was this?"

"Little place called Twitchell. It's not much more than a wide place in the trail." It was the hometown of the real Lon Williams, who at the moment was locked up in the Colorado state penitentiary at Cañon City. Rogers had arrested him four months earlier for stagecoach robbery, and Williams had volunteered the information about the shooting back in Missouri. Some telegraphs back and forth had established that the hombre Williams had shot hadn't died after all, so he could serve out his sentence for the robberies before being sent back to face attempted murder charges. The real Lon Williams had never ridden with the Bell-Poole gang, but he could have; the timing fit. Rogers knew about Bell and Poole being cousins because it had come out while Bell was being questioned after he'd been placed under arrest. Both those elements of Rogers's story would check out if anybody went to the trouble of looking into it.

So would the details about other crimes Williams had been involved with that Rogers added, including being part of a rustling ring that had operated in western Kansas. He didn't elaborate too much, just enough to make it clear that he was a wanted man with a history of crime and violence and not much in the way of scruples.

The man on the other side of the table smiled. "You're a real bad man, aren't you?"

"I'm a man who plays the hand he's been dealt," Rogers snapped. "I never figured it made sense to be any other way."

"How come you split from Bell and Poole when you did?"

Rogers shrugged. "I had a bad feeling about that bank they were planning to hit. That settlement was a pretty rough cow town back in the trail drive days. I figured there might still be quite a few folks around there familiar with which end of the barrel the bullet comes out of, if you know what I mean. Turns out I was right . . . but I didn't take no pleasure in it when I heard about what had happened."

"Well, all that sounds reasonable enough, I reckon."

"So, are you hiring?" Rogers hoped he wasn't pushing too hard, too fast.

"Me?" The man smiled and shook his head. "No, I'm not hirin'. All I'm doin' is roundin' up strays, I guess you could call it. I'm puttin' together a group of men to ride with me back to where they'll meet the man who *is* doin' the hirin'. You interested in bein' one of that bunch, Williams?"

"Is there money to be made?"

"You don't want to know what the job is?"

"I already asked the question I want an answer to."

That brought a laugh from the man. "Then yeah, there's money to be made. One of the biggest ranches in Colorado to be looted, before we're done." He extended his hand across the table. "They call me Muddy Malone."

Rogers gripped the outlaw's hand. "Pleased to meet you, Muddy."

CHAPTER 28

Two more days of riding had Denny as stiff and sore as she had ever been. She had thought of herself as an excellent, experienced rider, and she had worked together with the crew on the Sugarloaf enough so that long hours in the saddle didn't bother her. Or so she had thought.

Putting in those long hours day after day was different, she had discovered on her way north. Riding the buckskin and leading the paint wore down a person and put a deep ache in the muscles and bones.

It was with a sense of relief that she rode into the settlement that had to be Elkhorn. Sure enough, she spotted a sign over a business's door that read ELKHORN GENERAL MERCHANDISE, V. TRAMMELL, PROP.

It was late afternoon. The streets were starting to empty out. As Denny slouched along, she saw men and women dressed like townies hurrying here and there. They cast nervous glances around them and over their shoulders, almost like they were afraid and wanted to get wherever they were going before the sun went down and night settled over the town.

She wasn't sure where somebody who was looking to recruit rustlers would set up shop, so to speak.

Probably in one or more of the saloons. Certainly not in a general store. But a store was a good place to pick up information about a town, as she had discovered back in Carterville.

That thought brought a brief frown to her face. She hadn't been dogged by a guilty conscience about the man she'd been forced to kill. Her sleep since then had been untroubled by anything except sore muscles. But the memory of that moment was still with her and probably always would be. She was sure her father didn't remember all the men he had ever shot. Such a feat would be impossible. She didn't expect to have to kill that many men in her life. It would be all right with her if she never had to kill another one.

She angled the buckskin toward the store and dismounted in front of it. Elkhorn looked like it had more saloons than anything else, but the two stores appeared to be doing quite a bit of business. A couple women came out while Denny was tying her horse. They glanced at her and then scurried away with their purchases like she was a mad dog.

That bothered her for a second before she remembered that was the impression she wanted to create. Well, maybe not of a mad dog, exactly . . . but she wanted people to think she was an hombre it wouldn't be a good idea to cross.

As she approached the mercantile's front door, it opened again and a man hurried out. He wasn't watching where he was going closely enough, and his shoulder jolted heavily against hers. Denny took a stumbling step to one side before she caught herself.

The man who had run into her was a townsman. He backed away, clutching a paper-wrapped bundle to his chest as he stared at her in fear.

Remembering the sort of hombre she was supposed

to be, Denny rasped, "What the hell! Are you clumsy, mister, or just stupid?"

She rested her right hand on the butt of the Colt.

"I . . . I'm sorry," the man said hastily. "I wasn't paying attention. I never meant to bump into you that way. It's all my fault—"

"Damn right it is," Denny told him.

"Please, I . . . I apologize. You're not . . . you're not hurt, are you?"

Denny let out a contemptuous grunt. "Hurt?" she repeated. "From runnin' into some pasty-faced hombre like you? Not hardly, mister."

"Then is it . . . is it all right if I go . . . ?"

Denny jerked her head and said, "Git."

The man turned around so fast he almost slipped and fell. He caught his balance, then scrambled to get going and hurried away along the boardwalk.

A voice came from the store's doorway. "I appreciate that. It would've been my responsibility to scrub up the blood if it was on the walk in front of my store, and it's almost impossible to get it out of the boards."

Denny looked over and saw a short, wiry man with white hair and spectacles standing there. He wore a gray canvas apron and was clearly the storekeeper.

"Anyway, I'd hate to see Calvin Hughes gunned down," the man went on. "He may not be a very good barber, but he's the only one we've got."

"You really think I'd kill a man for bumpin' into me?" Denny asked.

The man shrugged. "Some fellas around here probably would. Not that I plan on naming any names, mind you."

"That's wise, more 'n likely. Why was that hombre in such a hurry? Why does *everybody* around here act like that? Folks have to be off the street by a certain time?"

"There's no curfew, not in a legal sense. Of course,

there's not really anything in Elkhorn you can say is in a legal sense. That's a notion we've learned how to do without. Law, I mean."

"Just the way I like it," Denny said.

The storekeeper studied her. "Kind of young to be such a hardcase, aren't you?"

Denny glared at him. "Maybe you ought to be as worried as your barber friend was."

"I don't know. If you shoot me, I won't have to clean up the blood, now will I?"

Denny couldn't help but laugh a little. "You've got some bark on you, old man."

"I've been in these parts longer than just about anybody who's still alive. Came here as a civilian scout for the army, back in the Indian-fighting days, stayed to help tame the place. You modern-day owlhoots can't come up with anything worse than what I've already seen."

"What's your name?"

"Virgil Trammell." The old man pointed with a thumb at the sign above his head. "Proprietor."

"I'm Denny West."

"You don't call yourself the Palo Duro Kid or something ridiculous like that?"

"You're a prickly sort of hombre, aren't you? No, just plain old Denny West. I'm looking for a place to get some good grub and then a drink."

Trammell aimed a finger down the street. "Lu Shan's café isn't bad. He's a Chinaman, but he cooks food that you can actually tell what it is. His steaks are a little tough, but if you've got good teeth they're tasty. Need any washing done, his brother Lu Sung owns the laundry. They're old-timers around here, too, came to the States to help build the Central Pacific, then drifted up here when that job was over. As far as the drink goes, the Silver Slipper is as good as any in town and better than some. A fella comes out of there every now and then with the blind staggers, but I don't recall anybody ever actually dying from the whiskey they got there."

Denny nodded. "I'm obliged to you. If I need any supplies before I leave town, I'll be sure to come here."

"I don't turn away anybody's trade, even gunmen. How long do you plan to be in Elkhorn?"

"Depends on how long it takes me to find some good-paying work. I can use it."

"Tapped out, are you?"

"Don't start prying," she snapped.

"What sort of work are you looking for? If that's not *prying*."

"I told you. Good-paying. Other than that, I don't care what it is."

"Well, you'll probably stumble onto something," Trammell said. "This is a town with a lot of things going on. None of it's pretty, but some of it is lucrative."

Denny nodded and went back to her horse. The sun was down, and shadows had begun to gather. Night would fall quickly.

She said, "I guess you'll be closing up now, since all the honest citizens are hiding in their houses."

"I generally stay open a while. Like I said, I don't turn away anybody's trade."

Denny led the buckskin and the paint along the street, leaving the crusty old storekeeper standing in the doorway with the light behind him. If he had been on the frontier for a long time, he had to know of Smoke Jensen, Preacher, and the other members of the Jensen clan. He might have even crossed trails with some of them. He would have been surprised to find out that he was talking to the daughter of Smoke Jensen, she thought.

She came to the café and saw that a lamp was still

burning inside. Maybe Lu Shan had the same idea as Trammell and was willing to do business with the outlaws who drifted through Elkhorn. She tied up the horses and went inside.

A stocky, middle-aged Chinese man was stacking the chairs on the tables so he could sweep out. "Just closing up," he told her in a voice devoid of any accent, then added quickly, "No offense, mister."

"You people in this town are the edgiest bunch I've ever seen," Denny said. "Always afraid somebody's going to take offense."

"We just don't want any trouble." The man hesitated, then went on. "I've got a little stew left in the pot. I guess you can have it if you want."

"I'd appreciate that. I've been on the trail for a while and I'm gettin' a mite sick of my own cooking, such as it is."

That was actually true. One of the things Denny really missed about the Sugarloaf were the fine meals her mother and Inez prepared.

"You mind turning around the CLOSED sign for me?"

"Nope." Denny turned the sign in the window, then said, "You're Lu Shan?"

The man looked a little surprised. "That's right. You're new in town. How did you know my name?"

"The old-timer over at the store mentioned it. He said you cooked up a pretty good meal."

"Ah, Virgil. He and I are friends."

Lu went into the kitchen and came back out with a bowl and spoon. He filled a cup with coffee from the pot on the stove and set that on the counter with the stew. Denny sat down and dug in. The stew was flavorful, although the chunks of beef in it were on the tough side. Evidently that was how Lu Shan liked to cook meat.

"You just rode in this afternoon, didn't you?" he asked as he leaned on the counter.

"That's right."

"On your way anyplace in particular?"

"Nope. Wherever I can find work and make some money."

"What sort of work?"

She raised an eyebrow. "I ain't never been particular, except about the money."

"You seem like a decent young man. Maybe you should try somewhere other than Elkhorn—"

Denny drew the Colt and set it on the counter next to the bowl with a slight thump. She didn't want to seem like a decent young man. "I ain't payin' extra for talk, Chinaman."

Lu straightened, moved back a step, and raised both hands, palms out. "Sorry," he muttered. The same sort of nervousness Denny had seen in the barber's eyes was evident on Lu's face. "I didn't mean anything by it. I've heard there's a fellow in town looking for men who are good with their guns."

"Sounds interesting. Where can I find him?"

"He's usually in the Silver Slipper, of an evening. Or so I've heard."

"Maybe I'll take a *paseo* over there when I finish this."

"Take your time. And, uh, there's no charge. Like I said, it was the last of the stew left in the pot."

Denny shrugged. She didn't figure the gunnie she was supposed to be would argue with that gesture.

She finished the stew, drank the rest of the coffee, and stood up. "The Silver Slipper's just across the street. I'm gonna leave my horses tied up in front of your place for now." She didn't make a question out of the statement.

"That's fine," Lu said without hesitation. "No one will bother them."

"Nobody with any sense, anyway."

Denny swaggered out, closing the door behind her with a little extra force. Remembering to be a jackass was harder than she had expected it to be, she reflected.

She walked diagonally across the street, dodging the numerous piles of horse droppings, and stepped up onto the boardwalk in front of the Silver Slipper. She had just about reached the batwings when they suddenly swung out toward her, forcing her to step back quickly to avoid being hit. She burst out, "Damn it! Doesn't anybody in this town watch where they're going?"

The two men emerging from the saloon stopped short just outside the batwings.

Maybe her angry exclamation—which had been half genuine, half feigned—was a mistake, she thought. In Elkhorn, these hombres might be the sort who would take offense and demand satisfaction at gunpoint.

The first man looked rough but not particularly threatening at the moment. The second one stiffened as if he were angry then moved slightly to look past the first man to see who they had almost collided with and to size him up.

Then he raised his head so his hat brim no longer concealed his face and looked directly at her. Denny couldn't stop herself from reacting. Her breath hissed between her teeth in surprise.

She was looking at Deputy U.S. Marshal Brice Rogers, and he was staring right back at her with unmistakable recognition in his eyes.

CHAPTER 29

Recognition was like a punch sinking into his gut.

His brain had never worked faster in his life. If Denny Jensen blurted out his secret, he was a dead man. She would probably doom herself, too, if she spilled the truth.

With that spinning madly in his head, Rogers lunged past Muddy and grabbed her around the throat—the only thing he could think of to make sure she didn't say anything.

Realizing he needed a reason, he yelled, "You bastard! Thought you'd never run into me again, didn't you?" He shoved Denny up against one of the posts supporting the awning over the boardwalk, put his face right up in hers, and snarled curses at her. Between them, he whispered, "Don't say anything"—then louder, "You double-crossing polecat!"—he finished the whispered entreaty—"about who I am!"

Her eyes were wide with shock. He was choking her harder than he wanted to, but he had to make it look good. Then her gaze began to smolder with anger, and he felt something hard poke against his belly. He didn't have to hear the sound of a hammer being pulled back to know it was the barrel of a six-gun.

She wasn't really going to shoot him, was she?

Having a gun shoved in his stomach was a believable enough reason to let go of her throat. As his fingers fell away from her flesh, she rasped, "Back off, or I'll blow your backbone in two!"

Muddy said, "Williams, have you gone loco? Who the hell is this hombre?"

Denny grimaced. "Yeah, Williams, tell your friend who I am." She felt like she had been swept up in a flood, whirled around and around, and washed away. Her brain was stunned, and it was all her taut-stretched nerves could do to hold themselves together as she struggled to navigate through the unexpected torrent of confusion and danger.

"You're the good-for-nothing skunk who left me to deal with that posse back in Kansas," Rogers said with a furious glare of his own as he cooked up a story in his head as fast as he could. "You made off with all the loot we took from that store, too!"

"You were plannin' to do the same thing to me!" she challenged right back at him. "Nobody does that to Denny West and gets away with it! I just made my move first, that's all."

He had known she was smart. He quickly realized she was quick-witted, too. She had just let him know the name she was using, and in a way that wouldn't make anybody suspicious. Obviously, she was trying to pass herself off as a young man. With her hair cropped off crudely and her breasts flattened somehow—he felt his face warming slightly at that thought—she might be able to pull off the masquerade.

"Listen here," Muddy said. "If you two got a grudge to settle, I won't stop you, Lon, but I was countin' on you ridin' out with me in the morning, remember? Can you take this kid in a shoot-out?"

Denny sneered and practically spat, "Not on his best

day, mister!" Words were coming out of her mouth, formed largely by instinct.

"Maybe we ought to find out." The last thing Rogers wanted was a showdown with Denny, but he had to keep acting the way a double-crossed "Lon Williams" would have, at least for a little while longer.

Muddy rubbed his chin and said, "The two of you used to ride together?"

"For a while," Rogers replied. "Before I threw in with Bell and Poole and their bunch." Might as well feed Denny as much information as he could, he thought.

"I could've warned those two not to trust you," Denny said. "I'll bet you ran out on 'em!"

Muddy chuckled. "Sounds like the kid knows you pretty well, Lon. You actually did leave the gang not long before they ran into that bad fracas."

"I didn't know anything about what was comin' at the time," Rogers said in a surly voice. "I never ran out on a pard in my life, unlike some. And I never would."

"Listen, maybe the two of you ought to just have a drink instead of tryin' to kill each other," Muddy suggested. "One thing you got to remember . . . once water's flowed under the bridge, it's gone and it ain't comin' back."

"From what you've told me about what your boss is doing, he doesn't feel that way."

Muddy's face tightened. "Hush up about that in front of strangers."

"But I'm not a stranger," Denny declared. "I used to ride with this son of a bitch, and now he rides with you." She turned her head to glower at Rogers again. "You're mixed up in some sweet deal, Williams. Don't bother tryin' to deny it, you weasel. Well, by God, I want in on it!"

It was like acting in a play, she realized, but the lines

weren't written out for her by some hombre who had the luxury of going back and changing them if he decided he didn't like them. She had to come up with them on her own, without hardly any time to think about it, and if she said the wrong thing . . . well, that was just too bad.

Rogers was staring at her and she wondered suddenly if he had said something to her she had failed to notice. Was he waiting for an answer? If this was a play—albeit one where the stakes were life and death—whose line *was* it, anyway?

"That's just like you, West. Always trying to come along later and horn in on somebody else's deal." He'd just taken his time about answering.

She hadn't missed anything. "The only reason I ever horned in on any of your deals," she shot back at him, "is because you were never up to carryin' them out on your own."

"All right, that's enough," Muddy said, starting to sound irritated. "If you two ain't gonna go to shootin', you might as well stop all this snarlin' and hissin' at each other like a couple mangy alley cats. Just go your separate ways and forget about it."

"Wait just a damn minute," Denny said. "Who in Hades are you to be tellin' me what to do, mister?"

"My name's Muddy Malone. You got a bone to pick with me, son, you're liable to regret it."

The name didn't mean anything to her, but she was starting to put together everything she had seen and heard. The only explanation for Brice Rogers's presence in Elkhorn was for him to be there for the same reason she was.

He was pretending to be an outlaw and trying to get inside the gang of rustlers and killers so he could bring them to justice and keep them from attacking the Sugarloaf again.

That was an admirable thing for the young deputy marshal to be doing, but it sure played hell with her plan.

Malone had to be one of the gang, or at least connected with it. Denny wanted to stay close to him until she figured out exactly what was going on. "Look, Malone, I didn't ride into town lookin' for trouble. Maybe I got a mite too proddy there. It's just that seeing this hombre again"—she jerked a nod toward Rogers—"has got my back up."

"I reckon I can understand that—"

"Hey!" Rogers interrupted, clearly offended—or at least pretending to be.

"If the two of you used to be partners and it didn't end well," Muddy went on, "of course there are some hard feelin's. But the way I figure, if it ain't worth gunplay, it ain't really worth worryin' about, now is it?"

"I suppose you're right about that," Denny said with grudging acceptance. She and Rogers had pushed the argument far enough, she decided. Their phony identities and past relationship were well established, and all they had to do was stick to that and be careful. "Look, just to show I'm willing to forget about the past, why don't we have that drink you were talking about a minute ago, Malone?"

"Sounds like a good idea to me."

Rogers looked intently at her for a second, then nodded. "Fine," he said, his voice curt. "On one condition. You pay for those drinks. You were the one who ran off with that loot back in Kansas, after all. I'm sure it's long gone by now, but . . ."

"Reckon I can go along with that," Denny said.

A grin stretched across Muddy's round face. "Now, ain't it better to be friends?" He put his right hand on Denny's shoulder, his left on Rogers's. "Come on back inside. Lon and me were on our way to the stable to check on our horses before we turn in for the night, but that can wait a little while. I want to hear more about the days when the two of you were ridin' together."

Denny wasn't happy about that—it would mean making up more false history—but she was the one who had suggested the drinks again, so she couldn't back out, though she did say, "Aw, there ain't that much to tell. We pulled off a few jobs, but nothing spectacular."

"You've forgotten about that train in Nebraska," Rogers said as Muddy steered them back toward the batwings.

"The two of you held up a train?" the outlaw said, sounding impressed.

"We took over a flag stop in the middle of the night, waited until the train pulled in, and grabbed the conductor before anybody knew what was going on. The express messenger opened up the safe to keep us from putting a bullet in the fella."

"Really? I didn't think they'd do things like that, even to save the conductor's life."

Rogers shrugged. "We'd found out that the conductor and the messenger were brothers. Turned out blood meant more than either hombre's job."

"Smart!" Muddy said as they headed for the bar.

"It was my idea," Denny said.

Rogers glared at her for a second but didn't contradict the claim.

"This was a few years ago?" Muddy asked.

"Yeah," Rogers said.

"But how's that possible? The kid here looks like, well, a kid. A few years ago he would've been too young to be ridin' the owlhoot."

Denny said flatly, "I'm older than I look. I figure it's because of clean livin'."

Muddy looked at her, then burst out in a laugh. "You're a caution, kid." He signaled to the bartender and told the man to bring them drinks.

"Make it a bottle," Denny said.

When Rogers frowned at her, she continued. "Maybe I'm not as much of a spendthrift as you think I am, Lon."

"Could be you've changed," he allowed, still playing his part. "It's been a while."

Denny dropped a coin on the bar, then picked up the bottle and three glasses the bartender placed in front of them. She inclined her head toward an empty table. "Come on. If we're not gonna kill each other, we might as well make this a reunion."

CHAPTER 30

Denny had never acquired much of a taste for whiskey. Young ladies in Europe might sip a glass of port or sherry now and then, but that was about all the drinking they did. It was a far cry from guzzling down raw whiskey that might well have been mixed up in a tin washtub out back.

She managed not to gasp and choke and pound on the table when she downed the first shot, but it took some effort to control that impulse. The liquor didn't seem to have much effect on Rogers or Muddy Malone. She hoped her insides, from her mouth on down, would stop burning sooner or later.

To postpone taking another drink, she said to Rogers, "Tell me about this deal you're working on, Williams."

"It ain't Lon's deal to tell about," Muddy said as he leaned forward in his chair. "It's mine."

"Well, then, you tell me about it. Unless you think I can't be trusted."

"Don't go gettin' another burr under your saddle, kid. It ain't that I don't trust you. It's just that, well"—Muddy looked a little sheepish—"maybe I sorta spoke out of turn. It ain't really my deal, neither. But the boss sent me up here to look for some fellas who might want to throw in with us, fellas I figured might be trustworthy."

"And you picked this one?" Denny said skeptically as she nodded across the table toward Rogers.

"Now hold on," the lawman said as his face flushed with anger again.

"Don't start up," Muddy snapped. "Look, kid . . . Denny, was it? If what Lon says is true, you're the one who double-crossed him. That doesn't sound like a fella I can really trust."

That clever son of a gun! Denny thought. Even though Rogers had been making things up off the top of his head like she was, he had hit on a phony story that would make Malone less inclined to believe her about anything, including her desire to join the gang. He really and truly *didn't* want her horning in on what he was doing, even though his motivation was completely different from what Malone believed it to be.

"Well, here's the thing," she said slowly. "Lon's telling the truth, but I was younger then, more impulsive. And I really did believe he was planning to run out on me as soon as he got the chance. But I was wrong, and I'm man enough to admit it. Here's something else: I'd like to make it up to you, Lon. I done you wrong, and I want to make it good."

He regarded her with a wary frown as he asked, "What do you mean by that?"

"Give me the chance to be part of whatever this deal is," Denny said, "and I'll give you half of my share until I've paid back everything I took. We'll be square then, and we can start over."

Rogers's cautious frown turned into a glare. He could see how neatly she had turned that around on him.

Muddy could, too, and grinned in appreciation. "You're pretty smart, Denny. Maybe you ought to ride south in the morning with me and Lon and a few other fellas who want to throw in with us."

Rogers said, "I'm not sure that's a good idea—"

Muddy held up a hand to stop him. "Not your decision to make, Lon. No offense. Don't get touchy at *me*, now."

"No, I'm not." With a visible effort, Rogers forced a shrug. "It's up to you if you want to bring the kid along. You won't blame me, though, if I keep a pretty close eye on him."

"That's fine. You watch him and I won't have to, any more than I'll be keepin' my eye on all of you."

Denny asked, "Where is it we're going, anyway?"

Muddy shook his head. "You'll find out when the time comes."

"When we meet this mysterious boss of yours?"

"That's right."

Denny asked the obvious question. "What happens if he decides he *doesn't* want us to be part of his bunch?"

"Well . . . that'll be a real shame. By then you'll know where the hideout is and what's going on, and if you're not one of us—" Muddy stopped and reached for the bottle. "Ah, hell, why worry about things that ain't likely to happen? We got a bottle and empty glasses, and by God, we'd better do something about that!"

Denny's head was spinning. Even though she hadn't drunk as much as Rogers and Malone, she had put away enough of the whiskey to feel it. She was unsteady on her feet as the three of them left the Silver Slipper and stepped out onto the boardwalk. Luckily the railing at the edge of the walk was close, so she was able to lean on it casually to keep from stumbling—or falling down.

That wouldn't do at all for a hardened outlaw like she was pretending to be.

Rogers's speech was a little slurred, but Denny couldn't tell if he was really drunk, too, or only pretending as he said, "Listen, Muddy, I'll check on your horse for you. You can go on back to the hotel and turn in. Get a good . . . a good night's sleep."

"Well, now, that wouldn't be fair—"

"Sure it would. Anyway, Denny's got to take his horse over there, too, so we'll go together."

Muddy squinted at him. "You two ain't gonna get in a ruckus again, are you?"

"Hell, no," Rogers said with a laugh. "We've put all that behind us, ain't we, Denny?"

"You . . . you bet." She hiccupped and then went on. "Me an' ol' Lon here, we're pards again." She was feeling the liquor physically, but her brain was still sharp enough to maintain the masquerades they were both carrying out. At least she hoped it was. Maybe she was too drunk to notice if she made a slip.

She knew any slip would likely be a fatal one, and that knowledge was enough to dispel some of the fog hanging over her brain, anyway.

"All right, then," Muddy said. "I'll see you fellas in the mornin'. We'll all get together at the Chinaman's place for breakfast, then ride out. I want to be on the trail not long after sunup. We got a three- or four-day ride ahead of us."

Three or four days would put her right back in the vicinity she had started from, Denny thought. Back to the mastermind who wanted to ruin Smoke Jensen and then kill him.

"Night," Rogers said to Malone. "See you in the morning."

Muddy walked off, stumbling just enough to demonstrate that he was feeling the whiskey, too.

Rogers let him get out of earshot, then said sharply from the corner of his mouth, "Get your damned horse."

"Watch your mouth . . . *Lon.*"

He looked over at her. "You're pretty quick on your feet, aren't you?"

"Quicker than you ever would've given me credit for."

"You're drunk, too."

"Aren't you?"

"Not so's you'd notice. Come on. If Malone looks back, I want him to see us heading for the livery stable."

That made sense. Denny stepped down from the boardwalk and grasped the hitch rail to steady herself again. "My horses are tied up across the street, in front of Lu Shan's café." She sighed. "It's a long way over there."

Brice put a hand on her shoulder. "I won't let you fall on your face in a pile of horse droppings."

"I'd appreciate that," Denny said.

They started across toward the café. Denny pointed a shaking finger at the buckskin and the paint and identified them as hers. As she walked and breathed in the cool night air, the fog cleared a little more and her steps steadied. Feeling that, Rogers took his hand off her shoulder.

Denny sort of missed the touch, then told herself that was loco. The grudge between "Denny West" and "Lon Williams" might be purely fictional, but the two of them weren't exactly friends, either.

She untied the buckskin. "Which way is the livery stable?"

Rogers took the paint's reins. "Come on. I'll show you."

He led her toward a barn not far from Virgil Trammell's store. The big double doors on the front were closed. Rogers lifted the latch and swung one of the doors open. The barn's interior was dark, but Denny smelled horseflesh, hay, and manure, and heard tails swishing and the occasional stomp of a hoof against the hard-packed ground.

"The liveryman sleeps in a shack out back," Rogers said as they led the two horses into the barn. "No need for us to roust him out. We can take care of these animals. You're not too drunk to unsaddle a horse, are you?"

"I'm not as drunk as you think I am."

"Good, because if you were, you'd probably be passed out by now."

"You just take care of yourself, Williams."

His voice was a whisper as he said, "You don't have to call me that when nobody else is around."

"Reckon I'd better," Denny said. "We don't want to forget who we're supposed to be."

"That's true. There were some empty stalls back here earlier. We'll see if they still are."

He snapped a match to life with his thumbnail, then held the flame to the wick of a small lantern hanging on a post. The feeble glow lit up one corner of the barn but provided enough light for Denny to pick out a couple empty stalls.

She started unsaddling the buckskin. Her fingers fumbled several times at the task.

Rogers stepped closer to her and reached out. "I'll take care of that for you."

"I can unsaddle my own horse, damn it."

His hand had already fallen on hers where she was gripping one of the cinch buckles. Denny caught her breath. She wanted to jerk her hand away, but for some reason she didn't.

He was close beside her, close enough to breathe so no one else could hear, "You crazy little fool. What are you doing here?"

"Same thing you are," she whispered back. "Trying to pick up the trail of those rustlers and killers."

"But you're just—"

"A girl?" she cut in. "No, I'm not. I'm Denny West, outlaw and fast gun, and if you try to ruin that for me, mister, I'll make sure you're sorry."

"How?"

"I'm not the only one with a secret."

"You're threatening me?"

"Stop and think about it, idiot," she muttered. "Neither of us can give the other one away without ruining things for ourselves. Is that what you want?" When he didn't answer right away, she went on. "For God's sake, Malone's going to take us right where we want to go! The only way not to ruin that is to work together."

He was silent for a moment longer, then said, "You're right. That doesn't mean I have to like it."

"I don't give a damn whether you like it. All I care about is putting a stop to the threat to my family."

"How do you think your father would feel about what you're doing?"

"He'd be mad at first." Denny smiled in the near-darkness. "And then he'd be proud of me for going after those varmints."

"Are you sure about that?"

"I reckon we'll find out sooner or later."

Rogers grimaced. "Yeah, if we don't get killed first."

CHAPTER 31

There was one actual hotel in Elkhorn, as well as a couple saloons that rented small, squalid rooms in the back, with or without the company of a soiled dove, depending on what the customer was willing to pay. Denny planned on staying at the hotel, if a room was available. Under the circumstances, sharing a room could present some problems.

She was lucky. The hotel had several vacant rooms, and the pasty-faced, oily-haired clerk was glad to rent one to her. She slid a coin across the desk to him—nothing as formal as signing a register.

He leered and said, "I can send out to have a girl keep you company if you want."

"I thought this was a respectable place," Denny said.

"Oh, it is, it is. Only the finest, cleanest girls, that's what I'm talking about."

Denny shook her head. "I've been on the trail a long time. Just want some sleep."

"Suit yourself," the clerk said as he took a key from a hook and handed it to her. "Room Seven, top of the stairs and turn right." As she turned away from the desk, he added, "And if you rest a while and then change your mind about the company, just let me know. I got a room in the back. Knock on the door anytime, and I'll go rustle up some companionship for you."

Denny just grunted and went on to the stairs. Simply being around the clerk was enough to make her feel like she ought to soak in a nice, hot tub for a while to get some of the grime off.

Brice Rogers had a room there, too, and had gone upstairs already while she was making arrangements with the clerk. He had told her he was in Room Eleven, two doors down the upstairs hallway, which didn't really matter because she didn't plan on seeing him again until the next morning. Muddy Malone had indicated that he was staying there as well, although Denny had no idea in which room.

The place wasn't fancy, by any means, but the bed looked comfortable. She lit the lamp, drew the thick curtains closed over the single window, and made sure she had locked the door when she came in. Then she took off her vest, shirt, and long underwear and unwound the bindings from her torso, sighing with relief as her breasts came free.

She sighed again as she ran her hand over the ragged, bristly blond hair on her head. The masquerade had its drawbacks and discomforts, that was for sure, but she could tolerate them for the sake of her father and the rest of her family, she told herself.

Stripping down to the bottoms of the long underwear, she blew out the lamp and crawled into bed. The sheets were coarse and the mattress was a little lumpy, but after several nights of sleeping on the trail, she didn't mind.

Slumber didn't come quite as quick as she thought it would, though. She couldn't get Brice Rogers out of her mind. It complicated things having him around, that was true, but at the same time, she had an unexpected ally. She believed she could count on him for help if any trouble broke out.

On the other hand, having two of them working undercover doubled the chances that something could go wrong, didn't it? If one of them was exposed, the other would be, too.

Unless the one whose secret *wasn't* exposed was willing to let the hand play out however it would for the unlucky one. And that hand was almost certain to end badly . . .

Denny finally drifted off to sleep, hoping it would never come to that.

Hoping she would never have to make such a decision.

Rogers was waiting in the hotel lobby for her when she came down the stairs the next morning.

"Muddy's already gone down to the café, but I told him I'd wait for you." He smiled. "He said that was fine as long as I wasn't intending to ambush you over that old grudge."

"Water under the bridge, like Muddy said," Denny declared. She tugged her hat down tighter on her head as they stepped out onto the boardwalk and headed for Lu Shan's place.

Not many people were out and about that early, and the ones who were appeared to be some of the honest citizens of Elkhorn rather than the lawless drifters who accounted for most of the settlement's population those days. No one paid any attention to Denny and Rogers; in fact, people seemed to be going out of their way to avoid them.

That allowed them to speak freely as long as they were discreet about it.

Rogers started off by saying quietly, "I hope you've changed your mind since last night."

"Changed my mind? About what?"

"About going through with this loco scheme of yours."

"You mean finding the gang's hideout? Nothing loco about that. It's what has to be done."

"It's also a job for the law."

"Well, the law didn't seem to be doing too good a job of it." She heard Rogers's breath hiss sharply and knew he had taken her words as an insult. She hadn't meant them that way, exactly. To her it was more of a matter of stating the facts. "My father wound up shot and nearly killed. I would have left things to my uncle and my cousins if they'd been around, but there's no telling when they'll show up. They might not get the message for weeks or even months."

They walked along for several steps without Rogers saying anything. Then he surprised her a little by telling her, "You might be right. But even so, this is too dangerous for you to be mixed up in, Denny. I want you to tell Muddy that you've changed your mind and will be drifting on along by yourself."

Anger flared as she looked over at him. "Is that an order? An official decree from the federal law?"

"I can make it one, if that's what it'll take to get some sense into your head."

"Go to hell, *Lon.* Nobody tells me what to do."

"You stubborn, bullheaded—"

"You're repeating yourself." If he responded to that, she didn't hear it, because she angled out into the street and cut across it to reach the café.

As soon as she went in, she spotted Muddy Malone sitting at a large, rectangular table with several other men. Platters of flapjacks, biscuits, eggs, steak, ham, and bacon filled the table, and the men were helping themselves to the grub. He waved her over to join them.

She took one of the two empty chairs at the table and nodded to the other men, who all had the look of hardcases and outlaws about them. She had never seen a more dangerous, disreputable-looking bunch.

And she was going to try to pass herself off as one of them? For a second, doubt attacked her. She must have been loco, just like Rogers said, to believe her scheme would work.

Thinking about Rogers stiffened her resolve. If her plan succeeded, not only would she be helping her family, she would be showing that stiff-necked young deputy marshal it was a mistake to underestimate her. She picked up one of the coffeepots sitting on the table and filled the empty cup at her place, then began piling food on her plate.

"Where's Williams?" Muddy asked. "He said he was gonna wait at the hotel for you. I hope the two of you didn't get in another squabble."

"You didn't hear any gunshots, did you?" Denny said.

"No, I didn't," Muddy replied.

"He'll be along in a minute. I'm just a mite faster than him, that's all." She grinned. "In all the ways that count."

The door opened, the bell hung over it jingling a little, and Rogers went in, still frowning.

One of the other men at the table jeered, "Hey, Williams, this old pard of yours was just tellin' us how slow you are when it counts."

"Yeah, well, nearly every word out of his mouth is a lie, and you'd all do well to remember that."

Muddy said, "If you two keep goin' on like this, I'm liable to decide I can't trust either of you and that you oughta just go on your way instead of comin' with us."

"No need for that," Denny said. "I can tolerate him."

"And I can put up with him," Rogers said as he took the other empty chair, which thankfully wasn't next to Denny. "Right now I'm more interested in this coffee and grub."

Like Denny, he dug into the breakfast. No other customers were in the café at the moment, but Lu Shan was kept busy anyway, bringing more food and pots of coffee. While they ate, Muddy introduced the other men to Denny, nodding to each of them around the table as he supplied their names—Moran, Truett, Long, Watson, Calder, Hamlin, and Daly.

Denny nodded pleasantly to them and tried to remember what each of them was called, but she figured it didn't really matter much. In a few days, they would all be members of the outlaw gang out to destroy the Sugarloaf.

Her mortal enemies, in other words.

One of the men—Moran, Denny believed it was—asked, "How long is it gonna take us to get where we're goin'?"

"Three days, four at the most," Muddy replied. "Unless we run into real trouble, like the law. I'm pretty good at steerin' clear of star packers, though." He grinned. "I can sniff 'em out, kinda like a bloodhound."

Denny didn't say anything, and she was careful not to glance in Rogers's direction. Let Malone believe whatever he wanted. He would find out how wrong he was, soon enough.

When breakfast was finished, Muddy paid Lu Shan for everyone's meal. "Don't get used to it," he warned the others. "Everybody pays their own freight in our bunch. Reckon you can call this a bonus."

"We're obliged to you, boss," Daly said.

Muddy shook his head. "Don't call me *boss*, and damn sure don't get in the habit of it. Where we're goin', that could get you in a heap of trouble. There's only one boss, and you'd best not forget it."

"What's his name, Muddy?" Rogers asked.

Always fishing for information, he was. Denny had to give him credit for that.

"Like everything else, you'll find out when the time comes." Muddy jerked his head toward the door. "Go get your horses saddled and ready to ride, then meet me in front of Trammell's store. I told that old man to put together some supplies for us, and I got a pack mule to load 'em on." He thumbed his hat back on his head. "I don't know about you boys, but I'm ready to get started."

"Not me," Rogers said with a grin. "I'm ready to be there and start earning some of that money you promised us."

Amen, Denny thought. She didn't care about the money, but she was ready to arrive at the gang's hideout and discover just who it was that wanted her father dead.

CHAPTER 32

The trip was generally miserable. It rained a lot while they were riding south, so they spent a lot of time wet and cold. When it wasn't raining, thick clouds continued to gather over the mountains and the foothills, not even allowing the sun's rays to warm and dry the riders. Every gust of wind had sharp teeth in it.

Denny was glad she had brought the extra blankets. Even with them, she still woke up shivering most mornings.

She rode with her head down and her hat pulled low over her eyes. The faces of the men were heavily beard-stubbled and she didn't have any to display. She was able to get a handful of mud and smear it over her cheeks and jaws when no one was nearby to make her beardless state less obvious. Any time she had personal business to take care of, she had to sneak off into the brush. No one seemed to have noticed that so far, but the possibility that they might realize what she was doing worried her. She was glad the journey was only going to take a few days. That much less time for the others to figure out something about her was off-kilter, she thought.

The fourth and final day of the trip dawned clear

for a change. Denny was glad to see the sun. With the clouds and mist that had been hanging over the mountains finally gone, she was able to get a better look at them and realized with a slight shock that some of the peaks looked familiar. They were less than thirty miles from the Sugarloaf.

Rogers drifted over close to her while she was saddling the buckskin. None of the other men were close by. He said quietly, "Got to be getting pretty close now."

"Yeah, I think so." She pulled a cinch tight. "We ought to get to the hideout today. Then what?"

"Then we'll figure out some way for you to get out of there and go for help. I'll stay behind to cover for you."

Denny frowned. "Why don't we both get out? If you stay there, it's going to be mighty dangerous."

"Not necessarily. I'll just make it sound like you double-crossed us and ran out again, like you did back in Kansas."

"Don't go thinking that was real," she snapped.

"You'd better believe it was real. If you act like it wasn't, you could get us both killed in a hurry."

He was right about that, she supposed. She finished getting the saddle in place and gave a curt nod.

The group mounted up and rode on. The farther south they went, the more familiar the landscape was to Denny. Knowing that she was less than a day's ride from home made her long to be there, to see her parents and brother again. She had only been away for a little more than a week, but she couldn't help but wonder what had happened during that time. Had Louis been able to convince their mother and father that she had gone back east? Was Smoke still continuing to recuperate from his wound? If he'd had a setback, a turn for the worst, and something had happened to him while she was gone, she didn't know if she could ever forgive herself for not being there.

Her more pragmatic side reminded her that she had been gone a lot more often than she had been there. Smoke could have died a hundred times over while she was on the other side of the world. But he hadn't. He was the strongest man she had ever known, and she saw no reason that should change.

Muddy Malone's course angled west, deeper into the foothills. The terrain grew more rugged. Huge, rocky shelves thrust up a hundred feet or more, forcing the riders to detour around them. The vegetation was sparse, mostly clumps of tough grass and small but hardy pine trees. Denny didn't recall ever exploring that particular area. It wasn't on Sugarloaf range, although she estimated the ranch's northern boundary was only a few miles away.

They dropped down into a stretch slashed by ravines. A rider could get lost pretty easily in that labyrinth, but Muddy seemed to know where he was going. He led the way down a broad, caved-in bank into a gully about twenty yards wide. That gully twisted and turned but provided a way through the badlands.

Brice nudged his horse alongside Denny's, and when she glanced over at him, he darted a look down at the ground. Denny's eyes followed his gaze and spotted the same thing he had. The ground was too hard and rocky to take many prints, but here and there cattle tracks could be seen. At some point in the not-so-distant past, cows had been driven through the gully.

Stolen cows, Denny thought. Stock rustled from the Sugarloaf.

That came as no surprise. After all, the whole plan had been to find the rustlers' hideout. Those tracks were welcome confirmation that she and Rogers were on the right trail.

The gully ran for several miles and then rose and ended at a level stretch of ground. Half a mile away loomed another of those massive rock shelves, that one split by a small opening. Denny's heart slugged faster at the sight. She sensed that the cleft led to her destination.

She was even more convinced when Malone rode straight toward it. He took off his hat and waved it back and forth over his head three times in what had to be a signal. As the group approached, two men holding rifles stepped out from behind some boulders clumped at the entrance.

Muddy reined in and greeted the guards. "I've got some fellas who want to ride with us, just like the boss was lookin' for."

One of the outlaws gave the newcomers a hard stare. "They know they've come too far to turn back now, don't they?"

"Nobody wants to turn back. They're all good hombres."

"You'd better hope so," the guard said. "Your neck is ridin' on this, too, you know, Muddy. Turk convinced the boss to put you in charge of this, but he can't save you if you've fouled up."

"That ain't gonna happen," Muddy snapped. "Too many of you fellas have been doubtin' me. You'll soon see that I done a good job."

"Hope so . . . for your sake, Muddy." The guard stepped back and used his rifle barrel to wave them on through the opening in the cliff. The other outlaw just watched impassively as they rode past.

Denny took in all the details of the narrow canyon leading to the hideout and knew Rogers was doing the same thing. She counted the number of bends and noted that a guard was posted at each one. Getting to the other end of the canyon wouldn't be easy. A small number of defenders could hold off a much larger force.

Smoke had probably been near there and might know another way in, if one existed. Once he knew where the hideout was located, he would be able to come up with an effective battle plan, even if he was still too weak from his injury to take part in the show-down. Denny was certain of that.

Even in the middle of the afternoon, it was shadowy inside the cleft. The only time the sun would shine down into it would be at noon, during certain times of the year. Because of that, the air had a permanent chill to it.

The canyon was narrow enough that only a handful of cattle could be driven abreast through it. That was workable—plenty of cows could be moved through there as long as you didn't mind having a long line of them—but they couldn't be kept penned up in such close quarters. Knowing that, Denny figured the canyon had to lead to a larger area. She wasn't surprised when they rode around another bend and she saw sunlight up ahead. The bright rays were flooding across a wide, cliff-enclosed basin as the group emerged from the passage.

Quite a bit of work had gone into that hideout. There were corrals and an old prospector's cabin that had been fixed up. Tents were pitched, giving it a re-semblance to a military camp. A large fenced-off area where the rustled stock must be kept was empty at the moment, telling her that the gang had already disposed of their last haul.

Men were scattered around the basin, but Muddy ignored them and rode straight toward the cabin with his companions trailing out behind him. A figure appeared in the structure's open doorway.

Denny was a little surprised to see that it was a woman. She had long, straight brown hair and wore a simple dress cut low enough in the front that the upper swells of her breasts were visible. She might be a whore the gang had brought along to service them—or she might be the boss outlaw's wife—or anything in between. She didn't seem surprised to see Muddy and the others, though. She turned away unconcernedly and disappeared into the log cabin.

As Muddy reined in and motioned for the others to do likewise, a man stepped out, buckling on a gun belt. He was fairly well-dressed and neatly groomed, with a close-cropped mustache and sleek dark hair. His hawklike face was intense but bore the stamp of intelligence. He walked with a limp, but it didn't seem to hinder him too much.

Another man, stocky and sandy-haired, came quickly toward the cabin on foot. As he strode up, he spoke first. "Glad to see you're back, Muddy."

"Told you I could do the job, Turk." Muddy gestured toward the others on horseback. "Got nine good men here to throw in with us, the best of the bunch in Elkhorn."

"I'll be the judge of that," the hawk-faced boss snapped.

"Uh . . . sure, Nick," Muddy said hastily. "I never meant otherwise." He paused. "You, uh, want 'em to get down off their horses?"

The boss nodded. Muddy motioned for the group to dismount.

They swung down from their saddles and stood by the horses, holding their reins. Denny's paint packhorse was tied to the buckskin's saddle, so it wasn't going anywhere. She kept her head down, but she was

watching everything closely with eyes shaded by the
brim of her hat. Rogers was behind her somewhere.
She wished she could see him but didn't want to turn
around to look. That might draw more attention to her.

The woman came out of the cabin again, leaned a
shoulder against the doorjamb, and folded her arms
across her ample bosom. She studied the newcomers,
too, and that made Denny uneasy. Would another
woman be more likely to realize that she wasn't a man?

It was too late to do anything about that. More than
ever before, she truly had to play the hand out and see
what happened.

The boss walked toward them and looked them
over. He didn't come up and study each of the newcomers at close range. Denny was grateful for that.

After a moment he said, "My name is Nick Creighton. I reckon you've probably heard of me."

Denny hadn't, not at all, but under the circumstances she sure wasn't going to admit that. Some of
the hardcases nodded slightly to indicate that they
were familiar with Creighton's name. Whether or not
they actually were, was anybody's guess.

"Not far south of here is a ranch called the Sugar-
loaf," Creighton continued. "It belongs to a man named
Smoke Jensen." A cold smile curved the outlaw's lips.
"I reckon you've heard of *him*, too."

One of the men—Calder, Denny thought it was—
glared at Muddy Malone. "You didn't tell us anything
about goin' up against Jensen."

The others looked a little surprised, too, and even
nervous.

"Jensen's laid up," Creighton said. "He's got a bullet
through him from the last time we tangled. I nearly
killed him then, and next time I *will* kill him. Him and
everybody he cares about. And then, once that's
done . . . we're going to loot that ranch. We're going

to drive off every head of stock on it and burn every building to the ground. We're going to soak the Sugarloaf in blood, gentlemen, very soon. When we're done, we'll be rich men, rich enough to go wherever we want without the law touching us. If you want to be part of that, you've come to the right place."

One of the men said, "You sound like you've got a powerful grudge against this fella Jensen, to want to wipe out him and his whole family."

Creighton patted his left thigh. "I got a bullet through here five years ago. It broke the bone and put me in bed for months. The damn doctors told me I'd likely never walk again. But I knew I would, because I had to be on my feet to get my revenge against the man who shot me—Smoke Jensen."

Denny cast her mind back, trying to remember if her father had ever mentioned a man named Nick Creighton around her, or in any of his letters. She drew a complete blank.

She wondered fleetingly if Smoke himself would recognize the name. Or was Creighton just another of the almost anonymous owlhoots Smoke had gunned down over the years?

She got the answer as the man went on. "While I was mending, I didn't think about anything else except killing Jensen. It took a long time before I was ready to face him again. Then I rode to Big Rock, because I knew I'd find him there sooner or later, and bided my time until I saw him on the street one day. I went out to meet him, walked right toward him . . . and then he looked at me and didn't have the slightest idea who I was. He'd forgotten completely about shooting me." Creighton was breathing harder from the depth of the emotions gripping him. "I never hated a man more than I did right then . . . and that was when I decided that just killing Jensen wasn't enough to even the score. I had to make him suffer before he died. Suffer by knowing that he'd lost everything. I'd bleed his ranch dry, then kill him." Creighton closed his eyes, lifted his hand, and rested the fingertips against his forehead for a moment before he looked up again. "No, I never hated anybody like that before . . . until Jensen—or one of his men—killed my little brother. After that, it wasn't enough to just ruin Jensen and then kill him. His family had to pay, too."

The man was loco with hate and the lust for revenge, Denny thought. She could see the insanity in Nick Creighton's eyes. But that didn't mean he was any less dangerous. She felt cold inside, knowing that she was one of the objects of the outlaw's twisted wrath, that her mother and brother were also in danger.

Creighton drew in a deep breath and blew it out. "So that's what you're signing up for. If you've got any qualms about killing, you'd better mount up and ride away now."

"The hell with that," one of the men said. "If any of us tried to leave, your men would put bullets in our backs."

Creighton smiled thinly. "Well, that simplifies your decision, doesn't it?"

The man who had spoken shrugged. "I've never minded spillin' a little blood if the payoff was good enough. Sounds like this one will be."

"It will," Creighton said. "How about the rest of you?"

Nods and mutters of agreement came from the other men.

Denny mumbled, "Damn right," loud enough for Creighton to hear.

The hawk-faced killer stepped past her and said sharply, "What about you? What's your name?"

Denny glanced over her shoulder and saw that Creighton was confronting Brice Rogers.

Rogers didn't hesitate. "They call me Lon Williams. And I'll kill just as many Jensens as you want me to kill . . . boss."

CHAPTER 33

Since it was fairly late in the day when the group arrived at the hideout, Denny didn't expect anything else to happen right away, and she was right.

Turk Sanford, who seemed to be Muddy Malone's friend and Nick Creighton's second in command, told the newcomers they could use the tents that had belonged to the men killed in the previous clashes with the Sugarloaf. "I don't expect any of you are sensitive-natured enough to be bothered by that.

Disdainful grunts were the only answers he got.

Actually, Denny didn't feel that good about bedding down in a dead man's tent, but she wouldn't let any of the outlaws see that, or Brice Rogers, either. The real problem was that the men were expected to share tents, and Denny didn't want to risk one of them finding out that she was really a woman.

She contrived to be next to Rogers as they were unsaddling their mounts and said quietly, "We'd better wind up in the same tent."

"I was thinking the same thing," he said, being equally discreet.

"Is that so?" Denny arched an eyebrow.

"Don't make anything more of it than it is," he

advised. "The two of us sharing a tent shouldn't look too funny, since Muddy believes we used to ride together."

"We haven't acted like we're exactly friends these days, though."

"We were cordial enough during the ride down here, at least most of the time. I reckon he'll accept that we've declared a truce."

Denny nodded. "I hope so. Anyway, we don't have much choice. Anything else is too much of a risk."

"You're right about that," Brice agreed.

Once they had put the horses in the corral, they carried their saddlebags and other gear toward one of the empty tents. No one was close by, but they still didn't say anything that would give away their true identities.

A couple members of the gang were building up a cooking fire in the middle of the basin. The sun dropped below the mountains to the west, and night closed in on the cliff-enclosed hideout. The light from the fire spread out into a wide circle, but it didn't reach to all parts of the basin, Denny saw as she and Rogers emerged from a tent after putting their gear in it.

Since there was still no one near enough to overhear, she risked saying, "We need to start thinking about how we're going to get out of here and bring back a posse."

"We?" Rogers repeated.

"If only one of us goes, that'll make the gang suspicious of the one who stays behind, won't it?"

"If we both disappear, Creighton will *know* that something's up, instead of maybe just suspecting it. He'll be ready for an attack. It's going to be hard enough as it is to get in here and bust up this bunch. Remember, you've got a history of running out on your partners. You go, and it'll look like you just got cold feet and took off again."

"Damn it," Denny said. "Lon Williams has got a history of running out on his friends, too."

Brice grimaced. "I was just trying to come up with a good story for Malone, so I used for background some things I knew really happened, namely what happened to the Bell-Poole gang. It didn't make me look *too* bad."

"I reckon that's a matter of interpretation," Denny said coolly.

"Maybe, but our best shot is still for you to sneak out and for me to stay behind and wait for you to show up with reinforcements. When you do, I can get the drop on as many of them as possible from in here."

"You'd never make it out alive," she said, her voice flat.

"I could sure cut down the odds against the rest of you, though."

"Blast it! You can't just throw away your life like that."

"I have a job to do," Rogers said. "I'll do it the best way I see fit."

Emotions tore at Denny. She didn't want to like Brice Rogers, but she had been around him enough to know that he was a decent man. She didn't like the thought of him dying in the lonely basin, at the hands of no-good outlaws working for a crazy man.

But lawmen always ran the risk of dying, she reminded herself. They knew that, every time they pinned on the star. Rogers, of course, wasn't actually *wearing* his badge, but the concept was the same.

"Let's leave the question of who stays and who goes until later," Denny said. "How does whoever goes . . . get the hell out of here?"

"Now that is a damned good question."

"With half a dozen guards posted along the canyon, it would be mighty hard to slip past all of them."

"A person might be able to climb one of the cliffs. It would have to be at night, though, or else he'd be spotted too easily. And climbing those cliffs in the dark"—Rogers shook his head—"would be pretty dangerous. Even if you got out, you'd be on foot. How far is it to anyplace you could get help?"

"It's twenty miles or more to the ranch headquarters. I might run into some of my father's hands on the way there, but there's no way of knowing where or when."

"Could you find your way in the dark?"

Denny smirked. "What do you think?"

Rogers chuckled. "I'd be surprised if you couldn't. It would be a lot better if you didn't have to make the trip on foot, though. You could be back with a posse by morning."

"More than likely. But there's no need to talk about that, because while that buckskin of mine is a pretty good horse, it can't climb a cliff."

"There might be a way for you to ride out of here after all."

"If there is, I sure don't see it."

"Let me think on it for a while," Rogers said. "We've got a little time."

"Yeah, but we don't know how much. Now that Creighton's bunch is close to full strength, we don't know how long he'll wait before striking at the Sugarloaf again." She nodded toward Muddy Malone and Turk Sanford. "There's something else for us to worry about." She had spotted the two outlaws walking straight toward them.

"What's that?" Rogers asked.

"Looks like we're about to have company. Whatever

those two have in mind, I'm willing to bet it's not anything we're going to like very much."

Rogers tensed, then made a visible effort to relax. He hooked his thumbs in his gun belt and waited for the two outlaws to reach them. Denny tried to seem as casual.

"The boss wants to see the two of you," Turk said as he and Muddy walked up.

"What about?" Rogers asked.

"Nick's not in the habit of explaining everything to me, Williams. He just tells me what he wants done, and I do it. You'd be smart to do likewise."

"Never intended anything else," Rogers said. "I was just curious, that's all."

Turk grunted. "In this bunch, it never pays to be too curious. Nick's got his own way of doing things, and the rest of us have learned to go along with that. He generally steers us right."

"Funny," Denny said, "I thought the reason Muddy went to look for more men to join the gang was that the last two jobs got a heap of you killed."

"That's enough of that kind of talk," Turk snapped. "Now come on, unless you've changed your minds about throwing in with us."

"Nobody said that." Rogers glared briefly at Denny. "That mouth of yours is gonna get you in trouble one of these days, kid."

Denny snarled. "Get your mind off my mouth,"

Muddy leaned his head toward the cabin. "You two quit snipin' at each other and come on. The boss don't like to be kept waitin'."

As the four of them walked toward Creighton's cabin, Denny wondered how much of the friction between her and Rogers was for show and how much was real. They had a tendency to rub each other the wrong way, that was for sure. She knew she was guilty of provoking some of it, even though she didn't always mean to.

The cabin door was closed. Turk thumped a fist against it.

From inside, Nick Creighton called, "Come in."

Turk opened the door and jerked his head to indicate that Denny and Rogers should go in first. She hoped they weren't walking into a trap, but whether they were or not, they couldn't back out.

Creighton was sitting on a bench at a rough-hewn table, rolling a cigarette. A half-full bottle of whiskey and an empty glass were on the table at his elbow. Across the room, his woman sat in a rocking chair held together with strips of dried rawhide. She rocked back and forth gently, just enough for the motion to be visible. A reddish glow came from the embers of a fire in the stone fireplace, but most of the light in the room came from a lantern sitting on the mantel.

He didn't get in any hurry to acknowledge the newcomers or Muddy and Turk, who'd stopped just inside the open door, alert in case of trouble. Creighton finished rolling the quirley, then scratched a kitchen match to life on the bench next to him and set fire to the gasper. Only after he had taken a couple puffs did he look up. "Tell me your names again."

"I'm Lon Williams," Rogers said. "This is Denny West."

"Kid can't speak for himself?"

"That's my name," Denny said. "What I go by now, anyway."

"Not everybody here goes by the name they were born with, that's true," Creighton said. "Happens I do. Muddy tells me the two of you used to be partners."

Rogers nodded. "That's right."

"But there's bad blood between you now."

"I wouldn't go so far as to say that," Denny told the

boss outlaw. "What's past is past. I'm more interested in the money I can make in the future, and I reckon Lon is, too."

"That's right," Rogers said. "Hell, if there's a good payoff involved, I can work with anybody."

Denny grunted and said dryly, "Thanks a heap for putting up with me."

Creighton waved his cigarette. "In this bunch, we all have to trust each other. Everybody's life could depend on it. If either of you is going to have any trouble going along with that—"

"No trouble," Brice interrupted. "You've got my word on it."

"Mine, too," Denny added.

Creighton studied both of them for a moment, then nodded. "I just wanted to talk to you and see for myself if I could believe you. I think I do." Creighton's voice hardened as he added, "Don't give me any reason to think I made a mistake."

"You won't be sorry you let us throw in with you," Denny said.

Now that was an outright lie . . . she hoped. She hoped Nick Creighton would be sorry as hell when he went to prison—or died with Jensen lead in him.

"All right, you can go on about your business," Creighton said with another wave of his hand. He stood up.

Turk and Muddy stepped outside, and Denny and Rogers followed them. Creighton ambled along behind them, still smoking. He paused just outside the doorway, evidently intent on getting a breath of the night air.

The cooking fire was burning pretty big under an iron pot of stew. The glare from it spread to the edge of a clump of scrubby trees about fifty yards from the cabin. Denny happened to be looking in that direction when she saw the firelight reflect redly from something in the trees. She caught her breath as she realized it was a rifle barrel being thrust past one of the trunks.

Pure instinct sent her diving off her feet as flame spouted from the rifle's muzzle.

CHAPTER 34

The dive carried her toward Nick Creighton. Her shoulder crashed heavily against his side. Since he wasn't expecting the collision, he wasn't braced for it. The impact drove him off his feet and sent him sprawling to the ground as the crack of the shot reverberated through the basin. The quirley flew from his fingers and its coal traced an orange arc through the air.

Denny felt something pluck at her vest in midair and knew it was the rifle bullet whipping past her as she fell to the ground beside Creighton.

"Somebody just took a shot at the boss!" Turk yelled as he clawed at the gun on his hip.

Muddy grabbed his iron and both of them opened fire on the trees. Bark flew as slugs pounded into the trunks. Some of the bullets clipped branches and made them fall.

Rogers weaved to the side and threw lead at the trees as well. All over the camp, men were shouting and running toward the cabin to see what was wrong.

Creighton scrambled up. He reached his feet just as Denny made it to her knees. He grabbed her arm and jerked her the rest of the way up. "That shot was meant for me," he said, panting a little. "How'd you know, West?"

"Caught a reflection of the firelight off the rifle barrel." She didn't like being that close to the outlaw. Her skin crawled at his touch, but it was more than that. She worried he would take too good a look at her. Her hat had fallen off when she lunged and knocked him out of the way.

Something suddenly occurred to Creighton and he exclaimed, "Molly!" He let go of Denny's arm and wheeled toward the cabin door.

It was still open. Given the bushwhacker's location and where he had been standing, the bullet that missed him might have gone on into the cabin where the woman was.

Creighton plunged through the doorway, hampered a little by his limp but not letting it slow him down much. Denny grabbed her hat from the ground, jammed it back on her head, and followed him. The shooting had stopped, so she assumed the bushwhacker was no longer a threat.

Molly stood next to the table, breathing hard. At first glance she appeared to be unharmed. She pointed toward the fireplace. A splash of lead on one of the stones showed where the bullet had struck.

Creighton grabbed her arms anyway. "Are you all right?"

"I'm fine, Nick. Just startled, that's all. What happened?"

"Some son of a bitch tried to kill me," Creighton answered grimly. He let go of Molly and swung around toward Denny. His hand hung near the gun on his hip, and she tensed, thinking he might be about to draw on her.

He didn't. "West caught a glimpse of the bushwhacker and knocked me out of the way. Saved my life, more than likely."

Denny lifted her right shoulder in a tiny shrug. "Just did what any of the other fellas would have done, boss."

"Most of them wouldn't have seen the bastard in time to do anything about it. I owe you, West."

Maybe she could turn the unforeseen incident to her advantage, Denny mused.

Before she could think any more about that, Turk appeared in the doorway, gun in hand. "Were you hit, boss?"

"No, I'm fine," Creighton told him. "What about the man who tried to ventilate me?"

"He's shot to pieces," Turk said, "but he's still alive. Probably not for much longer, though."

"Good," Creighton snapped. "I want to talk to him, find out who he is, and why he tried to kill me." He stalked past Turk and out into the night.

Turk followed him outside.

As Denny started to follow them, she caught Molly staring at her. The scrutiny made Denny nervous, and she muttered a curse under her breath as she went out.

A glance back showed Molly standing in the doorway, one hand raised to rest on the jamb as she watched the men.

Several outlaws stood around a figure on the ground. The circle parted to let Creighton through. He stood there looking down at the wounded man for a moment, then knelt beside him.

Denny moved up closer so she could see and hear what was going on. She found herself standing next to Rogers, who gave her a speculative glance.

Somebody brought a torch from the fire and held it up so the flickering light washed over the bushwhacker's face. Denny wasn't surprised to see that he was one of the men Malone had brought to the hideout, the one called Daly.

"Why did you try to kill me?" Creighton demanded. "I never even saw you until—wait a minute. I *do* know you, don't I?"

A worm of blood had crawled down from the corner of Daly's mouth across his chin. His shirtfront was black in the torchlight, soaked with more blood. He coughed and tried to focus his eyes on Creighton.

"D-damn right . . . you know me," Daly gasped. "I rode with you . . . five years ago . . . Went by . . . Al F-Fitzgerald then. That was . . . my real name."

"I remember you now," Creighton said, nodding.

"Didn't know . . . when I rode down here . . . from Elkhorn . . . that you were the boss of . . . this bunch. That fella Malone . . . he never told us . . . your name."

"What the hell do you have against me?" Creighton said. "I never did anything to you."

"There was a girl . . . You took her . . . away from me . . . Always swore . . . I'd get even—"

The words stopped and the man's breath came out of him in a rattling sigh. He was gone.

"The stupid son of a bitch," Creighton said. "He tried to kill me because of a grudge over a woman? Some saloon slut?"

Turk Sanford said, "You never know what's gonna be important to some fellas, boss. More important than anything else."

Creighton jerked a hand angrily. "But he never would've gotten out of here alive. Even if he'd killed me, he would have wound up just like he is now, shot full of holes."

"Maybe that didn't matter to him. Maybe it would have been worth it."

Creighton uncoiled from his kneeling position and turned away from the dead man. His eyes sought somebody else, and he found his quarry as Muddy

Malone tried to draw back unobtrusively behind some of the other outlaws.

"Malone!" Creighton shouted. He yanked his gun from its holster.

The men standing between him and Muddy scrambled out of the line of fire. "Malone, you brought this . . . this murderous viper into our camp!"

"I didn't know, boss!" Muddy said as he continued to back away. He held up his hands as if they would stop a bullet. "How could I have known? I wasn't ridin' with you back then, and Daly . . . Fitzgerald . . . whatever the hell his name is! . . . never said nothin' about havin' a grudge against you. I didn't tell any of those new fellas your name because that's the way you said you wanted it!"

"Stop your damn babbling." Creighton's voice was thin and hard with menace. "I ought to put a bullet in you." He inclined his head toward Denny. "If it weren't for West here, I'd be dead now and everything would be ruined."

Turk said carefully, "Boss, I don't see any way Muddy could've known that loco son of a bitch had it in for you. If he had, he never would've brought him here. None of us would have, in those circumstances."

Creighton whipped around, his gun swinging in front of him.

Men drew back from its threat.

"What about the rest of you?" he demanded. "Anybody else here have a grudge against me? Anybody want to kill me so bad you're willing to pay for it with your life?" He lowered the gun and stuck it back in its holster. "Well, go ahead, damn you! Go ahead and take your revenge. See what it gets you!"

Coming so close to death had made Creighton almost hysterical, Denny thought.

"Nobody wants to do that, boss," Turk said. "We're all on your side."

Denny was careful not to look at Rogers. *She* wanted Nick Creighton dead. He was responsible for the deaths of several Sugarloaf riders, as well as what had happened to Smoke. She supposed she would be able to accept it if he was locked up for the rest of his life, but she would much prefer to see him blown to hell or strung up at the end of a hang rope.

But she didn't let any of that show on her face. She kept her features carefully impassive.

For a long, awkward moment, nobody said anything. The only sounds were the uncomfortable shifting of a few feet as the men stood there under Creighton's baleful scrutiny.

Then Muddy swallowed hard. "You . . . you're not gonna kill me, boss?"

Turk groaned quietly as if he wished his friend had just kept his big mouth shut.

"Kill you, Muddy?" Creighton said. "No . . . No, I reckon I won't do that. You're too stupid to know any better." He looked at Turk. "I want all those other new men rounded up and brought to my cabin later. I'm going to talk to all of them . . . except for West and Williams. I know they're all right."

Denny knew she ought to feel relieved at that vote of confidence, but somehow she didn't, not completely.

On the other hand, she *had* saved Creighton's life . . . the life of the man she had set out to kill, or at least make sure he was stopped from carrying out his vengeance on her father. She hadn't even hesitated before she knocked him out of the way of that bushwhacker's bullet.

Sometimes acting on instinct could be damned inconvenient, she thought.

Creighton owed her, and he seemed like he intended to pay that debt. If nothing else, he trusted her.

Maybe that was a good thing and maybe it wasn't.

Creighton turned to her. "West, come on back to

the cabin with me. You'll eat supper tonight with me and Molly."

Denny nodded. "Sure, boss. I'm obliged to you."

What else could she say?

He clapped a hand on her shoulder. "No, I'm the one who's obliged to you. Don't get any ideas, though. I'm still the boss here, and you're still taking orders from me."

"Wouldn't have it any other way, boss."

"Call me Nick."

That was one of the last things Denny wanted to do, but she forced herself to smile and nod. "Sure, Nick."

As they started walking toward the cabin, she saw the worried look on Rogers's face as they went past and hoped he wouldn't be too obviously concerned about her.

Creighton ordered over his shoulder, "Do something with that carcass. Take it out through the canyon and throw it in a ravine somewhere. I don't want it drawing scavengers here."

They continued on their way, Creighton limping, Denny holding her long-legged strides in check so she wouldn't get in front of him. Up ahead was the cabin, with Molly still standing in the doorway watching them, the intensity of her gaze making icy fingers tickle their way up and down Denny's backbone.

CHAPTER 35

"Want a drink?" Creighton asked Denny once they were in the cabin.

"Sure, boss," she said.

"Molly, fetch us another glass. West, take your hat off and relax."

Relaxing was just about the last thing she was capable of doing, Denny thought, but she had to try. She had to make Creighton believe she was relaxed, anyway. She took her hat off and hung it on the back of a chair.

Molly brought her a glass with a couple inches of whiskey in it and smiled slightly as she held out the glass. "Here you go. Denny, isn't it?"

"That's right." Wondering what was behind the smile, Denny took the glass. She found Molly's expression unnerving. "Thanks."

Creighton filled his glass and lifted it. "Here's to you, West."

"And to you, boss." Denny glanced at Molly. "And your lady."

"I need to tend to the stew," Molly murmured. She turned away as Denny and Creighton drank. The outlaw threw down his whiskey, but Denny knew she would choke and start coughing if she tried to do that.

She pretended to take a healthy swallow but let only a little of the fiery liquor down her throat.

"Sit down," Creighton told her, gesturing toward one of the empty chairs at the table. He resumed the seat he'd had earlier. "Tell me about Williams."

She pulled out a chair and sat. "Lon? Told you earlier, boss, everything's fine between him and me. We figured we'd both come out ahead if we just let bygones be bygones."

"That's smart. Most hombres in our line of work really aren't that smart, though. Are you sure he's not just waiting for a chance to double-cross you?"

Denny laughed. "If you asked him, he'd probably say he was worried about me doin' the same thing." She shook her head. "No, Nick, I've made my peace with Lon. As far as I'm concerned, you don't have to worry about us."

"Well, that's good to hear," Creighton said, nodding. He poured more whiskey into the glass, which almost emptied the bottle. He held it up, cocked an inquiring eyebrow. Denny shook her head. Creighton thumped the bottle back on the table.

Molly brought over bowls of beef stew with wild onions and beans in it, ladled from a pot on the stove, along with chunks of bread torn from a fresh-baked loaf. She filled cups of coffee and set them in front of Denny and Creighton as well, then got her own food. As she sat down at the table, she asked, "Where are you from, Denny?"

"I was brought up in Missouri," Denny said, remembering her father's family history. She believed she would be safe if she stuck to that, less likely to get mixed up and caught in an inconsistency. "My ma and pa had a farm in the Ozarks." It was actually her grandparents who'd had that farm, she recalled from Smoke's stories.

"In the mountains? That's not very good land for farming, is it?"

"It's sure not. Reckon that's why we were always dirt poor."

She had never been poor in her life, Denny realized. By the time she and Louis were born, the Sugarloaf was a successful ranch, and Smoke had his gold claim in reserve, too. She had never known anything but luxury and comfort. The past week and a half had been the roughest she'd ever had it and yet she hadn't actually lived the sort of hardscrabble existence her father and so many other pioneers had. The whole experience was going to be good for her . . .

If she made it out the other side alive.

Creighton said, "You probably left the farm and struck out on your own as soon as you were old enough. That's what I would have done."

"Yep, just about," Denny agreed.

That enigmatic smile appeared on Molly's face again. "That probably wasn't all that long ago. How old *are* you, Denny?"

"I'm twenty-one. Been on my own six years."

"You don't really look that old."

Denny shrugged. "Clean livin', I guess."

That brought a laugh from Creighton, then he said, "Enough talk. Dig in."

They ate in silence, washing down the stew with sips of hot, strong coffee. Denny continued trying to appear relaxed, but she was sure going to be happy when the meal was over and she could get out of there.

Finally, she mopped the last of the juice from the bowl with the final bite of bread and popped it into her mouth.

Creighton said, "There's plenty more if you want it."

"I appreciate that, boss, but I reckon I'm done."

Denny drank the last of the coffee in her cup. "I thank you for the food."

Creighton nodded toward Molly. "She's the one who cooked it."

Denny summoned up a smile and told the woman, "Thank you, ma'am."

"Ma'am," Molly repeated with a quiet laugh. "Not many have called me that. I'm not exactly a fine lady."

"You, uh, you are as far as I'm concerned, ma'am."

"Well, it's nice of you to say so. Sure you don't want anything else?"

"I'm sure. Thanks anyway." Denny grinned. "Reckon the other fellas will already be jealous of me, gettin' special treatment like this."

"Don't worry about that," Creighton said. "Nobody's going to give you any trouble."

"Not if they know what's good for 'em," Denny said.

That brought another laugh from Creighton.

She scraped her chair back and stood up. It felt good to settle her hat back on her head. Her face had been altogether too much out in the open without it. She hoped the grime worn into her skin kept her lack of beard stubble from being too obvious.

She nodded good night and headed for the door. A soft footstep behind her made her look over her shoulder. Her heart sank as she saw that Molly was following her. Denny kept going, hoping Molly would stay in the cabin.

She didn't. She stepped out of the cabin behind Denny and said, "Wait a minute."

Denny stopped and half-turned. "Ma'am?"

Molly eased the door closed. "You can drop the act. I know you're a girl."

Denny caught her breath. Instinctively, her hand moved closer to her gun.

"Forget that," Molly went on. "All I have to do is yell

and you'll be dead in ten seconds. Anyway, I don't mean you any harm. Do you really think you're any sort of threat to me? A skinny little thing like you?"

"Ma'am, I don't know what the hell you're talkin' about—" Denny began.

"Please. Men never notice anything if it doesn't have to do with horses or cattle or guns. If there hadn't been another woman here, you likely would have gotten away with it. And since I don't have any interest in exposing the truth, maybe you *have* gotten away with it."

Denny should have accepted Molly's attitude as a good sign, but she couldn't bring herself to believe it was true. On the other hand, if Molly wanted to ruin her masquerade, she could have already done it and easily.

"I suppose Lon Williams must know," Molly went on. "You didn't show any qualms about sharing a tent with him. The two of you are lovers, aren't you?"

Denny stiffened. "I don't see as how that's any of your business."

"You're lying to Nick about who you really are," Molly snapped. "That makes whatever you do my business." She waved a hand. "But I don't care what you and Williams do as long as you're not threatening Nick. I figure you've got your own reasons for dressing like a man and packing a gun. Back in the old days, Calamity Jane used to do the same thing. I've heard she even passed as a man some of the time while she was scouting for the army. Maybe you'd rather *be* a man. I've heard of such things."

The only reason Denny had for posing as a man was so she could find the son of a bitch who wanted to hurt her father. She had done that. Once she had seen that justice was done, she had no desire to conceal her true identity. She figured she could wear pants and ride horses and work cattle and still be a woman.

None of that was important at the moment, though. She couldn't afford to waste time worrying about anything beyond the here and now.

"I'm not here to cause trouble for Nick or anybody else," she lied. "If I was, I would've let that fella shoot him a while ago instead of knocking him out of the way."

She wished she had thought quickly enough to let Daly kill Nick Creighton. Without Creighton's fanatical grudge against Smoke Jensen, the gang might well have broken up and drifted apart. The threat to the Sugarloaf would be over.

As it was, Denny's instincts had betrayed her and she was still in deadly danger as long as she was among the outlaws, as was Brice Rogers.

"You saved his life, all right," Molly said, nodding slowly. "I took that into account when I was deciding whether or not to tell him the truth about you. That's a big reason why I decided to let you keep on playing whatever game it is you're playing. But I warn you." She leaned closer to Denny. "If you do anything to hurt Nick . . . if I even start to suspect I've made a mistake by trusting you . . . I'll tell him everything I know, and you and Williams will be in big trouble."

"You don't have to worry about us," Denny said.

"I'd better not." Molly turned and went back to the cabin.

Denny watched her go, then took a deep breath and drifted on toward the tent she was sharing with Rogers.

So Molly believed the two of them were lovers. Denny hadn't done anything to convey that impression, at least as far as she could remember. She certainly hadn't tried to make anybody think that, least of all Rogers himself. He was already insufferable enough most of the time without him feeling like she had fallen for him. That wasn't going to happen.

A little annoyed at wasting time and energy even thinking about romance, she pushed that subject away in her mind. A much more pressing problem was the question of how one of them was going to get out of there and bring back reinforcements to wipe out the gang of outlaws.

The light from the fire allowed her to make her way across the basin. As she approached the tent, she spotted Rogers sitting on a log nearby.

He saw her, too, and got to his feet. "I was getting a little worried about you," he said quietly. "You were in that cabin a long time. And then when you came out, Creighton's woman followed you—"

"She knows who I am," Denny said.

Rogers went stiff as a board and swung his hand closer to his gun, ready to fight.

"I'm sorry. I didn't mean she knows I'm Smoke Jensen's daughter. But she knows I'm a woman. With my hat off, in good light, I couldn't fool another female."

"I told you it was a loco idea," he muttered.

"Creighton doesn't know," Denny said sharply. "Neither do any of the others."

"You can't be sure about that."

"Sure enough. We can go on with our plan. Or at least we could if we actually *had* a plan."

"We do," Rogers said. "You're getting out of here tonight and heading for the Sugarloaf. We can't trust Creighton's woman, and we can't afford to wait."

"We've been through that," Denny said. "If I climb out over the cliffs, I'll be on foot. No telling how long it'll take me to bring back help. Anyway, when Creighton realizes I'm gone, he's liable to send men after me, and they'll stand a good chance of hunting me down before I'm able to get far enough away."

"Not if you're on horseback. In a little while, when things start to quiet down for the night, you're going to drift over there toward the corral. Can you ride bareback?"

"Damn right I can."

"Good. When the time comes, you jump on the buckskin and get out of here. When you do, stampede the other horses if you can."

"What about the guards in the canyon?"

"They'll be in here along with everybody else. Trust me, I'm going to create enough of a distraction that the whole gang will come to see what's going on, and nobody will be paying any attention to you."

"How the hell—"

"Don't worry about that. Just leave it to me."

Without thinking about what she was doing, she reached out and took hold of his arm. "Damn it, Brice, you're going to get yourself killed, aren't you?"

"No, I plan to live through this just as much as you do, Denny. They're not going to be paying any attention to me, either. When I make my move . . . trust me, all hell's going to break loose."

CHAPTER 36

They went back to the tent they were sharing, where she had to badger him for quite a while before he finally gave in and told her his plan.

"I was looking around earlier and found a tent nobody was using, set off by itself a little ways," he said, keeping his voice so quiet it couldn't be heard outside the darkened tent. "When I looked inside, I saw that it's being used for storage. There are some crates of supplies in there, along with a case of dynamite. I took half a dozen sticks from it."

Denny's eyes widened in the shadows. "Dynamite!" she whispered. "You've got it with you now?"

"Yeah, along with some fuse and blasting caps."

"Here in the tent?"

"That's right."

"You loco fool! You're going to blow us to kingdom come!"

"No, I'm not. Unless it's old and has been sitting around for a while, dynamite is stable enough as long as you know how to handle it."

"How do you know how long that's been sitting around?" she wanted to know.

"I can tell by the feel of it, how greasy it is. I've

been around the stuff before. I worked on a railroad construction crew for a while when I was younger. They had to blow out some cuts through hills and ridges."

"Did *you* set off any explosions?" Denny said.

"Well . . . no. But I saw it done plenty of times."

"Yeah, you're gonna blow us up," she said bleakly.

"You just let me worry about that."

She grunted. "That's easy for you to say."

"Listen to me, all right? You wanted to know what I'm planning."

Denny didn't respond for a moment. Then she said grudgingly, "Go ahead."

"In a little while, once they're all sound asleep, I'll sneak over to the other side of the basin, as far away from the horses as I can. I'll set off the blast, and everybody will go running over there. I'm betting the guards in the canyon will abandon their posts, too, because it'll sound like the army is attacking. If any of them stay behind, you'll have to get past them, but I don't think that's going to happen."

"Where do you plan on being when that dynamite goes off?"

"Don't worry," he told her. "I brought plenty of fuse with me. I can get far enough away to be safe from the blast and then light it."

"You can't tell for sure how far it might fling some rocks."

"I'll take that chance. You'll be running some risks, too. We can't avoid them completely."

"No, I reckon not," Denny said. "I suppose you'll just join the crowd after the explosion and act like you don't know what's going on any more than they do."

"That's right. If I'm slick enough, nobody will know I had anything to do with what happened."

Denny thought it all over, then admitted, "It might

work. Creighton will know something's going on, and when he realizes I'm gone, he'll probably blame it on me. But you and I are supposed to be partners, so he may hold you responsible, too."

Rogers chuckled. "Not once I get through ranting about what a no-good, double-crossing polecat you are."

"You'd better be convincing."

"I think I can do that."

Denny glared in his direction in the darkness, but then she had to laugh softly, too. "When you first told me you had some dynamite—once I stopped thinking about how crazy you are—I wondered why we didn't just toss it in the cabin and blow Creighton to hell. But then I realized—"

"That would be cold-blooded murder," Rogers said sternly. "Double murder, because that woman Molly would be in there, too."

"Yeah, yeah, I reckon. I just said I thought about it. I didn't say we really ought to do it."

"What I'm wondering now is if you wouldn't have time to slap a saddle on that buckskin of yours. That would make it easier for you to charge out of here."

"With so much commotion on the other side of the basin, I think I'd have time to saddle up."

"You can give it a try," Rogers said. "Just don't take too long. If it looks like you might get caught, get on out of here, even if you have to do it bareback."

"You sound like you're actually worried about me," Denny said with a trace of amusement in her voice.

"I am."

Something about the way *his* voice sounded made her reach out in the darkness. Her fingers touched his shoulder and she tightened her hand on it for a couple seconds. "Don't blow yourself to hell when you're messing with that dynamite."

"I'll do my best not to," he promised.

Time dragged maddeningly as they waited for the camp to settle down for the night. Rogers stuck his head out of the tent now and then to check on the outlaws.

Finally he said, "I don't see lights anywhere, and the cooking fire has burned down to embers. I think everybody has turned in for the night."

"Maybe we should give it a few more minutes, just to be sure," Denny suggested. She didn't like to admit it, even to herself, she was scared. However, that wouldn't stop her from doing what needed to be done. She was confident of that.

When their nerves were stretched too tight to wait anymore, Rogers said, "All right, let's go. I'll give you ten minutes to get to the horses. Then I'll light the fuse."

"Be careful."

"I intend to be. I—"

Denny leaned closer and planted an awkward kiss on his mouth, surprising both of them. She drew back quickly. "For luck. That's all. Don't get any ideas."

"I, uh . . . I reckon I won't. And good luck to you, too." With that he was gone, slipping away into the shadows.

Denny stayed where she was, heart pounding heavily, but only for a couple seconds. She knew she couldn't afford to waste any of the time he had given her.

Despite what he had told Denny, having a bundle of six dynamite sticks under his shirt was more than a mite unnerving, Rogers thought as he made his way across the basin toward the far side. Sure, there was no real reason for the paper-wrapped sticks to explode on their own. They needed some outside force, like the blasting caps, to detonate them. But the thought of what would

be left of him if they *did* happen to go off—not a hell
of a lot—was enough to make anybody tense.

All the more reason to get this over with, he told
himself. He was counting off the seconds in his head,
and as soon as he had allowed enough time for Denny
to get her horse saddled, he would provide the distraction she needed to get out of there. A very loud,
violent distraction.

Denny shoved everything out of her mind except
the need to escape from the outlaw hideout and return
with help from the Sugarloaf. She moved quickly and
silently through the night toward the corral. No one
else was moving around the camp, as far as she could
tell. Even though everything seemed to be all right,
her pulse boomed like thunder inside her head as
she approached the enclosure. The horses inside the
corral shifted around slightly but didn't spook.

She had to take it easy, Denny told herself. Too
much of a commotion among the animals would
surely draw attention.

Speaking of distractions, Rogers thought . . . he
could still taste the kiss she had given him.

He had never expected that from her. Sure, they
had been working together and getting along all right.
And even though he thought she was headstrong and
reckless to the point of being loco at times, he couldn't
help but admire her courage and determination. It
took one woman in a million to attempt the audacious
course Denny Jensen was following. Not only attempt
it, but so far succeed in it.

And there was no doubt she was a beautiful woman,

even with most of her hair hacked off and dirt smeared on her face . . .

Denny spotted the saddles sitting on logs dragged up near the corral, and the rest of the tack hanging from pegs driven into tree trunks. She found the buckskin's bridle, then slipped between the poles into the corral. Enough starlight filtered into the basin for her to spot the buckskin—lighter in color—among the other horses. She made soft, calming sounds as she moved up next to the horse and got the harness on it.

Leading the buckskin, she lifted the rawhide strap holding the gate closed and swung it back. She took the buckskin out and pulled the gate to but didn't fasten it. She wanted to be able to open it in a hurry when the time came. She thought the explosion would stampede the horses, but if it didn't, she would ride among them, swat a few rumps with her hat, and start them running that way.

With quick, efficient motions, Denny got her saddle on the horse. She didn't need much light for that. It was all automatic, and thankfully, she and the buckskin had grown accustomed to each other enough that the horse cooperated.

Reaching the far wall of the basin banished thoughts of Denny from Rogers's head for the moment . . . except for the idea of helping her escape. He took the bundle of dynamite from under his shirt and pressed blasting caps onto two of the sticks. Having already cut a couple lengths of fuse, he attached one to each of the caps, then twisted them together to make a single strand, the way he had seen men working for the railroad do when they were getting ready to blast out a cut.

Burning at about a foot a minute, Rogers's four-foot-long fuse would give him that much time to put some distance between himself and the blast. He thought that would be enough. He wedged the dynamite into a dark crack in the rock wall, then held the fuse in his left hand while he used his right to fish for a lucifer in his shirt pocket.

Before he could find one, a voice behind him asked sharply, "What the hell are you doin' there?"

Ready to go, Denny thought as she pulled the last cinch tight. All she was waiting for was the dynamite blast Rogers was supposed to set off. She'd been trying to keep rough track of the time in her head and thought the blast ought to be happening any moment.

Brice stiffened. His first instinct was to reach for his gun, whirl around, and open fire. But that could rouse the whole camp and ruin everything. It might lead to Denny being caught, and he couldn't stand that. He controlled the impulse, let the fuse fall quietly from his hand, and turned slowly and carefully. He thought he recognized the voice, so he said, "Muddy, is that you?"

"Yeah," the outlaw replied. "Lon? What in blazes? What are you doin' over here?"

"I could ask the same thing of you."

Muddy grunted. "Followin' you, that's what I'm doin'. I had to take a leak, and while I was doin' it, I spotted somebody skulkin' outta camp and headin' in this direction."

Brice thought rapidly, casting about in his mind for

a plausible explanation. "So did I! While you were following me, I was following whoever it was sneaking around the camp."

"Dang," Muddy breathed. "Did you get a good look at him?"

"No, I never did. He got over here in the shadows next to the cliff and I lost him."

Starlight winked on the barrel of the gun Muddy lifted. For a second Brice thought the man was about to shoot him.

Then Muddy said, "So he could still be lurkin' somewhere close by. Might even be fixin' to bushwhack us."

"He could be." Rogers used Muddy's reaction as an excuse to draw his gun and step closer to the outlaw "We oughta get out of here."

He should have lit that fuse by now, Rogers thought. Denny probably had her horse saddled and was waiting for him. Every second that ticked by increased the chances she would be discovered. He couldn't afford to wait. He had to get close enough to strike without warning. A swift blow from the gun in his hand, and Muddy would slump to the ground, out cold.

"What's that?" Muddy said.

"Where?"

"Stickin' out of that hole in the rock." Muddy started to step past Rogers, closer to the cliff. "Son of a bitch! It looks like dynamite—"

Rogers struck, slashing at Muddy's head with the revolver.

Something warned the man and he twisted aside just enough to avoid the full force of the blow. The gun skidded down the side of his head, ripping at his ear, and thudded against his shoulder.

Muddy managed to hang on to his gun and triggered it as Rogers tried to hit him again.

The bullet didn't hit him, but the shot was so close that the noise slammed against Rogers's ears and deafened him. Burning flecks of powder stung his face. He reeled back and tried to bring his own gun to bear, then held off on the trigger as he suddenly realized Muddy was right in front of the dynamite. If he fired and missed . . . and the slug struck the stuff . . . it could set off an explosion that would blast them both to bits.

Rogers lunged at the outlaw, hoping to get close enough to knock his gun aside and batter him into unconsciousness. Another shot slammed out and Rogers felt a terrific blow against his body. He wasn't sure where he was hit, but the impact drove him backwards. He couldn't get his breath, couldn't force his muscles to work, though he felt Muddy kick the gun out of his hand.

"You son of a bitch!" Muddy said as he bent over Rogers. "What the hell are you doin', tryin' to blow us all up?" His free hand fumbled at Brice's midsection. "Well, you're gut shot now, you bastard. You're the one who's gonna die—What the hell!"

Rogers heard the startled exclamation. He felt sick and all the air had been knocked out of his lungs, but there wasn't any real pain. Maybe he was just numb to it.

"What's this?" Muddy said as he straightened. He lifted his hand and stared as the starlight revealed what he clutched.

Rogers saw it, too. Muddy had his badge.

"A lawman!" Muddy howled. If the shots weren't enough to bring the rest of the camp on the run, that strident cry would be.

CHAPTER 37

Denny sprang up into the saddle as soon as she heard the shots. She leaned over and jerked the gate open. The dynamite could still go off, but even if it didn't, stampeding the gang's horses was bound to help her chances of getting away. She drove the buckskin among the other mounts and slapped left and right at them with her hat. She gave a low cry that spooked them even more. All it took was one horse bolting through the open gate, and then the rest followed, running wildly through the darkness.

She wheeled the buckskin and raced out of the corral after them. The shots had come from the far side of the basin, half a mile away. She didn't know what had happened, but it couldn't be good.

Brice Rogers might be dead now, drilled by those two slugs. The thought made a chill go through her, followed by a burst of white-hot rage.

If those bastards had killed him, they would be sorry. It might be completely illogical for her to think such a thing, one lone young woman against two dozen hardened killers, but she swore it anyway.

Although the quickest way to reach the area where the shots had sounded was to gallop straight through the outlaw camp, she didn't go that way, figuring the men might try to stop her, might suspect a fast-moving rider was trouble.

She swung the buckskin wide around the cluster of tents and the cabin. Faint shouts drifted through the night, barely heard over the horse's drumming hoof-beats. Denny knew the outlaws would be scrambling out of their tents, guns ready, looking for something to shoot. Although well out of handgun range, she was a little surprised they didn't fire blindly at her as she rode around the camp.

Angling back in the direction of the shots, she urged the buckskin on. A few moments later, she heard shouts coming from up ahead.

A man bellowed, "Boys, get over here! I caught a damn lawman!"

Denny's heart sank as she recognized Muddy Malone's voice, and the outlaw's words made it even worse. He somehow knew Rogers was a deputy U.S. marshal. Not only was the plan to set off the explosion likely ruined, but his true identity had been exposed, dooming him.

Unless somehow she could get both of them out of there, Denny thought. She poured on the speed and came within sight of two figures standing up ahead, one with a gun thrust out while the other was bent over in apparent pain.

Brice is hurt! That thought shot through her as she closed in, not even realizing she'd begun to think of him on a first-name basis.

She drew the Colt and leveled it as she hauled the buckskin to a stop.

Muddy didn't recognize her at first. He laughed. "Look here! I got me a law dog! It's that fella Williams—" He howled a curse as he realized who she was and tried to jerk his gun toward her.

Denny fired first, but Malone was on the move and

her slug just nicked his gun arm, but it was enough to throw off his aim. She heard the bullet whine past her head.

The next instant Rogers threw himself forward and crashed into the outlaw, swinging short, powerful punches that drove Malone back against the cliff. His knees buckled as his head banged against the rock.

Rogers caught him, wrenched the gun out of his hand, and then let him fall to the ground, stunned.

Denny pouched her iron, held out her hand, and called, "Brice, come on!"

A quick step took him within reach of her. He clasped her wrist and swung up behind her. "You were supposed to get out of here!"

"Not without you," she said. "We'll make a run for it. I scattered the other horses, so we've got a chance."

But maybe not much of one, she thought grimly as she heeled the buckskin into a run away from the cliff. All it would take was for a few outlaws to catch horses and head them off. Even if they reached the canyon leading out of there, the guards would be on the alert and would try to stop them. They would have to shoot their way out . . . and the odds of that weren't good at all.

Shots boomed behind them.

Muddy Malone must have had another gun stashed somewhere on him, Denny thought, and he had regained his senses before they were out of range. She felt Brice twist around behind her on the buckskin's back as he kept one arm around her waist to hang on. The revolver he had taken away from Malone roared a couple times as he returned the fire.

Then the whole world blew up.

That's what it sounded and felt like, anyway. The explosion pounded against Denny's ears like giant fists. The ground jumped under the buckskin's flashing hooves. The horse stumbled and started to go down as a wave of heat and flying debris washed over them. Denny hauled up hard on the reins and kept the buckskin plunging forward. Gradually the horse regained its stride.

"Brice!" Denny called. "Are you all right?"

"Yeah," he said, his mouth close to her ear as he leaned forward. "Feel like I've been in a fight from the pounding those flying rocks gave me, but I don't think anything's broken. I'll be one big bruise tomorrow, though . . . if I live that long!"

"What happened?"

"One of those shots I fired must've hit the dynamite. Pure luck, but I'll take it!"

"Malone?"

"He's not there anymore."

Denny shuddered in horror. Malone had been so close to the blast it must have engulfed him and blown him into a million little pieces.

She hoped the explosion had disoriented the rest of the gang. That would give her and Rogers the slimmest of chances to get away. She pointed the buckskin toward the canyon mouth.

Men ran in front of them, yelling questions. "Back there!" Rogers shouted at them as he waved an arm toward the site of the explosion. "I think it's the army! Gotta find the boss!"

That was actually plausible, Denny thought as she leaned forward over the buckskin's neck. The little knot of outlaws parted to let her and Brice through. She barely slowed down as she galloped past them.

That might not work a second time . . . but it had gotten them that much closer to the canyon.

Wild, riderless horses tore past. Some of the outlaws were trying to catch them, without much success. The canyon mouth was only a couple hundred yards away.

"Stop those two, whoever they are!" The ringing command came from Nick Creighton. He ran awkwardly toward them, guns blazing in both hands.

Bullets whipped past Denny's head, but she didn't slow down. Speed was the best weapon they had.

Rogers returned Creighton's fire as they flashed past the gang leader, but Denny couldn't tell if any of the shots found their target.

Then the buckskin's hoofbeats echoed back from the towering stone walls as they galloped into the narrow canyon.

"When we get to the first bend, don't slow down any more than you have to," Rogers told her. "The guard won't shoot when he doesn't know what's going on."

Denny hoped he was right about that.

As they pounded up to the bend, he shouted, "The army's attacking! Light the signal fire and then go help the boss!"

The man didn't try to shoot them, and then a second later the signal fire went up with a *whoosh!*

Denny glanced back, saw it blazing brightly, and said, "It worked!"

"That explosion was enough to throw everybody for a loop, but some of them may have heard Malone yelling that he'd trapped a lawman. It won't take long for them to figure out we're gone and decide that one of us is the star packer. They'll be coming after us as soon as they round up some of the horses."

Denny didn't doubt that for a second.

Seeing the innermost signal fire lit, the guard at the next bend set his pile of wood ablaze, as well. The explosion must have left the man so shaken he didn't think about the fact that the fires were supposed to be lit *in the other direction* in case of trouble. The uproar had everybody spooked and confused.

Rogers waved at the second guard and told him to

go help Creighton, too. The buckskin lunged around the bend and left the signal fire behind.

That scenario repeated itself at the next bend, and then they had only to get past the sentries at the canyon mouth. These two men were more cautious than the others, however. One of them yelled, "Hold it!" When Denny didn't rein in the horse, the guards began blazing away with their rifles.

Bad light and the horse's blinding speed saved the two fugitives. Denny didn't know how close the guards' lead came to them, but neither she nor Rogers nor the horse were hit. Six-guns erupted with muzzle flame as they returned the fire and sent the guards leaping back into the shelter of the boulders.

Then, just like that, they were out of the canyon. Denny jerked the buckskin back and forth in a zigzag course across the open ground in front of the entrance. The guards fired after them, but the buckskin never broke stride.

They reached the gully and dropped down into it, safe for the moment from any more flying bullets.

"I can't believe we got out of there!" Denny cried exultantly.

"They'll be after us," Rogers warned. "We know where the hideout is, so Creighton can't afford to let us get away."

Denny's brief sense of triumph vanished. "We've forced his hand. If he's ever going to strike at the Sugarloaf and get his revenge on my father, it's got to be now! If he's going to have a chance to win, he's got to hit the ranch before we can warn everyone."

"You're right. As soon as he can get all his men together, he'll come boiling out of there and head straight for your father's place. That means we have to get there first and let them know what's coming."

He was right, Denny knew. They were in a race and

would be at a disadvantage because the buckskin was carrying double. But even so, it was a race they had to win.

The stakes might well be life and death for everyone on the Sugarloaf.

CHAPTER 38

Nick Creighton had wrenched his leg when he dived aside from Lon Williams's bullets, which made his limp even worse as he stalked around shouting orders at his men. Fury filled every bit of his being. One of the men had said he heard someone shouting about capturing a lawman. That had to be Williams—the traitor—Creighton thought, which meant the other person on horseback with the son of a bitch was probably Denny West, more than likely also a lawman.

Although if that was true, why had West saved his life? He could ask West that question once the two fugitives were caught, Creighton told himself. He would torture the answers out of them . . . assuming they weren't killed before then. If that was the way it turned out, Creighton supposed he could live with it. He had more important things to worry about.

Turk Sanford trotted up to him and reported, "I can't find Muddy, boss."

"Malone? He should be around somewhere."

"He's not." Turk shook his head. "Everybody else is accounted for except him, Williams, and West. Some of the boys caught sight of those two riding double on their way out of here. But nobody's seen Muddy. I'm thinkin'"—he swallowed hard—"maybe he got blown up in that explosion."

Creighton didn't give a damn one way or the other, except that losing Malone meant he had one less gun on his side. But he remembered that the two had been friends, so he said, "I'm sorry, Turk. That's one more score to settle with those bastards. Luckily, I reckon we can find them where we're going as soon as all the horses are rounded up."

Turk was pretty sharp for a gunman. "We're gonna hit the Sugarloaf tonight?"

"As hard and fast as we can," Creighton said. "That's where Williams and West are headed. I'm sure of it. It's the closest place they can get any help. Now that we're back up to full strength, it's time we wiped out Jensen."

"Not quite full strength," Turk muttered.

Creighton knew he was talking about Muddy Malone. "Get the men mounted and ready to ride. We're going after those two. We'll try to catch them before they get to the Sugarloaf. I don't want them warning Jensen."

As Turk hurried off to see to that, Creighton started reloading his guns.

"Nick," Molly said as she came up behind him. "Are you all right?"

"I'm not hurt," he told her as he continued to reload. "I just don't like being betrayed. It really stings about West, after what he did earlier this evening—"

"West is a woman."

Creighton frowned as he looked around at her. "What?"

"Denny West is a woman," Molly repeated. "Her

hair's cut off short and I'd be willing to bet her breasts are bound, but she's as female as I am."

"You're loco!"

Molly shook her head. "I've never lied to you, Nick, and you can take my word for this. I knew it while she was eating supper with us."

Creighton's frown deepened. "And you didn't tell me about it?"

"I didn't see any reason to at the time. I figured whatever reason she had for pretending to be a man, it couldn't have anything to do with you. Maybe I was wrong about that. I just thought she and Williams were probably lovers."

"One of them is a damned undercover lawman," Creighton bit off. "Maybe both." For a moment his rage was directed toward Molly. He felt like backhanding her across the face. But that wouldn't solve anything, he realized, so he controlled the angry impulse.

"I'm sorry, Nick," she said. "I see now I should have told you."

"Yeah, you should have. No more secrets from now on, right?"

"No more secrets. Right. What are you going to do?"

Creighton leathered both irons. "We're riding for the Sugarloaf and putting an end to this."

Having caught the horses, the rest of the gang were mounted and clattered up. Turk led Creighton's horse. Creighton took the reins and swung up into the saddle, too caught up in his hate to pay attention to Molly as she said his name plaintively and held up a hand. He jerked the horse around and led the charge out of the basin, leaving her standing there staring after him and the other outlaws.

* * *

The buckskin had traveled far enough in the past week and a half that it didn't have the reserves of strength it might have had otherwise. Denny felt the horse beginning to flag a bit after she and Brice had covered less than two miles from the hideout.

The buckskin was valiant, and pride and a strong heart kept it going.

Pride and a strong heart could only go so far, Denny thought.

Rogers realized the same thing. "This horse can't carry both of us, Denny. Not as far and as fast as we have to go."

"We get away together or not at all," she snapped.

"If neither of us get away, there's nobody to warn your folks. I don't see that wild bunch behind us now, but you know they're going to be after us as quickly as they can. They're probably on the trail already, closing in on us. If you drop me off, you'll have a chance to get away and alert everybody at the ranch."

"And let them kill you!" She shook her head. "I can't do that."

"It's dark," he argued. "I'll find a place to get out of sight, and they'll charge right on past me without ever slowing down. I'll be perfectly safe."

"If that's true, then let me do that while you go on to the ranch."

"I'm not sure that would work," Rogers said. "Your pa barely knows who I am. He might not take my word for what's about to happen. If you show up and tell him about Creighton's bunch, he'll believe you. You know he will."

Denny couldn't deny that. It was true she stood a better chance of warning everyone at the Sugarloaf headquarters. Not only that, but looking at the situation logically, she weighed less than Brice, and the buckskin would have an easier time of it with her aboard, rather than him. The horse would make better time that way.

But the thought of leaving him behind was unexpectedly difficult for her. They had spent enough time together and gotten to know each well enough that she felt *something* for him. Not affection, she wasn't going to admit to that, but respect, maybe. Friendship. Yeah, that was what it was.

"The trail goes by a ridge up ahead with some rocks on top of it," she said. "You get up there among those boulders, Creighton and his men will never see you."

"That's exactly what I was talking about."

"I guess we can give it a try."

"Good," he said, "because the moon's fixing to rise, and they'll be able to spot us pretty soon."

Denny slowed the buckskin as they reached the stretch of trail that curved around the rugged upthrust of rock.

Still holding on with his left arm around her midsection, Rogers squeezed lightly and told her, "This'll do."

She reined to a halt and turned her head to say, "Damn you. Be careful."

"That's a mighty tender sentiment."

"Just get out of sight and stay there."

Rogers leaned forward, pressed his lips to the line of her jaw, and murmured, "Yes, ma'am." He slid off the buckskin and landed lightly on the trail, gun in hand.

Denny looked back at him. He waved her on.

She went, and soon the swift rataplan of the buckskin's hoofbeats faded.

Rogers heard a growing rumble in the other direction and turned to look toward the inevitable pursuit. As the pounding grew louder, he recognized it as the sound of many horses, moving fast. He shoved the gun he held behind his belt and started to climb the ridge toward the boulders that loomed at its crest.

It didn't take long for the outlaws to show up. Denny had less of a lead on them than he had hoped. Now that the buckskin wasn't carrying double, she might be able to maintain that lead. Some of the gang's horses were fresher, which was worrisome.

Crouched in the thick shadow behind a slab of rock, Rogers leaned out to watch the killers approach. Creighton was mounted on one of those fresh horses and was a short distance out in front of the others, who strung out in a line behind him along the trail.

An idea sprang to life as Rogers saw the way they were scattered. Carefully, sticking to the shadows to avoid being spotted, he slid down the slope until he reached a boulder that thrust out almost over the trail.

Spread-eagled atop that massive rock, he waited, judging the progress of the gang by listening to the rapid hoofbeats. He crawled forward, risked a look, and saw three of the outlaws still to his left, galloping along the trail. Two of them were ahead of the other man, who lagged about ten yards behind.

The moon was up, peeking over the lower ranges to the east and casting silvery light. He would have only one chance, so whatever he did had to be perfect. The two outlaws riding together raced past him. He raised himself slightly. The man bringing up the rear was almost there, almost . . .

Rogers leaped, sailing off the top of the rock and flying through the air until he came down on the horse's back, right behind the outlaw in the saddle. Rogers grabbed the startled owlhoot with his left hand while his right jerked out the revolver behind his belt. He struck with blinding speed, slamming the barrel against the man's head. The man sagged, knocked senseless by the blow.

The two riders up ahead had no idea what had happened. Rogers kicked the man's feet free of the stirrups and gave him a hard shove that toppled him off the horse. He crashed to the trail. Rogers looked back as he levered himself into the saddle. The unconscious outlaw was a motionless heap in the middle of the trail.

It had worked out better than he'd dared to hope. He rode hard, keeping up with the other men, ready to strike at them unexpectedly from behind when the time was right.

CHAPTER 39

Denny swayed in the saddle and clutched the horn to keep from falling. The buckskin was stumbling with exhaustion but somehow managed to keep going. With the moon fairly high in the sky and the position of the stars, she could tell that the time was long after midnight.

She had been riding for hours, and both she and her mount were exhausted. She reined in, knowing the buckskin had to rest for a few minutes. Otherwise the horse would collapse and she would be left afoot.

At first Denny thought it was just the frenzied pounding of her heart she heard. Then she knew better. She lifted her head and listened.

Hoofbeats. They were less than half a mile behind her, she estimated. She had heard them before during this long night, whenever she stopped to let the buckskin blow, and gradually they had come closer and closer.

Creighton and the other outlaws had almost closed up the gap, she thought. She groaned, unable to hold it in. "I'm sorry," she said to the buckskin, who stood with head down and foam-covered sides heaving. "I know you've given me everything you have, but I have to ask for a little more." She lifted the reins. "We have to go."

A gentle prod of her heels against the horse's flanks started the buckskin moving again. It tried to break into a run, couldn't do it, and settled down to a lope. That wasn't enough, Denny thought bleakly, but any more would likely burst the animal's gallant heart.

Maybe it *would* be enough, she thought. The range around her was familiar. The ranch house was less than a mile away. She patted the buckskin's shoulder and muttered, "Just a little while longer. Just a little while . . ."

She had ridden just a couple hundred more yards when riders surged around a bend in the trail behind her. They must have spotted her in the moonlight. She heard shouts and looked back, saw them charging ahead and gaining on her.

"Whatever you've got left," she told the buckskin, "we need it now!"

The horse stretched its legs and broke into a gallop.

At least the outlaws didn't open fire on her. They must have known they were close to the ranch and didn't want to alert anyone that trouble was coming. They would stand a better chance of winning the battle if they took the Sugarloaf's defenders by surprise. The numbers would be about even, Denny knew, so the element of surprise might be enough to swing the victory to the owlhoot side.

She couldn't allow that. As she leaned forward in the saddle and urged the buckskin on, she reached down and drew the holstered Colt. As soon as she came in sight of the ranch headquarters, she would start firing warning shots into the air.

Horse and rider swept around another bend. Up

ahead, the ranch house and the other buildings lay dark and quiet in the moonlight. Denny sobbed in relief, pointed the revolver at the sky, and pulled the trigger. Boom after boom rolled out as she emptied the cylinder. The yellow glow of lamps being lit bloomed in the darkness. Denny sagged. The gun started to slip from her fingers, but she tightened her grip on it. That was her father's Colt, and she wasn't going to lose it.

Since those shots had blasted out, the outlaws had nothing to gain by being quiet. They opened fire, a sheet of muzzle flame spurting from their weapons. Denny rode low, feeling the smooth play of the buckskin's muscles beneath her. Somehow, the horse had reached deep inside itself and found a core of strength that neither of them had known it possessed. The buckskin was running its heart out, running the race of its life.

Then it gave a final leap and collapsed.

Denny felt the horse going down and kicked free from the stirrups. She flew forward, momentum carrying her. While she was in the air, she caught a crazy glimpse of the ranch house. It seemed almost close enough for her to touch . . .

Then she crashed into the ground with stunning force and rolled over and over, the breath gone from her lungs, her muscles limp and useless, her brain stunned almost into insensibility. She came to a stop practically at the feet of a tall figure who quickly knelt beside her, took hold of her shoulders, and turned her onto her back.

Denny blinked dust out of her eyes and looked up into a familiar face. She recognized the lean planes of it, the fair hair, the neatly trimmed mustache sported by the middle-aged man. She whispered, "Uncle Matt . . . ?"

"Denise!"

Matt Jensen didn't allow himself to be surprised by the sight of his niece for more than a split second. Not with a horde of gun-wolves bearing down on them. He slid his arms under Denny's shoulders and knees and lifted her easily as he surged to his feet. Bullets kicked up dirt near his feet as he turned and ran toward the ranch house with her.

More figures appeared on the porch.

Matt recognized them as his nephews Ace and Chance Jensen, his brother Luke's boys. "Cover us!" he shouted at them, then ducked his head and kept running as Ace and Chance opened fire from the porch.

Cal, Pearlie, and the rest of the hands were emerging from the bunkhouse, too, roused from sleep by the gunfire but always ready to fight at a second's notice. More shots crashed out from them, and as the hail of lead ripped into the unknown attackers, the onslaught blunted their charge. The compact group broke up.

But they kept coming, and in the blink of an eye, the area between the ranch house and the bunkhouse and the barn was a wild melee of individual gunfights. Matt leaped onto the porch with Denny in his arms, touching only one step along the way, and lunged into the house with her.

Smoke and Sally were at the bottom of the stairs. Sally had hold of Smoke's arm, but he shrugged free of her and stepped toward Matt, exclaiming, "My God! Is that—"

"It's your daughter, I think," Matt said.

"Denise!" Sally cried. "Is she all right?"

"Can't tell for sure, but I believe so. She took a bad spill outside when her horse collapsed."

"Put her on the sofa," Sally said, directing Matt into the parlor.

Smoke followed. He looked at the gun Denny was holding. "That's my Colt. I wondered where it had gone."

"Pa . . ." Denny murmured as Matt lowered her onto the sofa. She blinked her eyes open. "Those men . . . outside . . . they're the rustlers . . . who've been after you . . . The boss . . . is a man named . . . Creighton."

Matt glanced at Smoke, who shook his head. The name didn't mean anything to him.

Matt straightened. "I need to go help Ace and Chance and the others." He hurried out to get back into the fight.

Smoke and Sally dropped to a knee beside the sofa.

Sally ran her hands over Denny's body. "I don't see or feel any blood. I think she's all right, Smoke. Thank God!"

Smoke rested a hand tenderly against Denny's cheek. "You tracked them down, didn't you? When you disappeared, I knew that's what you'd gone to do."

"I just wanted to . . . help."

"You did. You brought them right to us." Gently, he took the gun out of Denny's hand. "Now it's up to us to finish the chore."

"Smoke—" Sally said as he stood.

"Take care of our little girl." He reached down and slid a handful of cartridges from the loops on the shell belt strapped around Denny's hips. His voice was flat and hard as he added, "I'll see to this."

"You haven't recovered—"

"I'm well enough," Smoke said, thumbing the fresh

rounds into the Colt's cylinder. He snapped it shut and headed for the door.

Creighton. That was the name Denny had said.

That was the man Smoke wanted.

When the shooting started, Rogers prodded his horse ahead. He'd been hanging back on purpose, so none of the outlaws would notice that he wasn't who was supposed to be on the horse, but that didn't matter anymore. It was time for action.

As he drew even with one of the men, he leaned over in the saddle and lashed out with the gun he had taken from the late Muddy Malone. The barrel ripped a gash on the outlaw's head and toppled him from his horse. The man riding on the other side of him yelled, "Hey!" and tried to bring his gun to bear on Rogers, but the young lawman fired first. His bullet ripped through the man and drove him out of the saddle.

The shots didn't attract any attention since gun-thunder already filled the air. Rogers shot another outlaw off his horse, then the attack faltered and the gang began to scatter. Rogers reined in as one of the mounted men plunged at him from the side.

"Williams!" Turk Sanford bellowed. "You dirty, double-crossin'—"

The gun in Turk's hand ripped across Rogers's ribs and twisted him in the saddle. He felt himself falling but triggered his gun as he went over and slammed into the ground. Turk's head jerked back. The slug had bored a black hole in his forehead, a third eye that spouted blood as he fell, landing in a loose sprawl of death.

Pain from the wound in his side flooded through Rogers's body, but he pushed himself to his feet and stumbled toward the ranch house. Denny was up there somewhere. He had to find her, had to make sure she was all right.

He was concentrating on that so much he almost didn't hear the hoofbeats coming up behind him until the rider was practically on top of him. He turned and brought up his gun, gasped, "Creighton!" as he caught a glimpse of the man's face, and tried to fire.

Before he could pull the trigger, flame filled his eyes and something slammed into his head with such terrible force that he was blasted backwards into a deep black oblivion, darker than anything he had ever experienced.

His last thought before that darkness claimed him was of Denny Jensen.

The shooting had just about stopped by the time Smoke stepped out onto the porch. Bodies of men and horses littered the ground. A gun blasted here and there as some of the surviving outlaws tried to put up a fight and were finished off.

Matt, Ace, and Chance stood on the porch, watching a man on horseback about twenty yards from the house.

The man called, "Smoke Jensen!"

"He just rode up and started yelling for you, Smoke," Matt said.

"We could have blasted him out of the saddle," Ace said.

"Figured you might want him for yourself," Chance added.

Smoke gave a curt nod, went down the steps, and called, "I'm Smoke Jensen. You'd be Creighton, I expect."

The man slid down from the saddle and shooed the horse away. He walked closer, moving with a pronounced limp. "Nick Creighton. You're the one who made me a damn gimp, Jensen. Shot me through the leg five years ago."

Smoke shook his head slightly. "Sorry. I don't recollect every snake I've shot. There are too many of them."

"You killed my brother!" Creighton cried. "My brother Blue is dead because of you!"

"I reckon he must have been part of your rustling gang. I'd say that makes his death your fault, Creighton, not mine."

"You son of a bitch," Creighton panted as he limped closer. "I swore I'd kill you, and I will. I wanted to take everything away from you first, but I'll settle for seeing you die here and now. That damn girl tried to ruin everything, but she didn't succeed. I'll still see you dead."

"Creighton!"

The shout came from the porch. Smoke turned slightly, just enough to keep one eye on Creighton while the other saw Denny standing with Sally on one side of her and Louis on the other, holding her up.

"That damn girl is Smoke Jensen's daughter!" Denny cried. "When you take on one Jensen, you take on all of them!"

"That's right," Matt said. He and Ace and Chance were at the foot of the steps.

Cal, Pearlie, and the rest of the crew drifted toward the house from the other direction.

Smoke smiled faintly. "The smart thing for you to do, Creighton, would be to drop those guns and surrender."

Creighton's face twisted with insane rage. He howled a curse and yanked up both revolvers.

Barely seeming to move, Smoke raised the Colt and shot him in the chest. The gun roared and flame gushed from the barrel and Creighton rocked back a step as his eyes widened with pain and shock. He had both guns almost level, but they sagged as he pulled the triggers, and the bullets slammed harmlessly into the ground. He reeled back another step, then dropped both guns and fell to his knees, staying there for a second. As blood dribbled from his mouth, he pitched forward on his face, not moving again.

The moon hadn't set, but the sky was gray with orange streaks heralding the approach of dawn. The light was good enough to see better.

Denny's gaze touched one of the sprawled figures. She broke away from her mother and brother and rushed down the steps, breaking into an unsteady run. "Brice!"

Smoke followed her. She dropped to her knees beside the man and pulled his bloody head into her lap. Smoke recognized him. He didn't know what Rogers had been doing in the middle of this fight, but Denny seemed to. She was sobbing and clutching the young man fiercely to her.

Smoke put his hand on his daughter's shoulder. "Denny. Denny, listen to me."

She looked up at him, tears streaking her face. "He's dead."

"No, he's not," Smoke said. "That's what I wanted to tell you. Look at his chest. He's breathing. Looks like he got creased in a couple places, but he's not dead."

Denny's eyes widened. She looked down at the young lawman, back up at Smoke, down at Rogers again. And then she started to sob even harder.

"Leave her alone," Sally said softly as she came up

and took Smoke's arm. "She'll be all right. And you, mister, need to get back to bed."

"But the fight—"

"This fight is over," Sally told him. "Lord knows there'll probably be another one, sooner or later, but this fight . . . is over."

CHAPTER 40

Denny stepped out onto the porch. It was a clear, cool, beautiful day, and she was moved to take a deep breath of the fresh, invigorating air.

"Pretty as a picture," Brice Rogers said from the rocking chair where he sat.

Denny jumped a little. "Don't sneak up on a girl like that."

"How could I sneak up on you? I was sitting right here. You just didn't see me, that's all."

"Well, you'll be fit enough to travel in a few more days, and then you can stop lurking around here."

He still had a bandage around his head where Nick Creighton's bullet had creased him, and his torso was wrapped up in bandages, too, a result of being shot by Turk Sanford. Neither of those outlaws would ever hurt anybody else. They were buried in cheap pine coffins in the potter's field section of Big Rock's cemetery, along with most of the other members of Creighton's gang. The few who had survived were locked up in Monte Carson's jail, awaiting trial.

"I reckon your father and uncle and cousins will all be glad to see me go, too," Rogers said. "They seem to have the crazy notion that I'm interested in courting you."

Denny snorted. "That'll be the day. Even if you had a loco idea like that, it takes two for any courting to happen, you know."

"Yeah, that's what I thought. Not going to happen."

"Nope. I guess we did a pretty good job helping to bust up that gang of outlaws and killers, but that's all it was."

Rogers nodded. "I couldn't agree more."

"You got anything else to say?"

"Not a thing."

"All right, then," Denny said. "Go ahead and sit there and heal up." She went down the steps and walked toward the corral next to the barn. The buckskin saw her coming and tossed his head in welcome. Finding the horse lying on the ground after the battle had been a repeat of what had happened with Rogers. Denny had thought the buckskin was dead, but that turned out not to be the case. She didn't know if he would ever be fit to ride again, but either way, he would live out his days on the Sugarloaf as an honored friend of the Jensen family.

She reached through the fence and stroked the horse's sleek shoulder. He put his nose against her hand and nuzzled it. Denny laughed, content at that moment as she hadn't been for quite a while.

Several days had passed since the bloody, predawn showdown. Since then, Smoke had continued to recuperate. He was strong enough to have ridden up to the outlaws' hideout with Matt, Ace, Chance, Sheriff Monte Carson, and a couple deputies. They had found the hidden basin deserted. Molly was gone, and there was no way of knowing where. When Creighton and the others hadn't returned, she obviously decided they were all dead and had moved on. Likely, they would never see the woman again. That would be fine. Denny was grateful to Molly for keeping her secret, but the way things had worked out, it hadn't mattered much.

They hadn't found any remains of Muddy Malone among the rocks that had been scattered by the explosion, but that was no surprise, either. He had been too close to the blast to survive.

With things settled down on the Sugarloaf, Denny's uncle and cousins would be moving on. Even though Matt, Ace, and Chance were middle-aged, well into the time of their lives when most men settled down, Denny didn't expect that to happen any time soon. They were too fiddle-footed for that. Smoke Jensen, the fastest gun of them all, the daring adventurer of the frontier, was the only one of the bunch who had put down roots and surrounded himself with family and friends. There was a certain irony in that, Denny mused, but she was grateful things had worked out that way.

The clip-clop of hoofbeats made her look around. A lone rider was approaching the ranch headquarters, and after a moment she recognized Monte Carson and hoped it wasn't more trouble bringing the sheriff out there.

She gave the buckskin a final pat and then walked over to meet the lawman. "Hello, Sheriff," she said with a smile. "What brings you out here today?"

Monte nodded toward the porch. "I've got a telegram for your friend over yonder."

"My friend?" Denny said. "Oh, you mean Deputy Marshal Rogers."

"Yeah." Monte dismounted and led his horse toward the house as Denny walked with him.

Rogers gave him a friendly greeting as well. "How's everything in town?"

"Quiet . . . for now. I know better than to expect it'll stay that way for too long, though." Monte took the folded piece of paper from his pocket and held it out. "Got a wire for you. Fella at the telegraph office had it sent over to me, and I figured I'd better bring it out to you."

Frowning, Rogers took the telegram and unfolded it. He glanced at the signature and said, "It's from the chief marshal." He read for a moment, then looked up and went on. "Do you know what this says, Sheriff?"

"I didn't read it, but I've got a pretty good idea," Monte said. "I got one from Marshal Horton, too. Sort of a professional courtesy, I reckon. He didn't have to ask my permission to assign you to this area permanently."

"What?" Denny said. "You're going to be staying in Big Rock?"

"I suppose I'll make that my headquarters," Rogers said, "but my job could take me anywhere in these parts."

"So you're not going back to Denver?"

"Not for the time being, anyway." He smiled. "Reckon you can put up with me?"

"It doesn't look like I'll have any choice in the matter," Denny said, glaring. "But it doesn't really matter to me one way or the other. I'm going to be too busy to pay attention to whether you're around or not."

"Busy doing what?"

"Learning how to run this ranch."

"You're going to replace Smoke Jensen?"

"Nobody could ever replace Smoke Jensen," she said. "There's only one of him and only one ever will be."

"That's what I figured."

"But there's only one Denny Jensen, too, and I'm just getting started! Which means that you'd better just stay out of my way, mister."

"Happy to . . . as long as you stay out of the way of me doing my job!"

Neither of them noticed that Monte Carson had chuckled and gone on into the house. Nor did they see the two people watching them through the parlor window, Sally with a slightly concerned expression on her face, Smoke grinning so big with pride he looked like he was fit to bust.

*Keep reading for a special preview
of the next installment in the bestselling series
from William W. and J. A. Johnstone!*

FLINTLOCK:
HELL'S GATE

Raised in the wild. Armed to the teeth. Sam Flintlock
is no ordinary bounty hunter. But sometimes even a
man who *sets* traps for a living can *step* right into one.
Sometimes the hunter becomes the hunted—in the
ultimate kill-or-be-killed showdown from bestselling
authors William W. Johnstone and J. A. Johnstone . . .

ONE WEEK IN HELL

After crossing the dry Arizona desert—and missing
six meals in a row—Sam Flintlock is flat-out desperate.
For food. For work. For lodgings. Luckily he finds all
three in the high timber country east of the Mogollon
River. A very young and pretty heiress, Lucy Cullen,
has an unusual proposition for the bounty hunter.
She will pay him cold hard cash to spend one full
week in the Gothic mansion of her murdered uncle.
What's the catch? The place is haunted . . .

Flintlock ain't afraid of the dead. It's the living
he's more worried about—namely, Hogan Forde,
the murderous Texas gunslinger who just happens
to be skulking around town. Toss in a few unfriendly
locals and a missing treasure map, and you've got
all the makings of a pretty terrifying campfire story.
The difference is, these restless spirits are
very much among the living, and they've got
Flintlock slated for his own afterlife . . .

Visit us at www.kensingtonbooks.com.

CHAPTER I

In a raging thunderstorm any shelter is welcome and the cabin set among the foothills was a pleasing sight to Sam Flintlock. He said as much to O'Hara, his half-breed sidekick, who agreed that the place fit the bill.

But the bullet that kicked up a startled V of dirt a foot ahead of Flintlock's horse was less than welcoming and the racketing roar of a heavy rifle was warning enough to stay the hell away.

Flintlock drew rein, waited until lightning scrawled across the sky like the signature of a demented god and thunder boomed over the blunt peaks of the Carrizo Mountains to the west, and then said to O'Hara, "Do you think that bullet was meant to scare us?"

The breed looked around him, at an empty, untamed landscape, and said, "I reckon so. There's nobody else in sight but us two."

Rain ticked off the brim of Flintlock's hat and ran down the front of his slicker. "That there shot didn't come from a friendly party," he said.

O'Hara said, "Sam, I'm always amazed at your grasp of the obvious." Then, "I guess we should try and find a place out of the rain to make camp."

"We got no coffee, no grub, and I'm too damned wet for a cold camp," Flintlock said.

"So what do we do?" O'Hara said, his eyes scanning the cabin. "The traveling preacher we met told me there's a stage station to the north of us at Rock Creek on the old Oregon Trail."

"You mean the feller with the one arm?" Flintlock said.

"The very same. He said he lost that arm at Chancellorsville and maybe he did."

"How far?" Flintlock said.

"How far what?" O'Hara said.

"Damn it, you can be annoying by times, Injun," Flintlock said, scowling. "How long away is the stage station?"

"It's a few years since I've been this far west, but I reckon we're about four miles south of the trail, maybe less."

"And then when we get there we have to hunt around for a stage stop in a wall-to-wall downpour," Flintlock said.

O'Hara nodded, "Yeah, there's always that."

"Well, we got a cabin right in front of us with smoke coming out the chimney, and I'm sure I can smell coffee on the wind. I say we—" a thunderclap that shook the ground obliterated Flintlock's words—"and we'll be made right welcome."

"I missed that." O'Hara said. "What did you say?"

Flintlock shook his head and rain cascaded from his hat brim. "You don't pay attention, that's always been your trouble, O'Hara, you just don't listen. I said we'll ride on in a-grinnin', like we're visiting kinfolk. Nobody's gonna gun grinning kinfolk, especially in a thunderstorm."

"We ain't grinning kinfolk, and he'll know it," O'Hara said. "Try it and we're dead men."

"Trust me, O'Hara."

"Remember all the times I've trusted you before?"

"And you're still alive, ain't you? Anyways, this time will be different."

Flintlock kneed his horse forward and again a bullet kicked up dirt a couple of feet ahead of him and put an exclamation point at the end of the warning to steer clear. A cloud of gray gunsmoke drifted from the cabin's cracked-open door, and Flintlock caught the glint of a rifle barrel. He felt the burn of O'Hara's hostile gaze and said, "If the party in the cabin wanted to kill us he'd have done it by now. We can ride in real slow, a-grinnin' like a bushel basket of possum heads, and we'll be just fine."

O'Hara glanced at a turbulent sky as black as mortal sin and said, "Whoever he is, he ain't going to invite us in for cake and ice cream and that's a natural fact."

Rain driven by a gusting north wind drummed on the shoulders of Flintlock's slicker and his wet horse tossed its weary head and made the bit chime. "We'll give it another try," he said.

"Suppose he shoots again?" O'Hara said.

Flintlock's eyes narrowed. "Well then he'll make me good and mad and I'll go in there a-hollering and a-shooting."

O'Hara grimaced. "Hell, Sam, he'll blow you right off that buckskin before you even cover half the distance."

"Maybe he's been trying to hit us and missed every time. Ever think of that?"

"No, I never thought of that. I've thought of other things but that never crossed my mind."

Flintlock kneed his buckskin forward. "Let's go, O'Hara. The coffee is bilin' in the pot and maybe there's a stack of bear sign cooling on the plate."

"And maybe pigs will fly," O'Hara said.

Thunder crashed and lightning scraped across the sky but there were no more shots.

"Only a pair of damn fools would ignore two warning shots from a Sharps fifty," the man on the cabin porch said. He was a scrawny, tough-looking old coot, the white stubble on his right cheek parted by a wicked knife scar. The muzzle of his rifle was pointed right at Flintlock. "Did Nathan Poteet send ye?" he said.

"Never heard of the man, and you're less than hospitable, old-timer," Flintlock said. "In fact you're one unfriendly cuss."

"Man and boy, I never was a friendly cuss," the old man said. His Sharps didn't waver. "State your name and your intentions."

"My only intention is to come in out of the rain. My name is Sam Flintlock. There are them who know it and others who fear it."

"Big talk, mister." The old-timer cradled his rifle, reached into the pocket of his vest, and produced a pair of pince-nez spectacles that he clamped onto the bridge of his nose. He craned his head forward and stared at Flintlock for a long time and then said, "Ach, I ken ye fine. You're old Barnabas Feeney's grandson, a right homely kid turned into a homelier man. You still got the thunderbird on your throat?"

"It's there," Flintlock said. Rain lashed at him and lightning gleamed on the shoulders of his slicker but the oldster was a talking man and didn't seem to be in a hurry.

"I mind the time back in '42 me an' Barnabas an' Kit Carson joined John C. Fremont's expedition to survey the Platte and the Sweetwater as far as the South Pass. That was the time Barnabas fought a mounted rifle duel with Black Faced Dave Cosgrove over an Arapaho woman. Dave got a bullet into Barnabas but he cussed off the wound, rode straight at Dave, and shot him in the belly. Dave hollered in pain and said he was done, but Barnabas drew his pistol and put a bullet in his head. Well sir, Dave lingered for a while, but his brains were running out of his skull, so he didnae last long." The old man cackled. "But after all that the Arapaho woman spread her blankets next to a Yankee surveyor and Barnabas lost out. He was all for killing the surveyor, mind, but Fremont brandished a horse pistol and said he needed all his surveyors alive. And that was the end of that. He was a rum one, was ol' Barnabas."

The old man lowered his rifle and said, "My name is Jamie MacDonald, Scotland born and bred, as ye probably can tell. There's a barn around the back where you can put up your horses. There's hay, but if you want oats it will cost you fifty cents an animal, so think carefully on that. And be careful of my mule, she does not care for strangers."

"Your ankle is bruised but it's not broke," MacDonald said. "She kicked you, you say?"

Irritated but mindful of the weather outside, Sam Flintlock bit back a sharp retort and said, "Yeah, that's what I say, damn mule kicked me all right."

"Well, let that be a lesson to ye, never get behind a cantankerous mule," MacDonald said. "Now ye'll be wanting coffee, you and the Hindoo?"

"His name is O'Hara and he's half Irish," Flintlock said. "But as far as I know when it comes to religion he's all Indian."

"Ah, weel, the Scots and Irish are brothers under

the skin separated by differing views of Christianity, so you're welcome to my home, Mr. O'Hara."

"That's most gracious of you," O'Hara said. Flintlock gave the old man a sidelong look, surprised at his politeness.

"And now I'll get the coffee and later I'll boil us up a mess of porridge, or as some say, oatmeal," MacDonald said.

Flintlock and O'Hara exchanged horrified glances and the old mountain man laughed. "I always say that to my guests just to see their faces. You need not be alarmed. I've got a nice beef stew on the stove that will stick to your skinny ribs."

The old man cackled and busied himself with the coffee and Flintlock looked around him. The cabin was small but the wood floor was meticulously swept, and MacDonald's few sticks of furniture glowed from polish and much elbow grease. A fire burned in the stone fireplace and above the mantel was a painting of a self-assured young man wearing armor, a blue sash over his shoulder and a fancy powdered wig.

"That's Prince Charles Edward Stuart, known to Scots the world over as Bonnie Prince Charlie," MacDonald said, seeing Flintlock's interest in the painting. "He should have been the king of Britain but his cause was lost." The old man shook his gray head. "He risked all on one final battle against the English, was defeated, and had to flee Scotland, never to return. Forty-two years later he died in exile in Rome, of the drink they said." MacDonald raised his cup to the portrait. "To you, my Prince, and a tragic but noble figure you were."

MacDonald took a chair beside the fire opposite Flintlock. O'Hara, as was his habit when no other chairs were available, sat cross-legged on the floor.

"So, young Sam, tell me how Barnabas fares? Does his shadow still fall on the earth?"

"No, he's dead," Flintlock said. "Well, more or less."

MacDonald looked puzzled, but he never asked the question framed on his face because from outside in the rain a man's voice called out, "MacDonald! Jamie MacDonald! Show yourself and make an accounting."

The old man rose to his feet, grabbed his Sharps from the gun rack beside the mantel and yelled, "Nathan Poteet, is that you?"

An answer from outside, "You know it's me, old man. You've had your week to decide if a map is worth dying for. Speak up now, what conclusion have you reached?"

MacDonald stepped to the door and yelled, "Poteet, there is no buried gold. There never was any buried gold. Mechan Cully died penniless. All he had left was the big house. He drank and gambled away the rest and there are some say he lay in sin with fallen women."

"Get out here, old man," Poteet said. "My talking is done."

To emphasize that statement a bullet shattered through one of the top panes of the cabin window, hit Bonnie Prince Charlie and sent him crashing to the hearth, and then thudded into the far wall, splintering timber.

"Damn ye for a scoundrel, Poteet, you broke my window and shot my bonnie prince," MacDonald said. "And twice damned to ye for a rogue!" The old man flung the door open, and Flintlock yelled, "No!"

Too late.

Jamie MacDonald angrily stomped onto his porch, raised his rifle, and was immediately hit by a volley of bullets that punched great holes in his thin frame. Flintlock heard a thud as the old man fell, and he pulled his Colt from the waistband.

"Easy," O'Hara whispered. He stared through the open door. "I see six but there could be more."

"You in the cabin!" This from Poteet.

"What do you want?" Flintlock said.

"Step outside and identify yourselves. My quarrel is not with you."

"Damn you, you murdered the old man," Flintlock said.

"He had been notified," Poteet said. "Come out now or we'll shoot the cabin down about your ears."

O'Hara hollered, "We're coming out!" Then, "For God's sake put the gun away, Sam. There's too many of them, and I think I see Hogan Lord out there."

"You're seeing things. Hogan never leaves the Brazos River country," Flintlock said. "It isn't him."

"Even if it isn't him, there's still too many guns out there," O'Hara said.

He stepped out the door into teeming rain that hissed like an angry dragon. Reluctantly, Flintlock shoved his revolver back into the waistband and followed.

Six men wearing yellow rain slickers sat their horses in the downpour, Winchesters at their shoulders. Flintlock saw no friendly faces, but then one of the gunmen lowered his rifle and said, "Hell, it's Sam Flintlock. I'd recognize that beak of a nose and sour disposition anywhere."

Flintlock now remembered the face and a shooting scrape from a few years before. "Howdy, Hogan," he said. "It's been a while."

"Four years, to be exact," Lord said. Rain dripped from his hat brim. "That time we both went after the same mark. Remember?"

"Yeah, I remember. His name was Link Liddell, and we caught up with him in Ciudad Juárez down Chihuahua way. He was wanted for rape and murder, and you scattered his brains all over the front door of the Church of Christ the Redeemer. As I recollect, the priest got real mad over that."

As always, Lord's smile was wide but without warmth. "That town was a dung heap."

Flintlock nodded. "So was Link Liddell. Sorry I didn't stick around to share the reward with you, Hogan. I took one look at the money and decided that three thousand pesos just wasn't enough for two people, doesn't go very far, like."

"If I'd found you that day, Sam, I would've gunned you," Lord said.

"You were always too quick to go to the gun, Hogan. I always considered it a character flaw in you," Flintlock said, staring at the gunman, thinking about things.

Could Hogan Lord shade me on the draw and shoot? Damn right he could and on my best day.

"Well, now that we're all reacquainted, tell us what you're doing here, Flintlock," Poteet said. "Be honest and straight up, like a white man."

"What I'm not doing here is murdering old men," Flintlock said.

"Self-defense, Sam," Lord said. "MacDonald was fixing to cut loose with the Sharps. Mr. Poteet here was in fear for his life."

"It took six of you to kill one old man?" Flintlock said.

Poteet shrugged. "That's the way his hand played out." He looked past Lord to the other riders. "All right, boys, go earn your day's pay."

Now that his quick anger had subsided and he no longer saw through a red haze, Flintlock realized that the four men who'd climbed out of the saddle and stepped onto the porch were of a different stripe than Poteet and Lord. Low-browed and coarse, these were common thugs, dark alley specialists, skull and boot fighters more at home with a sap, billy club, brass knuckles, or a knife than a Colt. All four wore plug hats and the townsman's lace-up boots, and when they talked to one another their accents were not of the West but of the rank, violent slums of the big northern cities. They were trash, but hideously dangerous, and they'd attack in packs.

"Tear the cabin apart, boys," Poteet said. "If the map's in there, find it." He stared at Flintlock, his eyes hard as stone. "You thinking of taking cards in this game?"

"I reckon not," Flintlock said. "I know when I'm facing a stacked deck."

"You, breed?" Poteet said as crashing, smashing, and splintering sounds came from the cabin.

"I'm not the law," O'Hara said. "I've got no call to be involved."

"Wise man," Poteet said, dismissing O'Hara with a disdainful glance reserved for anyone not of the white race.

Poteet and Lord sat their saddles for the best part of an hour while the cabin was wrecked. They ignored the torrential rain as though it was a matter of no consequence.

Finally, one of the thugs stepped out the door onto the porch and said, "It ain't there, Mr. Poteet."

Poteet didn't hide his disappointment. "You sure?"

"Look for yourself, we tore the place apart. Two hundred dollars in a cigar box but no map." The thug shook his head. "It just ain't there."

Poteet, a big man whose claim to handsomeness was sabotaged by the cruel hardness of his mouth and his dead gray eyes, said, "Dave, you and the others share the two hundred among you, a bonus for getting wet."

"Obliged to you for that, Mr. Poteet," the scarred

bruiser named Dave said. Then, as the other three joined him, "You want us to ride to Mansion Creek with you?"

Hogan Lord answered that question. "No. You four got too many wanted dodgers on your back trail and you could be recognized. And that goes for you too, Nathan. Stay close to town and I'll send for you when I need you."

"Need him for what, Hogan?" Flintlock said. "Does he have more old men to kill?"

Poteet's face hardened into hewn rock. "Take my advice, don't push it, Flintlock," he said.

"Listen to the man, Sam," Lord said. "Mr. Poteet will take only so much."

"And then I get the urge to kill somebody," Poteet said. "Keep that in mind."

"Sam, let it go," O'Hara said, his voice urgent. "This isn't the time or place."

"Listen to the breed, Sam," Lord said. "If you stop in Mansion Creek look me up. I'll buy you a drink."

"Poteet, you didn't put the crawl on me," Flintlock said. "What's your opinion on that? Sum it up, now."

"We broke even, Flintlock," Poteet said. "That's my opinion."

"Sam, you can live with that," O'Hara said.

Flintlock nodded. "So be it." But there was a rage in him that scalded like acid.

CHAPTER 2

"We done well by the old man, buried him decent," O'Hara said.

Sam Flintlock nodded. "I reckon. He had two mourners and a marked grave. That's more than most mountain men could hope for."

The rain had stopped during the night, and Flintlock and O'Hara had buried Jamie MacDonald by lantern light, neither feeling much inclined to sleep. Now, as they took to the trail again, the sky was serene and white clouds drifted across its blue depths like lilies on a pond. The air smelled fresh after the rain had settled the dust and was heavy with the scent of pine and juniper. An east wind rustled in the grass like the whispers of dead Navajo. Ahead of the two riders rose the twin peaks of the Pastora and Zibetod mountains. Nestled between them in a grassy meadow ringed by stands of juniper, pine, and mountain oak lay a one-street settlement that Flintlock decided must be Mansion Creek.

O'Hara was of the same mind. "Maybe we can get breakfast. I should've shot the ranny who tipped out MacDonald's stew."

"But you didn't," Flintlock said, drawing rein.

O'Hara smiled. "I've lived among white men for a long time, but I'm still not completely crazy. Hogan Lord is not a man to antagonize."

"Unless you have to," Flintlock said. "You're the banker. How much money do we have?"

"Enough for coffee, bacon and eggs, and then we're done."

"Maybe we can find some work."

"Maybe. Saloon swampers are always in demand."

Flintlock grimaced. "I was thinking more of something in the restaurant trade. At least we'd eat regular."

"Dishwasher?"

"If that's all I can get."

O'Hara shook his head. "I'd rather rob the town bank."

"It may come to that," Flintlock said. He kneed his horse forward. "Did you see Barnabas at the graveside?"

"I saw him," O'Hara said. "He didn't seem to be cut up about MacDonald's death."

"For Barnabas it's way too late for sorrow," Flintlock said. He shrugged. "Or maybe when he was alive he didn't like the old man. Barnabas didn't like many people."

O'Hara smiled. "Who did he like?"

"Beats the hell out of me. I only know that whoever they were, I wasn't one of them." Flintlock's eyes rose to the sky above Mansion Creek. "Hell, look at that, there's buzzards drifting above the town."

"A bad omen for somebody," O'Hara said.

Flintlock sighed. "You know I have the strangest feeling that we're not heading into a happy time."

"But maybe your ma is there in town, Sam," O'Hara said. "There's always that possibility."

"Something is there all right," Flintlock said. "But I don't think it's my ma. I don't think she'd turn the air black."

"What is it then?"

"Wicked things," Flintlock said. "Like hell has emptied out and all the devils are right there in Mansion Creek."

Connect with Us

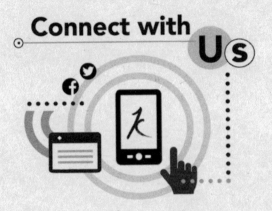

Visit us online at
KensingtonBooks.com
to read more from your favorite authors, see books
by series, view reading group guides, and more.

Join us on social media

for sneak peeks, chances to win books and prize packs,
and to share your thoughts with other readers.

facebook.com/kensingtonpublishing
twitter.com/kensingtonbooks

Tell us what you think!

To share your thoughts, submit a review,
or sign up for our eNewsletters, please visit:
KensingtonBooks.com/TellUs.